At The Pleasure of the President

Shayla Black and Lexi Blake

At the Pleasure of the President
Perfect Gentlemen, Book 5

Published by Black Oak Books LLC

Copyright 2019 Black Oak Books LLC
Edited by Chloe Vale and Shayla Black
ISBN: 978-1-939673-11-4

Cover by Rachel Connolly

Dedication

Through friendship, anything is possible.

"Shayla Black and Lexi Blake never fail to heat up the page, and the Perfect Gentlemen series is no exception. Hot and edgy and laced with danger, the stories in the Perfect Gentlemen are just that—perfect."

—J. Kenner, *New York Times* and international bestselling author of the Stark series.

THE NOVELS OF SHAYLA BLACK ARE...

"Sizzling, romantic, and edgy!"—Sylvia Day, #1 *New York Times* bestselling author

"Scorching, wrenching, suspenseful... A must-read."—Lora Leigh, #1 *New York Times* bestselling author

"Wickedly seductive from start to finish."—Jaci Burton, *New York Times* bestselling author

"The perfect combination of excitement, adventure, romance, and really hot sex."—Smexy Books

"Full of steam, erotic love, and nonstop, page-turning action."—Night Owl Reviews

THE NOVELS OF LEXI BLAKE ARE...

"A book to enjoy again and again... Captivating."—Guilty Pleasures Book Reviews

"Utterly delightful."—Night Owl Reviews

"A satisfying snack of love, romance, and hot, steamy sex."—Sizzling Hot Books

"Hot and emotional."—Two Lips Reviews

PRAISE FOR THE MASTERS OF MÉNAGE SERIES BY SHAYLA BLACK AND LEXI BLAKE

"Smoking hot! Blake and Black know just when to turn up the burner to scorching." —Under the Covers Book Blog

"Well done...full of spicy sex, and a quick read."—

Smart Bitches, Trashy Books

"Steamy, poignant, and captivating... A funny, touching, lively story that will capture the reader from page one and have them wishing for more when it ends." — Guilty Pleasures Book Reviews

"Very well written. With just the right amount of love, sex, danger, and adventure... A fun, sexy, exciting, hot read."

—Girly Girl Book Reviews

Prologue

Zack and Liz
Three Years Before
Memphis, TN

As Zack Hayes looked across the linen-draped table of one of Memphis's most exclusive restaurants at the woman in front of him, an odd contentment settled deep inside him. Some part of him he'd never known existed suddenly slid into place. He was a bit horrified that mysterious something might actually be his heart—a thing he hadn't believed existed until now. Simply by looking at her, he could breathe more easily. Being near her felt good. Times were changing, and he was going with the flow.

Because Elizabeth Matthews was the magical, mystical unicorn he'd always believed was a fantasy. She was *the one.*

Only Elizabeth had made him realize there was more to life than work and the never-ending pursuit of ambition. Only falling for her had convinced him to want more than the path he'd been set on forty years ago.

And the only thing holding him back from hauling her into his arms and making her his was the little problem of his marriage—to another woman.

"Zack, I know the polling numbers aren't what you wanted, but the election isn't over. Anything can happen." Liz's clear blue eyes were so earnest and reassuring.

He smiled. Those same blue eyes could go icy as fuck, of course. And damn if that didn't do something for him.

He took a cautious glance around the private dining room. Except for the two of them, the room was empty. Not surprising since the staff was well trained. They'd also been handsomely paid to deliver the drinks, then disappear. For the first time in forever, no one was listening in. No reporters or pundits hovered to catch a few stray sentences they could turn into the evening's headlines. He was alone with Elizabeth, and that was the way he liked it.

"I didn't ask you here to talk about polling numbers." Though she was wrong about those. No one suddenly surged ahead after being four points down less than a week before election day. His race was over. Of course he would go through all the motions, do everything to appear as though he'd fought until the last minute, but he'd already written his concession speech.

And he was shockingly okay with that.

His whole life, he'd worked to sit behind that desk in the Oval Office. He'd spent every waking moment—and lots of the sleeping ones, too—preparing for his presidency. He'd carefully organized his life, right down to his calculated marriage, so that one day he would be the most powerful man in the free world. Now after all that plotting, the vision was slipping through his fingers because according to the American public he was too cold and detached, not a man of the people. They liked his platform and ideas, but the other guy was the kind they could see themselves sharing a beer with.

With the exception of letting down his best friend, Roman Calder, he wasn't upset about losing. In fact, he felt lighter now that the weight of responsibility was mere days from being lifted off him for good. All because he had a fresh cause, something else to focus on, a new reason to care. He had Elizabeth.

Well, almost.

Last night, he and Roman had shared a shockingly expensive bottle of Scotch and planned for a future that didn't require a Secret Service detail. They were going to put their law degrees to work and make some life choices that would likely get them used as tabloid click-bait for a while. But hey, they were Perfect Gentlemen—two among the wildest group of rich boys to ever roll through prep school and the Ivy Leagues. Sure, he and Roman had always been the most circumspect of the six, but no one would be truly surprised when he and Joy announced their divorce. There might be some eyebrows raised when he started dating his media consultant. And there would likely be outright gasps if his best friend married his ex-wife, but Zack felt sure they would weather the storm.

"Of course you didn't ask me here strictly to talk polling numbers. I'm sorry, Zack. I understand," Elizabeth said with a sad smile. "I'll clear out of the bus."

"Why would you do that?" They still had a few days before the election. No matter what the polls indicated, he couldn't shrug and walk away yet. "Are you quitting?"

She frowned. "No. I thought you were firing me."

He reached across the table and tangled her fingers with his. Her eyes widened as she pulled her manicured hand away, discreetly scanning the room to see if anyone was watching.

Undeterred, Zack reached for her again, this time holding firm. "Why on earth would I fire you? And you can stop looking around. Our team and the press are both too busy prepping for tonight's rally to come all the way across town for lunch. I reserved this private dining room for us and ensured we won't be disturbed so we can talk freely."

She relaxed a bit. Even better, she stopped trying to tug her hand away. "All right. I assumed you would fire me because I haven't done a good enough job at getting your message across to the American people. But there's still a few days left. You know as well as I do that lots of voters are undecided. Some major social influencers—senators, celebrities, newspapers—still haven't formally endorsed anyone. Heck, if you got a nod from a Kardashian, it could totally sway the election. And you never know, an October surprise could pop up and change everything."

He needed to quell her worries here and now. "You've done a fabulous job, Elizabeth. As far as I'm concerned, you're the best in the business. The fact that I'm even within striking distance of the White House, despite being a first-term senator running against a popular VP who's served for the last eight years, is incredible. It simply wasn't our time. And quite frankly, the pundits are right about some things. I am too intellectual. I do come off as cold and elite at times."

Now she squeezed his hand in support before tangling their fingers together once more. The feeling of rightness stole even deeper into his heart. He wanted—needed—to be connected with this woman. For years, he'd worked with her. During that time, he'd befriended her. He'd also slowly fallen in love with her, too. For him, she was it.

He wasn't entirely sure how she felt about him.

"Zack, you're none of those things," Elizabeth swore, her tone soft. "Well, you're intellectual, of course. You're one of the smartest men I've ever met, but you're not cold at all. Somehow, we have to convince the American public of that because you're also incredibly generous and kind."

"You only think so because I've been careful around you." She was going to see his ruthless side very soon. "Because I've wanted you to think of me that way. I can be brutally ambitious."

"Of course. That's one of the reasons I wanted to work on your campaign." She leaned in. "I don't know if you've noticed, Senator Hayes, but I can be brutally ambitious, too."

Oh, he'd noticed. Elizabeth was sweet most of the time. It was her usual Southern charm that made her effective when she let loose her inner lioness. It didn't happen often. Usually, she delegated the nasty details to her second in command precisely to keep her perfectly manicured claws from showing until she truly needed to bare them. But when he got a rare glimpse...damn that did something for him, too.

It was also why he was so nervous about what he planned to say next. Elizabeth Matthews was determined to make a name for herself. Could she love a failed politician? Could she really tie herself to a man determined to walk away from the very world she'd set out to conquer?

"Elizabeth, I'm going to lose this election."

She shook her head, lips firming. "You can't think that. And if we do lose, we'll concentrate on taking back your Senate seat when the midterms come around."

"No." He had to stop her there. She needed to understand that he was plotting a different course this time—his own. "I'm walking away. Roman and I have decided to open a law firm in New York. I'm leaving DC altogether."

Manhattan was the right choice. He and Roman would be close to Mad and Gabe. Dax could visit them all easily when he was on leave from his ship. And one day, when Connor's location was no longer classified, he would return to find his friends waiting. *If* Connor came home alive.

That worry sat in Zack's gut. One of the perks of being in government was being able to keep something of an eye on his CIA operative friend. But since he wasn't going to be commander in chief, Zack had to trust that Connor could take care of himself.

Elizabeth's hand slid out of his. "You can't do that. You're too gifted to walk away."

His stomach took a deep dive. It wouldn't be the first time a woman had rejected him, but it would be the only time that mattered. Because Elizabeth mattered. She was everything to him...even if she didn't know it yet.

God, he hadn't been this nervous when he'd asked Joy to marry him. Of course, he'd known she would say yes because her father had told her to. Their marriage had been carefully orchestrated, all the way down to his proposal. And they'd agreed to the dissolution of their loveless union in a similarly thoughtful and emotionless manner.

It's for the best, Zack. I care about Roman in a way I wouldn't have believed possible. Let's get through the next few days. Then we can quietly pursue the lives we want.

A genuine smile—one that reached her eyes—had stretched across Joy's face. He hadn't seen her look that happy in years.

So it was done. The time had come for him to be happy, too. That meant finally getting his hands on the woman across from him and making her his.

What if she didn't want him?

"Elizabeth, my mind is made up. I'm leaving politics, moving to New York to open a law firm with Roman and"—he dragged in a bracing breath—"Joy and I are divorcing."

She gasped, lifting her delicate hand to her mouth. "Divorcing? But...Joy hasn't mentioned a thing. I don't understand."

Zack wanted to pull her into his arms. But he forced himself to stay in his seat. He couldn't touch her until he knew where she stood.

"Yes, you do. You know my marriage is nothing but a contract between two parties, and I failed on my end. Joy was meant to be a First Lady, not a wife, not a lover. I failed to earn her the position she deserves, so we have nothing more truly between us. Joy and I made this decision together, and we're both happy about it."

He suspected Joy had been in love with Roman for a long time. And Roman seemed enamored, too. Oh, he tried to hide it, but Zack knew his best friend too well. If Roman eventually pursued Joy, he would be making a mistake. But Zack doubted that Roman wanted to hear, especially from him, that Joy's placid temperament wouldn't make his hot-headed friend the perfect wife. The way he saw it, Roman was still hung up on Augustine Spencer.

To this day, Zack didn't understand precisely what had gone wrong between Roman and Dax's sister. He only knew that Roman hadn't been the same since their affair decades ago. Even now, he lit up when Gus entered a room…and not always in a good way.

Hell, who knew? Maybe Joy would bring Roman the peace he claimed he needed.

One thing Zack knew? He was damn sure seeking more than polite civility with Elizabeth.

Across the table, she wore that slightly pensive look that told him she was thinking through a problem and ticking off some list in her head. "All right, if the worst happens with the election, I'll spin the story of your divorce to make you look more human. You and Joy can remain friendly in the press. If you don't start immediately dating a supermodel, the gossip should die off quickly. Then if you decide to run for your Senate seat again—"

"I won't. And since when do I date supermodels?"

She shrugged. "Your friends all do. I assumed…"

"Mad and Gabe do," he corrected. "Look, I don't need you to spin anything. I didn't call you here to get your ideas on how to handle my divorce in the press."

"Then why did you call me here?" The question came

out terse, as though she was getting emotional.

He knew her tells. He'd studied her for years. She was nervous and on the edge. It was a good sign.

"Elizabeth, I called you here to ask you on a date."

Her eyes widened, and she froze, as though she was trying to process his statement. "A date?"

"Yes. A date, a real one." He leaned closer and lowered his voice, despite the fact he knew they were alone. "I've cared about you for a very long time. The day I met you, I realized I'd made a mistake marrying Joy. We were never in love. We do love each other—but as friends. Neither of us ever felt any spark between us. I didn't even believe such a thing existed...until I met you."

She gaped. "You felt a spark? When you met me?"

What he'd felt had gone beyond mere lust, although that had certainly been present. He'd taken one look at the gorgeous blonde in the white business suit and the sky-high red Louboutins, and his world had shifted. His half-dead libido had come alive again.

"Yes, and it's done nothing but get stronger over the course of this campaign."

She frowned. "Zack, a campaign like this is a pressure cooker. It's easy to feel close to someone when you're with them twenty-four seven, when you're forced to depend on them. But—"

"Tell me you didn't feel something the day we met."

He remembered that fateful introduction so clearly. Was it possible she hadn't felt the same? Could he have mistaken her lighthearted, flirtatious nature for deeper attachment?

"Of course I did," she admitted, meeting his gaze, eyes soft. "You must know... I'm crazy about you. I haven't even considered dating another man because I think about you all the time."

Relief flooded his system. She was going to be his.

A grin slid across his face. "I'm crazy about you, too. And you should know that Joy and I...we haven't been physical in a long time."

"I shouldn't be happy about that. But I am. Does that make me a terrible person?"

"It would if she had feelings for me." Zack needed Elizabeth to understand that he and Joy hadn't had any sort of normal marriage. "I've talked to her about you. She knows I'm here today asking if you'll see me after the election. She's the one who told me to order the vodka gimlet for you. She said it always puts you in a better mood."

Elizabeth laughed, the sound magical to him. She was the single most radiant woman he'd ever met.

"Well, she knows me." Elizabeth shook her head, but she wore a wry smile. "This is surreal. This is crazy! I had no idea you felt this way..."

"Is that a yes? I know we should probably wait a while, but I don't want to. I want to finish out this campaign and get on with my life."

"By going on a date with *me?*" Her tone told him she was wowed by that notion. "Yes! But you should know, Senator Hayes, that I'm a lady. I require a man to be a gentleman."

Hey, it was practically his nickname. "I have no problem opening car doors and holding your seat for you. You'll find me exquisitely polite."

"You already do all those things. I know how exceptionally well you take care of a woman in public. But that's not what I meant. I'm definitely going to require you to be a gentleman in bed. A perfect one," she insisted, and he wondered if she knew every word out of her mouth was heating his blood. "And I don't mean polite, Zack. Underneath all that civility, I know there's a bad boy. I want that part of you—and all the others you keep hidden—to myself."

His groin tightened and he was even more glad he'd reserved a private dining room. "I want to kiss you."

"I want that, too," she admitted breathlessly. "But not here and not now. Not with Joy and the cloud of the election hanging over our heads. I want it to be special. I want to know when we kiss for the first time that we don't ever have to stop again."

"Agreed. Where would you like to go on our first date? I say we steal Gabe's plane and head to Paris. I'll get a room with a view because you probably won't get out much."

He'd meant to go slow, to ease her into a relationship, but she'd just hit the gas and he didn't have any intention of pumping the brakes, not when it meant he could have her—and soon. He wasn't a man given to impatience, but then he'd never craved anyone the way he did Elizabeth.

"Paris sounds lovely, but I'll be happy with the view from my side of your bed." She gave him the flirtiest grin he'd ever seen.

He'd suspected that, under her gracious charm, she would be sexy and sassy. No playing coy games. Elizabeth wasn't girlish, after all. She was pure woman, and he suspected she would take him on the ride of his life—one that would last for the rest of his days.

Finally, he had no doubt that he and Elizabeth were perfect for each other. She would make all the difference in his life because now he would have more than his ambitions. He would have his friends near and his soul mate beside him.

Reassurance and contentment wrapped a warm hand around his heart and cradled his soul. Suddenly not being the most powerful man in the world seemed pretty damn sweet.

He sat back and repositioned his napkin in his lap as the waiter appeared on cue to take their order. He couldn't stop smiling. Despite the decades and the dramas, he felt like a dumbass kid again—this time, one with the world open to him.

Tonight, he could give his stump speech with perfect confidence. He would say and do all the right things. Shake hands, kiss babies—and it wouldn't do a damn thing to win him the election. In a few more days, he would be free. Then Elizabeth would be all his.

He sat back and stared at her, barely holding in a smile. She did the same, her gaze eating him up from under her long lashes as she "accidentally" bumped his foot under the table. Life was good. The promise of tomorrow was right in front of him, so he was content to simply be near her—for now.

* * * *

Later that night

Liz stood numbly in the middle of the nondescript hallway of the hospital, unable to move. Hell, she could barely breathe. She kept replaying the sound of gunshots in her head.

"Ms. Matthews? You're Senator Hayes's media consultant. Do you have any update on his wife's condition?" a reporter she vaguely recognized asked. "Is she expected to live?"

Someone pressed a microphone in Liz's face. The lights glared too brightly. She blinked and froze.

God, she made a living responding to the press on Zack's behalf, and she was damn good at her job. But right now, she was dumbfounded. She could hardly focus on the question, much less a coherent answer. All she could manage was an endless looping replay of Joy falling from her chair, her body limp, blood splattering everywhere.

"You're not supposed to be here," a deep voice admonished.

Connor Sparks moved in, and suddenly the camera was out of her face.

She caught a glimpse of men in black suits swarming the area, their eyes mirrored by identical aviator sunglasses, despite the fact that night had already fallen.

The Secret Service agents hustled the film crew out in seconds. Liz watched, processing in slow motion.

Had it really been mere hours ago that she'd sat in a restaurant with Zack, planning their future?

Connor turned to her. "Are you all right?"

God, he had blood on his shirt. She recoiled, even as she knew she had to get it together.

"Where's Zack?" The question slipped out, then she shook her head. She shouldn't ask about him first. "And what about Joy? Is she out of surgery?"

Joy wasn't dead. She was alive. She had to be. The paramedics had gotten her to the hospital within minutes. Liz hadn't seen them move her, but she'd seen the mob of first responders on the stage working to save the woman's life.

Connor's face went blank. "No one's told you?"

Her stomach took a dive. "Told me?"

"Liz! Liz!" a familiar feminine voice called out.

Augustine. Her dear friend stood at the end of the hallway, held back from entering by security guards.

God, she needed Gus.

"Let her through," Liz implored the uniformed sentries. "Please."

They didn't move.

"Let her through." At Connor's command, the guards parted like the Red Sea for Moses.

Immediately, Gus rushed down the hall, for once looking less than perfect. Her usually impeccable caramel hair was in a haphazard ponytail. Normally, she was dressed to the nines. Tonight, she'd thrown on ripped jeans and a simple white T-shirt.

"I caught a friend's private jet and got here as fast as I could," Gus said in a rush. "Oh, god, Connor. Tell me it isn't true. Moments ago, the media said...they said she's gone. Joy's gone."

A shocked sob stuck in Liz's throat as she whirled to Connor. Since he'd just left Zack's side, he would know. But no, it couldn't be true...

Maybe they were deceiving the press. That made sense. They didn't want anyone to know that Joy was okay. Because she had to be alive. Joy was sweet and kind. God, she'd had tea with the woman this evening before Zack had taken the stage. That woman couldn't be dead.

"Joy died on the operating table. Single gunshot to the heart." Connor's tone was softer than she could ever remember hearing it. He put a bracing hand on Gus's shoulder. "Zack... They had to sedate him. Liz, I know this isn't fair, but someone has to make a statement. It can't be Zack. I can't do it. I've already been filmed too much tonight. Roman is..."

"Oh, god." Tears flowed down Gus's face. "Roman can't do it. I will."

But this wasn't Gus's job.

"No." Liz shook her head. "I'll do it. I just need a couple of moments to think this through."

Because what she said next would be important. It would be everything.

Connor stared down at her. "Are you sure? Liz, do you understand what's happened?"

He wasn't asking if she understood that Joy had been murdered. He wasn't ensuring she grasped the fact that someone had attempted to assassinate Zack and offed his wife instead. He wanted to make sure she knew full well that one act of violence had shifted the balance of power forever.

She glanced over at the large-screen TV in the waiting room. It was filled edge to edge with the shocking moments following the shooting. Yes, the footage showed panicked people scurrying for safety. But in the middle of the stage—and plastered across every TV in America—the video played something real, something heartbreaking and visceral.

It displayed Zack Hayes holding his dying wife, his face a mask of shock and anguish. It revealed him in his most human moments.

"Zack is going to be president," Liz murmured. "We're going to win the election."

They would be swept into the White House on a wave of sympathy.

History had been changed with a single bullet.

At her side, Gus nodded and took a deep breath. "I'll help you. Let's fix your makeup."

"No. I go on like this. I'm not going to clean up a thing. I want the public to see what was done today. I want them to feel it. Connor, brief me on everything we know about this tragedy. I'll take questions."

Gus squeezed her hand. "I'll be right by your side."

But Zack would not. He would be the president of the United States.

So she would remain alone.

* * * *

Mad and Sara
Manhattan
Three years later

"Are you sure you have to go?" Maddox Crawford wasn't

usually anxious, but the evening had kind of gone to hell. It was supposed to be peaceful, damn it. This was the penultimate evening, the night before his engagement. Engagement Eve. Not that Sara Bond knew that. It was a secret he'd only let Augustine Spencer in on.

He'd shared the info on the down low with Gus because he hadn't trusted himself to buy the right engagement ring. Despite his ridiculously privileged upbringing—or maybe because of it—he tended to think big when it came to jewelry and forgot about things Sara would value, like elegance and good taste. Apparently, shoving a diamond the size of his fist on a band of the most expensive platinum wasn't the way to go. Who knew?

So that was why he had a half a million dollars' worth of princess-cut diamond set on a pavé-encrusted rose gold band sitting in his dresser drawer, nestled in its velvet box, just waiting. Tomorrow night he would drop to one knee and beg the best woman he'd ever met to marry him. He'd done everything he knew to make the event romantic and sweet…but he'd hoped he would be spending Engagement Eve doing nasty stuff to his soon-to-be bride. He needed to remind her that while he came with some baggage, he also came with a super flexible tongue that could vibrate at just the right speed. Sure, she might be able to find some other scandalous billionaire who would love her—because who wouldn't?—but she wasn't going to find his tongue on any other man.

Of course, he'd already done the one thing that might ensure she married him. He'd gotten her pregnant. Not on purpose…but that fuckup didn't hurt his cause.

Two days earlier, she'd cried and admitted her "terrible" state. He'd figured out he was supposed to be upset. So he'd frowned and told her they would make the best of it. Mentally, he'd danced a fucking jig and high-fived himself, then started planning exactly how he'd close that trap behind her forever.

Sara turned to him with a groan. "Yeah, I have to. I'm sorry, babe. I'm exhausted and I have to be up super early for that meeting. Besides, I know what will happen if I stay at your place. You'll do that tongue thing and I won't ever get out of bed."

At least they agreed on that. "You don't have to go to the meeting at all, you know. I happen to know the boss, and he's cool with you missing that sucker. In fact, you can have the meeting moved to my place."

Her warm chocolate eyes held mirth even as she rolled them. "Oh, that will impress my manager. The other employees are already whispering and speculating. Once we attend that gala tomorrow night and everyone realizes we're together, there will be even more gossip. Is it too much to hope that people will be more interested in your new head of security? I haven't met her yet."

Oh, but she would. "Everly Parker will do great things. I'll set up a meeting between the two of you when she gets back from the conference she's attending this week. She's young and smart."

She was also his half sister.

He'd discovered the affair his normally good-for-nothing father had engaged in with his secretary years before. It had sparked an investigation that had led him to discover his shared blood with Everly. Unfortunately, he was almost certain she had no idea the father she'd grown up with hadn't given her his genes. Mad wanted to tell her sooner rather than later…but he had no finesse. Luckily his almost fiancée had it in spades. Once he and Sara were engaged, he would get her advice on how to not freak Everly out. Because if he plopped his ass on a corner of Everly's desk and suddenly said, "hey, sis, Dad was a bastard, wasn't he?" she would probably lose it.

Sara grinned up at him. "Excellent. I'm glad you're

hiring more women. If Gabe doesn't do the same, I'm going to protest outside my own family's company. I swear, if I have to sit through another board meeting where some rich, entitled guy mansplains the world to me, I'm going to turn homicidal."

He loved her idealistic side. "You know those rich guys kind of run our world."

"Not when women like me and Everly Parker start taking over," she shot back. "I've been thinking... We should steal Augustine from Zack."

He also loved how confident she was. Sara knew damn well he and Gus had been fuck buddies for years and she didn't feel threatened. It probably helped that he'd explained most of those late-night booty calls had been more about needing to not be alone than wanting sex.

Mad pulled Sara to his side, wanting his hands on her. Soon they would be at her building and he would have to let her go. "No can do, baby. I worked too hard to get her that job at the White House."

She cuddled close. "Why? I always assumed Gus would head Crawford legal one day. I would try to convince Gabe to hire her, but we're too small. Gus needs serious red meat. You get sued way more than we do."

Ah, but soon they would share all those fun lawsuits—along with their lives. "I sneakily convinced Roman to hire Gus because he's been in love with her since we were kids."

He was sick of watching those two wreck their lives. If they didn't get it together soon, he was fairly certain they would both end up alone and miserable, and his tender heart couldn't take it.

He'd figured out long ago that all the biblical stuff about time was right. There was a time to be born and a time to die. A time to enjoy strippers and cocaine, and a time to get married and not do either of those things anymore. Roman didn't understand that lesson yet, but he was going to.

Sara sat up as the limo rolled to a stop. "Huh, that kind of makes sense. I thought Roman loved Joy, but he always seems more alive when he's near Gus."

Exactly. Roman was a dumbass for refusing to admit that. Not that Joy hadn't been lovely, but Mad had never been as enthralled with her as the rest of the gang. She'd seemed so implausibly sweet that her demeanor sometimes felt false. Sara was sweet like pure cane sugar. Joy had been saccharine.

"Roman and Gus had an affair a long time ago." The rest of that story was theirs to tell. He owed Gus his silence about the baby she'd lost, but he could use Sara's help to play cupid. "I don't think either one of them got over it."

Sara cupped his face in her palms. "You are not at all who I imagined you were. You are so much kinder and more thoughtful. You're loving and charming and… You're everything, Maddox Crawford."

He was glad she thought so, but that was only because he was so good at hiding the fact he was a needy asshole. "I wasn't until I met you."

She leaned in and brushed her mouth over his. "You met me when you were twelve."

"And that was the day I became a man." He put his hand on her belly.

God, he couldn't wait until he could feel their child there. Sara was going to be so gorgeous all round and full, and he was going to be the best dad-to-be ever. He would rub her feet and agree with everything she said.

He would be the kind of dad he'd always wanted, one who loved his wife and kid. One who put them first.

She laughed, the sound filling his soul. "I love you. And now I have to go. We're really on for the reception at the Met tomorrow night? No second thoughts?"

Oh, they were so on. The Met was one of his favorite

places. He'd found solace there as a kid, and he couldn't wait to share it with his own. But tomorrow night would be even more perfect. The Met was debuting a new exhibit, one that Crawford Industries had sponsored. Tons of socialites and gossip writers would be there, so it was the perfect event for him and Sara to go public and announce their engagement.

"None at all. I'll pick you up at seven." When she pulled away, he tugged her back. "Hey, you don't have to go yet. You know, we could do it right here."

She groaned, but her smile was wide as she maneuvered out of his grasping hands. "We can't."

"I'll be quick." But he wouldn't be. He would get her under him and not care that they were sitting in the middle of Park Avenue making the ground shake.

"I've always said you were the devil, Maddox Crawford." The door opened, and his driver helped her out of the car. "See you tomorrow."

He hated letting her go. After tomorrow, he would never have to do it again. He would be an engaged man, and he would make sure Sara understood that when she accepted his monster good-taste ring and his last name, she'd also accepted his neediness.

Mad also hoped she accepted what would likely be his latest lawsuit because he was going to fire Tavia Gordon as soon as he figured out her scheme. Something fishy was going on with the Crawford Foundation... But he refused to think about that now. Instead, he watched as Sara walk into her building, the doorman closing the door after her. She was safe for the night. And it was his last one without her.

God, that sounded sweet.

He hit the button that connected him to the driver.

"You can pull out, Bill. Let's head home." He wouldn't sleep. He'd probably call Gus and pray she wasn't on a date with some skanky too-young dude with abs of steel because he wanted to go over tomorrow night's plan again. Everything had to be perfect.

"I'm very sorry, Mr. Crawford." Bill's voice shook over the intercom. "I didn't want to do this, but I, um…owe some people. You're actually a pretty nice boss, and I'm…I'm sorry."

The comm went dead, and the door suddenly opened. What the hell?

Then Mad found himself looking up into dark eyes that held the promise of violence.

"Mr. Crawford, my name is Ivan Krylov." The big man shoved his way into his limo and sat squarely across from him.

A chill dashed through Mad. He forced himself to sit back since he had the definite feeling that if he tried to escape, he wouldn't be allowed.

This had to be about the investigation into the foundation. He'd discovered a connection between Tavia, the head of his charitable foundation, and the Russian mob. It was obvious he was going to get a stern talking to about looking into things he shouldn't.

Maybe he wouldn't be firing Tavia after all. Maybe he would be bringing in the police instead.

For now, he swallowed and tried to play cool. "I'm afraid I don't do business anymore by partying with perspective clients, Mr. Krylov. If you have a proposal, schedule a meeting with my assistant. I'll get back to you."

When he risked reaching for the door on his left, it opened. Another large man blocked his exit, slid in, and shut it solidly behind him.

Bill was so fired. And he, unfortunately, was trapped.

"I will be giving you my proposal in person now, Mr. Crawford," Krylov said, his Russian accent thick. "Because I cannot wait. I must return to my friends in Moscow, you see."

"You need a ride?" He reached for the bottle of Scotch he kept in the limo as his heart raced. But he couldn't let these men see him sweat or smell his fear. "I'll be happy to drop you off. I'm friendly that way."

Thank god Sara was up in her apartment.

"We are here to...talk. Let's go somewhere quiet so I can discuss a situation with you. I think you have some misconceptions about one of your employees. I will fix this now. Unless you think it's better for us to go upstairs to your girlfriend's home. We could speak there."

His heart threatened to stop. "Girlfriend? Are you talking about Sara? She's my best friend's sister. I did her brother a favor by letting her intern at my company. I was just giving her a ride home from work." Thank god he and Sara had been beyond circumspect. For months, she'd insisted he keep her out of the tabloids, so no one had seen them together. "Trust me. She's not my type. I'm into one-night stands. That one is practically a virgin, and I don't have any use for a woman like that. The only one in my life right now is my housekeeper, and she's gone home for the day."

"This is good for her," Krylov said. "Unfortunate for you, though. Since no one is at your home, we will go there and have a nice, long chat."

He put on his best devil-may-care grin and held up his Scotch glass. "Whatever you say, buddy. I like an adventure."

He forced himself not to fight as the limo rolled away. He focused on finding some way out of this mess. There had to be one, right? He just had to find it.

But nothing mattered as long as Sara and the baby were safe.

Nothing.

* * * *

Three hours later, Mad clutched his stomach as he rolled to his side and spit blood. Every muscle in his body ached. He thought he'd known pain, but what Krylov and his associate had given him was next level. The men had laid into him with a long, agonizing "speech" about how Mad should stay out of their business. Every word had been punctuated by violence.

Then, finally, the mobsters had left, certain they'd made their point. Mad had to admit Krylov's message was crystal clear. Butt out of the Crawford Foundation's irregularities.

God, he wanted Sara. He wished like hell he could call her and beg her to come over and hold him. She would take him to the hospital and baby him. For a few hours, the world might feel safe again.

Except he knew it wasn't. And it might never be again.

Tonight had changed everything.

Mad closed his eyes, hissing as he rolled to his back again. The marble felt cold as fuck against his clammy skin. He didn't usually spend much time in his kitchen, but Krylov was a thoughtful torturer. Just before he'd taken the first punch, he explained that he'd chosen this room because blood could be mopped up more easily here.

Wincing, he tried—and failed—to get up. In a weird way, his pain was good news. If he could feel it, that meant he was still alive.

"They got you good, huh?"

Panic flaring, Mad opened his eyes and tried to inch away from the red-haired intruder. "Who are you?"

Shit, had Krylov changed his mind and sent someone to finish him off after all? Maybe, but this guy didn't sound Russian.

"Hey, I'm not here to hurt you. I hoped I could stay underground a little longer, but things are moving now, so I can't wait." He sighed. "God, I never expected *you* would be the one out of the bunch I'd have to work with. I'm not even sure this is a good idea." The lanky man paced the floor, stepping around the blood. "You could be in on it, after all."

Mad shoved himself up, managing to sit, despite the agony screaming through his system. Grimacing, he forced his back to the ridiculously expensive gray cabinets a designer had told him Sara would love. He'd remodeled his place to trick her into thinking he was a good catch.

If Krylov had any idea how much he loved her, that she was having their child, or the lengths he would go to keep them safe, the Russian would have far better methods of controlling him than mere pain.

Of course if what he'd said was true....

"In on what?" Righteous anger was rapidly replacing his fear. Did everyone think they could waltz in and out of his fucking house tonight?

The intruder glowered. Despite his russet hair swept around his ears haphazardly and his Howdy Doody face, the tall man managed to convey a very real sense of danger, especially when he propped his hands on his hips, revealing his lean strength—and the holster at his shoulder.

"The conspiracy." His hands twitched slightly as he stared down at Mad.

Krylov hadn't used that word, but the big Russian's mission had been to give him fear, not information. Even so, Mad had grasped enough to understand.

"Zack Hayes isn't a Russian plant."

He couldn't be. Mad had known Zack for the vast majority of his life. Zack was an all-American hero. Krylov had only suggested otherwise to keep him from calling in the biggest gun he could.

"Which is exactly what you would say if you were in on it."

Mad did not appreciate the irony. "Look, asshole, I

don't get—or believe—half what that Russian fucker said to me, and I have no idea who you are but I need to get to a hospital."

The man shook his head and dropped to one knee to more closely inspect the damage. "You can't, but you'll be fine. I've got a friend who can help you."

"A friend? I could be bleeding internally. What the—"

"They're too careful for that. You're more useful to them alive than dead or you'd already be fish bait. Besides, I want you to think about what happens if Maddox Crawford goes to a hospital and the press finds out."

Then Sara rushes to his side, and their relationship is outed. And that wasn't all. "The police get involved."

"Yep, and once the police get involved, everything gets exposed. That's something they want to avoid at all costs. But if that happens, they'll be looking for a scapegoat…and they won't care about collateral damage."

The stranger was right. As much as it burned him, he had to stop looking into what was going on at the Crawford Foundation. But once he did, Krylov would know he had a weak spot, a button that could be pushed again and again to make him do whatever the syndicate wanted. Mad wasn't foolish enough to think this mess was over simply because he'd promised to stop his investigation.

"Fuck."

"Exactly. So as much as that sucks, if you don't keep your mouth shut, they'll have no choice but to get rid of you, like they got rid of Constance Hayes."

"What?" They'd offed Zack's mother? Sure, she'd died suddenly and under somewhat mysterious circumstances, but… "How do you know?"

The stranger rolled his eyes. "Pull your head out of your party-boy ass and follow the trail of bodies. Who else shoved his nose in, got too close, and paid the ultimate price? Admiral Spencer."

Holy shit, they'd killed Dax's father, too? "No. He committed suicide."

"Don't be naïve. They faked his fall from grace. And when that didn't get him out of the way, they faked his self-inflicted death."

These suggestions were so next level, they were blowing Mad's mind. "You've got to be kidding."

"This shit is too significant for me to joke about. Come on. Keep thinking. Who else's death was suspicious. Whose was the most shocking of all?"

It couldn't be. It just couldn't. But the name still slipped out. "Joy Hayes?"

"Someone get the guy a prize." The stranger smiled acidly.

"Joy would never have investigated the death of a fly, much less a Russian infiltration."

He shook his head. "You're right. She had a bigger purpose to serve. What would have happened without her death?"

Mad's thoughts were racing. This guy had to be a loon…but what he said was starting to make a weird sort of sense. "Zack wouldn't have become president."

"Bingo."

And the Russians had wanted Zack to be elected? Why?

Oh, fuck. This conspiracy was a rabbit hole, bigger and deeper than he could have possibly imagined. He didn't know what his friend and his president had to do with the Crawford Foundation, but they both had shady Russians pulling the strings.

No, this was just a nightmare. A bad dream. That must be what was happening. He would wake any second now. Sara would be in bed beside him. He would stop worrying about finesse and he would propose. Then he would tell her about Everly. She would help him figure out how to handle her. He would wake up. They would laugh about this stupid dream and they would...they would make plans to become a family.

"The Russians have been planning this for a *very* long time. Sergei is not only on US soil, he's in the White House. I need to figure out what Zack Hayes knows about him. Or...if Zack Hayes is him."

"No." Mad refused to believe that one of his best friends was a traitor.

"Take off your rose-colored glasses. It's possible the president of the United States is actually a Russian citizen, and that he's working for Russian interests."

Stunned, Mad laughed, mostly because he didn't know what else to do. For once, he had nothing to say, not even a smartass comeback.

The grave face of the man looking down at him didn't appear amused. "It's time to get serious, Crawford. I need your help."

"Why me?" Mad shook his head. "And who the hell are you?"

"You can call me Freddy." The stranger stood and offered him a hand. "Let's get you cleaned up and talk about what happens next. I've been trying to unravel this mess by myself for years. It might be nice to have a partner."

Seeing that he had very little choice, Mad reached out a hand. Freddy hauled him up. His entire body protested.

And he realized he wasn't going to wake up soon. He was going to dive headfirst into the nightmare of this Russian conspiracy mess because he didn't have a choice. He had to get smart, think fast, protect the people he loved...by giving them all up.

As much as he hated it, this was now his life.

* * * *

Two Months Later

Sara sat inside the Church of St. Ignatius of Loyola, facing the urn. Fury and heartbreak churned inside her. How had she gotten here?

Around her, people rose from their pews and began shuffling down the aisles. Some approached the urn, quietly paying their respects to a man who hadn't respected much of anything.

Maddox Crawford certainly hadn't respected her or he wouldn't have broken her heart.

Augustine stood and touched a bracing hand to her shoulder. "Sweetie, Gabe said the car is coming around."

Sara had tried to sit through the service alone, but Gus had slid beside her at the last minute, holding her hand during the long, sometimes ridiculous funeral that Mad had apparently arranged himself.

Had he planned his own death? Her mother had always wondered if Mad was unstable.

"All right." She still didn't move. It would be a few moments before the car got through the dense Manhattan traffic. If she stood, people might see her and try to talk to her. As it was, Sara was barely holding herself together. Or worse, she might catch sight of the woman Mad had left her for.

Was Everly Parker mourning her lover, too?

Gus frowned. "Gabe and the guys are going to go to a nearby pub to drink and reminisce. I suspect you're headed home?"

The last thing she wanted to do was hang out with her brother and his friends. She'd been around them all her life and she'd been smart enough not to get tangled up with their antics and dramas. They were Gabe's friends, not hers. Sure, she'd gotten to know a couple of them, and she'd certainly developed close relationships to some of the women in their circle, but she'd been smart enough not to fall for one of the men the world called the Perfect Gentlemen.

At least until she had.

"Do you want me to tell Gabe to hold the car?" Gus asked.

"I'll leave when the crowd clears out a bit." Sara fell quiet again, but the question she hadn't stopped asking herself gnawed again. "Do you think she was here?"

She shouldn't care. Mad had treated her more like a hundred-dollar hooker at the end of the night than the woman he'd professed to love. Even telling herself that she was better off didn't help. There was still a horrible, gaping ache in her heart where Mad used to be and she didn't know how to fill it. On the one hand, she wanted to weep and wail and beg for someone to send Mad back to her. On the other hand, she hoped he was rotting in hell.

Gus sighed. "I don't know what Everly Parker looks like. Besides, it doesn't matter if she was here because Mad wasn't having an affair with her."

So Gus kept insisting. Sara wasn't convinced. She'd heard the rumors over the water coolers at Crawford Industries. She'd been a massive idiot to think Mad would ever settle down.

Then why had he told her he loved her?

Because it's what I do, sweetness. And I totally loved you. Long and hard and well. Now it's time for me to love someone else. I'm not dad material. Find yourself some boring, stable IT tycoon. There have to be a few hanging around. I've got to go. My date is waiting.

Sara had their whole breakup on her phone because he'd done it via text.

She'd been dressed and ready for the gala at the Met. She'd spent all day plucking, waxing, painting, and grooming to make sure she looked her best. Then she'd spent the evening staring at the wall of her bedroom trying to figure out what had gone wrong and who the hell he'd left her for. She'd called and texted, tried to reason with Mad.

He'd never spoken to her again.

The headlines of the tabloids the next day had spoken volumes though. No, he hadn't taken Everly to the Met that night, but it hadn't taken long for him to start having a lot of closed-door meetings with her at the office.

"Sara, you have to believe me," Gus insisted, sitting beside her again.

All around them, people from Mad's life mingled as they slowly filed out of the church to get on with the rest of the day. The rest of their life. Mad had touched each of them, many of them intimately and in ways that would make most blush.

She'd known he was a manwhore. She'd known it before she knew the word. Even when they'd been kids, she'd been sure she shouldn't lose her heart to him. "It doesn't matter now."

"It does matter." Gus put a hand on her shoulder. "Sara, something is incredibly off with all of this. He loved you. He was going to ask you to marry him."

Maybe it had crossed his mind for a moment or two. Maybe he'd even believed it. Mad had been impulsive and mercurial. The night she'd told him she was pregnant, he'd seemed excited. Two days later, he'd completely washed his hands of her and the baby. That was Mad.

"He changed his mind."

"Or something happened."

She couldn't waste the energy to unravel Mad's "logic" now. She had to think about her baby. "I'm going home."

"All right. I'll take care of my one task and come by your place. Then we can go out to the Hamptons. You can unwind, and we can talk there," Gus offered. "I can call Liz. We'll make it a girls' trip. I would contact Holland but she's being a stubborn butt."

Sara shook her head. "I want to be alone."

Standing, she carefully smoothed out the Prada sheath she wouldn't be able to fit into after another week or two. Or maybe she would be able to wear it a bit longer. She hadn't felt much like eating lately. The doctor said the calorie deficit wasn't a big deal yet, but soon she needed to stop being furious and grief-stricken and start taking care of her baby.

Yes, it was *her* baby. Not his. He hadn't wanted their child. He'd made that perfectly clear. He'd even offered to pay for her abortion in his flurry of breakup texts.

Fucking bastard.

Why did she miss him with every ounce of her soul? She'd hated him in those last weeks when she'd been forced to watch him date other women and hear all the juicy gossip about him and Everly heating up the chairman's desk. But not once had she contemplated a world without him.

Some foolish part of her had hoped Mad would eventually miss her and come back groveling. At the very least, she'd thought he would change his mind about the baby once she or he was born. Now any chance of Mad returning to her life in any way was gone forever.

Gus stared at her. "Are you joining Holland in the mulish brigade?"

Sara sent her a cutting glare. "Or maybe I don't want to spend the week listening to Mad's old mistress tell me why I should forgive him." The minute the words were out of her mouth, she wanted to call them back. She reached for Gus. "I'm sorry. I didn't mean old in terms of age. I meant former. But you weren't his mistress, really. And I never meant to imply that he owned or possessed you in any patriarchal way. I'm trying to say I can't handle much of anything right now."

Gus chuckled as she cupped Sara's shoulders. "I

understand. What if I promise I won't mention his name unless you want to talk about him?"

But Sara always wanted to talk about him. She wanted to scream at him, wanted to ask him why. God, she'd do almost anything for one more moment with him.

She'd always thought she was strong, but in the wake of Hurricane Mad, she felt like nothing more than a pathetic girl in love. It was time to grow up and give her love to someone worthy: her baby.

"I need to be alone, Gus. I'm sorry I snapped."

"I suspect you'll snap a lot, and that's okay," Gus replied. "You've been through some serious emotional turmoil. Besides, you know I've got thick skin. I can handle whatever you dish out. And if you need a friend, call me. I'm going to poke my nose into a few things that aren't adding up. I won't involve you except to promise it will be okay." She withdrew her hands. "I'll let Gabe know you'll be ready to go in a few minutes. Oh, and don't think I'm letting the stubborn-bitch thing go for too long."

Sara knew better. Gus would be on her doorstep long before she was ready.

For now, she took a deep breath, staring at the picture of Mad they'd placed by his empty urn. Even now, Mad was smirking, but she'd seen his real smile. She'd seen his whole face light up like it was Christmas morning.

"I can't believe she showed up," a voice whispered behind her. "Do you think the boss left her a little something?"

"You mean, like, in his will? If anyone would leave his mistress a really lavish final parting gift, it would be Mad Crawford," another voice said.

"Yeah," quipped another. "I'll bet Everly gets paid after all. I never bought that innocent act. I live not far from her, so I know he spent tons of time at her place."

Sara didn't look back at the gossipers, merely turned

and walked down the aisle. She wouldn't look at Mad's picture again. She would try her best not to think of him at all.

"It's you and me, baby," she said quietly.

It would have to be enough.

Chapter One

Present Day
Washington, DC

Zack Hayes stared, utterly shocked, at the dead man sitting across from him.

Minutes ago, he'd slid into the presidential limo for a short ride to Marine One so he could chopper over to Camp David for the weekend. Thanks to the guy across from him, he put that plan on hold.

"For someone dearly departed, you don't look any worse for the wear. Did you use a parachute?" It was the wrong thing to ask first, but Zack had so many questions, he hardly knew where to start.

What he really wanted to do was throttle the man who'd once been among his very best friends.

Maddox Crawford, as impeccably groomed and urbane as ever, sat back and crossed one leg over the opposite knee as he knocked back a glass of expensive Scotch. Apparently perishing tragically in a plane crash hadn't been too rough on the guy.

"Of course. It wasn't easy. After I discovered the bomb on board, I had to time my jump just right. I needed to reach a location where cameras wouldn't catch me bailing out. My escape would have gone off so much easier if I'd flown west. The east coast is awfully crowded these days. Ever thought of moving the White House to Wyoming?"

Death hadn't changed Mad's personality one bit. He was still an irreverent ass. "I take it you weren't actually coming to see me then. That was all part of whatever ploy you'd cooked up?"

Now that he knew Mad was alive, Zack saw clearly that the last several months had been a carefully crafted drama. But why? Sure, Mad had once been all about grabbing the headlines, but even he wouldn't go so far as to fake his own death simply for a media splash.

"When you wouldn't talk to me before my plane took off, I realized I had to find another way to get your attention."

Zack remembered that fateful day well. It had been one of the worst of his life. Mad had called that afternoon, wanting a meeting. Zack had dodged him. A few hours later, Mad had been "dead." Since then, Zack had wondered what his friend intended to say.

"When you called I'd just gotten off the phone with Gabe. He'd asked for advice on how to deal with you. I was angry. I didn't have anything civil to say so I didn't want to talk."

"That day, Gabe wouldn't listen to me either. We met for lunch at Cipriani's. I looked across the table at my best friend in the world, who was beyond pissed at me for the way I treated Sara, and I almost told him everything. Then I realized someone was filming our exchange—and not because he was interested in gossip. The Russians had already paid me a visit once, and they were following me. Probably had been for a while."

"The Russians?" Zack frowned because nothing made sense. "But why you? You've never been interested in politics."

"Politics, no. A money trail, yes. Long story. But after that aborted lunch with Gabe, I knew I had to do something radical. Thanks to my prior run-in with some Russian mob heavies, I started working with Matthew Kemp. He was actually the one who found the bomb on the plane, since he routinely checked all my vehicles. When he found the explosive device a few hours before I took off that day, I knew what I had to do."

"Pretend you were coming to DC to patch things up with me while faking your own death? That's crazy, even for you, Mad."

He shrugged. "Everyone believed it. And I needed them to."

"Even your best fucking friends? Do you understand the hell you put everyone through? The crushing guilt I've lived with because I believed that if I'd simply answered your call that day, you'd still be alive?"

"You're my friend—and the president—not an actor. The grief, the funeral—all of it had to look real. It was Matt's idea, but we all went along with it. And the plan served its purpose. It got you all thinking in a way nothing else would have."

For a time, Matthew Kemp, one of his Secret Service agents, had seemingly betrayed Zack. Or that's what he'd believed. But the man had died protecting Augustine Spencer and Roman Calder from a rogue MI6 agent working for the Russians.

"How did you start working with Kemp, of all people?" Zack was curious. Of course at this point, he was curious about pretty much everything.

Mad frowned, clearly choosing his words. That worried Zack because he hadn't been aware Mad thought at much beyond where to put the fiver in a stripper's G-string. "I don't know how much I should tell you, Zack."

That made him sit up straighter. Fuck, he didn't want to deal with this. Every time he considered the possibility that his mother might have accidentally smothered the real Zack Hayes in infancy, and he might be a Russian-born imposter, it made him physically ill. And ever since Mad's "death," Zack had become very aware that he was the focus of a global conspiracy. He'd spent his whole life striving to be president of the United States. Apparently, the Russians had been playing a long game with the same intended outcome for reasons Zack still didn't know. But he had some ugly guesses.

"You think I'm Sergei." He dropped the code name for a Russian agent at the center of this vast conspiracy they'd all been trying to unravel.

Mad raised a brow. But why mince words or draw this out? Mad was back from the dead for a reason, and he obviously knew far more than Zack would have believed a billionaire manwhore perpetually in search of a party would. Clearly, Mad had been investigating, too.

Zack was still pissed…but he was also kind of proud.

More importantly, the time had come to figure out if he was the real problem—the ultimate sleeper.

With a sigh, Mad poured himself another Scotch. "Maybe. We should have a meeting."

Though there was nothing humorous about the situation, Zack threw back his head and laughed. Of all the things he'd expected Mad to say, he hadn't imagined the man would want to gather the Perfect Gentlemen.

Over the decades, the six of them convened whenever they'd found themselves in trouble more serious than tossing back a drink or punching someone in the face could solve. They'd called their first meeting in eighth grade to handle the bully fucking with Connor in Spanish class. Two days later, Harold Tally hadn't bugged anyone again, and they'd set a pattern.

Was Mad trying to circle the wagons now?

"This isn't some problem with grades or a girl, man. We're talking about treason. If you know something, tell me now so I can get this over with."

Mad regarded him wearing his signature smirk. "I should have known you'd play the martyr."

Savage anger hit Zack. He leaned forward, looking one of his best friends straight in the eyes. "This isn't one of your games, Mad. It's not some prank we'll all laugh about later. People have gotten hurt. For fuck's sake, people have died."

Elizabeth had gotten hurt. And now she loathed him.

God, had Elizabeth betrayed him, too?

Mad leaned in, his stare unwavering. "The mother of my unborn child hates my guts, so don't act like I don't know people have gotten hurt. I lost everything. I gave it all up to protect her and my family."

"You don't have a damn family, Mad. And you're right. Sara won't speak to you again."

Mad paled, then whipped his gaze around to stare out the window of the limo. He took another drink, his hand clearly shaking. "I kind of thought you guys were my family."

All of Zack's rage dissipated. They'd been together for decades. Mad, Gabe, Dax, Connor, and Roman were his family. Always. They'd gotten him through everything from physics to his presidential campaign. He had to have some faith in them.

It hit him suddenly that Mad wasn't actually dead. Zack didn't have to mourn anymore. Maddox Crawford was sitting here in all his audacious, Scotch-drinking glory. Emotion rose hard and fast as he looked at the man who'd been a brother to him for decades.

Mad looked his way again, his eyes appearing to mist over. "I'm sorry I couldn't tell you. I know how hard it must have been on all of you. I love you guys. You might be pissed with me, but I'm going to explain everything. And I'm going to get us out of this shit storm—as soon as I figure out what's truly going on. That's why I'm here. It's gotten too big, and I need help."

Zack mulled that over. In the past, they'd stuck together and always come out on top. Granted, comparing calculus grades to international espionage was a stretch...but none of them had managed to solve this yet. Why not try together?

Zack couldn't take Marine One to Camp David since there was the obvious issue of having a dead man on board with him. At this point, Zack wouldn't be surprised if all his current Secret Service agents, not just Thomas, were in on whatever scheme Mad had going. But the press might have a collective heart attack at the sight of Maddox Crawford's return from the dead.

Good thing Zack had other means of reaching his destination.

"Who else was in on your plan? You didn't trust any of us enough to reach out, but you've been saying 'we.' Who *did* you trust enough to help you deceive us?"

"It wasn't lack of trust or a deception," Mad argued. "I was trying to save you. Do you honestly think I've been sleeping in shitholes for months, flying in cargo planes, and eating fast food for some kind of practical joke? In case it's not clear yet, you're in trouble, Zack. The entire damn country is, and it all comes down to you and your family." He pressed his lips together for a somber moment. "For what it's worth, I don't believe you were in on it."

His gut twisted because he knew exactly what Mad meant. "Do you mean my mother's murder? Or my wife's?"

"Any of it. There's a string of bodies that stretches all the way back to Moscow, Zack. This conspiracy goes deeper than you realize."

"Or maybe I know everything. *Mozhet byt, ya syn russkikh roditeley, kak ty eto dumayesh.*" Zack knew well his Russian accent was so perfect, he could fool even a linguist.

You have to speak their language, son. This is important. You have to make them believe you're one of them. That's the key to life. Let them think you're one of them until you no longer need them.

His father's voice rumbled through his head often. The man had dementia now, but he'd fed such nuggets of wisdom to Zack from infancy to adulthood because his father had groomed him to be president. So while some kids were taught to share their toys, Zack had learned Russian and the art of manipulation.

Mad scowled. "You are not a Russian son. I won't believe that. I'm sorry if it seemed like I doubted you earlier. It's been a tense few months."

Zack blinked at his old friend. "Since when do you speak Russian?"

"Since the day one nearly killed me and destroyed my life as I knew it." Mad sat back, his lips forming a mulish line. "I want a meeting. I don't want to tell this story five times."

"Well, you're in luck. The guys are on their way to meet me at Camp David. We can shelve this discussion until then." He let his driver know to change course and take him directly to the secluded retreat. "We should be there in half an hour."

Mad nodded and fell silent.

Zack did the same, oddly at a loss for words.

The guys would get to Camp David roughly thirty minutes after he and Mad did. Then they could start fixing this clusterfuck. That thought cheered him.

But he had to make some decisions first. Hell, he

should probably start by firing his entire detail and finding another since Mad had infiltrated them all.

Others would tell him to have Mad arrested and renditioned somewhere where they could torture the fuck out of him and get the answers they needed. But all those years of shared friendship sat between them. Mad had protected him from bullies' fists and shown him an entirely different way to look at life. Mad had given him a group of friends who'd become so much closer than family. Mad had brought them all together.

Zack refused to turn his back on his old friend now.

He reached for the Scotch. "I'm glad you're not dead."

Mad sent him something that looked too pensive to be a smile. "Me, too."

"Though I should warn you that Gabe will probably kill you."

Mad grimaced. "I think he'll understand once I explain."

"Nope. He's going to be so pissed. I think your sister will be, too. Thanks for the heads-up on that, by the way. Everly is good with a gun, you know."

"Come on, Zack. They'll be happy I'm alive. And it wasn't like I totally left you."

"No, you sent an army of Deep Throats after us."

Mad snorted. "I thought it was clever."

"You know that has a historical reference, right? Not a pornographic one."

Mad tried not to, but he still giggled like they were twelve again and someone said "boobs."

"Who were all those informants?"

"Just actors taking their cue from me through their ear piece. I hired a different one every time. I didn't want any of them getting too involved with the investigation or trying to figure anything out, so I told them all I was playing an elaborate prank on friends."

"The fact that the fate of the American people is even slightly in your hands makes me want to drink more." Zack took a long swallow, the alcohol burning a familiar path down his throat.

"That makes two of us, brother. Shocked the fuck out of me."

They fell silent again. Zack didn't pry. He'd hear Mad's story with the rest of their gang since they'd been in this together from the beginning. If he was being used as some pawn in a Russian game, he didn't want to hear that news without his brothers around him.

But Zack had one question he couldn't keep silent about a minute longer.

"Elizabeth…is she a part of this?" Elizabeth Matthews, with her long blonde hair, intelligent blue eyes, and seemingly innocent heart-shaped face. Had she been sent to ensnare him? Was she another string his enemies wouldn't hesitate to pull until he danced to their tune?

Mad's face went solemn. "I don't know. I hope not, but there's something happening at the White House. They have someone on the inside. Or at least someone wants us to think so."

That was all he would get for now. Zack eased back, his thoughts on the woman he couldn't seem to stop wanting…no matter what she might be guilty of.

* * * *

From his position by the fireplace at the back of the room, Maddox Crawford heard the door open. The raucous sounds of his friends greeting each other drifted his way. Excitement and anxiety each grabbed half his guts and squeezed until he felt wrung tight.

He heard Dax first since the naval officer was the loudest, bitching about the car trip then inquiring about a cold one. Connor didn't say a word, but there was no way Sparks hadn't come.

"I'm ready for some quiet time," Roman said. "We've got Gus moved in, which is great. But now I have to deal with bridezilla Gus. Work Gus was already a handful, but bridezilla Gus makes her look like a kitten."

"Like that's a surprise," Gabe returned. "I'm so glad my wife works at Crawford. If she looked into Bond's security, I would never hear the end of her horror about our lax cyber-safety protocols."

Their voices were drifting closer. *Shit.* This was it.

Mad took another long drink to quell his anxiety. The Scotch was excellent. It was so fucking good to be back in civilization, back to familiar things. Freddy had the world's cheapest tastes, mostly because he lived his entire life off the grid and on the run from whatever happened to be chasing him that week. Mad had deeply missed indoor toilets, and right now he wanted nothing more than to curl up in a real bed, take a hot shower, and forget about the rest of world for a while.

It's going to be okay. The guys would be happy to see him, right? They were his best friends...whom he'd lied to and walked out on and gotten one of their sisters pregnant before viciously dumping her in a very public way.

Who was he kidding? They were going to make this hurt.

"Gabe, wait," Zack said. "I should tell you something. All of you. We have a visitor. I need to explain."

This was the tactic they'd decided on during their ride out to Camp David, the president's playground, as some in the press had dubbed the sprawling estate in rural Maryland where a president could always be assured of privacy. A month after Zack had been inaugurated, he and all the guys had come out here, sat around a fire to talk about Joy and everything Zack had lost on his way to victory.

How did he explain everything now that the losses were stacking up and amounted to far greater than any of them had imagined?

"Okay. Let me set this down, and you can tell me about our visitor. But it better not be a stripper. I'm a married man now. Everly would kick my—" Gabe walked around the corner, then stopped in the opening of the great room, his jaw dropping.

"Hi." Mad wasn't sure what else to say.

Of all his friends, leaving Gabe had hurt the most. They hadn't exactly drifted apart the way so many friends did after college and relationships and high-powered jobs. They'd stuck together through it all. Not that he wasn't attached to them all, but Dax spent most of his time on a ship. Connor's location had been classified for the last decade. Roman and Zack had always been on the campaign trail. But Gabe Bond had been by his side day in and day out for decades.

Dax entered behind Gabe, Connor on his heels. They all stood frozen and mute.

Mad cleared his throat. "Gabe, I'm sorry I couldn't tell you. You have no idea how often I've wanted to call you these last months."

When Gabe didn't answer, Mad swallowed tightly. How had he ever thought this would be easy? He'd anticipated that seeing Sara again would be wrenching and painful, but somehow he'd fooled himself about this reunion with his friends. For the last four months, he'd done nothing but dream of this moment. He'd envisioned himself as the white knight riding in to save everyone, so in his head they'd all been so freaking happy he wasn't dead that they instantly forgave him.

There wasn't an ounce of forgiveness in Gabe's eyes as he crossed the space between them. Fuck. Zack had been right. He was about to die.

Mad began backing away. "Now, Gabe…"

Gabe wasn't hearing it. He simply reared a fist back and punched him squarely in the face. Unlike the Russians from the night this ordeal had started, Gabe wasn't trying to be conscientious or careful about where his blow landed. Those professionals had left his face intact so he could make public appearances without raising brows. Oh, he'd pissed blood for a week, but his mug had been perfectly beautiful.

That would not be the case today. Already, his nose stung and throbbed like a bitch. He hoped it wasn't broken.

"You asshole," Gabe growled, teeth bared.

"Well, I called that." Connor stood back, shaking his head. "I knew he wasn't really dead."

"You didn't call anything," Dax argued. "Gabe, don't kill him—yet. I want an explanation first."

"And I'd love a couple of pounds of flesh." Roman tossed his jacket aside, looking ready to join the fray.

Thanks to Freddy, Mad had picked up some new moves. He hadn't spent his whole time in hiding merely learning Russian and how to use an outhouse. Now he ducked and bobbed out of range, even though he had two sides to protect. "Look, I'm willing to take one punch. I deserved it from Gabe. But Roman, I will fight back."

"I have a cat because of you. A freaking cat. There's an entire cat shelter in the UK I now have to maintain." Roman grumbled like getting a feline companion was the worst thing that could happen to a man.

"You also have a fiancée," Mad pointed out, fists still raised to protect his face. "You're welcome."

Roman and Augustine Spencer would never have gotten together if it hadn't been for his meddling. Not that Roman deserved her.

"And I have a sister who cries every night." Gabe fisted his hands at his sides, his face mottled with emotion.

The idea of Sara crying kicked Mad in the gut. "I know

you won't believe me, but I did this for her. And for you. For Everly. Hell, for all of us. Punch me later. But listen to me now. We're in trouble, Zack especially."

That leeched the rage out of the room.

"Mad and I had a chat on the way up here. He wanted to call a meeting. It seems that while he was on the 'other side,' he learned a thing or two about our Russian adversaries," Zack said.

Connor stared pointedly at Thomas, who stood inside the door. The rest of Zack's detail patrolled the grounds. "Should we talk right now?"

Zack shrugged. "Thomas is a plant and has been for some time. We can't tell him anything he doesn't already know."

"He's not a plant in the way you think." They were going to be difficult. "He's on your side, just like I am. Thomas was in the military with the guy who helped me plan my "death" and caught on to the conspiracy before anyone else. That guy, along with Matthew Kemp and Thomas, made sure the Russians didn't embed anyone else in the president's detail. We've already identified two sleeper agents working for the White House and denied them access. We believe there are at least three more who were actively spying on the president and his staff."

"That's not…" Roman stopped. "Holy shit, is that why I lost Janice? She up and quit because she said she needed to 'find herself.' She didn't look lost to me."

"No, but she decided to find her way back to Europe after we threatened to expose her ass," Mad explained. "And Thomas took care of the Secret Service agent they managed to plant."

Thomas stood at attention, staring ahead at no one in particular.

Zack stepped into his line of vision. "Is this true?"

"Yes, sir. We've been investigating quietly. We

couldn't afford to stir too much, and we're not entirely sure who we can trust," Thomas replied, his voice deep but efficient. "I managed to ferret out the agent in your detail and the woman who ran the background checks that allowed him to get through. After some...persuasion, she was very helpful in letting us know who she'd placed, as well as where she and her handlers intended to target next. But we still don't know about people here for a while, especially those embedded in your campaign staff."

"Shit." Roman's shoulders slumped. "I want every bit of information you've got. If it involved our staff, I need to know."

Zack stood in front of the man who'd been his protector since he'd taken the oath of office. "Who are you loyal to?"

"I am loyal to the United States of America and to the office of the President," Thomas replied.

But not to Zack Hayes. Mad groaned. He'd hoped Thomas would play this with more finesse, but he should have known the man was too much of a straight-shooter to tap dance around the truth.

After a moment of silence, Zack held out his hand. "That's what I needed to know. If ever there comes a time that I, for any reason, compromise this office, I expect you to do your job."

"I will, sir. But this evening, I'll do it from outside. You six have some talking to do," the agent said with a hint of a smile. "I've informed the detail that this is a boys' weekend. They will be appropriately discreet."

Thomas stepped outside. Then Mad was alone with his friends again.

The time had come to tell them everything, but he had to start with the worst news of all, the news that would shake them to their very core. News that should only be disclosed in mixed company.

"I know you planned an all-boys weekend, but you

should call in the women. They're involved, too. The reason I'm back now is that there's a clear and present danger to the president's life. Zack, someone is planning to assassinate you."

Chapter Two

Elizabeth Matthews was having a hell of a day, but then they all seemed long lately.

"We've got fifteen requests for interviews," Vanessa said as they headed down the hall. "Three from CNN alone. There's apparently a story circulating that Zack is going to open talks with European officials about the natural gas pipeline. The BBC says it has some notes from the meeting with the prime minister last month."

"They're fishing." It would hardly be the first time a reporter alluded to some mysterious record or informant, only to reveal it was a carefully baited trap. Liz refused to fall for that. Hell, she'd practically invented the game. No way was she officially commenting on that damn pipeline. It was a land mine they'd collectively stepped on and barely managed to avoid detonating in their faces on a recent trip to London. Now, they were all standing as still as they could, trying to find a way to avoid the damning explosion. "And it's President Hayes, please."

Vanessa frowned, yet somehow managed to make the

expression look pretty. Then again, the woman had been blessed with shiny dark hair and a pouty mouth that could grace the cover of a magazine. And Liz supposed when one was barely twenty-four, it was hard to look haggard.

"When did we get so formal?" the press office admin asked.

Liz wondered if Vanessa would catch Zack's eye at some point. It was blatantly obvious the man was done with her, so why wouldn't he start looking at the lovely, intelligent women who worked around him? Until now, he'd dated high-profile figures, but she knew Zack. He would eventually want someone in his sphere.

"Since we went to London, and I realized your behavior could be more professional. If the president doesn't mind you calling him Zack in private, that's your business. Otherwise, he's to be referred to as President Hayes or Mr. President."

Vanessa's eyes widened. Liz wondered if her associate knew how on edge she felt.

"All right," the young woman said. "So does the president or the White House have an official stance on the natural gas pipeline?"

Just the thought of that pipeline sent a shiver down Liz's spine. Someone powerful in Russia wanted that pipeline killed, and they were willing to play very dirty to get their way. Of course, Liz didn't have all the facts. She wasn't an insider. But she did know the president—and those around him—had been threatened with blackmail if he didn't shelve the project and allow Russia to continue their stranglehold on the natural gas supply in Europe.

"At this point, the president is weighing all the options. The pipeline is an important issue, so he's talking to the head of the Energy Department and his advisors about how to proceed. We're waiting on several reports regarding the environmental and economic impacts. The United States will proceed in a thoughtful way around this very important issue. That's all you need to say. If the reporters choose to show these so-called notes they found, it's a free world."

She'd spent a lot of time thinking about the events that unfolded in England. Professionally speaking, how could she think about anything else except the fact that Zack— President Hayes—had been forced to shelve plans to announce the pipeline because of the blackmail threats? Worse, she'd been the one to find that envelope detailing all the ways the blackmailer could bring down every single member of Zack's inner circle. The perpetrator had left it on her bed.

Liz remembered clearly the moment she'd walked into the bedroom she'd been assigned while in London and seen it coiled there like a snake. Even before she'd opened the envelope, she'd known something malicious awaited.

She'd asked herself one question over and over: Why had the blackmailer left the threat in *her* room. Why not someone else's?

Of course, Liz was asking herself a lot of other questions these days, too. Why was she even still here? When she'd tried to quit her job, Zack had refused to accept her resignation—which made no sense. She couldn't breathe anymore, not since the day she'd realized Zack had lost whatever interest he'd had in her that magical afternoon in Memphis, before the nightmare of Joy's murder. Now, he'd moved on entirely. Why wouldn't he let her do the same?

"Liz?"

She blinked, then realized she was in the middle of the press office, Vanessa staring with a concerned expression that said Liz had been standing there for a while. "Sorry, lost in thought. What were you saying?"

"She was saying she'll handle it and you don't have to worry about a thing," a familiar voice cut in. Augustine Spencer stood in the doorway wearing one of her power suits and sky-high heels, brow raised. "After all, it's part of her job."

"Of course, Ms. Spencer. I will ensure everyone who needs our response has it." Vanessa tossed her shoulders back, gaze sharpening. The woman was young but hungry. She was a lioness in the making, and she knew when to go for the kill. She also knew that in this room, right now, she was merely a cub. "I've also heard some tabloid rumors that might interest you two."

Liz felt her stomach roll. They had so many secrets. They'd been careful, but she knew rumors were surfacing about a relationship between her and the president. It was precisely why he should have accepted her resignation when she'd tendered it. In the beginning, she'd put up with all the talk because she'd believed one day they would be able to act on their feelings. Now, the gossip would only put a stain on her professional reputation. "And what is that?"

"That Sara Bond is pregnant," Vanessa replied, her lips curling up. "She's kept to herself, but a photographer who was following some ridiculous reality star caught a picture of her coming out of an OBGYN's office in Manhattan. According to this source, she has a definite baby bump."

This was Vanessa's true talent, ferreting out bits of seemingly innocuous information that, if known, would shake their world. If anyone learned Maddox Crawford had fathered Sara Bond's baby, the press would be all over that. The questions and speculation might prove too much for Sara to take.

"I want a name." Gus managed to infuse each word with arctic frost.

"I'll get you one," Vanessa promised, obviously satisfied someone seemed interested in her news. "Have a good weekend. I'll be here working if you need anything. It will be nice to have a quiet office for once."

She turned and strode back toward her small office.

"I don't like her." Gus stared at Vanessa, not bothering to keep her voice down.

Liz smiled since Gus didn't like many people. "She's been with us for years and she's good at her job. We should actually thank her for giving us that heads-up so we can plan how to deal with it. We can't keep the press from talking about Sara forever, but only those close to the president know about her relationship with Mad. So all we have to do is keep our mouths shut, maybe devise a story about a vacation fling, if necessary. Then it'll be a fifteen-minute story. But if you start making the paparazzi cry now, they'll know we're hiding something."

Gus shut the door. "Screw crying. I'd like to hide the body of whoever is trying to make a buck off my friend."

"Then you'll be hiding a lot of bodies." Liz started toward her office.

The day was almost over. Since Zack had refused her request to be relieved of duty, she refused to work overtime. At least today she did. Now that she was definitely outside the inner circle, Liz was so tired of trying to figure out what was happening. Sure, Gus was one of her best friends, but now that she was engaged to Roman, Gus knew plenty she couldn't divulge. The Perfect Gentlemen kept their secrets—and their significant others did the same.

Liz changed the subject. "Did Roman get off okay?"

"Roman got off quite nicely." Gus followed behind her. "That desk of his is comfy, let me tell you. I will never complain about his overly traditional tastes again. It's sturdy, too. But if you're asking if he left for Camp David on time, the answer is yes. All the men are away now, so I think the women should play. Let's consider tonight a dry run of my bachelorette party. I know we're all supposed to be on high alert and shit, but between Everly and Holland we'll be perfectly safe from the assholes trying to influence Zack. Although we might give them more blackmail material."

The last thing she wanted to do was hang around all those happy women who would undoubtedly talk about their recent or upcoming marriages. It would send her straight into a tailspin. She was happy for them, but every word was a bleak reminder that Zack no longer wanted her any way but professionally. It was as if his desire for her had begun a slow death the day Joy died.

"I'm so sorry. I know I said I would go, but I can't. I'm meeting with my sister's new attorney on Monday, so I want to do some research on him this weekend."

The blackmailer trying to manipulate Zack into stopping a US natural gas pipeline had threatened to divulge her sister's teenage stint in a mental hospital. It was something her soon-to-be ex-husband didn't know and could use in their upcoming divorce and custody proceedings. Liz couldn't let that happen.

In fact, the blackmailer had threatened everyone even remotely close to the president. He'd vowed to expose the emails Roman and Joy had exchanged during the campaign when they'd been having a non-physical but emotional affair. He'd procured a sex tape Gus had made with a past sexual partner. Both Roman and Gus had offered to release their "sins" to the public to render those threats pointless. But the blackmailer had even more damning dirt.

Following Mad's death, the FAA had opened an investigation into the crash. The blackmailer claimed he had proof Zack had pressured the organization to halt their inquiries so Gabe wouldn't be implicated in their friend's death. Gabe swore he'd had nothing to do with Mad perishing, just as Zack vowed he hadn't interfered with the investigation. But how would that play out in the court of public opinion? Collectively, they might be able to weather the storm, but the blackmailer also had information about Connor's involvement in a CIA op that resulted in the death of a cartel head's son. If word got out that Connor had participated in that raid, the cartel would stop at nothing to destroy him. And while the operative could handle almost any threat that came his way, they wouldn't hesitate to take their revenge out on his gentle wife, Lara.

More than once Liz had offered to quit so the blackmailer could no longer use her sister's past to threaten Zack, but he'd merely fired the lawyer Anne had hired and sent in a high-priced pit bull to deal with the fallout.

Liz frowned. Zack didn't want her, but he refused to let her go. It made no sense.

"You don't have to do anything at all," Gus promised. "The new attorney is handling everything. Besides, that case is based in Atlanta, and you're not going there for the weekend. You're confined to DC, right? We all are. Bastards."

The men were concerned something could happen to one of their wives/fiancées since Zack hadn't given the blackmailers what they wanted. But Liz didn't know why she'd been included in the restrictions. It wasn't as if she mattered to Zack personally anymore.

Unless Zack suspected she would betray him.

After weeks of consideration, that was the only logical reason she could figure for his insistence that she stay on his staff and remain confined to the White House. Keep your enemies closer and all that.

Liz sighed. When had they become enemies? She couldn't pinpoint a moment. After that fateful day in Memphis, he'd pulled back. Not surprising since he'd become a widower and been elected president in the same week. But instead of getting closer to her as he healed and found his feet, he'd grown more distant. Then recently, he'd told her that his feelings for her had changed, and he now thought of her as a sister. Nothing could have stabbed her heart any more.

She would never be able to think of him as a brother. Never. She couldn't look at him in one of those tailor-made suits, with his broad shoulders and that granite-cut jawline, and feel any sense of familial connection to him—unless she counted the fact that she'd once thought she might have a family with him.

"No, I'm going to talk to him on the phone," Liz admitted. "I just want an update on how it's going."

"You have to know Zack won't allow anything to happen to your sister." Gus crossed her arms over her chest in that "big sister is about to lecture you" way. "There's more going on than we imagined, Liz. Be patient with Zack. He has his reasons. I don't know all of them, but I believe with every fiber of my being that man is still in love with you."

He'd never been in love with her. Maybe he'd thought so once, years ago. Maybe it had merely been lust. But no one who loved another person could be as cold as Zack had been recently. He'd seemingly turned angry, too. She couldn't soothe him anymore. In fact, her presence only seemed to perturb him.

Liz was prepared to argue the point when a brisk knock sounded on her door. Gus opened it.

Vanessa paused in the portal. "I told him you were about to leave."

As the officious man skulked through the door, Gus groaned. Liz was tempted to join in. Vice President Wallace Shorn hadn't been chosen to round out Zack's ticket for his charm. The older man, whose suit was a bit too tight around the middle, projected calm and experience, at least according to Franklin Hayes before he'd succumbed to dementia. Together with Joy's father, they'd selected Shorn, a senator from Florida, to balance out Zack's northeast-elite vibe.

"What are we doing about all the rumors flying around

following the meeting with the prime minister?" Wallace demanded, a frown creasing his face. "Does the president even understand what he did by refusing to talk about the pipeline? I've put months into that project. Mind you, I told him it was a bad idea in the first place. It's going to get us into a war we can't win, but I was willing to go along with it because I'm a team player. Then he announced it's all up in the air without even consulting me. My neck is on the line here. I've made promises. Hell, I've got a meeting with the gas lobby next week, and I have no idea what to say."

"You should talk to the president," Gus replied. "Somehow I don't think the press secretary has the answers you need."

Wallace sent a withering look Gus's way. "Do you think I would be in here if Hayes would take my calls? He's avoiding me. Calder set up a lunch for next week, but I need answers now. What's going on? And what the hell happened in England? I've heard talk of someone from the prime minister's contingent going missing. For that matter, how did we lose a Secret Service agent? No one is talking."

Liz didn't have any of those answers since Zack had shut her out. He used to tell her everything. She'd been the one he came to at the end of a day to share whatever had happened. He'd often asked for her advice. Sometimes they had dinner with Roman in the residence, and the three of them talked things out and planned their strategy. Often, they'd talked so long into the evening, she'd stayed in one of the White House's many guest rooms. Every time, Zack walked her to the door, and she'd pretend they were everyday people on a perfectly normal date.

Had it really only been a few months since she'd straightened his tie before they'd attended a private fundraising party? She remembered the evening like it was yesterday. They'd flown up to New York together, and she'd ensured he'd worn the right suit. He hadn't protested when she'd fussed over him. If anything, he'd eased closer. Then he'd told her how beautiful she looked.

That night, his stare had vowed it was only a matter of time before mourning and circumstance would no longer keep them apart. That expression had promised they would find a way to be together.

That expression had lied.

"I'm sorry, Mr. Vice President. I know as much as you do about the president's current thoughts on the pipeline. He chose not to announce his reasoning in England." She wasn't getting in the middle of that fight. She would do her job and run the press office. She would stand in front of the press corps and dutifully answer every question to the best of her ability. She wouldn't organize Zack's life anymore, nor would she be the buffer between him and his annoyances any longer. Roman could manage that. He was chief of staff and an insider. Liz had become merely an employee, and he didn't pay her enough to deal with this crap.

"Don't treat me like I'm stupid. Everyone knows who to go to when they need something from the president. I want a meeting with Hayes and I want a full briefing on all the pipeline's developments," Wallace insisted, staring pointedly. "And while you're at it, keep him in a better mood. He's been irritable lately."

She bristled. "What exactly is that supposed to mean?"

He rolled his eyes. "Everyone sees through the two of you. For god's sake, apologize for whatever you've been fighting about and take care of the man so he'll be in a better mood."

Gus stepped between them. "Listen up, Wally…"

Liz had to intervene before this altercation turned ugly. Of course Shorn's intimation was a sexist insult. But the last thing she needed was Gus dressing down the vice president of the United States in front of the whole press office.

Maneuvering around her friend, Liz carefully blocked anyone in the outer office from seeing her expression and she lowered her voice. "Let's be clear about one thing: the only way I take care of the president is by being his press secretary. Your insinuation that my only value is in keeping the president sexually satisfied is offensive. I'm excellent at my job, which is restricted to relaying the president's message and keeping unfavorable stories about him out of the press. I also assure you that if I'm capable of stopping the negative, I can release it, too. I might look like a sweet little woman, but I've made a career of ferreting out helpful information. For instance, Mr. Vice President, I know all about your wife's little incident at Bloomingdale's last month. It's not the first time she's been caught shoplifting, is it? The pattern of behavior suggests she's got a problem. Oh, you've done a good job covering it up. I'm better, so I suggest you watch your mouth around me."

"Is that a threat?" Wallace asked, clearly shaken.

"It's a promise."

Shorn's behavior reminded Liz of something she'd suspected for some time. She'd let the last few years soften her up. She'd spent more time crying over Zack than she had asking the right questions. Something was going on behind the scenes, but she'd been far too caught up in her own heartache to decipher the problem.

That stopped now.

"You should leave." A shit-eating grin stretched across Gus's face, which only widened when the older man huffed as he complied. The moment the VP was out of the office, Gus shut the door behind him. "That was classic Liz. I've missed your badass side, my friend."

"You know what? I have, too. I'm going to drop one last press release off with Vanessa, then I think I will join you this evening. I could use some girl time."

"All right." Gus gave her a thumbs-up. "We're going to

rock this town. Maybe we can even find you a hot stripper."

It was funny how quickly Gus's mood could turn when the occasion called for it. Minutes ago, she'd been preaching patience. Now she was talking strippers. "I thought you said Zack still loved me."

"He does…but pictures of you with a hot exotic dancer is bound to get him off his ass. Besides, I'm dying to see how Lara handles some guy in a G-string with his junk in her face. She'll either protest or try to talk him into finding a line of work that more appropriately honors his body. Personally, I can honor a guy's hot bod just fine with cash."

Gus was incorrigible. Perhaps a night where Gus led her posse into wild times was exactly what Liz needed. She grabbed the last of her paperwork off her desk. "Or maybe she'll go the sex-positive route and praise them for not having sticks up their asses. I'll be right back."

She grabbed the press release she needed to distribute about the White House's upcoming social events. She wasn't going to manage those personally anymore. It was the First Lady's duty. She'd played that role for the last time. Vanessa or Gus could do it from now on.

As she walked toward the copy machine, Liz overheard some of the interns talking.

"I don't know what to do. I don't think he's supposed to be in that room. I was only up there because I was taking a couple of pictures for the website," said one young woman.

A brown-haired senator's son shook his head. "How did he get in that office? What do we do when the president isn't around?"

"Doesn't he have a nurse or something?"

Damn it. There was only one person they could be talking about. She refused to let this be her problem anymore. When Zack had shut her out, he'd also forfeited her willingness to deal with his father's dementia-related episodes. So she felt zero guilt about walking away from

Franklin Hayes. Someone else could deal with it.

Except Frank could be difficult. They'd hired four different nurses in the last couple of years, and every one of them had abruptly quit. For all she knew, the latest had decided he'd suffered enough and left without notice, so now Frank was ambling around the White House without supervision. Usually he didn't get out of the East Wing, but the staff was thin late on a Friday afternoon, especially because the president wasn't in residence for a few days.

Liz sighed. As much as she'd like to, she couldn't leave the man to wander. What if he hurt himself? Or if someone saw him, stories might leak to the press that Zack didn't take care of his father. When she thought about it that way, helping Frank really was her job.

"Vanessa, could you get this out on Monday?" she said, handing the other woman the paperwork. "And call me if you hear anything going on with the vice president. I don't need him causing trouble. I have to go hunt Frank down."

Vanessa groaned. "He's out again? They need to put that old codger on a leash."

Liz would have admonished the younger woman…but she was kind of right. Frank could be a handful. Sometimes, he thought it was still 1960, and every female in the vicinity needed to see him mooning the Harvard football team.

She shuddered. There were some things she could never, ever unsee.

After asking the interns where they'd last seen Frank, Liz rushed to find him. With a huff, she climbed the stairs to the second floor, which housed the residence. At least she could be thankful that Frank almost never wandered downstairs.

As she started toward the small, private study known as the Treaty Room, she caught sight of a middle-aged man in hospital scrubs racing from the back of the East Wing.

"I'm so sorry. He was asleep when I went to the

bathroom." The man Liz recognized as Frank's second-shift nurse approached, looking flustered. "He's probably playing with paperwork or something. He likes to pretend he's working."

Liz frowned. "That door is supposed to be locked."

But someone somehow had managed to open it.

"He's very good at getting into places he shouldn't be able to," the nurse complained, pushing through the door.

And out of places that should be secure, which was why Frank now lived in the White House.

Zack had tried putting his father in a memory care facility. But the older man had been belligerent and combative whenever the facility managed to contain him. But too often he'd escaped, walking the streets of DC in his pajamas and attracting the attention of the press while looking for his son. It was a PR nightmare.

After his latest escape had been plastered all over the news, she and Zack had sat up late one night, and he'd opened up to her about his mixed feelings where his father was concerned. Franklin Hayes had pushed Zack hard, always demanding the best from his son. It had been something of a relief to not live with the man, and he should have been getting far better care in the facility than anywhere else. But in the end, Zack agreed that his father wandering the streets was too much of both an optics problem and a security risk, so it was better to keep him close.

Zack was obviously doing the same with her now. He saw her as a liability. She recognized his behavior since she'd been the one to teach him this tactic.

"Mr. Hayes, you're not allowed to be in here. Let's get you back to bed."

Dressed in blue pajamas, a thin maroon robe, and slippers that could have come out of the 1950s, Frank peered at them with a scowl. To the outside eye he appeared perfectly normal, like any other upscale man of means at an advanced age.

He turned back to the desk and shuffled through the papers now scattered across the surface. "This is my office. Where are my papers? Don't you know I have to meet with the Kremlin in two days? Where is Constance? Don't tell me she's crying again. She has to get over that."

The moment he opened his mouth, Liz was reminded that appearances were deceiving and that Frank's mind was lost in the past. She also knew from experience that she had to take a firm stance with him. "Mr. Hayes, this is your son's office, not yours. You do not work in the Russian embassy anymore. You're in the White House, and you need to go back to your rooms."

It was obvious he'd been going through the notepads Zack often used when he was working. He'd also turned on the laptop there.

Zack preferred this office to the Oval when he wasn't meeting with people. When he was alone, he liked the privacy of the Treaty Room. But Frank didn't know that. He probably came here because it was close to his rooms. Poor old guy...

"My son is a child." Frank paused and looked around. "This isn't my office. Where am I?"

Liz grimaced. When Frank was having a really bad day, he couldn't remember more than a few moments at a time.

The nurse took over, gently easing the man back out into the hallway. "It's okay, Mr. Hayes. We'll get you back to your room."

"Where is my son? I would like to see him before his bedtime. Shouldn't he be here?" Frank ambled out with a glower. "Tell me he's not with those boys from the school. Bad influences. That's what they are, especially that Crawford brat."

Liz sighed and glanced down at the desk. It no longer

looked neat and organized, the way Zack kept everything. The man was practically obsessive compulsive. She squashed the impulse to put it all back to order so the chaos didn't bother Zack.

Her fingertips glided across the notebook, over his clean, masculine handwriting. She missed him. Even when he was an asshole, she missed him like she'd lost a piece of her own soul. The ache was that deep.

"Ms. Matthews?"

A deep voice startled her, and she turned with a yelp to find a Secret Service agent standing there, Gus at his side.

"Sorry, I came up here to see if I could help with Frank. He was up and about again," she explained, closing the notebook. She shouldn't be in here, either. She wasn't welcome anymore. "What's up?"

Gus handed her the Prada bag she'd been so excited about when she'd bought it in New York. That had been her last good trip with Zack.

"Sorry about the scare, but this one insisted we find you. Apparently our girls' night out has been canceled. I told Mr. Serious here that he was costing us strippers."

"Ma'am, I've been instructed to bring you to the president." The agent stared at her with a cold, stony expression—a seeming prerequisite for getting a Secret Service job.

Was Zack finally going to let her go and he'd elected to release her in person? Why couldn't he kick her to the curb via text? Isn't that what all the hip people were doing these days? That would be far less humiliating.

Liz frowned in confusion. "Why? Isn't he at Camp David with his friends?"

"Yep, but I'm getting nabbed, too. And Roman isn't answering his phone to explain. He's so in the doghouse."

So she wasn't getting fired, most likely. Then Liz had no idea what this presidential summons was about or why he'd roped Gus in too. But she didn't want to see Zack, not after Wallace Shorn had made the staff's perception of her relationship with the president clear. Not when she was feeling a bit maudlin and vulnerable.

"What if I don't want to go?" she asked.

The agent's lips curled up. "I'll be forced to bring you. And I have a pair of handcuffs you would look spectacular in."

Well, at least he was flirting with her. Made a girl feel wanted. She needed it because she was pretty sure she wasn't going to feel wanted in the least after this meeting with Zack. "Fine. But I want a limo—and there better be booze in it."

"No luck," Gus said. "We're taking a chopper, and I've been informed they've already nabbed Holland and Lara. Since they seem serious about getting us there, I suspect they're intending to cordially command Everly and Sara, too. But I stole a bottle of tequila." Gus held a ridiculously expensive bottle of the booze in her fist.

"Ma'am, I don't think…" When Gus sent him the kind of stabbing glare that would make any human bleed, the agent stopped and nodded. "We'll try to keep the flight smooth for you ladies."

Even the Secret Service feared Gus, so that was one small blessing. But something was up. There were only so many reasons the Perfect Gentlemen would want the women to crash their boys' weekend, none of them good.

Liz followed the agent and her friend, her heart in her throat.

* * * *

Sara Bond stared out the window of her room in her brother's DC condo, the lights of the city flickering on in anticipation of the coming night. The condo had a majestic view of the city, but then Gabe always sprung for the best. Their parents had taught him that. Money had never been a problem in her life.

She put a hand on her growing belly. At least she had that security. Her baby wouldn't lack for food or clothes. When she thought about her life from that perspective, she hadn't been dealt a bad hand. Her child would grow up with the love of a father figure because her brother would step in and play the role for his niece. She had a good, secure future. As single momhood went, she'd hit the lottery.

So why wasn't that enough? Why did it always feel like she was missing something vital?

"You ready? Damn, girl. That dress is stunning on you." Her sister-in-law walked in, giving her a once-over. "You're rocking that bump. But...are you sure you want to risk this? There could be photographers. A lot of people are interested in Gus and Roman since they got engaged."

Her "bump" was growing, and she wouldn't be able to hide it much longer. She'd disguised it well until now, but in the last week she'd had no choice except to wear maternity clothes. The dress she'd donned tonight was definitely designed to accommodate her swelling middle, and Sara was surprised by how much she liked seeing the evidence of her precious baby growing inside her. That made needing to hide it for as long as possible even more odious.

"I know the press will find out I'm pregnant at some point. For now, I'll drape a long sweater around my body and try to stay in the middle of the crowd. I'm going to talk to Liz tonight about how to announce my pregnancy to the public soon."

As it was, people would speculate about the baby's father. Mad had left all his worldly possessions to Gabe, who intended to hand Crawford over to her after the baby's birth. When she took the helm, speculation would become outright gossip. People would probably guess Maddox had fathered her child. The business world would almost certainly respond, and the tabloids would splash her across their pages. At some point, she would have to admit that Maddox Crawford had gotten her pregnant and dumped her. Then...he'd died.

All these months later, that was the most crushing reality of all. She was still trying to come to terms with it.

"I'm glad Liz is coming with us. I was worried she would back out." Everly looked chic and camera ready in her vibrant orange sheath and killer heels. Everly didn't have to wear black to give the illusion that she hadn't swallowed a basketball.

Oddly, though, black felt right since she was still in mourning. How could she hate a man and yet mourn him with her whole heart?

Sara grabbed her Judith Leiber clutch and forced her feet into sensible kitten heels. She would be the shortest in the squad tonight, but she had to accept that. Her feet could not handle five-inch stilettos right now, given the slight swelling she often had at night and her sometimes irregular balance. "Why wouldn't Liz want to come?"

Everly's face flushed slightly, but she shrugged. "Well, she's been really busy since we just got back from London, and she's handling a lot since she's Gus's maid of honor. Let me tell you, Gus is insistent this wedding will be perfect, so I'm going to hunker down, do whatever bridezilla says, and survive until she says 'I do.'"

Something about Everly's expression made Sara suspicious. Granted, she'd been out of the game for a while, hiding away at her parents' place in the Hamptons, but once she'd been an excellent poker player. And Everly was bluffing.

"That's not why. Tell me the reason Liz wouldn't want to come with us. What's going on? Is she upset that Gus and

Roman are getting married? I assumed she and Zack were waiting until after his reelection campaign to tie the knot."

"No, she's happy for Gus and Roman." Everly sighed. "The truth is, Liz and Zack were never really together. Not in a romantic way."

"Of course they were." No one could deny the chemistry between those two. "She's basically played the role of the First Lady since day one. I know Zack has been in mourning publicly since he was elected, but he's also crazy about Liz. I can tell. It's only a matter of time before they acknowledge their relationship."

Everly shook her head. "While you've been in the Hamptons, you've been out of the loop. I didn't want to spend our time together gossiping, but...Zack's been dating."

That shook her world a bit. Zack was Superman. He always did the right thing. "Dating? But not the woman who has stood by him for years?"

Everly frowned. "Nope. His first date was with a supermodel."

Sara felt a growl forming in the back of her throat. Normally, she was perfectly sweet and feminine. She was a good executive, too. Not as cutthroat as Liz or Gus, or as badass as Everly and Holland. She probably fit in best with Lara. But she fucking hated supermodels. After Mad had broken up with her, he'd gone on a supermodel tour. He could probably write a Zagat-style rating guide of the supermodels' vaginas.

Everly held up her hands, obviously trying to ward off the beast. "Whoa, hold your horses. There's more at play here than Zack wanting cheap sex. Not that it's actually cheap. I'm sure those ladies are incredibly expensive."

Sara narrowed her eyes because she still wasn't getting the whole story. "What do you know that I don't know?"

Everly bit her bottom lip and winced. "I can't talk about

it until I discuss it with Gabe. I'm so sorry, Sara. There's...a lot going on."

She waved a hand. She knew the drill. She'd been around the guys all her life, and they kept a close circle. When she'd been ready to spend her life with Maddox Crawford, she'd thought she might break into their confidence, but it didn't matter anymore. Best to stay focused on her baby. "I'll let it go, then. I know better than to meddle with my brother's brothers. Besides, I'm probably better off not knowing. But for a bunch of manly men, you have to admit they have *so* much drama."

"You have no idea," Everly agreed, nodding. "But seriously, don't hate Zack. You don't know the whole story."

There was one good thing about being on the outside. She could so judge. "And I never will, so as far as I'm concerned Zack might be a great president, but he's an asshole. I can't get drunk with the rest of you tonight. Not on alcohol, but I can totally get drunk on self-righteousness and judgment. I think Liz is going to be my bestie for the night."

She was actually mindful about the way she discussed Mad, especially with the ladies. She didn't want to seem bitter and tried not to vent her emotions to others...except Gabe when he caught her in the occasional weak moment. But tonight, it would be a nice change to have someone whose man had done them wrong. Someone who understood what it meant to spend time with all the happy couples and be thrilled for them, while dealing with her own grief and loneliness.

Everly eased beside her, walking down the hall toward the front door. "I'm just glad you agreed to come to the city and spend time with us. I hate thinking about you all alone up there."

"Alone? I wish. Gus shows up all the time," she

complained good-naturedly. "Or you need help shopping and no one else has my sense of style. Yeah, I caught that one, sister. Connor and Lara rented the house next to mine, then pretended like they didn't remember I would be their neighbor when they decided to spend a long weekend in the Hamptons."

"We're all worried about you. We love you."

She linked her arm with Everly's. "And I love you. I'm good, Ev. I'm finally coming out from under the cloud, and I can't thank you guys enough for always letting me know that I wasn't alone. I'm going to forgive Mad. I don't want to have this baby and hate her dad. I've decided to move on and face the future."

A future without Mad. Somehow even when he'd been dating other women, she'd thought he would grow up and want to see their child. She would never have gone back to him. He'd closed that door, but she'd envisioned a future where they found a way to be good parents, maybe even friends.

Now that would never happen, and she'd finally managed to find a sad peace in that knowledge. She'd spent hours looking over the water crashing on the shore, thinking about everything that had happened, and eventually finding closure. She'd even had her own funeral for Mad on the beach one night. She'd started a fire and burned the last pictures she'd had of them together, not in anger but so she could finally let go. She'd cried and screamed and wailed out at the moonlit ocean. Afterward, she'd slept better than she had in months.

Everly squeezed her arm. "It's going to be okay. You'll see. In a couple of months we'll have a baby to love and while we'll all miss…"

"You can say his name." Everly had lost a lot, too, and in the beginning Sara hadn't been at all easy on her. Of course, she hadn't understood why Mad had turned to

Everly. Sara knew now that he'd been leaning on his sister, not a new lover. She often worried she'd overshadowed Everly's mourning with her own.

"We'll have a piece of Mad to hold on to," Everly finished solemnly.

Sara nodded. This was what the passing of all these months had given her. "We will. God, I hope she gets her personality from me. I don't know if I can handle a female Mad."

Everly laughed. "Oh, she would be a terror. But regardless, she'll be unforgettable because this baby is going to be the best of both of you." She sniffled and shook off the emotion that had threatened to overtake the moment. "I can't wait for you to lead Crawford. I'm literally counting down the days."

"You might not be if our stock tanks when the announcement is made." It was something Sara worried about. She had a business degree from an Ivy League school and she'd spent plenty of time working at Bond, but this would be her first time as a CEO, and she had no idea how the market would react.

"The board will be firmly behind you. It's going to be great, and I've already talked to Liz and Gus about how to garner good press. The new onsite day care and parent-friendly work environment will be amazing. We'll take Crawford to a whole new level," Everly promised.

It would be a welcome challenge and a good way for her daughter to learn the value of hard work. After all, she would inherit the company one day.

The future. That was Sara's focus now.

She and Everly had almost reached the door when a hard knock resounded through the apartment.

"Must be the car service. We're meeting at Gus's and taking a limo from there." Everly glanced at her watch and frowned. "They're a little early though."

Sara opened the door. Immediately, she knew the man standing there wasn't from a car service. The broad, hard-looking man in his perfect black suit wearing aviator sunglasses had never driven a bunch of partying girls around town. Nope. He was a serious man.

She reached out for Everly because sometimes men like him came bearing terrible news. What had happened to Gabe? She could actually feel her heart constricting with fear.

"I've been sent by the president to bring you to Camp David."

"What?" Everly asked, her voice going breathless. "Has something happened?"

The man's face remained stony. "Everyone is safe, but the gentlemen require your attention."

Sara exhaled. Thank god, she could breathe again. Maybe this was some prank the boys were pulling, and she'd never been a part of that. Yes, she'd been looking forward to a night out with her friends, but it might be nice to stay home and read a good book.

She stepped back. "I'll be fine here, Ev. Call and let me know you got there okay, will you?"

"Your presence is required, too, Ms. Bond," the man in black said. "The others are taking a chopper, but the president felt, given your condition, that it would be more comfortable to drive you out. We need to leave in five minutes, so retrieve anything you'd like to bring with you now. I was told you shouldn't worry about toiletries. They will be provided. And someone will bring you whatever clothes or other items you might need."

She shook her head. "I'm not married to any of the guys, so why am I required?"

Required was such an odd word in this context…

"Ma'am, it's my job to get you to Camp David."

And he would do it. She looked to her sister-in-law for

answers.

Everly shrugged. "No idea. Maybe it's a surprise for Gus? Let's go with it. I'll grab your prenatal vitamins. Need anything else?"

"Nope. If Zack wants to kidnap me, he can pay for everything I'll need while I'm in captivity," she shot back with a tart smile.

Everly went to the bathroom while Sara got ready for her night to be hijacked.

Sometimes, like now, she really missed liquor.

Chapter Three

Zack sat back, taking another long drink as Mad continued to insist that he'd done what he'd done to protect them all, yadda yadda, yadda.

He sighed. Why hadn't he punched Mad in the face? Gabe had taken a swing before asking questions. Even Roman had threatened Mad with physical violence. Zack wished now that he had a do-over.

"I'd like to discuss this whole conspiracy from top to bottom." Connor sounded far calmer than Zack felt.

He and Dax were actually taking this whole return-from-the-dead thing pretty well. Maybe the military and the Agency taught their operatives how to handle such scenarios better than the pencil-pushers at Harvard Law.

"Yeah, but the explanation will be more complete if we include the guy I've been working with," Mad explained.

Gabe frowned, watching Mad like he wasn't sure the other man wouldn't disappear at any moment. "I thought you were working with the Secret Service."

Those two hadn't hugged it out yet, but it was obvious

Gabe was relieved Mad was no longer among the dearly departed.

"Only Thomas and Matthew Kemp." Mad's face grew solemn. "I can't tell you how sad I was that the Russian agent managed to kill Matt. He was a good man. But he wasn't the brains behind this op."

Connor snorted. "Op? Seriously? That sounds ridiculous coming out of your mouth."

"Hey, I'm practically a spy now, brother," Mad quipped, going from solemn to witty in a second.

Then again, Mad had always been mercurial. In fact, he'd been properly named something close to the Mad Hatter.

"But my partner is the real thing," his recently risen friend insisted. "I admit, he's insane and he's got serious issues. Despite that, I'm hoping you'll let him join us here."

Roman pointed out that the stranger would need clearance, then he and Mad started arguing. Zack merely watched from the sideline, taking in all his friends.

He couldn't quite feel anything except somehow separate from them. Suddenly, he was twelve again and just meeting this group of cool kids. That's what they'd been back then. And Zack hadn't been at all sure about his place in their circle. After all, he'd been the nerd always fearful of not living up to expectations. His father had made him vividly aware that, because of his difficult birth, his mother couldn't have more children. So, their every ambition fell on his shoulders. Meeting Mad, and subsequently the rest of the guys, had been the first time he'd felt any camaraderie with other kids, but it had taken years before he'd really felt as if he belonged.

Now he was back on the outside because he might be a Russian plant sent to destroy the country they all loved. His very DNA could make him a traitor. Hell, Mad had been investigating him. Zack wasn't sure he should even be sitting here among his own pack anymore.

Equally disquieting, Elizabeth Matthews would walk through that door soon. Any moment, the chopper should arrive, and the car not long after that, depending on the traffic out of DC. All the women would be here with their men—and he wouldn't be able to touch his. Because he wasn't sure he could trust his.

For the hundredth time, Zack asked himself why, when he and the guys had decided to bring the women closer, he had insisted Liz should come, too. The minute Mad suggested the women should be here, the room had exploded in chaos. But they'd all agreed on one thing: their women needed protection and they needed to understand the risk. Events were forcing them to huddle up, and he hadn't been able to stand the thought that Elizabeth might be on the outside.

"Mad, I want real explanations now," Roman demanded. "You can't just show up and expect us to wait around for...what? Do you have a presentation set up? You do. You asshole. You have a presentation, don't you?"

Mad shrugged. "I can't help it if I know how to put on a show. And everyone involved needs to see it. I shouldn't have to tell you how serious this is. I know you're all pissed at the way I went about this. My ass may not be the only one at risk, but I'm the one who's been alone all this time."

No, Mad was wrong about that, Zack mused. Lately, he'd felt so damn alone without Elizabeth. Since he'd forced himself to put distance between them, he realized how much he'd come to depend on her being part of his everyday life. She was often the first person he saw in the morning and the last person he spoke to at night. Even if he wasn't with her, he would call her before he went to bed. Oh, he would say he had business to discuss, and he always managed to come up with something relevant. But then he would ask her about her day, and she would tell him all the crazy stuff that had gone on in the press room or laugh about how Gus had managed to take down some annoying lobbyist. Eventually, he would look at the clock and realize that hours had passed.

He missed her so fucking much.

"Apparently, you weren't alone," Dax argued. "You had Matthew Kemp, Thomas, and whoever this mystery guy is."

Zack listened with passing interest. Sure, he was curious about the mystery guy, too. Well, he should be. But he had an almost fatalistic acceptance that nothing they said or did would truly matter. If he was Sergei, then his whole life had been a lie and everything he knew, especially his days as president, were over. Even if he survived his resistance against the Russians, he would have to resign in disgrace. Then everything he'd worked for would have been in vain.

Yet he could remember a time when the notion of not being the president had been the most freeing thought of all. If he hadn't won the election, he might have had a life with Elizabeth...presuming she wasn't a Russian operative. Maybe he would have embraced the career of his choice while bringing up a family differently than the way he'd been raised. He could have embraced love above duty for once.

Without Elizabeth, all Zack had was the presidency and his legacy. Didn't that sound empty as fuck?

"You have to understand my partner in all this is actually quite intelligent. When I nudged you to look into him, I didn't realize you would go crazy and fall in love." Mad huffed at Connor. "I actually prayed you wouldn't kill the pacifist chick because she was so obviously wrong for you, but I suspected from her blogs that she had valuable information. Except about Zack's penis. I didn't need to know any of that. But I was pretty sure Everly would work well with her. But most of all, she was close to my partner...and at the time I didn't really know him, so I needed you to investigate."

Connor's jaw had dropped. It might be the first time Zack had ever seen Connor Sparks completely at a loss for words. In fact, they all were.

"Are you talking about Freddy?" Zack scowled.

Freddy Gallagher had been living next to Lara Armstrong when Connor investigated her and her website, Capitol Scandals, which had been the bane of Zack's existence since it hit the DC scene. Connor had gone in to find out what she knew about Mad's "death" and the surrounding conspiracy. Her neighbor Freddy, a longtime conspiracy theorist, had discovered the proof that Joy's death hadn't been the result of an assassin's bullet meant for Zack gone astray. Someone had intentionally murdered Joy to sway the voting public into sweeping Zack into office— and the plan had succeeded.

Mad nodded. "Yeah, that's him. At the time, Freddy wasn't too keen on sharing what he knew, so I maneuvered Connor where I was sure he would come into contact with Freddy. Lara was the vehicle since I knew Freddy would peg Connor as a government suit and be too suspicious to talk to him outright. I gambled that Lara was aware of Freddy's investigation and that Connor's instincts would kick in. I worried like hell that Connor would fuck everything up. I never imagined he would get down and dirty with the vegan princess."

"Oh, he did both." Dax looked like he was going to go pop some corn and enjoy the drama.

Connor turned on his best friend. "Hey, since my courtship of my wife didn't include marrying another woman and wasting years of our lives, unlike some people, I'm the smart one here. I had Lara under control in a couple of weeks."

"Really? Are you talking about the same woman who

recently ran an 'exposé' about all the ways my company is polluting the earth?" Gabe asked with a sigh. "Because it doesn't feel like you've got her under control."

"She loves the earth." Connor shrugged. "Look, she and I have a deal. I don't get involved with her protesting and she doesn't ask me about my CIA contacts. Or why I sometimes have blood on my clothes when I come home. But she's excellent at getting that out of dress shirts. Saved me a ton of money." He turned back to Mad. "We need to have a serious discussion about Freddy. He's a lunatic."

"And a menace." For the first time since they started talking, Dax looked serious. "I barely survived breaking into his apartment. Did you know about that, Mad? Did you know about the land mine in his foyer? Walking into that place was like an obstacle course in a deadly *Three Stooges* cartoon."

Mad looked at him as if he'd gone mental. "Why do you think I didn't go in myself?"

Glowering, Dax stood.

If Mad wasn't careful, he would get another beatdown. Zack didn't need to hang around for this. Clearly, Mad wasn't going to divulge any important details until he made a big production out of it. That shouldn't surprise anyone.

Zack rose as Mad and Dax faced off and walked to the bar, his thoughts turning.

How would Elizabeth take Mad's return from the dead? Would she be shocked he was alive...or did she already know? He would have to watch her carefully. Yes. That was why he was bringing her here. He needed to watch her, keep her close so he could monitor her every expression, word, and move.

Of course he couldn't get any closer than being in bed with her.

Maybe he'd played their game all wrong. He'd pushed her away so that no one would think to use her against him.

But if she was in on the conspiracy, drawing her close made so much sense.

All the better to eat you...

Yes, he was the Big Bad Wolf in this scenario, and she was sweet Little Red Riding Hood with her basket of treats. Damn, but he wanted a taste of that. Needed it. Had craved it for so fucking long.

"Can you believe this?" Roman had left the crowd to join him, empty glass in hand.

Zack refilled it. "We should have known Mad's death was a ruse when he made sure a good percentage of the 'mourners' at his funeral were his favorite hookers. Hell, nothing takes out Mad. He must have a deal with the devil."

"Sometimes I think he *is* the devil," Roman shot back, then glanced into the great room where the guys were arguing about which one got to take off Mad's head. "But I have to say, I'm fucking relieved he's not dead. Something feels right about the world again. Despite the fact that he could have just called and told us what was going on."

"You know why he couldn't do that."

Roman sighed. "You're not Sergei."

Zack sent him a pointed look. The evidence was not in his favor, and Roman needed to acknowledge that.

"Fine, we don't know anything, and Mad's not talking yet." Roman leaned against the bar. "But I know this. If somehow you are this mystical Sergei, you won't let the Russians use you. Their plans will fail because you're a man of integrity. You'll step down before you'll steer this country wrong."

"Will I?" He'd been sitting up every night asking himself that question. "Haven't I already let them manipulate me?"

He hadn't announced the natural gas pipeline that would free Europe from Russian control and fill American coffers. He'd put it off indefinitely. Was this the first compromise he would make in a long line of them to keep his loved ones safe? How easy would it become to give in just a little more each time?

"You know how to fix that. I'll release that correspondence between Joy and myself, and Gus doesn't mind if her sex tape gets out." Roman took a long swallow. "I will hate that part, but I bet she looks gorgeous. You've got Liz's sister handled."

"There's no way to manage the other threats. I'm at the end of my rope. Connor and Lara's lives will be in danger. Gabe and I can probably deal with the heat from the FAA investigation, though. I did not kill that report." According to everything they knew, someone from the press office had.

No, he needed to call it like it was. Elizabeth had likely killed the report.

She'd also been the one to "find" the blackmail letter. Everything pointed to her. She'd even been recommended by his father, who almost certainly knew something...or had at one point. Information had to be buried in that foggy brain of his.

His father was the key to unlocking this mystery, but Zack couldn't get the man to say anything lucid. He'd tried to question his dad many times over the last couple of months. He'd asked about the years they'd spent in Russia. He'd asked about his mother's death. He'd absolutely asked why his mother had talked constantly about a mysterious baby when she'd been drunk.

Had that baby been the real Zack Hayes?

But whenever he posed these questions to his father, the man always stared at him as if he didn't understand. Or he would melt down into a tirade, and Zack would have to bring in the nurse to sedate him.

"I'm looking into what happened with that FAA matter, but I have to be quiet," Roman murmured. "Connor is taking point on that. We'll figure this out. You haven't done anything to compromise yourself or the country. Honestly, now that we've got Mad back, I'm more positive than ever that we'll win this fight."

"We don't even know precisely who we're fighting."

Roman stared at him for a moment, an almost nauseating sympathy in his eyes. "We're going to have to deal with Elizabeth."

"That's what I'm trying to do."

"By bringing her to Mad? By letting her in on all of our secrets?"

"She already knows them. If she's half the spy you seem to think she is, I assure you she already knows everything there is to know about me."

"And if she's not, then you've wrecked the best relationship of your life. Don't pretend you don't love her and this isn't killing you. For what it's worth, Gus loves her, too. Honestly, I don't know what to think anymore and I'm sick of playing the bad guy. I'm only looking out for you."

If there was one thing in this world Zack could count on, it was that Roman Calder always had his back. "I don't want to believe Elizabeth had anything to do with this mess, but all the roads lead back to her."

"Maybe that's because someone's trying to divide us."

Zack clung to that suggestion like a damn life raft. "She would be the easiest one to get to. Mad admitted he isn't sure about Elizabeth, either. But maybe he has some insights. When I told him I was having her brought here this weekend, he didn't argue."

Roman held up a hand. "Look, regardless of whether she's done anything wrong or not, you're going to rest easier if you know she's safe. I think you should try to repair your relationship with her."

"Maybe, but—"

"There are two ways to think about this. If Liz isn't involved in this conspiracy, then someone on the opposite side is damn smart. They've figured out what she means to you and they're using her already. Pushing her away didn't stop them in the least. But if she's in on it…"

"Then keeping her close is the best idea." Zack always felt better having his conclusions seconded by a master politician. "And maybe if she's not involved, letting her in will go a long ways to repairing our friendship."

Roman rolled his eyes. "You mean you might finally get her into bed. *That* will go a long way to fixing you two. But just in case, maybe we should run a little test."

"What do you mean?"

Roman had his scheming face on. Of course most people would simply call that his face in general because Roman was almost always plotting something. "Give her some information no one but the two of us knows, something false. If it gets out, we know she's involved."

And if it didn't, then he might still have a shot at some kind of happiness, however temporary it might be. Though he had to consider all the ramifications of being with Elizabeth. "I still need to keep my distance. I don't want her tied too closely to me if it turns out I'm a Russian plant. I won't ruin her life that way."

"Let's take it one day at a time." Roman clapped a hand on his shoulder. "And tonight, let's just be happy our asshole friend isn't in the grave and that he might have useful information so we can end this once and for all."

Zack grimaced. "I know…"

"Come on, man. Don't feel guilty or wallow yourself into misery. Let's have one night where we're just happy that we're all together again. How much do you want to bet that Everly and Sara both slap the shit out of Mad?"

He smiled at that before reality intruded again. "Gabe needs to talk to Sara before she sees Mad."

How would the expectant mother handle her lover coming back from the dead?

"She'll be happy…eventually. She's got to understand he did this to protect her. I believe that part of his story," Roman said. "Now, let's take a deep breath and get ready for the storm. I hear the chopper coming in."

Zack felt his whole body tense because that meant Elizabeth was here. She would walk in any moment with Gus, Lara, and Holland.

Minutes later, he heard the door open. The *click-click-click* of Gus's heels followed. Naturally, she was carrying a bottle of his best tequila. He should have known if he disrupted that woman's party, she would simply make another one.

"All right, guys, we're here. Your explanation better be excel…"

Augustine Spencer looked across the great room and fell uncharacteristically silent. She simply stood, rooted, staring at the dead man who looked very much alive. Lara and Holland joined her, each blinking in shock at Mad with their jaws hanging open.

"Hey, Gus." Mad might care about the other ladies, but Zack knew damn well Mad had always adored Gus. She'd been his touchstone for years. "I thought you might forgive me for hijacking your party."

Roman stepped up beside him, watching his fiancée with concern.

Gus gasped and tears started. "Yep. You're forgiven." She walked toward Mad, her arms wide. "I knew you couldn't be dead. Something inside me kept insisting. You bastard."

But she threw her arms around him and cried.

Lara had her hands on her hips. "I'm glad you're alive, Mr. Crawford, and I'm eager for an explanation. But we'll need to talk about the environmental impact of your faked demise."

Connor managed to cup his wife's shoulders before she

could start the lecture. He knew exactly how to get her attention. He started kissing her.

Dax moved in on his wife, Holland, taking her hand and explaining with quiet words, stopping when she had questions.

Elizabeth stood apart from the rest. She still wore the suit she'd worked in all day. The Secret Service must have nabbed her before she could change for Gus's impromptu party. It didn't matter. She was the most gorgeous woman he'd ever seen.

And Zack didn't know for certain, but he'd bet she would be absolutely stunning wearing nothing at all.

She turned to him, and those crystal blue eyes caught his. *Caught* was the perfect word. Every time he looked at her, that's how he felt. Years ago she'd caught him, and even now she refused to let him go.

He couldn't think of another woman, hadn't been able to in forever. He'd gone out with several of the world's most celebrated beauties for appearances' sake. A few had even indicated they were receptive to far more than a friendly dinner. Zack couldn't stand the thought of touching them. Not a one of those women moved him.

He watched the moment Elizabeth decided to be brave. She squared her shoulders and those eyes went steely as she marched his way.

His heart rate ticked up, but he was sure no one would be able to tell. He'd learned early in life how to hide almost everything he was feeling. His father would have preferred that he feel nothing at all, but he'd been satisfied that Zack was usually quite good at putting on a bland face.

She wouldn't be able to tell that his dick had stirred to life the way it always did when she was around. He could ignore his physical needs easily—with the singular exception of this one woman. Sometimes, like now, he wished he'd never met her, never known how good it felt to be in love.

"Mr. President, I understand why I'm here now, but I'm going to need to get back to DC tonight. The Secret Service agent told me they're sending the chopper back shortly. I'd like to be on board so I can do my job."

She didn't understand anything at all. He hated the fact that she called him Mr. President now, even when they were alone. Sometimes, he played a sick game with himself to see if he could fluster her enough to let his first name slip past her gorgeous lips. He always felt a rush of triumph when it did.

"You've been assigned a room. If you need anything, let me know and we'll have someone get it for you. Since we'll be here for a few days, I've already sent one of the interns to your place to pack a bag for you."

Since Roman had joined his fiancée and the rest of the women, who were now peppering Mad with questions he likely wouldn't answer, they were mostly alone. Elizabeth stared at him for a moment. "I don't belong here. I don't even understand what's going on, but I'll spin this any way you want me to. I need some time to think, and I definitely need my computer."

He bet she did. "You're not here to work."

"Then why am I here?"

"Because someone's planning my assassination and they might use you to get to me. I've changed my mind about keeping you out of my problems. It hasn't worked, so we're trying something new. You'll stay close to the group, close to me. Settle in. It's going to be a long weekend."

He turned and walked away because if he remained beside her for a second longer, he would show her exactly how close to her he wanted to be.

Zack glanced down. His glass was empty. He was going to need a lot more liquor to survive the next few days.

* * * *

Mad hung back. He knew the guys all wanted him to talk, but he needed Freddy to round out the explanation. Freddy knew every last detail. He could answer each and every question, as well as corroborate the story Mad knew they'd all see as insane. But Freddy was also notoriously paranoid and convinced someone was out to get him. How much would he actually tell a roomful of virtual strangers?

A problem for later. Right now, Mad had to somehow hold everyone off until Freddy arrived. Thomas was looking for him now…but Freddy could be notoriously slippery. All Mad could do was hope the retrieval mission didn't take too long. Or that Freddy didn't give Thomas too much hell. Until then, everyone would simply have to wait and be patient. It wasn't right or fair to put off telling the whole story, but this way everything would make more sense to everyone. Hopefully then, everyone would be on the same page.

Except maybe Liz. Mad wasn't entirely sure which side she was on yet.

He stepped outside and dragged in a long breath. The rest of the guys were still inside, but somehow he felt a disconnect from them he hadn't expected. He'd genuinely believed that once he was standing beside his best friends again that he would find some acceptance, even peace. A connection to his old life. Maybe he'd been naïve, but he honestly hadn't expected their anger.

What happened next would make or break him. He had to explain everything he'd discovered, help them understand why he'd disappeared. Most of all, he had to convince them that every move he'd made had been for the sake of his family. To keep all of them safe.

But that was later. Right now, he still had to prepare for the last shock of the night. Everly. Since she was Gabe's wife now, she would be here soon. She would have a lot of questions, his sister. Mad would answer them and start being her big brother. If she let him.

He didn't know when he'd see Sara. God, soon, he hoped. He'd missed her so fucking much. He wanted her back. Wanted to start their life together. Wanted to be there for his baby's birth. Wanted to make Sara his wife.

A door closed behind him. Mad tensed. Gabe.

"I need to ask you a few questions. Not about what you and Freddy cooked up while you were gone. Personal stuff."

Mad had known this was coming. While he'd hoped Gabe had forgotten some of their personal drama those last few days before his "death," he should have remembered that Gabe had the memory of an elephant.

He kept his stare fixed on the trees swaying gently as sunset approached. It was more peaceful than seeing the resentment on his best friend's face. "Shoot."

Gabe moved in beside him. "Why did you have your Deep Throat tell Everly she couldn't trust me?"

That was an easy one.

Now Mad turned to face the man who had once been his best friend. "Because I overheard everything you said about her that first day you walked into Crawford. So I decided to protect my sister."

"From me?" Gabe's eyes widened. "What are you talking about?"

Mad had been so enraged when he'd heard Gabe casually discussing how he intended to "deal" with Everly Parker. "The way you talked to Connor about her in my office, like she was trash you needed to take out... It was bad enough that you assumed she was my mistress and intended to fire her. But when I heard that you'd met her at the funeral and used her for stress relief, then nearly let her go? Yeah, I was pissed. You acted like an asshole and you didn't deserve her."

"You had the office bugged."

He didn't feel any remorse about that. "I had to keep up with things. And it wasn't a bug, per se. Connor would have found that. There's a backdoor into the desktop in my office. I can control pretty much everything from there, including the microphones and camera. You and my sister have sex on my desk way too often."

Okay, he did regret parts of his scheme now—small ones. He should have shut his surveillance down when he'd realized Gabe and his sister were happy together. But he'd kept it open, desperate for those brief times when he heard anything at all about Sara.

"You really want to talk about sisters?" Gabe asked, his jaw tightening.

Oh, Mad was so ready for this fight. "Yeah. Yeah, I do. I want to talk about the fact that I begged you to believe me that day at Cipriani's and you wouldn't. I thought out of everyone who knew me that you would…I don't know…have a little faith. I told you I loved Sara."

"Then you left her."

"When had I ever said I loved a woman before Sara? When? Did I ever once confide to you that I was in love? Not fucking once, Gabe. So you should have known something was wrong. I promised you I would take care of her. I can be a massive asshole, but never once in all our years as friends, have I promised you something I didn't make good on."

Gabe pointed a finger in his chest. "It doesn't matter what you said. It's what you did. You walked out on her. You knew she was pregnant and you left her—cruelly. You dumped her over text and went out the same night with a fucking supermodel. What was I supposed to think?"

"What about Zack? He's done roughly the same thing. If you hadn't known about this giant conspiracy trying to bring him down, what would you have thought of Zack snubbing Liz?" Mad challenged.

Gabe paused. The guilt that crossed his face kicked Mad in the gut, even though he knew exactly what his friend's answer would be. Hell, he'd known it before he'd asked the question.

"It's not the same."

"Because Zack is Captain America, and I'm an overprivileged asshole who treats all women like crap." Mad backed away. "That was all I needed to know, buddy."

"Damn it, Mad. She's my sister."

"And she's the love of my life. I hope and pray she understands better than you."

She would, right? Sara knew him, after all. When this mess was behind them, he would stand in front of her and finally tell her everything. He hoped he'd see understanding and forgiveness in her eyes. And god, he hoped all this was settled before their baby was born.

But after his less than warm welcome tonight, Mad was beginning to worry...

"What is it you want me to understand?" Gabe gnashed his teeth. "You told her you would pay for her abortion. You *texted* it."

Mad had hated every word he'd tapped out—and himself—that night. But he'd also known it was necessary to protect Sara. "Another thing that should have tipped you off since, again, I promised I would take care of her. Do you remember what we did two nights before I left Sara? Remember running into those old Yale friends at that bar in Hell's Kitchen, then sitting in the park afterward and talking about how fucking sad they seemed?"

"Yeah. I do," Gabe replied, his tone softer now. "I remember joking that if I ever spent hours talking about baby crap you should shoot me."

"What did I say, Gabe?"

"You said it wouldn't be so bad. You said maybe we

were the sad ones because neither of us had been smart enough to find a woman who would put up with us. You said maybe it was time to grow up." Gabe sent him a speculative stare. "You already knew about the baby."

"I'd known for a few days," he admitted. "When Sara told me, it was the best night of my life. It took everything I had not to tell you about it while we sat in that park, but Sara wanted to wait to announce our good news until she'd followed up with the doctor. And she wanted to think about how to break it to you. I already knew I was going to marry her, but my proposal had to be special. Man, I had a plan. Everything was set for the night of the Met gala... And the Russians fucked it up."

Gabe ran a hand through his sandy-colored hair. "I didn't think about that night we talked in the park. I didn't think about anything except the fact you destroyed my sister."

"I nearly destroyed myself trying to save her, you, our baby—everyone. Don't think I don't understand how much she's been hurting." Mad sighed, trying to hold himself together. "But I get your anger. When I heard you talking about Everly that day in my office, I saw red. I'm just glad you two worked it out. Congratulations, man."

Mad turned away. He needed to decompress. He needed sleep—preferably in an actual bed. It would be the first time in months. Maybe everything would seem brighter in the morning.

Gabe grabbed his arm. "Mad, stop. I'm sorry. I was wrong. I should have talked to you that day we had lunch instead of yelling. And I should have had a little faith in you." He held a hand out. "I am glad you're alive. I'm happy to have you back."

Mad stared at the hand. It could be a trick. "So you can kill me?"

"So you can be a father to your kid. So I'm not left

alone with all these women." Gabe tried to laugh, then sobered. "So I can maybe find a way to be your brother again."

Mad reached out and shook his hand. Repairing all his relationships wasn't going to be as easy as he'd assumed, but he was determined to get his family back, especially Sara. No one in the world knew or loved him like she did.

Gabe pulled him in for a hug, slapping his back. "I really am glad you're back. I didn't like living in a world without you, man."

Mad had missed them all, too. He hated the fact that he hadn't been there when so many of them had gotten their shit together and committed to the loves of their life. Sure, he'd watched from afar, but he'd missed out on so much. "I hated that I missed your wedding. Tell me Connor and Dax gave you a proper bachelor party."

Gabe was smiling when he stepped back. "Not even one stripper."

The horror. "Maybe we should have an all-guys post-wedding bash."

A chuckle huffed from Gabe's throat. "Nope. I've been happily married and stripper free for a while now. It's a good life, man."

Yes, Mad wanted that life, too—with Sara. "I'd like mine to be all about us. Just the six of us hanging out with the wives and kids."

"Hey, I'll make that happen if you can actually convince my sister to forgive you. But I'm telling you now, it's not going to be easy."

Sara was the most forgiving soul he'd ever met. Once he told her why he'd left her and the lengths he'd gone to in order to save her, there was a chance the two of them could pick up where they had left off, right? Maybe…

"I'll go and see her soon. I'll explain and grovel like nobody's business. I swear." The minute it was safe, Mad vowed he would be on her doorstep, hat in hand, ready to love her for the rest of his life.

"You know we're bringing in *all* the women, right?"

Mad froze. "What do you mean?"

Out of the corner of his eye, he saw a car pull into the drive, but he couldn't think about that at the moment. He was too busy trying to decipher Gabe's words into sense. "But not Sara. She's at the house in the Hamptons."

Gabe shook his head. "She came down to DC this morning. The women decided to spend some time together while Zack, the rest of the guys, and I hung out here. When you showed up, Zack told the Secret Service to bring them all in. They'll be here any minute. I think I should talk to Sara first, lessen the shock."

But it was too late because that limo door was opening and she stepped out. Mad stopped breathing. God, she was beautiful. The sun was setting and the golden light reflected off her hair, enhancing the riot of colors. He'd always been fascinated by how lovely her hair looked, how silky it felt wrapped around his fingers when they shared pleasure. The color wasn't precisely brown or blonde, but a combination, coupled with an alluring hint of red that sparkled in the light.

She turned toward Everly, and he saw the curve of her rounding stomach, the proof that their child grew inside her. Mad felt rooted. His heart threatened to stop. He loved her so fucking much, and he was going to love that kid every bit as much.

If she let him.

Oh, god. She was here. Now. He didn't have a speech planned. He didn't know what to say. He only knew he was terrified that she didn't love him anymore.

"Mad, get inside before she sees you," Gabe urged. "Sara can't find out like this."

He was right, but then Everly caught sight of him. She

blinked like he might be a mirage. Then she raised her arm and pointed his way. His name formed on her lips.

Sara turned. Her eyes widened. She gaped in shock. She paled. Then she was falling.

Mad raced to reach her, praying like hell he hadn't fucked everything up.

Chapter Four

Sara was having the sweetest dream. She was back in New York, dressed and looking her best for the Met gala with Mad. This time, the night was so special and she wasn't left waiting. He even showed up early.

I couldn't wait. I had to see you. I don't like spending the night away from you.

She turned to him and smiled. *Then maybe you should move in.*

His lips curled up, part triumph, part mischief—all Mad. *Done. I won't ever go home again.* He paused then, growing serious. *You are my home. You and this short stack of pancakes.*

You are not calling our child a short stack.

He touched her belly. *I'll call that baby ours.*

Sara melted. She didn't want to wake up. This dream was the sweetest of her regularly recurring ones. She rotated between slumberous fantasies where she and Mad were still in love and nightmares where she was on the plane with him as it was going down. Either way, when she woke up she had to face the fact that he hadn't shown up that night. He'd texted her his cruel kiss off. And every morning when she opened her eyes, she had to remember that he was dead and he would never know their baby, much less give their little one nicknames that would horrify her as a teenager. Mad was gone, and Sara had finally accepted that he had never loved her.

But even though it wasn't real, she always wished she could linger in the lovely paradise of sleep for more stolen moments with him.

"I'll take care of her," a familiar voice she couldn't quite place said.

"Holland said she's fine," her brother put in. "She's just had a shock, but she didn't hit the ground, thanks to Everly. I'm wondering if we should have a doctor look at her, just in case."

"Absolutely," said that male voice that niggled at her brain. "Or maybe we should medevac her."

Oh, god, that was not happening.

Sara sat up, her vision still blurred and her head swimming. She must have fainted, but now she remembered why.

She'd seen a ghost.

After climbing from the limo, the sun had been at her back, and she would have sworn in that halo of blinding light that Maddox stood mere feet away. Sara felt sheepish now. It was one thing to have dreams about him at night, but if she was carrying those over to her days? That nonsense had to stop. "I'm sorry to make a fuss. I'm okay. I thought I saw—"

She turned and focused. And he was there. Not a mirage, not a hallucination. Maddox Crawford in the flesh.

Sara stared, blinked. "Oh my god."

He rushed to her side, kneeling beside the bed and taking her hands in his. "Baby, are you okay? I saw you falling out there and I couldn't reach you in time. I was so worried. We should get you to a hospital. I know Holland has some medic training, but she's not an obstetrician."

She closed her eyes. "I must still be dreaming."

"You're not." He curled his hands around hers. "I'm really here."

He looked like Mad, had the same piercing green eyes and dark hair as Mad. He even talked like Mad. She now recognized that smooth and deep voice. It had an almost intimate quality when he spoke to her. But this man couldn't be Mad. His hair was longer, curling over his ears. His hands weren't smooth and perfectly manicured, but rather rough and callused and stronger. His gaze held no hint of his usual devil-may-care spirit. Instead it glinted with terrible knowledge and an even more excruciating yearning.

"Say something. I know this must be a shock, but I'm here. I'm alive. And I can explain everything."

What was there to explain? Before they'd gotten together, Sara had been convinced he was a spoiled rich playboy who took nothing seriously. That's how the rest of the world had seen him. But when he'd flirted and smiled and touched her, when he'd whispered and kissed her and made love to her, she'd seen a whole different Mad.

No, she'd seen a façade. That soft, loving Maddox Crawford was a chimera. The one who'd texted her his unfeeling sayonara? That was the real Mad.

She put a hand on her belly and forced herself to sit up. She was in a bedroom apparently. She'd never been to Camp David before, but it was tastefully decorated, like everything surrounding the president. The room was fairly large, too. It needed to be since every single person in her life was currently here and crowding around her. "I'm confused."

Holland moved in, eyes soft with understanding. "Sweetie, you fainted."

"I know." Had she hurt the baby?

As the question pelted her brain, Sara gasped and cradled her stomach.

Holland seemed to understand her panic. "You're fine. The baby is fine. You've just had a shock. You're at Camp David in the Aspen Lodge. You're safe here. Nothing can harm you."

The president had the largest of the eighteen cabins that made up Camp David. She understood that. What she hadn't known about Camp David was it apparently could bring back the dead.

Her brother stared down at her, concern etched on his face. "Sara? Are you all right?"

"Well, her blood pressure is great. The baby's heartbeat is strong and well within normal range. Seriously, she's fine," Holland reiterated. "At least physically. Emotionally, well, I'd like to murder all of you because how could you break the news to her this way?"

"Drama," Gus said with a shake of her head. "The Perfect Gentlemen all love drama."

"We didn't mean to spring Mad on her," Roman argued. "Gabe was supposed to tell her gently. And Mad wasn't supposed to be outside. Did you forget that part, dipshit? Marines are crawling all over this base, securing it. You can't possibly have every one of them on the payroll the way you do the Secret Service."

Mad groaned. "Thomas is not on the payroll. I don't have a damn payroll. Did you forget the outhouse story?"

"I doubt the marines patrolling this area read tabloids," Connor pointed out with a raised brow. "None of them will recognize Mad without a martini in one hand and a hooker on his arm. He's also lost weight and his hair has grown out. I think we're safe, but he's got to be better about staying inside."

Sara tuned out because none of this chatter explained

how and why Mad was here. He'd been dead. The FAA had even sworn his remains were among the wreckage. She'd finally gotten to a place where she could breathe and now…

He was back. Alive. Real.

Where had he been all this time?

She forced herself to remain calm. She couldn't pass out again. She couldn't afford to be weak.

"I need a moment alone with Maddox."

Gabe took her hand. "I'm really sorry. I meant to intercept you before you came inside. I was going to ease you into this."

"You've known all this time?"

Somehow the idea that Gabe had been in on whatever scheme this was felt even worse than Mad's betrayal. Gabe had been her rock. He'd been the one person in the world she could count on. If he'd kept the truth from her… Sara couldn't fathom it. She would be utterly alone.

"He didn't," Mad insisted, still kneeling beside the bed. "No one did. I couldn't tell any of you."

"Why don't we let them talk for a bit?" Zack was a calm presence in the midst of the chaos. "Apparently Freddy has been located. Presuming Thomas can adequately calm Mad's paranoid friend, they should be here in ten minutes."

She didn't know who Freddy was and had no idea why the man should matter. She didn't care right now. "I'd like for someone to explain what's happening. Gabe, could you?"

"What? Sara, I'm here. I'll tell you everything."

Gabe squeezed her shoulder. "You should talk to him. We'll give you two some privacy. But to answer your question, Sara, I've only known that Mad's alive for an hour and a half, and I'm still processing myself. I'll be outside if you need me."

Slowly, they all walked out until she was left with the man who'd broken her heart.

Sara hated how vulnerable she felt around him, how unsure. She didn't know what to say. She had no idea what Mad wanted. Why was he even bothering to talk to her when he'd made it crystal clear he was done with her and wanted nothing to do with their baby?

When he tried to take her hand, she jerked away and swung her legs over the edge of the mattress. The last place she wanted to be with Mad was flat on a bed. It had always been way too easy for him to talk her into one.

Mad stood and started crossing the floor in long, rapid steps—a sure sign that he was disconcerted. He always paced like a lion in a cage when he was nervous or unsure how to handle a situation.

Then he stopped in front of her, fingers curled into fists. "Sara, I know you're confused right now."

She was, and even though she had moved on for the sake of her sanity, she felt torn between the traitorous urge to throw her arms around him and the desire to punch him in the face. Instead, she steadied her breathing to keep herself calm. "I wouldn't say confusion is all I'm feeling, though I would like an explanation. Did you get into some trouble that forced you to fake your own death?" A million scenarios ran through her head, all of them bad. "Did you sleep with someone's wife? Owe someone money? Oh, god, don't tell me there are problems at Crawford. What did you do to the business?"

He frowned at her, the formidable expression doing nothing to lessen his fallen-angel good looks. "No. I put the business in Gabe's hands because I knew if I didn't come back, he would turn it over to you. I didn't bequeath it to you directly because you're pregnant and didn't need the stress. And the press would have gone insane with speculation. I tried to think about you."

"You broke up with me via text."

His face flushed. "I had to. I did it to protect you."

"Protect me?" Who was he kidding?

Was he claiming that he'd been cruel to be kind? That vicious text had been his way of keeping her safe? She didn't need that kind of protection. She'd needed a partner, and he had proven a poor one.

"Sara, I was investigating something fishy at Crawford. Do you remember Tavia Gordon?"

Tall, gorgeous, always fashionable. "She was the head of public relations at Crawford."

"She also ran an organization that supported women and educated girls across the globe," Mad reminded her.

Sara was well aware of the woman, mostly because Mad had slept with her in the past. "Yes, the International Women and Girls Education Foundation. It died off when she was killed."

"And also because it was a front for the Russian mafia."

She shook her head, trying to absorb Mad's claim. "What?"

"Yeah. I knew something was off," he said quickly, as though he worried she wouldn't stay around for his explanation. "A worker at the foundation anonymously sent me a note telling me that a surprising number of the girls the foundation helped went missing every year. When I started looking into it, I realized quickly that Tavia was selling those girls and had rigged a financial component for their operation by using the funds from the annual gala the company held to support it. I intended to fire her."

"That's horrifying, but what does any of this have to do with us?"

Mad sidled close to her, sinking to one knee again. "Because the night before I broke up with you, the head of the Krylov syndicate came to see me."

A chill went up her spine. "What happened?"

His gaze shifted away. "Let's just say my body was black and blue for at least two weeks. There were moments

I was sure I was going to die."

Krylov had viciously beaten Mad? Even the thought made her sick to her stomach. She hated that some criminal had damaged both his body and his spirit. He'd always been so larger than life that it was sometimes easy to forget he was just a man. But that didn't really explain anything.

"Why didn't you call the police?"

"A lot of reasons. Mostly because Krylov alluded to the fact that Zack was involved with their plot. He intimated that if I brought him down, I would be taking Zack down, too."

"What?" Zack was one of the most honorable men she'd ever met. He was stalwart and stable. Solid. He would never be involved with anything criminal.

"I know. It threw me for a loop, too. So I did what I had to do."

"You suspecting Zack of being involved in a Russian mafia scheme is the reason you broke up with me?" That sounded far-fetched and illogical on so many levels. Sara understood that he'd probably been scared, but Mad had a huge network of people who loved him. He'd hardly been alone. "What did Zack say?"

Mad sat back, putting more distance between them. "I couldn't go to Zack. Sara, I couldn't go to anyone. I needed to figure out what was really going on first."

"You?" Of all people?

"Yes. Why not me?"

"You don't have any investigative skills," she pointed out.

"I couldn't trust anyone else. I didn't have a choice."

"You couldn't trust *me?*"

The truth hit her squarely in the face. Mad had never really cared about her at all. She'd been ready to raise a family with him, and all he'd done was lie, use her, and keep huge secrets.

"Of course I trust you. But these people meant business. They could have killed me. If they'd understood how much I loved you, they would have used you against me. They would have used the baby, too. I couldn't risk you both. The minute Krylov and his cohort started beating me, I knew I'd do *anything* to protect you."

She shook her head. "But you didn't protect me. You left me ignorant."

"I couldn't tell you, baby."

She stood and shook her head. "Sure you could have. Your mouth works, Mad. But for weeks, you dated other women instead. I was alone. Before you fake checked-out, that is."

"All those dates were a cover. You have to see that. I wanted the syndicate to think I was exactly who they believed me to be, a playboy with no real ties to any woman. If they had come after you, I would have never forgiven myself."

"So instead, you told me you would pay for my abortion."

"Because I knew you wouldn't do it, but I had to make our break seem real and believable. Without meaning to, I got myself deep into something dangerous and I had to keep you out of it."

Sara shook her head in disbelief. His explanation still didn't make sense. The fact she was talking to him at all barely computed, either. She'd made her peace with his passing. The wound had started to heal. Now, he'd ripped it open and poured salt deep into it.

"And it never occurred to you to tell me any of this? You know I can keep a secret."

He shook his head. "I couldn't risk them coming after you to find out what you knew. And to be honest, I thought you would guess that something was horribly wrong and that you would trust me while I fixed it."

"Trust you? Oh, I won't ever trust you again, Maddox."

The truth was, any trust she'd had in him evaporated the moment he'd sent that text.

He rose and faced her. "Don't say that. I did this for *you*. I did this so you would never know the danger I felt with Krylov. I did this so that, when it was all over, I could stand in front of you and be proud that I protected you and our baby the way a real mate and father should."

In Mad's twisted mind, he'd painted himself as the hero of this complicated tale.

"So you're saying the danger is over now, and you're back? But didn't Tavia Gordon die months ago?"

"Yeah, but since the plane crash, I've been digging deep, trying to root out answers. This criminal plot is more complex than I ever realized. Sara, you have no idea what I've discovered. The foundation barely scratched the surface. This conspiracy goes back forty years."

Should she be glad he'd decided to let her in on his secrets now? The whole gang was here, all the Perfect Gentlemen, along with their wives or fiancées. They'd even included Liz, presumably so she could be in the know, despite the fact that being around Zack only amplified the pain of her unrequited love.

Or was this sinister plot Mad had been trying to unearth the reason Zack had started dating other women? Had he taken a page from Mad's book and rejected Liz the same way Mad had dumped her?

"So why tell me now?"

Mad cupped Sara's shoulders. "Please understand…but I never meant to reveal any of this to you until the danger was completely over. I didn't realize you were in DC."

In other words, he hadn't asked to have her brought here. She'd simply been in the wrong place at the wrong time when Zack had ordered the Secret Service to bring all the women to Camp David. "You don't want me here. I'm not surprised."

"Oh, I do, baby. I've missed you so, so much. God..." His face twisted with something that looked like agony. "If you only knew. But you shouldn't be near me now. I need you to be safe," Mad insisted. "I never wanted any of this to touch you."

"Not touch me? Are you joking? Whatever *this* is has touched me in more ways than I can count. It's ruined my life."

"No. No, baby. It hasn't. I promise. It's merely postponed our future." He cupped her cheeks, staring into her eyes with that look that never failed to make her weak, the one that urged her to believe she was the only woman for him. When he looked at her like that, the world fell away. There were no more problems or worries, just the two of them, together always.

But that was another one of his lies. "We have no future."

"Don't say that. It's not true."

But it was.

Sara stepped back. "Whether you wanted me involved or not, I am now. Tell me everything that's going on."

He shook his head. "You should go back to the Hamptons. Believe me, I don't want to let you go, but I have to think about you. About our baby."

From what she could tell, he hadn't been thinking at all. "I'm not going anywhere. I'm staying here and I'm listening in on whatever you're up to."

"Sara, I don't think that's—"

"It doesn't matter what you think anymore, Mad. Let me make this very plain. It's obvious you thought I would be so happy you're alive that I would forget the way you treated me when you left me, but I can't. It doesn't matter why you broke things off so horribly. There were a hundred ways you could have played this, but you chose the way that hurt me most."

"I didn't do it for the purpose of hurting you. I never wanted to. Please——"

"You just said it yourself. You had to ensure I wouldn't come after you. Well, you did an excellent job. There's nothing between us now and there never will be again."

She started to brush past him, but he caught her arm, his gaze steely as he drew her back. "There *is* something between us. That baby in your belly is mine, and I'm not giving up my rights to it or to you."

This was a different Mad, a more forceful Mad. In the past, he'd always been an imp, an instigator. The man standing in front of her now seemed far more like a warrior.

"You gave them up the minute you sent that text." She couldn't back down. She couldn't let him see that he intimidated her. Nor could she think about the fact that she found this new Maddox even more intriguing than the old one.

Sara yanked her arm from his grip and walked out of the room. It was time to figure out her future.

On her own.

* * * *

Zack sat in the great room, surrounded by his friends. Yet he'd never felt more apart from them. It seemed completely surreal that Mad sat across the room at the bar, talking to the man who'd destroyed his whole world mere months ago. Sure, he'd suspected for a while that someone sinister was coming after him and his friends. Then Freddy had confirmed Zack's worst fears by showing him the terrible footage he'd compiled. Zack had realized then precisely why Joy had been murdered—and he'd been forced to confront the possibility he might be the very enemy he'd been hunting.

He glanced across the room. Elizabeth had chosen a seat as far away from him as possible, one beside Sara. He was pretty sure Mad's private conversation with his pregnant ex hadn't gone the way his recently risen friend had hoped. Both Mad and Sara had emerged from the bedroom looking utterly miserable.

Pretty much the way he felt.

"I understand they more or less brought Freddy in against his will," Roman whispered, sending a sidelong glance at the conspiracy twosome.

Mad and Freddy were an odd duo. Zack wished they'd vlogged the last few months when Mad had apparently lived in the wilderness with Freddy as his survival guide. He would pay to watch that reality show.

"Thomas brought him in. From what I gather, Mad expected Freddy to help him explain the last few months, but Freddy resisted because there were too many guards."

The steely man with the russet hair glared their way. He had a stare like a crowbar, trying to pry their intentions from their heads. Then he whispered to Mad. Unfortunately, Freddy's low tones were pretty loud. "Are you sure we should be here? Because it would be really easy to bury us in the woods. Did you notice this place is surrounded by woods? On the other hand, if tonight goes bad, we can probably live off this land."

He was in full-on Freddy mode—paranoia mixed with hyper intelligence and meticulous attention to detail, topped off with a dash of pure crazy. Zack had looked into Freddy's military records. The man's career as an intelligence officer had been impressive...until he'd been captured and held by the enemy for almost a year. Something had fractured inside him during his imprisonment. Shortly after the prior administration had negotiated his return, Freddy had been discharged. The mind of an intelligence officer was still there, just buried under all the other issues.

"I'm never living off the land again. I would rather die," Mad replied.

Zack couldn't help but grin. Yeah, Mad's version of camping had been a fire on the beach, imbibing a load of liquor, then going back to the beach house with a woman or two to either have sex or pass out.

God, sometimes Zack wished he could be back there, when the six of them had been really tight. When the world had been their playground. Not that they'd had a multitude of possibilities. Their paths had been set from birth, with the singular exception of Connor. But he'd chosen his road when he'd met the rest of them and gotten caught up in their undeniable destinies.

"Are you sure we should tell him?" Freddy glanced his way.

There was no question who the man meant. Mad nodded at Freddy. "The president needs to know. We agreed. C'mon, even you have doubts that he's in on the conspiracy. I know I've never wanted to believe it, but over the course of the last several months, Zack's actions haven't been those of a Russian operative."

Zack tried to smile. At least he had the appearance of innocence going for him.

He cast a sidelong glance Elizabeth's way. Her eyes were wide, and she blinked at Freddy like the loon he was. Zack had to hand it to her. If she was acting, she deserved an Academy Award.

Suddenly, she turned those blue eyes on him. They were full of sympathy.

God, he didn't want to believe she wasn't genuine. He wanted her to be exactly the sweet, caring, strong woman he'd met so long ago, the one he'd waited years to be with.

And if she wasn't? Did that mean he couldn't be with her? What if he could find a way to have her, even if she was a traitor? It occurred to him that being constantly on top of Elizabeth was a damn fine way to keep tabs on her.

Freddy rolled his eyes. "Of course not. He's smart."

Mad's patience was obviously wearing thin. "Damn it, I know you hated the army, but you were an excellent intelligence officer. What does all that training tell you?"

Freddy's lips went mulish, but he finally sighed. "That he's a pawn. He's not playing the game the way they hoped he would, so they're planning to sacrifice him and move a better pawn into place."

All kinds of crazy with a thread of sanity—that's how Lara had described Freddy. Though the man actively hunted for Sasquatch and believed that ancient aliens walked the earth, he was incredibly good at cutting through the smokescreens and the everyday BS to find the nuggets of truth others overlooked. Zack couldn't deny that Freddy had also ridden in to save the day when Dax and Holland had been in grave danger. Though now Zack suspected he'd done that at Mad's behest.

"All right. But if they murder and bury me in the backyard, I'm going to haunt your ass," Freddy vowed. "You know I promised myself I wouldn't be buried on federal land."

Because he was certain the government had made a deal with whoever ran the afterlife, according to Lara.

Connor's wife got to her feet and joined them. "Freddy, I promise nothing will happen to you."

Freddy turned, his eyes softening on her like he thought the world was a terrible place full of terrible people...all except Lara. "I know you would try to save me, but this goes deeper than even you know."

Mad put a hand on Freddy's shoulder. "If Zack kills you, he'll have to kill me, too. I'll make my last wish for you to be cremated, with your ashes carefully portioned out and scattered in safe spaces across the globe. They won't be able to bring you back."

Lara took over, working her magic on the man. "Did Zack deal with us fairly when I showed him proof that Joy was the assassin's real target?"

"What?" Elizabeth gaped in both shock and horror, looking his way with an expression that said she prayed it wasn't true.

He gave her a grim nod, then Gus stepped in, quietly explaining what the others knew. Zack was grateful to Augustine in that moment. She would know how to tell Elizabeth exactly what she needed to know without embellishing or sugar-coating the truth.

Freddy gave him a considering bob of his head. "Yeah, I suspected he might have me killed then, too. He could have sent someone after me."

"You make me out to be far more Machiavellian than I actually am," Zack pointed out.

He'd ditched his suitcoat and tie for the evening, but the women, except Elizabeth and Gus, were still in their cocktail gowns because they had nothing else to change into. He rather hoped their clothes wouldn't arrive tonight. If they didn't, Elizabeth would be given a clean white T-shirt to sleep in—his. He might not ever see her in it, but he could spend the whole evening fantasizing about it.

"Well, I voted to have you silenced, but not because of your investigation. I simply find you annoying as hell," Roman commented. "And for two guys who've managed to stay off the grid for months, you're not very good at whispering."

Zack repressed a grin. His friends could be assholes. But he loved that they often said the very things he couldn't.

Lara turned to glare at Roman.

Gus merely rolled her eyes. "I want to know how you found Freddy. Because he was Lara's neighbor?"

"We'll get to that. The better question is, why did Freddy try to out me to Lara? If he was working with you, why did he send the target of my investigation"—Connor gestured in his wife's direction—"a complete rundown on her new lover?"

Freddy had written a letter to Lara that Connor had intercepted, outing Connor as one of the Perfect Gentlemen. If Lara had seen it, the missive would have blown Connor's cover utterly. Zack felt sure the entire situation would have exploded in their faces.

"I obviously didn't know about that," Mad replied. "Nothing about that particular op went the way we thought it would."

"You were in love with her," Connor said softly.

Freddy didn't deny it.

"It's okay," Lara's husband assured. "I understand. She's incredibly lovable."

Lara smiled as Connor leaned closer and tugged her onto his lap. He kissed his wife, proving the morose bastard had become much happier than he'd ever been during his single days. Then again, Lara brought out her husband's lighter side.

Zack didn't want to dwell on the fact that every single one of his friends had a woman by his side now. Sara might be holding out, but she was also pregnant, and their baby would tie them together forever. Funny, he'd married before any of them, but it hadn't been for love, rather duty and politics. And now he was alone, probably for good.

Freddy returned Connor's gaze. "I was never going to make a move on her. I…I don't think I'll ever have a wife or kids, and that's for the best. There's a part of me that's broken. But I did…do care about her. You sleeping with her was never supposed to be a part of the plan. I didn't realize you were falling in love with her. I thought you were simply using her and would break her heart. Mad promised me she wouldn't get hurt, so I went around him and tried to separate her from you. Obviously it didn't work, and that's for the best. I know you treat her well."

Connor's lips curled up. "Because she's told you or because you still spy on me?"

Freddy shrugged. "Old habits, you know."

"We're going to have a talk about that, but I understand why you did what you did. We're cool," Connor said.

"I didn't count on you two getting together," Mad admitted. "Or Roman being such a massive asshole."

"Hey," Roman began, then stopped. "Okay, that's fair."

"To get back to business, I've explained what happened the evening Ivan Krylov visited me," Mad began.

Holland gaped. "The head of the Krylov syndicate?"

Zack looked pointedly at Dax. "I thought we all agreed to fill the women on what we know."

Dax winced. "I meant to, but I might have been excited to see my wife. We didn't have time to talk. My mouth was busy, if you know what I mean."

Holland groaned. "Really?"

Zack should have guessed. While Mad had talked to Sara, Zack and Roman had filled in Gus and Elizabeth about how Mad had risen from the dead. Gabe and Connor had spoken to their wives, but Dax and Holland had disappeared. Apparently they'd had way more fun than the rest of them. Newlyweds… Hadn't they gotten enough during their Maui honeymoon at that cozy bed-and-breakfast?

"Mad was investigating the situation with the girls' foundation when the head of the Krylov syndicate beat the piss out of him in an attempt to stop him," Zack explained. "What I don't understand is why the syndicate wouldn't simply kill him. And why, when they left him alive, he didn't call his friends. Why would you decide to investigate by yourself?"

He wanted Mad to put his whole truth out there. They'd been tiptoeing around the honest reason Mad had faked his death.

"I didn't know what to think, Zack. Ivan Krylov told me you were the one who sent him to silence me," Mad explained simply.

Lara gasped and scrambled off her husband's lap. "That's not possible."

"Of course not. We know that." Everly reassured her friend with a quiet squeeze of her hand, then pulled her back to the couch. "I don't know why Mad didn't come to the same conclusion...but let's hear him and Freddy out. I suspect there's a reason Mad has returned now."

"And it can't be good," Gus pointed out.

"Nope." Holland had gotten over her embarrassment and now stared at Mad and Freddy with a shrewd gaze, looking like the NCIS investigator she was. "The game has somehow changed or he would still be in hiding. I can only think of one reason to come out now. Someone is in real, credible danger. Have the Russians threatened one of us?"

Mad held a hand up and sauntered to the front of the room—exactly where he liked to be. "Let me explain from the beginning. I didn't call Zack that night because I was trying to think things through...while making sure my kidneys still functioned after the Russians beat the hell out of me. And I didn't want to bring them down on any of my friends. I especially didn't want them to know about Sara."

The women immediately started in on that.

"You tortured her to protect her?" Gus asked.

Everly shook her head. "Not going to work, Mad. We could have managed some diversion that didn't include Sara and me being at each other's throats."

Lara and Holland were having their says, too—all at once. The room threatened to erupt in chaos. Brow raised, Elizabeth looked to him. Zack knew if he didn't take control, she would.

"Stop." He didn't have to raise his voice. The room

went quiet instantly. "I'd like to get through this debrief as quickly as possible. Holland is right. Mad is here because he's uncovered a plot to assassinate me. He doesn't know exactly who's behind it, but apparently the Russians have infiltrated the White House and the Secret Service."

"But we vet all our people," Elizabeth argued. "Anyone who works for us has to have security clearance, and there are layers on layers of background checks."

Freddy waved that off. "They've infiltrated everywhere. Background checks can be faked. More likely the agents were sleepers."

"What Freddy is trying to say is that the operatives in place have likely been there for years," Mad said. "Like Tavia. She and her family had been in America for decades. She passed plenty of background checks. Some of the operatives are American-born and, for whatever reason, the Russians either persuaded or blackmailed them in to betraying their country. It's even possible their parents raised them to be operatives."

"We need to examine all those files personally," Roman said. "Re-vet every single employee ourselves."

"Freddy and I believe that's the right course of action." Mad's gaze shifted back to Sara, and he shoved his hand in his pockets, as if forcing himself not to touch her...but Zack didn't think that would last long. "It's one of the reasons we had to surface. We need access to those employee records."

Roman huffed. "You want access to White House files? That's not going to happen. Connor can do it, but I can't get you clearance to look at those records."

Zack knew he might need Connor doing other things, so he wasn't willing to refuse Mad yet. "I'll think about it. Now tell me what you've discovered."

He steeled himself for what would happen next. While Mad laid out his conspiracy, he would watch Elizabeth, study her every expression. Try to decide where her loyalties lay.

"Okay…" Mad nodded. "After Krylov paid me that visit, I met Freddy and we started talking."

Gabe scowled. "You couldn't come to any of us, but you cozied right up to a stranger about Krylov's threats?"

"I didn't find Freddy. He found me—lying on my kitchen floor, barely able to move and afraid I was bleeding out. It's sort of hard to ignore someone who's giving you the kind of first aid that might be saving your life."

"He'd been beaten badly," Freddy added with a nod. "But he was still a good listener."

Mad nodded. "Besides, Freddy was already up to his eyeballs in this shit. He knew way more than I did. After we compared a few notes, I knew I couldn't stop the investigation I'd begun with the girls' foundation. I'd already figured out that my father once had an affair with Tavia's mother, so I needed to discern how deep my family ties were to the Gordons. I thought I could dig in plain sight as long as I did it carefully. So I broke things off with Sara to keep her off the syndicate's radar, then I began looking into all the deep, dark rabbit holes. I know I should have talked to you guys. I didn't for the same reason I broke things off with Sara. I needed answers, and while I was getting them I didn't want any of you to meet Krylov the way I had. I'm convinced the only reason he didn't kill me that night was my high profile."

Connor nodded. "I think so, too. If you'd been found dead in your home, there would have been an investigation. The police would have been involved, and the press would have gone insane—like they did when your plane crashed. I take it that happened because you got caught snooping again."

Mad nodded. "Freddy helped me figure out the best way to proceed. He'd been working on the assassination plot for months. He spends a lot of time on the Dark Web.

That's how he made the connection between Krylov and Crawford, then decided to pay me a visit. He was hammering out a theory that a Krylov associate actually killed Joy, not the patsy Connor took down."

"I've got a tight group I trust," Freddy added with enthusiasm. "Candy Man124, StoneColdLA, and AliensAmongUs. Those are solid guys. But not CandyMan125. Don't get those two confused. 125 is an actual candy dealer, and he gets upset when you send him a graphic murder video and ask his opinion. But 124 is excellent at finding the seeming unrelated threads in a conspiracy."

"I'll remember that," Zack promised. "Was one of these Dark Web visitors a pretty vegan?"

"Oh, Lara didn't play around on the Dark Web," Freddy assured. "Well, not much. But I knew she was a journalist. I figured out she was behind Capitol Scandals."

"Only because you're a sneaky bastard," Lara huffed.

The former army officer shrugged. "When you moved into the building, I checked you out. My friends helped me. And…I might or might not have hacked your system. But probably more on the might side."

Mad nodded. "Freddy is the one who put Lara on my radar, and given what I'd found out about Tavia, her family, and their connections to my father, I was looking for someone not associated with any one of us, who could start shining a light on the information I'd unearthed. I actually intended to reach out personally to Lara until I found that bomb on my plane. Or rather Matthew Kemp did."

"How did Kemp get involved?" Dax asked.

"I met Matty when I worked intelligence," Freddy explained. "We'd known each other for about ten years. When I first ran across the whispers about the president, I reached out to him because I knew he was working for the Secret Service. He didn't believe me at first, but when we realized Ivan Krylov was interested in Mad, he agreed we needed to look into it. That's why I was watching Mad the night Ivan came for him."

"I still say you could have saved me from that," Mad complained.

"No, I had to let it happen. If I'd intervened, he would have known someone was onto him. And if he'd killed you, that would have been a helpful piece of information."

Damn, Zack was glad he hadn't needed Freddy as a partner. "So the head of the syndicate mentions that I'm working with him, and you don't bother to ask me if it's true?"

Mad's gaze found his. "C'mon, Zack. If you'd been guilty, what could you have done but deny it? It made more sense to do some digging. What I really hoped to find was concrete proof that you were innocent, along with something I could show you that revealed your enemies and their motives. And…in the midst of that beating, Krylov told me if I went to you or any of my other friends, I might be surprised at what I found. Then I overheard them say that Sergei wouldn't approve. I'm not sure of what. But they made a call and spoke to someone they referred to as Sergei."

Zack grimaced. He wished he'd never heard that name.

When he glanced at Elizabeth, he saw no recognition on her face at all. The others though, they'd stiffened at the mention. His friends knew that name well.

"I played the odds." Freddy took up the tale. "I waited until they left, then checked the dumpsters around Mad's building. Those guys always use burners. I found it and the dude hadn't pulled the SIM card. We were able to figure out they'd called another cell phone, and we narrowed it down to the Foggy Bottom neighborhood of DC."

His stomach twisted. "You think they called the White House."

"I was scared because that seemed like an awfully big coincidence," Mad admitted. "I had no idea what was going on. Then Freddy started showing me everything he'd figured out."

"He showed you the footage of Joy at all those rallies?"

Even thinking about those clips made Zack want to throw up. He had that first time. Freddy had assembled a montage of video from the rallies leading up to the Memphis event shortly before the election. To this day, he remembered hearing the shot and looking down at his own chest, certain he would see blood there. Everything had happened so fast, but in his mind those moments seemed to last forever.

At the time of the shooting, the whole country assumed the assassin's shot had gone wide and mistakenly killed Joy. Guilt had taken root in Zack's soul and fed his every decision since because he'd believed that his wife had died in his place.

Freddy's video had proven him so wrong by showing him that whoever killed Joy had been practicing his shot for a while, like he'd intended to sacrifice her all along. In multiple rallies prior to Memphis, the footage had shown a split second where a tiny red dot hovered over Joy's chest. He wasn't sure why the assassin had chosen Memphis over any of the other cities, but it was clear Zack had never been the target.

Mad nodded. "Yes."

"And you thought I had been the one to order the hit? So I could be president?"

Mad's face fell. "Maybe. I didn't know, damn it. I should have had more faith. By the day of the plane crash, I'd found a few things I thought we should discuss. I was getting on that bird to come face you. And then we found the bomb. That told me the Russians would do *anything* to keep their conspiracy buried. I also knew my time was up.

So we agreed to the plan and faked my death. We had to involve you guys clandestinely so you understood the threat was at your doorstep and it was real. And honestly, we had to operate so far in the shadows that you could do things we couldn't."

"You used us and our wives to investigate what you needed exposed." There was no small amount of accusation in Gabe's tone.

"I did what I had to do," Mad replied, his jaw tight. "Everly was already curious. I thought if I directed her, I could also keep her out of trouble."

"You didn't do a good job of that," Roman remarked. "She nearly died, and so did Gabe. Dax got shot."

"We couldn't have foreseen either of those events," Freddy explained. "And that night we had our own problems. Though the world thought Mad was dead, the syndicate realized something was fishy from the beginning. They had their own investigators, and that night one of them almost caught up with us. We barely got out of that firefight alive. It's why I insisted Mad not be anywhere near DC during the rest of the operation."

"Lara was on our radar because she was looking into the situation with Natalia Kuilikov at the time. Was Lara involved on your end because of Freddy?" Zack needed to speed up this explanation.

"Yes." Lara leaned against her husband's side. "I was working on a story for Capitol Scandals when Freddy helped me out. His information brought me into his investigation."

"Neither Freddy nor I thought we would be able to get close to Natalia." Mad settled into one of the big chairs. "But they didn't see Lara coming."

"Is Natalia Kuilikov my birth mother?" Zack needed to know.

Elizabeth gasped. "What? What are you talking about?

I know someone is trying to blackmail you, but you can't possibly think you're not Zack Hayes. That's ridiculous."

It wasn't, but that thought didn't occupy Zack's mind most. Elizabeth did. Besides being beautiful and intelligent, she was good with the press corps and quick on her feet. But he doubted she was capable of feigning such shock. That would require serious acting skills.

"The information we discovered Tavia Gordon was hiding led us directly to Natalia Kuilikov, who happened to be my nanny for the first seven years of my life. I didn't know until all of this began that she also had a child around the time I was born."

Elizabeth shook her head. "No. You look exactly like your father when he was young. I've seen the pictures."

"I didn't say I wasn't my father's son," he pointed out. "He had plenty of affairs."

"Fine." Elizabeth got to her feet. "We'll do a DNA test and put this to rest. Do we know what happened to the baby?"

"Russian records are difficult to locate. There was no Internet back then." Freddy picked up. "What we've been able to find suggests the official cause of death was SIDS, but who knows if that's true? Officials could have been bribed to say anything. But we interviewed several people who worked at the embassy. They said Natalia simply stopped talking about her baby one day."

Roman looked grim. "And we know Zack's mother talked about killing her child. That was what she told her doctor at that mental institution. She said she'd gotten drunk one night and heard a baby crying. When she woke up she had a dead child in her arms."

Elizabeth's eyes shone with tears as she shook her head. "No. I won't accept that your parents replaced the real Zack Hayes with you. Surely, a bombshell like this would have come out long before now. Even if it hadn't, you're still an

American citizen, eligible to be president."

God, if she was faking, she was brilliant. Maybe he should have faith in Elizabeth, believe that she was exactly who she claimed she was, and that these fucking blackmailers had subversively spoon-fed him false clues and suspicions with every intention to cut him off from his loved ones. So they could corner him alone.

"I don't think some people would see it that way. There would be a constitutional crisis if it turned out that I wasn't born how and when I said I was. I think the night my mother talks about in those tapes Roman and Gus recovered is the night she accidently killed her own son."

"We know there were several visits from top Russian officials during the time period the death likely occurred." Freddy leaned forward. "That's not so surprising. It is the American embassy in Moscow. But there were three known meetings between your father and a man who later became one of the heads of the KGB. This man was also a known associate of Ivan Krylov. We believe the syndicate used the women's foundation to place Natalia at the embassy. Nature took care of the rest since the ambassador's propensity for affairs was well known."

"We believe she was initially sent to spy on Frank." Mad now spoke in a shrewd tone Zack had never associated with his friend. "After the syndicate made contact with the KGB, they formed an alliance. We're not sure whether the Russian mob agreed to this arrangement out of patriotism or a desire to get the police off their backs. Either way, they traded information, and Natalia was the key. She became pregnant, and when the child was lost, they saw an opportunity because Frank was in a no-win situation. Whether the dead child was the real Zack Hayes or Natalia's baby, they now had the American ambassador in a corner."

"My father's only goal in the world has always been for me to be president of the United States." Zack had heard his whole life that it was his duty to lift up the family name by reaching the highest office in the land. Now he wondered how much of that had really been his father's ambition...and how much had been a deal he'd made with the devil—or in this case, powerful Russians. "My father would have done almost anything to keep that stain off the family name."

"But why would the Russians wait so long?" Everly asked. "Why pull the strings now?"

"They're excellent at playing a long game," Freddy said. "When all this happened, Zack was merely an infant, and they had the ambassador under their thumb. Oh, I'm sure they promised to keep the other baby's death hush hush and Constance out of jail. They would appear to be helpful like that because they could afford to be patient and wait to spring their trap at the right moment. After all, your father had no way to ever erase the stain of that child's passing. By the time you were grown, Zack, and they started manipulating your father, he surely had to decide whether he should tell you all this information. I'm betting he stayed quiet in case you had an attack of conscience and decided not to run for any office."

"We've been piecing together a similar theory. If I'd had proof, I would have gone to the Agency without hesitation," Zack assured. There was no question about it. "But the Russians waited until they had me in a corner, too. Until they could apply pressure I couldn't deny."

If they had merely threatened his presidency, he would have resigned in a heartbeat. But instead, they'd learned who he valued and how much he loved them. Now Connor's and Lara's lives were at risk. Gabe's future could be compromised.

"Wait, I'm struggling to understand," Elizabeth said. "I've heard your mother said outlandish things when she drank, but no one ever mentioned that she carried on about a baby."

"Most people didn't know. She never said a word about it when she was sober. My father did his utmost to manage her. But whenever she fell into a bottle, he had to keep her out of sight because her lips always got loose. I assure you she talked about the baby's death on more than one occasion. We now know Admiral Spencer was disgraced and murdered because he was looking into things my mother divulged to him when she was inebriated at my wedding. We also believe her car accident wasn't so accidental."

"It wasn't. We're almost positive Joy is the one who procured her a rental and checked her out of the mental facility that night," Mad explained.

That had Roman's head snapping around. "We've been speculating the same thing, but there's no proof. The doctor who treated Constance at the facility is dead. Almost no one else who worked there then is employed at the hospital now. We managed to track down tapes of her therapy sessions with her doctor and listen to them, but of course there's no tape explaining who took her from the hospital since she was dead."

"Well, I can find almost anything online," Freddy assured. "Even records people think have been deleted."

Gus gaped. "You hacked the firm that handles the facility's medical records—the ones they swore they couldn't find—and located Constance's?"

"What can I say? I'm talented." Freddy smiled. "The only thing that threw me off was the night Mrs. Hayes died, the nurse made a note that a family member checked her out. The nurse described this woman as a pretty young blonde. Joy was a brunette. But who else could it have been?"

"It wasn't Joy," Zack insisted. "She was in Paris on a shopping trip when we got the call about my mother."

"Was she?" Freddy challenged. "Really?"

Zack scowled. "What kind of question is that?"

With a toss of his hands, Freddy shrugged. "If Joy was supposedly in Paris, at least she was on the right continent…"

To help commit murder? No. Joy had loved Constance. Then again, so many things about this case weren't what they appeared to be.

Zack shook his head, unable to believe that sweet Joy had been capable of wanting anyone dead. "My wife wouldn't have arranged my mother's death."

But he couldn't shake the former intelligence officer's suspicions. Who else could it have been?

"Since your mother is gone and the records Freddy found don't specify, we may never know who took your mother from the facility that night," Mad admitted.

True, and Zack accepted that for now. After all, the truth wouldn't bring Constance back. "So circling back to the question of who my birth mother is, without DNA from a relative of either my mother or Natalia, we're screwed."

Lately, Zack had thought of little else except finding a way out of this web. Well, that and Elizabeth. He'd worried endlessly that she was the most dangerous part of the Russians' trap—the alluring bait he was no longer sure he could continue to resist. If she was merely a bystander caught up in this tangle, then he'd done her a disservice with his suspicions and he needed to protect her. If she wasn't…the knowledge might wreck him.

"There must be some relative somewhere," Elizabeth insisted.

"No. Natalia's body disappeared and Constance was swiftly cremated. Mother was the last of her line. No aunts, uncles, or cousins. I have no one to compare my DNA to. I assume the Russians don't have the same problem."

"They haven't played out that hand yet," Mad said

grimly. "Given what I know now, I worry the higher-ups have decided to force the issue one way or another."

"Force the issue?" Everly asked.

Mad's whole body tensed. "Our Dark Web contacts believe they have an assassin targeting the president."

Elizabeth paled. Her hands shook. In that instant, Zack knew that if he didn't act fast, they would have another fainting woman on their hands.

When Gus leapt to her feet and lunged toward her friend, Zack interceded. Elizabeth was his responsibility. He'd brought her here for a reason, and leaving her care to Gus wouldn't help him figure out his press secretary's role in this mess.

"Come on." He wrapped a steadying hand around Elizabeth's arm. "Let's get you a drink. I've got the good vodka in the freezer."

She didn't protest when he led her away, just followed silently until they reached the big kitchen. After he pulled out the vodka and a pair of glasses, he poured two shots.

Elizabeth took it and knocked the alcohol back, setting it down for another. "This must be an anxiety-laden dream, Zack. Tell me it is."

"I wish it were." He poured her another one. "It's very real, and now you're involved. Before you got here, Roman and I decided to use Lara's blog to float the story about his e-mail fling with Joy. You'll have to handle that fallout."

She nodded. "You want to expose as much of the blackmail threat as possible so it can't be used against you. I can get ahead of this story. Let me think about how to frame it. I'll talk to Gus. I think if neither of you seems upset by the news, it should die down quickly. Let's not put Roman on TV. We don't gain anything by doing that. But, Zack, you do understand that once you make this move, they'll know you're fighting back? They might come at you harder."

He and the others were as ready for that as they could be. He simply had to hope they could keep everyone safe as this played out. God knew, he was beyond ready for this threat to be over—one way or another. "Then I'll watch my back."

Chapter Five

Two hours later, Mad stood, watching his friends as they talked and drank. It was almost like old times…but not quite. They'd sat together at dinner. By some unspoken understanding, everyone shelved talk of the looming conspiracy they found themselves in, but the cheer around the room as they'd dug into their food felt frenetic. Afterward, the conversation had turned to Roman and Gus's upcoming wedding, as well as the happenings in everyone's jobs.

He felt so out of touch with all of them.

Beside Freddy, he'd watched these people he loved so much and had sacrificed everything for, wondering if he would ever again feel like he belonged or be the man he'd been before that terrible night changed everything.

Now, everyone was clustered inside, listening to nineties tunes and reminiscing, pretending like this weekend was some sort of party. The old him would not only have applauded, but instigated. Now he was perturbed no one was discussing the fact they weren't sitting around a bonfire because an assassin might take a shot at Zack.

So he stood at the back of the room, contemplating whether he'd be bunking with Freddy tonight or be relegated to the couch. Of course the joke would be on them. That couch would be the best thing he'd slept on in months. His spine would thank him.

Still, he was depressed by the thought.

He'd imagined his reunion with Sara so many times. In his every version, he'd spent the night with her, inside her. Of course she shouldn't be here now. When he'd realized the Secret Service had mistakenly brought her to Camp David, he'd been horrified. But now that she knew he wasn't dead, it probably made sense to fill her in. Mad didn't like it...but he suspected the endgame was near, and he couldn't stand the thought of not being there for his baby's birth.

Still, he'd been a fool to think he and Sara could pick up where they'd left off. He had been gone too long and done too much damage to their relationship for that. She hated him now. Loathed him. Would probably never forgive him. The night Krylov had dropped into his life, he'd died for all intents and purposes. He'd been nothing but a revenant since.

"What are you doing standing back here?" Gabe had a beer in his hand as he approached. "I'm not used to a Mad Crawford who isn't the life of the party."

"Well, I don't party much anymore." Neither did Sara apparently. She'd disappeared after dinner, and he'd been told she'd gone to bed. She was tucked away in one of the cabins, sleeping. Or fuming and trying to figure how to extricate him from her life permanently.

Gabe was quiet for a moment as he scanned the room. "I've been thinking all night."

"Good for you." He was getting bitter, and he hated the feeling. Mad knew he was lucky to be alive, but what was the point when he couldn't go home and everyone he loved wasn't exactly happy to see him?

"In your shoes, I don't know that I would have done anything different," Gabe admitted. "The whole time you were talking, I thought about what I'd been willing to do to keep Everly safe that night in the Crawford building, when Connor saved us. I would have gone to any lengths, even hurting her if that kept her alive. Now, I would probably make a different choice because I trust her and I've seen how strong she is. But then, I was so panicked. I would have done whatever it took to ensure that she survived."

"During my evening with Krylov, I was pretty sure I wasn't going to survive, and honestly, all I could think of was that my death would be worth it if Sara remained safe."

"You love my sister."

"Gabe, I never told you this because I didn't know how you'd react, but I've loved your sister since she was sixteen. I get it; I tore through women, but she was the only one who mattered. I fell for her that summer before we went to Yale. I didn't touch her. I never even kissed her until a couple of months after she came to work at Crawford, but I'd loved her for years by then."

"And you never told...Gus. You told Gus."

He nodded. "We shared the common bond of pining for people we could never have. I'm glad Roman came around."

Sara probably never would. While he'd been laying out the last couple of months of his life, she'd barely looked at him. She'd merely sat next to Liz, not far from Everly and Gabe, and stared without a word. He'd seen her brush away a few tears, and it had taken all of his willpower not to take her in his arms.

"Is Sara okay? Did you make sure she locked her door?"

Not that he couldn't get in. He'd learned a lot of questionable though useful skills lately, things he'd never thought he would master. Lock picking. Hacking. Hand-to-hand combat.

"Yeah. Look, Sara is confused and scared." Gabe tipped back his beer before continuing. "She's angry at everyone, even me, but she's too polite to show it."

"Why would she be mad at you?"

Gabe had been there for Sara. In fact, Mad had counted on his best friend to protect her and Everly. Thankfully, after Gabe had realized that Mad's interest in Everly wasn't romantic, he'd taken excellent care of her.

Unfortunately, his sister, like Sara, probably hated him.

"Because as we've learned more about this conspiracy over the last few months, I've kept her in the dark for the same reasons you did. And honestly, I wish she wasn't involved now since she's pregnant. I can't imagine how she would feel if something happened to the baby."

"I've done nothing but worry about her and the baby every second of every day since Krylov dropped into my life." He fell quiet for a moment, watching his half sister laugh at something Holland said. "Thank you for taking care of Everly."

"I love her more than I ever thought I could love someone," Gabe admitted. "We had a rough start, but I was protecting Sara and I didn't know what your connection was to Everly. My mind went to the obvious answer."

Mad made barfing sounds. "Eww. Dude, she's my sister."

"That information would have made my life so much easier. You could have left a note, man."

"Sure, I totally should have left a paper trail for the syndicate to discover."

"Point taken," Gabe conceded. "You need to talk to Everly. You left her behind, too."

"I doubt she wants to talk to me. The women are pissed. Even Gus. She punched me after dinner. She hits hard, too. That's where we went wrong. We let girls into our club."

Gabe chuckled. "Everly wants to talk to you. That could change if you let the silence between you go on too long. She's your sister, and you've barely said three words to her."

"I asked her how everything was going."

"Yeah, that went over gangbusters, brother. I know you're scared, but she's more likely to understand and forgive you if you at least try."

He was scared, mostly that she hadn't been happy to find out they were related. And that, like Sara, she would want nothing to do with him. But Gabe had a point. "It isn't that I don't want to talk to Everly. I've missed her. I got close to her in those last few months."

"I have a million questions about that, but you owe her the answers first. She can fill me in later." Gabe put a hand on his shoulder. "You know this means we really are brothers now."

"In-laws. Is it weird?"

Gabe chuckled. "Maybe a little, but we'll get used to it. She's alone now. Go talk to her."

Mad watched Everly wander away from the group to stare out the big bay window that overlooked the gorgeous Maryland forest. Moonlight streamed in, and he saw her pretty face reflected in the glass as he approached. He'd known she was his sister for months. This would be their first conversation since she'd learned that truth, as well.

His palms started to sweat. He wasn't fucking good at this. How did he explain his choices so that she would understand? That hadn't worked so well with Sara...

"I was wondering if you were going to talk to me." She kept her gaze steady on the night outside.

He knew her, though. Despite her stoic expression, she was emotional. Everly had one of the biggest hearts he'd ever encountered. "I was afraid to. I didn't know if you'd walk away, and I don't think I can handle both of the important women in my life rejecting me tonight."

"Mad, Sara was shocked. I mean, we all were. But I think if you keep trying, she'll come around. She was angry with you for a long time. I guess I've been angry, too. But she also loved you. If you still have feelings for her, don't give up." She turned to face him. "Why didn't you tell me?"

One of the things he loved about his sister was her forthrightness. Everly never prevaricated. She made it easy for him to get to the heart of the matter. "When I realized I very likely had a half sibling, I thought about simply showing up on your doorstep. Or sending you an e-mail."

She sighed. "As a security expert, I would have told you to do neither of those things until you had some idea of who I was, but, Mad, you took your secrets too far. I understand the PI. I would even have understood you talking to some of my friends to figure out whether I was a nutjob who would wreak havoc on your life. But you hired me. You befriended me. You hung out at my place and we talked a lot. At some point you could have said, 'hey, did you know we're related?'"

Mad felt as if he was beating the same drum repeatedly. "I was trying to protect you."

Her gaze narrowed. "I was your head of security, Mad. I was literally supposed to protect you."

He held his hands up. "When you put it like that, it doesn't sound logical. But I don't care how bad ass you are. This is a Russian syndicate, and if they'd had any hint of our relationship, they would have used you to get to me, the same way they would have used Sara. The night the syndicate nearly killed me, I had an engagement ring in my dresser drawer. I planned to ask Sara to marry me the next day. Once she said yes, I'd planned to talk to her about you, get her advice on how to tell you that we're half siblings. By that time I'd figured out the kind of person you were. I also realized the news might upset you, and I wanted to break it gently. So I intended to tell Sara everything. It seemed like a perfect plan, give her a massive diamond so the world would know she's mine, then enlist her help finding the right words so I could finally tell you about our connection. It seemed like a win-win."

"When I found out, I was shocked. Even if Sara had helped you find the most tactful way to tell me, I still would have been shocked."

"After I realized that you loved your father, I worried that you wouldn't want to know the truth. I don't know if you've noticed, but I'm not exactly good at big, emotional talks. It seemed wise to get to know you. Once I did, I realized the news would be a bombshell and that I'd be telling you that your whole childhood was a lie. I was going to ask Sara if she thought I even had a right to tell you."

"Mad, my childhood wasn't a lie. Regardless of biology, he was my dad. Finding out that he didn't contribute half my DNA didn't change how well he loved me. In some ways, the information made me love him even more."

He admired her calm perspective. Maybe he should have given her more credit all along.

"I don't know what it feels like to be that attached to a father," he admitted. "My parents weren't exactly loving. They never divorced because they both realized neither was capable of truly caring about anyone but themselves, and a permanent split would have been too costly. So after we met and it was clear that you and your dad were really close, I worried I'd be taking a good man from you and replacing him with the asshole who raised me."

"What you should have been thinking about was the fact you'd be giving me a brother."

Damn it, he didn't do this, get emotional. His eyes never watered—unless he fucked up and got cocaine in them. Except he didn't do that anymore. And he loved his sister.

"I was alone in the world. Yes, I had my friends, but I was an orphan with stupid one-percenter problems. I would walk through that big house and everyone I saw was someone I paid. When I found you, I thought at least I'd have one genuine family tie. Then, when someone would ask about my family, I would be able to talk about you. Most people don't consider that. They take family for granted because everyone has one, right? Not me. When I'd get asked about my family in social situations, I never had an answer. But once I knew about you, I thought I'd be able to say that my sister is doing well. I liked that."

She turned to him. Tears swam in her eyes, too, as she cupped his face. "Mad, your sister is doing well. So well. I missed you. Don't ever keep me in the dark or run out on me again."

Since the syndicate was still out there and still suspicious, he couldn't make any promises. But as he hugged her tightly, peace settled in his soul. He had a sister and she didn't hate him. Finally, he had a family.

And now, he had some hope.

* * * *

Zack sat back in the desk chair and stared at the bottle of Scotch he knew he shouldn't touch again. He wasn't close to drunk, but he could get there fast now that the happy couples had all found their cabins. He was alone with Elizabeth. Well, Mad and Freddy were occupying the other bedrooms in the main cabin. But he'd come to the library, knowing there would be no sleep for him tonight with Elizabeth just down the hall.

She might, even now, be taking off her clothes. If he knocked on her door, would she answer? Would he perhaps catch her right before a shower? Or would she already be tucked into bed? Had she taken one look at the shirt he'd left for her to sleep in and tossed it out? Or was she wearing it, feeling the fabric caress her skin the way he wanted to with his hands? He ached to brush his palms along her curves and let her soft heat sink in through his fingertips. He wouldn't leave an inch of her untouched. He would explore her body like it was a new country he could conquer.

And now he had an erection.

That woman was driving him insane.

He reached for the Scotch. Who cared if he got drunk or not? His whole life had been about self-control, and where had that gotten him? Sure, he was president, arguably the most powerful man in the world. But what good was that? He didn't even know his real name. And he couldn't touch the one woman he craved.

"Are you all right?" a soft voice with the sweetest Southern accent asked. "Tonight was awfully intense."

Zack looked up. Elizabeth stood in the doorway as though he'd conjured her from his thoughts. "I'm great. It's not every day we raise the dead, after all."

She was still in her business suit, but she'd let her classic French twist down and ditched the jacket. Her soft blonde hair tumbled around her shoulders and made him itch to sink his hands into it. He could control her with that hair, show her exactly how he wanted her to move, where to put that luscious mouth of hers.

"How are you handling that? I can't imagine how shocked you were to discover that one of your best friends is still alive," she said. "And I was happy to see that he and Everly have mended fences, but you must be angry with him. Zack, you can't honestly think you're a Russian plant. Mad should have come straight to you and told you his suspicions."

Elizabeth had always been loyal. Of course, if she wanted to earn his trust and get close to him, she'd said exactly what she should.

He couldn't deal with her tonight. Between all the bombshells, coupled with his fears, he felt too close to the edge of his restraint. Elizabeth being here—so close and yet so far away—was like dangling a match over the kindling of his self-control. But damn, she looked slightly disheveled. So sexy. All woman. Soft and vulnerable.

He was so hard and hungry.

And she was the perfect bait for a trap.

Normally when a day crashed in on him like this, when the pressure got to be too much, he'd go for a run. He'd jog for miles, until his body couldn't endure anymore. Then, exhausted, he would finally sleep. But he couldn't engage in the hard, punishing exercise he needed to chase away the shadows and burn off stress now. It was after midnight. He couldn't force his detail to run in the middle of the night. And he couldn't make himself an easy target for the Russians' assassin.

That bottle was looking better and better.

"I think it's safe to say we'll all need therapy after this weekend. It's late. You should get some sleep. We'll have a lot to talk about in the morning." His tone was curt. He hoped she'd take the hint and leave. He needed her out of the path of his frustration. If she went to bed now, closed and locked her door, she would be safe.

She didn't take his advice, merely stood her ground. "I think you and I should talk now. We won't have any privacy tomorrow."

"About what?"

"I understand why you've been acting the way you have." Her mouth tightened, telling him that she didn't like it.

"And what way is that, Elizabeth?"

Everyone else called her Liz. He liked Elizabeth. He enjoyed the way her name rolled off his tongue. He loved to watch her, especially like now when she tried to be assertive...but still hesitated as if she sensed danger. Smart prey. She sensed there was a predator in her midst.

He needed to end this conversation or he would gobble her right up.

She took another brave but foolish step toward him. "Have you been trying to protect me?"

Zack sucked in a breath and remained glued to his seat because nothing good would happen if he got closer to her. He didn't trust himself right now. There was still a desk between them, but he could too easily change that. "I didn't think you needed protecting. Obviously Sara felt the same way since she didn't end up forgiving Mad."

Liz cocked her head in consideration. "I think their issue is more complex than that."

"Is it? He loves her. He was scared for her. He tried to protect her. It seems simple to me."

"But it's not that simple between us, is it?"

Zack grimaced. She just wouldn't leave it alone. "Nothing is simple when it comes to you."

Her shoulders squared—a sure sign she was about to get stubborn. "Or you, Mr. President. Joy was killed simply because she was your wife. I had no idea. But you clearly have for a while. It makes sense that you tried to protect me. If you haven't been, then I'd like to know why you suddenly rejected me."

Like he'd had a choice...

Bitterness welled inside him, and something nasty took root in his gut. Or maybe it had always been there, simmering beneath his seemingly benign surface. "I didn't reject you, Elizabeth. I thought once that we might date, but the minute Joy died, any romantic possibilities for us were over."

She shook her head, blue eyes flaring with obvious frustration. "Why? Don't get me wrong. I understand we had to take a step back. The optics would have been terrible."

"The worst." Zack sent her a dismissive shrug.

"But it's been years, and I've always been in your corner. *Always.* Yet lately, you've treated me like something between a stranger and an enemy. And I'm tired of it. Maybe it's the threat hanging over your head. Maybe I'm tired of being alone. Either way, I won't go on ignoring the elephant in the room. So here's the truth: I still care about you. I think you still have some interest in me, but you won't admit it or act on it. And you won't give me a decent explanation why. After hearing that Mad split them apart to save Sara from the danger, I suspect that's exactly what you did to me."

Well, he'd never said she was dumb. "Ah, but there's a difference. Sara and Mad were lovers. We never were."

They had never lain in bed for hours, worshipping each other's bodies, never found comfort in one another's arms. Always they had been forced to maintain a polite, professional distance. It rankled, this leash he kept himself on. Deep inside, he started to growl and fight that fucking chain he'd been on all his life.

"Still…" Her voice softened. "I thought we were friends."

He couldn't remain in his chair a second longer.

Zack stood, bracing his hands on the desk in front of him so he didn't put them on her. "Friends? That's what you thought?"

She laughed, a sound without any amusement. "Oh, that's right. You think of me like your sister now. Sometime between that lunch when you asked me to go to Paris with you so we could fuck our brains out and last month, you changed your mind. I guess I should be glad we never got naked. Touching me would have been like incest, and I would have been deeply disappointed when you couldn't get it up."

The words sent a thrum of anger through him. They fueled his arousal because he ached to show her exactly how up he could get for her. Her barb tipped him right over the edge of his control.

She wanted to challenge him? There were a million reasons for him to walk out the door, and only one for him to stay. Because he wanted her. Damn it, he'd been a good boy all his fucking life, and despite that, it looked like his presidency and his reputation would probably end in disgrace. He'd become a footnote in history, either going down as a puppet or a traitor.

So why couldn't he have one damn thing he wanted just this once?

Fuck everything. He was going to have Elizabeth.

"A sister?" The question came out almost polite, but it was all veneer. The civilized Zack Hayes had left the building.

He'd given her every out. He'd even told her to leave. She hadn't. Now, she would feel the wrath of nearly five years of pent-up lust.

As he moved around the desk and prowled into her space, she didn't shrink away. No, not his Elizabeth. She stood her ground. Despite wearing those sexy-as-hell stilettos he'd dreamed of wrapping around his waist as he fucked her hard, she had to tilt her head back to meet his gaze.

"Yes." She raised a challenging brow at him. "Your words. Not mine."

She was being awfully damn brave for a woman who was about to become his feast. Couldn't she feel the energy rolling off him? Didn't she wonder whether that spark was the need for violence or sex?

His cock knew exactly what it throbbed for. "You want the truth? All right. The feelings I have for you are far from familial. I have tried to protect you. Happy?"

The moment she had her answer, she seemed to reconsider. "Zack, I-I shouldn't have pushed. I—"

"You're right." He backed her against the desk and caged her by gripping the edge on either side of her. "And you should have taken the out when I gave it to you. But you didn't, so I'm going to show you how far from brotherly my feelings are for you. You're going to let me, aren't you, Elizabeth? You're going to walk the eight feet to that door and lock it, then you're going to come back here and let me get my mouth on you. You're going to open yourself to me and I'm going to take all you have to give tonight."

"And if I don't?" The words came out breathy.

"If you choose to run away like a scared little rabbit, you'll never know how it feels to have me cover you with my body, to have me worship you like the goddess you are."

She swallowed, nodded, then stood taller, shoulders squared.

Zack forced himself to step aside. He had to see what she would do. This had to be her choice. "Elizabeth, if you walk out now, I'll go back to being polite."

It might kill him, but he would do it. He would drink the rest of that Scotch tonight and put all his armor on in the morning.

He would do his damnedest to forget her.

"And if I stay and lock the door?"

"You'll be mine until morning. I'll take you every way I want to, and you won't rest until I've had my fill. It will be my way all the way, so think about that before you decide. I won't go easy on you. I'm too hungry. So this won't be tender lovemaking. I'll fuck you until I can't remember anything except how good it feels when I'm inside you."

She gave him one last unreadable glance before she walked across the room, her heels clicking on the hardwood.

His fists clenched at his sides as he watched and waited. It took every ounce of his restraint to allow her this choice. If it were up to him, he'd bar the door so she would have no escape. Then he would hunt her, capture her, take her. Instead, he stood there, holding his breath, his gut twisting, his entire body pulsing and alive with anxiety and anticipation.

Finally, Elizabeth reached the door. She closed it, sliding the lock into place, then turned to him, chin raised.

She'd made her decision. She was his for the night.

He sent her a feral smile and sauntered closer, pure need coursing through his veins as he tore off that strangling mental leash that had held him back for so long and reached for her.

Chapter Six

Liz's hands shook as she turned the lock, shutting herself alone in the library with Zack. This was likely the single stupidest thing she'd ever done, but after years of pining for and being in love with him, she couldn't walk away without knowing how a night with him would feel.

She should be in her bed right now, trying to find sleep. But she'd seen the light on and known he'd be here. Like a freaking moth to a flame, she'd found herself leaving the safety of her bedroom and walking right into the predator's den.

After this evening, she understood him better. He'd pulled the same dumb play Mad had, shoving her away so she wouldn't get caught up in his danger. So she wouldn't become another Joy. Gus had been hinting at this for weeks, but her friend hadn't been able to betray her fiancé's secrets by being specific...and Liz had been too hurt to believe.

Trembling, she turned now and looked at the only man she'd ever truly loved. He needed her tonight. She saw it in his stare, in the way he clenched his fists at his sides. How much character and willpower had it taken him to allow her this choice? She admired him even more for finding the strength, especially since she'd long suspected that under his façade of intellectualism and perfect manners, he hid a beast.

Tonight, she would find out if she'd been right.

Liz had no illusions. He was capable of breaking her heart into a million pieces, and she'd try not to let him. But even if she only got one night with this man, she would take it because she would rather live with foolish regret than stubborn ignorance.

"Elizabeth."

His voice hummed in the quiet room, caressing between her ears, vibrating through her body. She flushed with arousal.

This was it. This was happening.

She'd wanted him the moment they'd met, but he'd been forbidden. Now, he stood in front of her with his broad shoulders and his dark hair. Not a president, but a man. *Her* man—at least for the night.

Liz tried to steady her breathing as she crossed the room to him. Finally, she had permission to touch him the way she'd always wanted. Of course she'd heard him say tonight would be his way all the way, that it wouldn't be tender, but she wanted one sweet moment she could cling to later before her man turned beast.

She stopped in front of him and reached up, brushing her fingers against the silver threaded at his temples—the only sign that he was aging. Naturally, it made him even more attractive.

He caught her hand, clasping it in his big one. "Be sure."

That was Zack, always putting others first, even when his whole world was falling apart. Even when he needed so desperately for himself.

Tonight, she was here for him in every way. Liz hoped with all her heart he understood that.

She would cling to him through the bittersweet hours until dawn, memorizing every touch. Tomorrow they would go back to their corners, and the turmoil would start again. It would be worse because she would know exactly how good it felt to be in his arms. But their passion could only be temporary because he was right, any chance they'd had at a future had died the day Joy had. After her murder and three long years, how could they ever hope for more?

"I'm sure," she murmured. "I want everything you have to give me tonight."

He released her hand to grip her waist. Immediately, he dragged her against his body. His free hand found her hair and sank in, tugging her head back. "I've waited forever for this."

His thick whisper sent a tremor through her. "Me, too."

Silently, Liz mourned the loss of their idyllic vow in Memphis that when they finally kissed for the first time, it would only be when they'd never have to stop. But she couldn't worry about the future when she and Zack only had right now.

He angled her face under his and her heart began to careen. He bent, crushed her lips under his, and groaned into their kiss. She could feel the moment he let go of his iron will.

"It's not going to last nearly as long as I want it to," he muttered against her mouth. "At least not this first time…"

Liz expected it to be fast and furious because neither of them could deny their desire a second longer. He needed her; she could feel it. Another reason she couldn't walk away. If he had merely sought sex, she might have found the will, but even if this wasn't a tender joining, it was about connection. They were both starving for it.

Again, he swept his lips over hers and devoured her.

There was no other way to describe the way he clutched her against every muscle and bulge of his lean body and took her mouth captive. She wrapped her arms around him and lost herself in passion.

He didn't waste time. With his tongue, he urged her mouth open, then he tugged on her hair again in sharp demand. She opened her mouth and welcomed him inside. Her body felt taut, like an arrow about to be loosed. While his tongue dominated hers, she explored the hard planes of his body with eager hands, wishing so badly that nothing came between them. The clothes she'd worn all day were now far too tight. She wouldn't be able to breathe if she couldn't feel his naked skin against hers soon.

Zack was already working on the problem. He didn't miss a beat, just wrapped his hands around the neckline of her blouse and yanked. In a single movement, the buttons gave way. Cool air and his hot stare stroked her skin.

She didn't have a handy set of clothes to change into tomorrow, but her protest drifted away as Zack stripped the crisp white blouse from her torso and stared.

His burning gaze inspired a wave of goose bumps all over her body.

"Take off your bra."

His rough voice urged her to stand in front of him, unclasp the garment, and let it fall between them. She did. He watched, sucking in a sharp breath as she revealed her breasts to him. His eyes heated, darkened. He didn't have to say a word for Liz to feel adored.

"Come here." He reached for her.

She was already so close that she could feel his hot breath and electric impatience. "If I come any closer, I'll be pressed against you."

He merely smiled as he caressed up her arm, then wrapped his fingers around it to draw her in. "Now that I've seen how gorgeous you are, I want to feel you."

His words were melting her when he spun her away and dragged her bare back against his chest.

"Zack?"

"I'm not going to last. It's been fucking years since…"

Since he'd had sex. He and Joy hadn't been intimate for much of their marriage, and he would never have cheated on his wife. Only when he'd thought he would lose the election and Joy said she was amenable to divorce had he tried to find his own happiness. But in the last few months he had dated all those lovely women. "You didn't sleep with Mimi?"

He dragged her skirt up with one restless hand while the other cupped her breast. "You know why I dated her and the other women."

To keep her off the Russians' radar.

He kissed her neck, while he rolled her nipple between his thumb and forefinger. She couldn't help but soften against him and give herself over. That hand on her thigh was getting closer and closer to where she ached for it to reach.

She could barely breathe. As Zack's lips moved up her neck, she felt the hard line of his erection pressed against her ass. "I'm sure it was Roman's plan."

Most of the bad ideas came from Roman. He was utterly ruthless, and she prayed Gus tempered his worst impulses. It made him an excellent chief of staff, not so great as her lover's best friend.

She couldn't think like that. Zack wasn't her anything except her forbidden temptation. What they shared wouldn't last beyond tonight. It couldn't matter tomorrow.

He grunted as he shoved her panties to the side and out of his way. "I'm not the one who was playing around with the Secret Service."

She'd had a light flirtation—mostly because she'd been perturbed at Zack's sudden fascination with supermodels—

and the whole time she'd only been able to think about Zack. "Nothing happened. He wasn't you."

He nipped at her ear, his voice a low growl filled with satisfaction. "Nothing happened. She wasn't you. None of them were."

The words warmed and reassured her. Then she wasn't thinking at all because Zack's fingers found her pussy. She gasped, tilting her hips up for more of his touch. "Zack, please."

"Everything about this pleases me. You're going to please me all night long." He delved deeper until he slid a finger over her clitoris. "But first... I've fantasized about feeling you, hearing you. Touching you. Come for me, Elizabeth. Then it will be my turn, and I won't hold back."

She didn't want him to.

Zack was so complex. He was smart and kind, yet ruthless and focused. He could be cruel when he wanted to be. He could also be incredibly giving. And she wanted everything he had to offer.

Right now, she especially wanted the attention of that clever hand.

"You're already wet." Triumph deepened his tone.

"Yes."

His hold on her breast tightened, and he stroked her nipple. Pleasure rippled. Then his thumb began to strum her clitoris while one long finger found her opening and sank deep. "And you're soft and wet and ready to take my cock, aren't you?"

He held her against him. Even if she'd wanted to, she couldn't escape the bliss he was heaping on her body. "Yes."

"You're going to spread those gorgeous legs for me and let me fuck you as long and hard as I want, right?"

Every word from his mouth went straight to her pussy, combining with the rhythm of his fingers to drive her higher and higher. Even the realization that Zack was demanding her pleasure pushed Liz close to the edge, so she didn't need much to fall over. The minute she'd realized she would truly know Zack as a lover, her body had taken over, shutting down all the parts of her brain that knew this was a mistake. So long denied, her body refused to wait much longer before knowing ecstasy at this man's hands.

"Yes!" She shuddered as the sensations built, then crescendoed. Her heart pounded. She gasped, then bit her lip to hold in her cry. Then orgasm bloomed over her and she came to a shuddering climax in his strong arms.

As she drifted down from euphoria, Liz closed her eyes and let herself feel his breath against her neck, his fingers moving inside her, his hand clutching her breast. Feel his desperation so like her own. Feel...him. Connected to him in a way she'd always known they should be.

Her body was flush with pleasure as she sagged against him, but Zack wasn't through. In one strong move, he bent and lifted her into his arms, holding her to his chest. He didn't bother to straighten her skirt. He simply carried her across the room to the couch where she was certain world leaders dialogued about critical treaties. But there would be no negotiations tonight, just her surrender.

He eased her onto the couch and stood, staring down at her intently. Slowly, he brought his hand to his lips and sucked his finger inside, tasting the arousal he'd created.

"God, I knew you would taste like heaven." He dropped his hands to the belt of his slacks, working it open with ease. His hands shook slightly. "Spread your legs, Elizabeth. Take me."

For the first time in years, the world felt dreamy and perfect because Zack was here. He was really with her. He wanted her—and he intended to have her now.

She didn't care that they weren't in the comfort of a bedroom or that tomorrow they would go back to being boss and employee. All that mattered was fulfilling the unspoken promise they'd made so many years ago. This library was hardly a bedroom in Paris overlooking the Eiffel Tower, but tonight Liz was damn happy for the satisfaction they would find together.

She watched, unblinking, as he shoved his slacks off. His swift efficiency at undressing afforded her only a glimpse of his cock. It looked long, impossibly thick, and hard.

Liz had wondered when she'd read Lara's tongue-in-cheek article about the president's penis whether his long-ago lovers had exaggerated about its legendary stature. Nope. Liz wanted to take it in her hand and stroke it, but Zack wasn't waiting. He followed her down to the sofa and covered her body with his.

"Wait. I need to get undressed," she whispered, though she could already feel him aligning his erection against her and nudging at her opening.

"No time." His normally perfect hair was mussed and his whole body was taut as he yanked at the delicate material of her panties and it tore like tissue paper.

He'd left her with almost nothing to wear, but Liz no longer cared the second she felt him thrust up and join their bodies. His cock invaded, stretching her with a delicious burn. Moments before she'd been satisfied by the orgasm he'd given her with his skillful fingers. Now every cell in her body screamed for the dizzying pleasure he gave her again.

"Wrap your legs around me." He held her down with firm hands as though he was afraid she might fight him and he was determined not to let her go. His eyes closed briefly as he rocked against her and forced the rest of his cock deep.

The moment he was fully seated, he sighed, a deeply content sound as he held himself there, seeming to revel in their joining.

He pulled out before rocking back in. His eyes opened as he filled her with every inch. He stared down, his gaze intense and consuming. A silent warning this wouldn't be easy.

Then he began a deep, unforgiving rhythm. Liz held on tight as he began to fuck her with all the strength in his body and all the determination in his soul. Over and over, he slammed inside, then jerked nearly free before repeating the process. With each hard thrust, he ground against her clit, sparking undeniable arousal through her system.

The couch moved and the floors groaned. A Secret Service agent stood outside the door. He could probably hear them, so Liz didn't let herself cry out in pleasure...though she cared a lot less about Zack's guard hearing than she should.

"Don't you fucking dare hold back on me." His stare captured hers as he worked inside her, stroking and thrusting. "I know he's out there, too, but he'll keep his mouth shut. Pretend he doesn't exist. Right now, there's no one but you and me. I want to hear you come again."

He kept shoving deep inside her, holding nothing back. She held on for dear life because he was a force of nature, and like someone in the path of a hurricane or tornado, she was caught up in him.

He picked up the pace. Her blood raced. Her heart chugged. Her fingers dug into his flesh as she lifted to meet him. Then she went over the edge, nails scratching up his back as her body stiffened with the pure pleasure at the orgasm sizzling through her. Zack shouted hoarsely as he seemed to lose all control. He shoved his cock even deeper inside her as he spent himself, sparking her system again.

Moments later, Zack shuddered and fell on top of her, not moving to keep his weight off her or to pull away even an inch. He simply lay on top of her, his face buried in the curve of her neck.

Between them, he cupped her breasts, one after the other, seemingly fascinated with the shape and feel of them, as he kissed her neck and nuzzled her cheek.

She sank into the sweet moment between them, closing her eyes and absorbing everything—his heavy breathing, his hair damp at the temples, his heart beating against hers, finally in sync. For right now, in this moment, Zack was hers.

Liz wrapped her arms around him, held him close, and prayed the night never ended.

* * * *

Mad walked into the kitchen at seven the next morning, following the delicious smell of coffee that hadn't been made from instant crystals and didn't have to be imbibed out of a tin can that also doubled as a handy vessel for shitty canned soup.

He was so not going to miss the wilderness. If he ever went camping again, it would be at the Four Seasons. He would teach his kid that roughing it was building a pillow tent in a suite where they had twenty-four-hour room service.

He stepped toward the coffee pot, then paused because he wasn't alone. Sara sat at the breakfast bar, perched gracefully on a stool. She'd arranged her hair into a stylish, efficient ponytail. She had worn jeans and a simple T-shirt that molded to her rounding belly. She looked achingly beautiful to his eyes, and there was nothing more in the world he wanted to do than be close to her, stroke his hand over the place where their child was growing, and feel them both. Instead, he stood, watching her, afraid to move in case she scurried away again. He observed her picking at her bowl of yogurt and granola with a mug of what looked like herbal tea in her hand.

Mad looked for something to say that would bridge the void between them. Something smart. Something emotionally intelligent that would explain the depth of his feelings and commitment to her.

"Did you sleep okay?" Unfortunately, he wasn't all that emotionally intelligent.

She stared at him for a moment, as though she had to remind herself he was actually here. "Fine. I got up early because I'd planned to insist that someone take me shopping, but apparently the Secret Service grabbed my bag from Gabe's house. It's weird that someone else brought my undies. How about you?"

He practically fell over in his haste to get closer to her. "I slept some. Not great because my mind won't shut off, but my back isn't screaming at me, so I'll call it a win."

"I still can't picture you roughing it," she admitted, wrinkling her nose. "You're not exactly a nature lover."

"I like nature, just from a distance," he quipped, grateful that she was talking to him at all. He would happily make fun of himself in any way if it amused her. "Is anyone else awake?"

She shook her head. "I guess they're sleeping in. From what the Secret Service told me, they were up late, so you're the only person not in uniform I've seen this morning."

He sat down across from her. "Security is pretty tight."

"Obviously not tight enough if you managed to sneak into Zack's limo."

"Well, it helps when you're working with the head of the president's detail." He didn't want to talk about what had broken them apart. He wanted to talk about her and their child. He had a million questions. "How is the baby?"

"She's fine."

Mad felt as if his world stopped. His whole focus narrowed down to her and her words. Until now, the baby had been an idea in his head, something out of a dream. But

Sara said they were having a girl. A girl was different. A girl wasn't merely a baby. A girl was a daughter, a sweet feminine presence in his life he could love and protect and adore. A vision of a little sprite with tawny hair in pigtails whispered across his brain, the thought so sweet he could swear his heart clenched. "It's a girl? They can tell so early?"

"It's not that early," Sara replied as though she hadn't just rocked his world. "I had a sonogram weeks ago. She's growing at a good pace. There's nothing to worry about. She's going to be healthy and perfect."

"Of course she is. I'll make sure she is. When this is over, I would like very much to come to the doctor's appointments. I hate the fact that you've had to go alone."

"I hate the fact that I've done everything in this pregnancy alone," she said in a tone that made him realize he'd walked into a field full of land mines. "I hate the fact that my daughter is going to get caught up in all of this."

He had to be so careful now or he would lose her for good. "I will do everything I can to shield her. I promise. Everything I've done so far has been to protect you both."

She sighed, giving him that forthright stare that never failed to pull him in. "I sat up a long time last night thinking about this. I get that you thought leaving was the best way to handle the situation. You were scared and you had this paranoid guy talking in your ear."

"Freddy knew a lot about the syndicate and what they were capable of." He wasn't sure what he would have done if Freddy hadn't shown up that night. He might have called the police, then been in a world of hurt because the syndicate had long arms. "Freddy saved me that night."

Her head shook and a tendril fell from her neat ponytail to caress her cheek. The pregnancy had done nothing but enhance her beauty. Her skin glowed with health. "He fed into your every worst instinct. You had options, Mad."

How could he make her understand what it had been like for him? The world had crashed and burned that night, and it had been up to him to figure out how to make sense of it again. "I had to move quickly. I couldn't do anything that would risk exposing our relationship to the public and putting you on the Russians' hit list."

"I do understand that."

Thank god. Apparently she'd only needed to sleep on it. He reached for her hands. "I'm so glad you do. Baby, I've done nothing but think about you, worry about you. Miss the hell out of you."

She pulled away. "But you never considered just talking to me? Treating me like a partner, rather than a liability you needed to martyr yourself to protect?"

"What are you talking about?"

She huffed, a frustrated sound. "There was a simple solution. You could have called me and told me what happened. You could have called Gabe. We would have helped you."

"And have you threatened for it? Potentially be murdered for doing it?" Mad pointed out. "No."

"I'm not an idiot. I wouldn't have rushed out to the press and given away everything. I want to protect my child as much as you do. We'd been careful about our relationship up until that point," Sara pointed out. "If you had told me about Krylov's threats, I would have been perfectly reasonable. I might have been scared, but I wouldn't have been destroyed. But you chose to take what could have been a simple decision and turn it into a grand drama. You didn't treat me like your partner, your equal. You texted me that you no longer cared. You're damn lucky I have pride or I might have shown up on your doorstep that night."

How could she possibly think that way? "This wasn't some college prank. I'm in the middle of a global conspiracy, and they're out to not only kill one of my closest friends but assassinate my president. They can do it, too. They've already murdered Dax's father, Zack's mother, and Joy."

"So the smart move was to alienate all your friends and tell the woman having your child that you're done with her?" Tears shone in her eyes. "I love you. I do, but I've realized that you don't love me the same way. We don't have the same view of relationships. If I'd been the one unfortunate enough to meet Krylov, I would have tried to protect you, too, but I wouldn't have savaged you to do it."

He'd thought about it, thought about what could happen if she'd decided to be loyal to him until the bitter end. "Tell me you wouldn't have tried to help me. I know how brave you are."

"Yeah, but I have more than you and myself to worry about. I have to protect my daughter. I would have been careful the same way I'm going to be careful now. I'm happy you're alive, but we're over. I'm going to ask you to think of our daughter and stay away from me. There will be an insane amount of press around you when the world learns that Maddox Crawford is still alive." Sara placed her hand on her belly as she eased off the stool. "We don't need that."

Mad stood in her path because they couldn't end on this terrible note. "Sara, you can't just walk away. You're here with me. You're involved now. Going back to New York isn't an option. That's another reason why I left so dramatically, as you put it. So you could just live and you wouldn't have to hide."

"I've been hiding, anyway. I've been avoiding life because I didn't understand how you could love me one day and find me utterly beneath your notice the next. Now it makes sense. Thank you. I can move on."

"Sara, baby—"

"No. Don't try to sweet-talk me, Mad. The truth is, you're not a grown-up. You're still living in this crazy world where it seems logical to do insane things on impulse. I can't live like that. I have to think of her. Of her stability." She caressed her belly as she placed her half-empty bowl in the sink.

"But I love you." He had changed, damn it. He wasn't the selfish bastard he'd been for most of his life. She'd changed him. Loving her had made him a better man. "I love you both."

"I know." She brushed a tear away. "That's the hardest part of all. You mean that…in your way. But I need more. I'm going to go back to my cabin. When everyone else is up, we need to talk about where I should stay long-term. I'm willing to go into protective custody if necessary. Like I said, I'm not too stupid to live. I'll see you later."

She turned and left the kitchen—left him—but not before Gus approached. She paused, watching as Sara put distance between them as fast as she could.

"I guess that didn't go well. Are you okay?" Gus had always been there for him, one of his truest friends. He needed her now. She would understand and make him feel better.

"No," he admitted. "But don't worry about me. Sara is the one who needs an ear. She thinks I left her all alone and…" Mad sighed, feeling like his world was caving in all around him. Then again, it was because he didn't have Sara. "Can you please talk to her? Maybe take her some tea and listen to whatever she needs to say? I'd do it, but…"

She didn't want him anymore.

"I know." Gus's eyes went soft. "Of course I'll do it. I'll even curse your name with her."

Gus grabbed the tea pot to make another cup of herbal tea for Sara. Morosely, Mad sat and watched, his need for coffee gone. He only needed one thing—and it looked like he really had lost her for good.

Chapter Seven

Morning light filtered in from the small gap in the curtains, but it was enough to remind Liz where she was.

Zack's room. She had spent the night in the president's room and she was naked. She didn't know what time it was, but everyone would be awake soon, if they weren't already. They would know that she and Zack had fucked like bunnies all night. Well, "bunny" didn't properly describe Zachary Hayes. He was more like a ravenous wolf who couldn't seem to get enough of her, but that wasn't the point. If she didn't find a way to sneak out, their secret wouldn't be a secret anymore.

She rolled over, but Zack was gone. His side of the bed was mussed, an indention where he'd lain his head on the pillow. His side? He didn't have one since the man took up most of the space, and he hadn't apologized for it. In fact, he didn't apologize for much of anything.

After he'd had her on the couch in the office, he'd stood and hauled her to her feet. He'd straightened his clothes and let her fix what was left of hers—she'd managed to grab her bra and clutch her blouse together—then walked out of the library, past the Secret Service agent standing in the hall, like she and Zack had merely had an everyday business meeting.

Nothing to see here, Agent Tall and Grim.

If she hurried out of bed and into some clothes, then acted as if nothing had happened, she and Zack might be able to keep their privacy. After all, the Secret Service were notoriously tight-lipped. Their friends, however, were not.

She needed to move, but every muscle was deliciously sore. Zack had been insatiable all night, as if he'd tried to make up for all the years they had lost. The minute he'd closed the door to this room, he'd been on her again, stripping off her clothes and tossing them aside. He hadn't even waited until they reached the bed. He had merely shoved her against the wall and impaled her on his cock.

On their third time he finally managed to make it to the bed, and even in between bouts, he hadn't given her any space. He'd molded his body to hers, his hands constantly stroking her skin.

It had been the best night of her life. Now, it was over. She had to face that fact and find the will to get up and pretend that she hadn't briefly been the president's lover. That she wasn't more in love with him than ever.

Apparently, Zack had made keeping their fling clandestine a little easier. He'd already gotten up and was probably out there with his friends, distracting them. She could sneak down the hall to her room and pray someone had retrieved her a bag from home. She would shower and join the group for breakfast, and likely spend the rest of her life trying to forget how good being with Zack had been.

She forced herself to sit up and glance around the room. She couldn't help but wince when she noticed her clothes were strewn everywhere. Well, except her panties. She feared they were still in the office where President Carter had probably brokered Middle East peace.

She had to sneak in there before someone cleaned the place up.

Liz was about to stand when the bathroom door opened, and Zack walked out with wet hair, wearing absolutely nothing but a smile. Her mouth watered at the sight. Mercy... Even if they had fifty years together, she would never get used to the sight of him in all his glory. If she'd thought he was gorgeous in a suit, she had no words to describe him in the nude. Sleek, powerful, predatory. Perfect.

"What are you doing? Get back in bed." He rounded the bed to her, looming close. The nearer he got, the more his cock engorged. "It's still early."

She'd seen the clock. "No, it's after nine. Everyone will be up by now."

"We're not up."

Zack wrapped his hand around her nape, and she could swear the temperature in the room went up thirty degrees. Then he leaned in and covered her mouth with his. After that, she didn't think anything.

Heavens, the man could kiss. After the frenzy of the first two times they'd had sex, he'd finally slowed down and taken his time. He'd moved her to the bed and kissed her for what felt like a lifetime. He seemed obsessed with sinking his hands in her hair and melding their mouths together. His fingers twisted and gripped her, sending thrills of desire cresting through her.

His kisses made her forget all her good sense, drugging her past logic. She found herself lying back, letting lust take over again. They didn't have to leave their intimate world for another hour or so. Maybe they could even have the morning to themselves. They could always say they'd been working. After all, she would have to handle the press once the news that Mad was alive broke. None of their friends would question the need for a strategy around that.

His tongue surged in, stroking against her own as he tumbled her back to the bed, his body covering hers. She loved the way he crushed her into the mattress. Her legs parted for him of their own accord. Or maybe he'd already trained her to spread them every time he came near.

She hadn't gotten her mouth on him yet, and she so wanted to spend time on his cock, learning its shape and feel and taste. She wanted to touch him, know that she could give him ecstasy in return.

She heard a brief knock on the door before it opened. Liz gasped and scrambled to cover whatever parts of her body Zack's wasn't hiding.

Zack didn't move. He merely looked up. "I'm busy right now, Thomas."

Her heart was in her throat. There was a freaking Secret Service agent in the room. She was fairly certain she'd turned a stunning shade of red.

"I'm sorry, sir. I'm unused to you being busy. I'll let the team know we have new protocols." If Thomas was embarrassed, he didn't sound that way at all. "The vice president has called three times already."

"Please tell the vice president that I am busy and will contact him when I have time." Zack's tone was arctic.

"Yes, sir."

"And Thomas, if anyone else tries to open that door, I expect you to shoot them. We'll be out when we're ready."

"Of course, sir." The door closed, but the unexpected visit still reminded her yet again that there would always be someone hovering nearby.

Zack started to lower his head again like nothing at all had happened. She could feel his cock nudging her, trying to find a way inside.

She put her hands to his chest. "Zack, we can't do this."

He tilted his hips so that his cock slid inside her,

proving they actually could. Despite the fact that she was sore, her body responded, softening and readying itself for more of the pleasure he bestowed so easily and thoroughly. "We can do anything we like, and I fucking love this."

He started to thrust at a leisurely pace, as though he was satisfied with merely penetrating her. He was forgetting a few things.

"Zack, everyone will know what's happening if we don't show up for breakfast. They'll put two and two together."

He didn't seem to care. He simply drew her hands over her head, pinning her. "They're all good at math, Roman especially. Those Ivy League schools know how to educate. When we're done here, we'll take a shower. Unless you're hungry now. Thomas can have food brought in. How do you like your eggs?"

He was missing the point, but god, he wasn't missing her G-spot. She could barely breathe. "Everyone will know what we're doing."

"They probably do already," he admitted, nuzzling her neck. "Roman and I were supposed to go for a run this morning. He showed up bright and early and I told him to go fuck his fiancée for exercise because that's what I intended to do from now on. Not his fiancée, of course. You, but I think he got the point. I'm pretty sure Roman told Gus, and Gus is a horrible gossip. God, you feel good. Jogging sucks. This...this is so much better."

He was right. Lord, he felt better inside her every minute. "I didn't think we wanted anyone to know. We agreed that we could only be together for one night."

He froze, his head popping up, his stare burning. His cock still filled her, utterly huge, not ceding an inch of her body back. "I never intended for this to be some one-night stand, Elizabeth. I told you to be sure."

She was sure how much she loved him, but the situation

was more complicated than that. "Just yesterday you were shoving me away. And we can't not talk about the fact that you're the president of the United States. Everyone is watching you. We can't have a fling."

"I'm not married. I can have a fling if I want one. Tell me right now if you intend to stay with me or not because I would rather not waste my time with a woman who doesn't want me."

"Of course I want you, but we have so many things to think about beyond how good this feels."

"Yes, we do. But the decision might have been made for us. I haven't used a condom."

At least she could alleviate that worry. "I'm on birth control."

His expression turned dark, and he thrust inside her to the hilt again, as though he couldn't control his hips...or didn't want to. "Then we have nothing to worry about."

He seemed almost disappointed. She wasn't going there with him. She skimmed her palms up the sides of his muscle-laden torso, reveling in the way he rippled, in his very vitality. "We have to worry about gossip."

He seemed to find that concern incredibly boring, since he devoted all his attention to nibbling her neck. "That's your job, but I have no intention of making some kind of statement. I also don't have any intention of sleeping alone anymore. Let them talk. I don't care. I want you. I'm going to have you."

He picked up the pace, getting serious now. He wasn't letting her go? He wasn't giving her up?

To the greedy part of her, that sounded like heaven.

It was a mistake, and she knew it. How—and why— had he gone from shoving her away at every turn to insisting she stay this close? But when he kissed her again, her thoughts all dissipated. Zack wanted her. Zack needed her.

She wasn't about to walk away from him now. He'd let

her into his inner circle and she intended to stay there, by his
side.

She held on to him and vowed they would find a way
through this mess, maybe even find that future they'd
promised themselves before tragedy and politics had
intruded. Maybe they could live happily ever after.

* * * *

Zack strode through to the kitchen as evening approached.
During the afternoon, everyone gathered at Camp David for
the weekend congregated to discuss the shitty situation they
were in. As the dinner hour drew closer, they'd all agreed
that pizza sounded great. Well, everyone except Freddy,
who claimed the food or the delivery—or both—could be
too easily compromised. As an alternative, he'd offered
them all the jerky and some trail mix he'd made. Mad had
sent the paranoid bastard a subtle shake of his head to let
Freddy know that wasn't going to fly.

And all Zack had been able to think about this
afternoon was Elizabeth—how gorgeous she looked with
her hair spread across his sheets, her blue eyes hot with need
as he worked her body from head to toe.

Fuck, he was getting another erection, while she was
off in Lara's cabin, probably sipping responsibly sourced
wine or something. Was she talking about him? Everyone
must know things had changed between him and Elizabeth.
Sure, he'd been perfectly serious while discussing the
conspiracy this afternoon, including the potential danger and
fallout, but when they broke to get ready for dinner, he'd
kissed her long and lingeringly without a second thought.

It was his right to kiss his woman. The other men did.
Roman didn't pretend Gus wasn't his. Gabe didn't politely
keep his hands off Everly. Lara had spent most of the
discussion sitting in Connor's lap. Dax and Holland kept

disappearing, and everyone knew what they were doing.

Still, she'd looked flustered as she'd followed Lara out. Afterward, Roman had tried to corner him, but Gus somehow sensed Zack hadn't wanted to talk and distracted her fiancé.

Zack sighed. He was going to have to explain and soon.

He made his way into the kitchen to grab a bottle of water before he returned the VP's phone calls. Despite being in over his head with the Russians and having the most stressful job in the world, he felt good. Relaxed. Almost invincible. Apparently enormous amounts of righteously dirty sex could do that for a man.

He grinned. He'd spent his whole life being circumspect. Unlike the rest of the Perfect Gentlemen, Zack had been thoughtful about dating. He'd had a few girlfriends, but they'd always been the kind his father approved of—ones who wouldn't distract him too much. If his father was in his right mind now, he would hate Elizabeth. She distracted him all the time.

Starting any sort of relationship with her was probably a mistake. After all, he still didn't know what, if any, role she played in this whole Russian mess. But Elizabeth was his mistake to make. Right now, he wasn't regretting her in the least.

He'd almost made it to the kitchen when he noticed a lone figure sitting outside. Mad lingered alone, a glass in his hand. It looked like he'd gotten into the Scotch early.

Things obviously weren't going for Mad the way he'd imagined or hoped. He hadn't spent the entire night and much of the morning in bed with his woman. In fact, Sara had barely looked Mad's way the whole time the group had been gathered this afternoon.

The damn VP could wait. Instead, Zack pushed out onto the elegantly appointed patio. "You want some company?"

Mad glanced up, and Zack saw shadows in his eyes. "If you're looking for the others, Connor is hiding out in Gabe's cabin while the women are in his. I could go hang out in my room if you need me to."

"I wasn't trying to run you off, though Roman will likely have a fit if he sees us out here in the open."

"We're well-hidden by the patio overhang and all the trees. I doubt an assassin can spot you, no matter how epic his scope. And Thomas won't let word of my 'resurrection' get out. Besides, it's not as if rumors about that haven't been flying for months." Mad gave him a humorless smile. "Rising from the dead will do nothing but enhance my reputation, anyway. Maddox Crawford, the man, the myth, the legend. Maybe when all this is behind us I'll do a road tour."

That was Mad. He covered up his pain with booze and sarcasm. "I take it Sara isn't happy."

"Sara doesn't want anything to do with me, and how can I blame her? She's figured out I'm a bad bet. Took her longer than most." Mad had obviously gone into posturing mode.

Zack barely managed not to roll his eyes, but he understood. As a kid, Mad's parents had only ever paid him any attention when he'd acted out. The bad-boy attitude had always been Mad's fallback position, his safe place. After all, if he never let on that anyone hurt him, how could they possibly know he cared?

"I think you're giving up pretty fast. Either you don't really love her or you're not as determined as I thought."

Mad's eyes narrowed. "I had a plan, Zack. A good one. She wasn't supposed to know about any of this until we were past it and I could come completely out of the shadows. I wanted her to know that I fixed this, made the world safer for her and the baby. But you brought her here. Right now, I have nothing to offer her except excuses she doesn't want to hear."

"I couldn't exactly leave her out there alone." Zack had known what he was doing when he'd ordered the Secret Service to bring all the women to Camp David. "You think you're the only one Sara can be used against? Gabe loves his sister. If they want leverage, she's a good weapon to use against any one of us. She can't be alone anymore."

"She was never alone," Mad said with a frown. "You think I didn't have someone watching over her? I hired a firm to keep an eye on her, through Freddy, of course. I never left her unprotected."

"Well, if you'd rather have your long-distance bodyguard protect her, then have at it."

"It's too late for that now. She knows everything. That makes it far too unsafe."

"Agreed." He could also think of other ways to handle Sara, ways that might give Mad more time with her. After all, being thrown together had worked for them once before. Sure, Sara had once held Mad off, when they were young. After they'd both grown up, working together had broken down Sara's reticence and bonded the pair. "Or we could find another situation."

"What do you mean?"

"I've been thinking about what to do with you."

Mad waved off the worry. "It's fine. I don't know what I was thinking, coming here. I could have called, but…I guess I chose to be dramatic and it bit me in the ass. I'll leave with Freddy in the morning. He's got some friends who can take us. Maybe you could loan us a car. I'm really sick of hiking."

Though he was still pissed at Mad, it was a low-level anger that would likely burn off far quicker than the anxiety he would feel knowing Mad was out in the world and unprotected. Zack refused to make the mistake of shoving away someone else he cared about. After all, it hadn't worked with Liz. "Or I can put you up. Being the president isn't without its perks, and one of them is an underground bunker where I can stash a couple hundred of my closest friends if need be. Of course, it's all pretty secret. Sara doesn't know how many rooms there are. I think I might only be able to loan you one. Trying times and all."

Mad stopped, eyes widening. "She wouldn't be able to leave. She would have to deal with me."

"Sometimes it's all about being patient and waiting out the storm. Unless you'd rather go wherever Freddy has in mind?"

Mad grabbed his shoulders, fervent gratitude in his eyes. "Freddy was planning on taking me to a guy in Colorado who lives in caves and patrols for aliens on a daily basis. Please. *Please* take me in. I swear I'll help the cause. I'll do almost anything you ask. I would even hand over the Scotch if it hadn't burned in that fire. You know, in all of this no one has mentioned that Gabe and my sister managed to burn down a perfectly good mansion of mine."

Ah, it was good to know he still could surprise Mad. The Scotch he referred to had been a Macallan 1926 that they'd all bid on when it had come up for auction through Sotheby's. A mystery bidder had slid in at the last minute and snatched it up. And that bastard had kept it hidden for years. "Gabe saved the Scotch. He came out of that fire cradling it like a baby he'd rescued."

"My Scotch is alive?" Mad asked hopefully, like the answer might bring light back into the world.

Zack felt his lips tug up in a ferocious grin. Actions had consequences—as Mad was about to discover. "Was alive and it was delicious, brother. Since you were dearly departed and all, we drank it at Gabe's bachelor party."

Mad's face fell.

"Hey," Zack said. "I'm sorry. I was teasing you, though we did drink it. I would offer to get you another one, but I'm pretty sure that was the last on the market."

Mad shook his head. "Actually, I wasn't upset about the Scotch. I bought it for just that sort of occasion, something big. I'm more upset that I missed Gabe's bachelor party. I also missed his wedding, Connor's wedding, and Dax's wedding—to the right woman. So…basically, I missed everything. That wasn't how I saw this unfolding."

"Sometimes life takes a turn. I assure you I never thought in a million years I would be wondering who I was at this point in my life. Not in an existential way, but in a real, visceral way. I don't even know my real name."

"Does it matter?" Mad asked.

"Of course it matters."

Mad's head shook. "I'm not going to lie to you. In the beginning I worried you might have known something or that your dad was still in on it, and that was why I hesitated."

Frustration welled inside Zack, and he wished Elizabeth was here. Even being able to clap eyes on her would calm him a bit. He wished they'd never gotten out of bed. "Anything my father might have known is gone now. I've questioned him, especially about Mother and what happened. He can't answer and he gets agitated when I mention that she's dead."

"Are we sure he's not faking the dementia?"

"Several of the top doctors in the world claim he's not." He'd thought about it, watched his father carefully. "I've had him under surveillance for months. He wanders around from time to time, but no one's caught him doing anything truly suspicious."

"I'd like to let Freddy watch him. On CCTV tapes at least," Mad said. "Freddy is surprisingly good with details, and he's an excellent hacker. I know it's not protocol, but he should look through your systems, too."

"I rarely work on a laptop," Zack admitted. "You do

understand that anything I put down on a computer is subject to the Presidential Records Act of 1978. I prefer to have conversations rather than writing emails or sending notes. And my work cell phone isn't supposed to be hackable. After all, it only connects to twelve other phones and has its own cell tower."

"I'm talking about the systems in the White House. I want to make sure no one is monitoring you," Mad said.

It seemed as if his old friend had learned a lot in the last few months. "We'll work something out. Thomas assures me he runs sweeps from time to time, but it's good to have fresh eyes. I'm sorry about Kemp. He seemed like a good guy."

He hated the fact that a Secret Service agent had been killed watching over him. Matthew Kemp might not have thrown himself in front of a bullet coming Zack's way, but he'd still been serving the office of the president.

"He was a good man." Mad sighed. "And a good friend. I sent him to England, you know. I should have backed him up." When Zack started to reassure him, Mad held a hand up. "No, you have your guilt, and I have mine. I need it. I need to remember always that this is dangerous and the decisions I make could cost us all."

Zack faced the same realization every day. It was something he tried to deal with in private. His friends didn't need to understand what this job cost him, but it appeared that Mad had learned this truth the hard way. "Keep his memory close and let it fuel you to be better. Kemp died upholding his vow. We have to uphold ours."

"That's the man I know. Thank you for giving me a perfect example." Mad cocked his head. "I've come to the conclusion that I know who you are. The rest is all semantics. You're Zack Hayes. You're the best man I know, and I've never met anyone I would rather have watch my back. It doesn't matter how you were born or to who. You are the man you are, and no DNA test is going to change that."

He should have picked up a glass because all the tender time he'd spent with Elizabeth couldn't save him from the way his gut twisted when he thought about the choices he might have to make. "If push comes to shove, I'll resign rather than give them what they want."

"If they're willing to assassinate you, then that might also give them what they want," Mad pointed out. "If they can't bend you to their will, I think they would rather take their chances with VP Shorn."

Zack nodded. He was caught in this trap unless he could figure out who was behind the blackmail. Even if he did, if they had the proof of his true identity, why hadn't they used it? He could answer that question himself. Because it would force a constitutional crisis, and if he didn't step down immediately, if he fought, it could tie up the office for months—enough time to start the pipeline.

Still, he had to be very careful. "We need information, and that means identifying exactly who they've worked with over the years. We're going to have to investigate anyone who had close ties to my family."

Mad's expression went grave. "You know that means we have to investigate Joy."

Joy. It was still hard to think about her and not feel guilty. She'd died so he could ascend. Or had she sacrificed herself for her true country? She'd been the one to insist on pushing through the rallies those final few days. He and Roman thought they needed to hit the Rust Belt swing states hard, but Joy had insisted they keep to the schedule. And Zack had capitulated. Honestly, at that point he hadn't cared. He'd wanted the whole thing over so he could go to Paris with Liz and start the life he wanted to live. He'd wanted to be free of forty years' worth of the chains of his father's expectations and the wife he'd taken out of duty. If he had cared about winning the election more than he'd cared about Liz, Joy would still be alive.

"Yes, I know. It will be easier for you to investigate if you're at the White House," he said, already mentally working through the problems they would face sneaking Mad and Sara into the tunnels that existed under the presidential residence.

"We're doing what now?" Roman sidled up, his brow furrowed. Gabe, Dax, and Connor were with him, each with a beer in hand. "Bringing Mad to the White House?"

Apparently, they had started the party without him.

That smooth smile of Mad's he wore whenever he thought the tides had turned his way broke across his face. "I'm back in the game, baby. The Mad Hatter is taking up residence and kicking ass."

"And hopefully groveling at my sister's feet," Gabe quipped, sinking into a nearby chair.

"I do not want to have to watch that," Connor said with a long sigh. "Reminds me of my own life. Hey, if you want to stay at my place, I've got an extra room. It's secure."

Mad's expression filled with horror. "Your place has tofu."

"And an aggressively sexual dog," Connor agreed. "Lincoln will hump your leg and you won't even have to grovel for it. He'll do that for free, and he is fluid with his sexuality. Man, woman, pillow, sofa. He'll hump anything. We're working on the problem."

"Hard pass." Mad lost the arrogance. "I only want to be close to Sara. I know she hates me right now, but I can't not try."

"Sara doesn't have it in her to hate," Gabe observed. "But she will distance if you give her the chance."

Dax tipped his beer Mad's way. "I learned that the hard way, brother. Don't take too long. And whatever you do, don't marry her best friend in a drunken stupor. You will never hear the end of it."

"See, no matter what I've done in my life, Dax is still the dumbest out of us all," Mad pointed out. "I don't want to give Sara more time to put her walls up."

"She won't have much of a chance if she's locked in a room with you twenty-four seven, investigating my personal nightmare." Zack liked the notion of playing cupid for Mad. His friend was rarely naïve, but he'd been foolish to think Sara wouldn't be angry.

Liz hadn't been angry. She had grasped that he'd been trying to keep her safe. At the time, he'd truly believed he had to sacrifice his feelings for her. Now? He wasn't sure if he could let himself love her...or how much he could stop his heart from doing it anyway.

How would she feel if she found out that he'd suspected her of working against him? If she knew he still had the slightest bit of doubt? That he'd simply decided he wanted her far too much to care what her true allegiance might be.

"I think it will be incredibly amusing to see how my sister handles this. I'll feel much better knowing she's in protective custody." Gabe got his serious face on. "But let's talk about how we're going to fix this situation because she can't stay there for too long. I think we should break up the research. Connor and I were talking. Collectively, we can handle this if we each take a piece."

Gabe continued on, but Roman tipped his head toward the house, an obvious request for a private word.

He'd been ducking Roman and all the man's questions since he'd walked into the kitchen with Liz to find the whole group eating lunch. Yep, they'd missed breakfast, and it had been impossible not to notice how badly their friends wanted to ask all the pertinent questions. He'd ignored their pointed stares and thanked his lucky stars that Gus had been in Sara's cabin because she wouldn't have been polite. He would bet Liz was getting interrogated at that very instant.

"We'll be right back." Zack stood because he wouldn't be assigned to do research. He hated that his friends would have to do work that should have fallen to him. Then again, he had a very stressful day job.

Roman followed, closing the door behind them. "Are you sure this is the right move?"

"Nope, and the sad thing is that that's my answer for everything you're asking, whether that's pursuing the blackmailer, bringing Mad to the White House, or being with Elizabeth."

Roman's hands fisted on his hips, like he was squaring off for a fight. "I'm definitely talking about Elizabeth."

Of course he was. "It's private, and you should stay out of it."

"It's not private. Nothing you do is private, and we're not sure she isn't in on the Russians' plans. You might be giving her the very access she's been waiting for."

"I don't think she's in on it." He'd thought about it while he'd watched her sleep this morning. She'd cuddled close to him and he'd woken sweetly tangled up in all that honey-colored hair of hers. He hadn't slept so well in years, and he'd felt a deep peace at seeing her look so serene lying there in his bed. He didn't want to believe she was anything but exactly what she appeared to be. "I watched her carefully while Mad was explaining everything yesterday. She was genuinely shocked. She was hearing all of that information for the first time."

"Or she could be an excellent actress."

Elizabeth could play her cards close to the vest, but not when she got emotional. "No. She can handle a press conference and anyone who wants to come at her work-wise, but she's never been able to hide her feelings in private. You know that."

Elizabeth often told Roman exactly how she felt, and in no uncertain terms or language. She and Roman frequently faced off over how to handle important issues. They were his two closest advisors, Elizabeth being the voice of his conscience, while Roman was the voice of his ambition.

"It could all be a mask, Zack. That's what I'm trying to tell you. If she's a sleeper agent, her whole personality is a setup. And if you let her get too close, she'll know how and when to play us all." Roman glanced back out at the guys, who seemed to be giving Mad some serious shit. "I don't think we should trust anyone who isn't family."

"Says the man whose fiancée is literally family." He wasn't giving Elizabeth up, not to feed Roman's paranoia. Roman got to go to bed with Gus every night. It was easy for him to tell Zack to push aside the woman he wanted.

If Roman heard the hard edge to his words, he didn't show it. He merely sent Zack the steely gaze he knew meant his chief of staff was digging in for a long fight. "I'm only trying to protect you. I know how you feel about her, but we have to be careful."

Zack loved her. He hadn't told her that yet. He wouldn't. They needed time to figure a few things out, but he knew the feelings that beat in his heart for Elizabeth Matthews.

Still, his niggling suspicion played at the back of his head, twisting his thoughts. She'd been the one to bring them the blackmailer's demands. The order to change the FAA investigation's status into Mad's plane crash had come through her office. How could all that be merely a coincidence?

Ruthlessly, Zack pushed the thoughts aside. He couldn't think about that now. He was going to put some faith in her, but that didn't mean he would be a complete idiot.

"I'll tell her about the meeting tonight."

The day before, he and Roman had decided to set Elizabeth up with a test of sorts, some disinformation about a secret meeting with his energy director on Friday to discuss the pipeline. Only she would know about the supposed talk. Zack thought it was an excellent way to get Roman off his back because Elizabeth knew how to keep a secret. But if word somehow spread, they would have another clue. And he would know for sure that Elizabeth was a beautiful traitor.

Chapter Eight

Sara looked around the Presidential Emergency Operations Center and prayed she wouldn't be down here for long. The White House, with all its elegant rooms and rich history, was right above her. "Is there a reason I can't just hole up in the Lincoln Bedroom? I promise not to give birth there or anything."

She understood that she needed to stay out of sight while everyone was investigating this global conspiracy. Yes, it was international espionage, so it was dangerous. But PEOC seemed to be nothing more than a series of sterile conference rooms and an endless collection of locked doors. It was a little intimidating.

"Ma'am, this is where President Hayes ordered me to bring you." Thomas held out a hand, gesturing for her to continue down the hallway.

It was a crappy way to start a shitty week after the rollercoaster ride of a weekend. They'd spent all day Saturday and Sunday at Camp David going over everything they knew about the Russian plot to manipulate Zack. Not that they'd spent all their time working. There had been hours of playing cards and catching up, when she'd forced herself to not stare at Mad, to not listen to the deep timbre of his laughter and think about how long it had been since he'd held her.

This morning, they'd all come back to DC. She'd managed to avoid a long good-bye. Mad had merely told her he would see her soon. That was it. He hadn't even tried to kiss her or sneak into her room once. He'd kept a polite distance, just as she'd asked. Why did that rankle? Apparently he wasn't going to try terribly hard to win her back.

It was for the best.

"It's not that bad down here." Gus touched her elbow and led her down the long hallway. "I'll bring you books and movies. Hopefully, you won't be down here for long."

"The other women aren't being sequestered in the bunker," Sara grumbled.

When she'd agreed to protective custody, she hadn't imagined it would be quite this isolated. She'd hoped they might put her up at a luxury hotel with some guards or send her off to the Maldives. Nothing bad ever happened there. That was a rule; she was sure of it. But plenty of bad stuff must happen down here since the bunker was a war room of sorts.

"The other women used more effective birth control," Gus pointed out in her matter-of-fact style. "I assure you if Lara pees on a stick this month and ends up with a plus sign, you'll have company here. Seriously, don't sweat this. I'll be nearby most days. Liz, too. I promise you won't be completely alone."

The crappy part was, while she'd chosen to be alone for the last few months, she was finally coming out of her mourning now, feeling ready to face the real world. Being with her friends over the weekend had shown her how much she was ready to interact and smile again. And now she was stuck in a cage for the foreseeable future.

Where would Mad be?

She'd watched him climb into the car with Connor, Dax, and Freddy, but she had no idea where they'd intended to drop him off. He would be out in the world again, fighting what he saw as the good fight. Sure, he'd changed in the last few months. He was no longer the billionaire whose only worry was whether the caviar was fresh enough. He'd come back with the heart of a warrior. But Sara still worried. These were dangerous people. Who would protect Mad?

She wasn't going there. She couldn't worry about him. She'd wasted months mourning his death—which hadn't even been real—while he'd been out there playing bad guys and spies. When he'd dumped her and lied, he'd given up all rights to her consideration and care.

"I'm not sure Liz will have time to visit me. The president seems to need meetings with her all the time now," she commented with a ghost of a smile.

It was better to concentrate on the happy couple, especially since it seemed as if Zack had learned something from Mad's idiocy and finally admitted his feelings for Liz.

"You mean he has a lot of meetings with her vagina." Gus was the queen of snark. Even normally stoic Thomas choked at that, though he went right back to his usual badass glower.

"I'm glad they're happy." She followed as they turned down the hall.

"Me, too. But I'm worried. I'm almost positive Roman is plotting something," Gus admitted. "I don't like the way he looks at those two. He's worried, and when that man is anxious and itchy like that, he can do truly terrible things."

"Why would he be worried about Liz?" Zack's Press Secretary hadn't grown up with the guys the way she and

Gus had, but she'd been part of their group of friends for a long time.

"My man always worries about everything, but he's veering close to paranoid now. I have to watch him like a hawk or he's likely to do something stupid. I haven't schemed and plotted all these years to get Liz and Zack together just to have Roman rumble in and destroy everything."

"Schemed?"

Gus waved a hand grandly. "Totally. I've been pulling strings for some time so that Liz and Zack can reach happy coupledom. I take credit for Dax and Holland, too. I didn't exactly get them together, but I did send them a gift that kept them alive. Gemma, the bodyguard, kicked ass on my behalf, so technically that's a win for me. And I often talk Lara out of doing crazy shit that would drive Connor off the deep end. Though I didn't manage to talk her out of chaining herself to a tree he wanted to cut down on their property. She said it was a squirrel's home or something. I'm pretty sure that's why he wanted to cut the sucker down."

"She chained herself?"

"Yeah, so Connor got creative. I'm glad whatever security footage he keeps around his perimeter didn't see the light of day." She stopped in front of the door that marked the end of the hallway. Like all the rest, it looked large, utilitarian, and unwelcoming. "And I'm definitely responsible for that little nugget there."

Gus put a hand on her belly. Sara didn't mind since it was Gus. Besides, the touch made her feel like she wasn't alone in caring for her daughter. But she did have some questions. "Why? Did you supply Mad with the incredibly breakable condom?"

Gus grinned. "No, but I totally scared off the other applicants for your job and persuaded Gabe not to flip his shit about you taking the job at Crawford. I actually even convinced Gabe that Mad would never sleep with you out of deep and profound respect for their brotherhood. It was a good speech. I swear I could almost hear the music swelling behind me."

Sara shook her head because Gus was incorrigible. "I don't know if I should thank you for that or not." But her baby was fluttering inside her as if she had her own opinion. "But I can't be too angry. I got something good out of it. I know you need to go. It was nice of you to come down here with me. Thomas can be very grim."

"It's a requirement of the job," Thomas offered almost apologetically, swiping his keycard over the door. The light turned green and the lock clicked open. "This is the only living quarters we have available. I'll let your roommate show you around."

"Roommate?"

She walked in. Then her purse fell from her numb fingers and onto the ground.

There sat Mad, lounging on the comfy-looking sofa, his dress shirt opened just enough to show off his new, outdoorsy tan and the beginnings of what she knew to be a spectacularly muscled chest.

"Hey, baby. These are some nice digs," he said with a heart-stopping grin. "Don't you think?"

Nope. This wasn't happening.

Protective custody, my ass.

She turned to insist Gus take her from here because she was *not* staying.

Instead, her friend waved as she began to shut the door. "I had absolutely nothing to do with this. Bye. Have fun, you two. Don't do anything I wouldn't do."

Sara watched in horror as the door closed and locked behind her.

Was this a joke? It had to be. She stood, blinking.

Waiting for Gus to open the door with a giggle and deliver the punchline.

It didn't happen.

Holy cow, this wasn't a joke. She was really stuck here with Mad.

She turned on him, her eyes narrowing. "You planned this. Now I know why you seemed so passive this weekend. You knew all you had to do was be patient and you'd have me cornered."

He didn't even try to look innocent. "I couldn't take the risk that I'd run you off before I closed the trap door behind you, baby. We're stuck here for our own protection. At least for a few days. Maybe weeks…"

"No. This"—she gestured between them—"is not happening. I won't stay here with you."

His gaze turned calculating. "So you're going to react emotionally and put yourself and our daughter at risk. I factored your safety into this plan. Last time, you were angry that I left you and kept you in the dark about all the deep, dangerous stuff. You can't say that now."

"Those are two completely different situations, you massive ass." She should have known he would pull something like this. It was a perfectly Mad Crawford thing to do. The man was never going to grow up. "I'm sure my brother will be more than happy to find me a place that's safe, preferably on another continent. So whatever you intend to say, get it all out now, Mad, because I'm leaving here in the morning."

"Gabe knows," Mad replied, patting the couch beside him. "He's happy with this plan because he doesn't have to worry about you while he and Everly are doing some hands-on investigation in Moscow."

Her heart flipped in her chest. "He's going to Russia?"

"Yes, he plans to talk to some people there about records we need. He's also in discussions with a company there about selling them private jets. It's a good cover."

"But he's not a spy." The idea of her brother walking into the lion's den terrified her.

"Except for Connor, none of us are. But we can't bring in outsiders. I managed to survive and I didn't have my own personal security expert, who also happened to be my wife, by my side. Gabe is smart. He'll put his hands on the information we need, and Everly will help him. She's really good. The one thing that could trip him up, though, is not knowing his sister is safe."

She crossed her arms over her chest because it was obvious he was fighting dirty. "That's emotional blackmail."

Mad simply shrugged. "No one ever said I played fair, and you should know it. Now, there's no TV in this place. Whatever shall we do?"

Sara scowled. He couldn't possibly be serious, right? Then again, this was Mad. "I am not having sex with you."

"I don't see why not. You know I can make you happy in bed, and there's absolutely no risk of further consequences now. You can't get more pregnant than you already you are. Consider me your pleasure slave. Use me all you like."

She ruthlessly shoved aside the dirty thoughts rolling through her head. Following the first three months of her pregnancy, which had been nothing but nausea and fatigue, she'd been horny, wracked by her aching body with no one on whom to release all her pent-up need. The idea of using Maddox's virile, muscular body as her living vibrator held a twisted appeal. But then she remembered what that incredibly talented cock was attached to. "No consequences? You know what you could give me? A big old STD. Nope."

He frowned as though he hadn't expected that. "Sara, I'm perfectly clean. You should know that since you made me take a test before you'd go to bed with me. Not the most romantic way to start a relationship."

Did he think she was stupid? "We've been apart for months, and you dated some of the skankiest models on the planet."

By skankiest she also meant beautiful and sexy and not carrying a soccer ball where their abs used to be. She knew Mad. He never went without. Sex was his drug of choice, and since he hadn't been getting his fix from her, he'd been getting it from someone else.

Mad stood and crossed the room to her, hovering in her space but not touching her. He reached up as though he wanted to touch her, then forced his hands back down. "Sara, I haven't touched another woman since the day I realized I might actually have a future with you. You're the only woman I've ever loved and I did not cheat on you. I wouldn't do that."

He sounded so sincere, and she wanted to believe him. Despite his reputation, Mad had never been a liar, especially not a skilled one. That was one reason she'd believed him when he'd texted those awful things to her. Damn it. It was *the* reason he'd texted rather than broken up with her face to face.

"You coward. You knew you wouldn't be able to say such horrible things and break up with me if you'd come to my apartment that day, so you texted all that vile shit."

He shrugged. "I also knew I couldn't be near you and not tell you everything. You don't understand how much I needed you that night. I know it doesn't sound manly, but I was scared and I wanted you so much." He paused, obviously trying to find the right words. "I know you think I made a mistake, but if I did, it's because I love you so much. We're stuck here for a while and yes, I trapped you here with me, but we have some things to work out because you were right about something else. Our daughter has to be our number-one priority now. She is everything. We have to find a way through the mess I made for her sake."

He stared at her belly, emotion naked on his face.

Was she going to have this child and keep her from her father? No. She would never do that. It wasn't fair to the child or to Mad. In fact, Sara would put up with a lot simply so her daughter had a relationship with her father.

She sighed. She and Mad did have things to work out. But she needed to make something clear to him.

"If you're doing all of this to get me back, it won't work. I'll be civil with you for our daughter's sake, but I'll never love you again." It was a total lie. She couldn't not love the man in front of her. The sad truth was, she simply couldn't trust him anymore. So they couldn't share their lives the way she'd dreamed of. They couldn't grow old together.

"Well, then all my work will be for nothing because, while we need to be civil, I also love you and I refuse to give up on us." He let out a long breath. "Now, we have a nice kitchen and I made you cookies. Don't get excited. They were break-and-bake, but they're your favorite— peanut butter—and I also made them stock herbal teas I know you love. So let's have a snack. I'll rub your feet and tell you all about the exciting job we have ahead of us. We're going to go through all of Joy's old notebooks and a ton of press clips about her to figure out if or how she was involved in this conspiracy. Did I mention I was keeping ten years' worth of her day planners just for you? We're going to have so much fun." He winked.

He was so damn charming when he wanted to be, and he knew exactly where her weaknesses lay. Peanut butter cookies for sure. Actually, she craved all things peanut butter even when she wasn't pregnant. And damn it, how did Mad know her feet hurt? When she thought about it, he owed her one hell of a foot rub since he was responsible for her weight gain. And for all he'd put her through.

"Fine. I'll take the foot rub. Maybe you could do my shoulders, too. But I've got a hard-core no-no zone, and it's all your favorite parts. Take me to the cookies."

The light was back in his eyes...and her heart threatened to melt. "All your parts are my favorites, and you have no idea what I could do to your toes. I'm incredibly creative. Not that I'm going to. These will be perfectly respectful fingers...for as long as you want them to be."

He headed toward the back of their appointed prison, and Sara prayed they wouldn't have to stay trapped together for long because being this near Mad might break her resistance—and her heart all over again.

* * * *

Three days later, Zack watched Elizabeth as she paced the Oval Office, staring down at her cell phone. She wore one of her power suits, this one a scarlet red. The skirt brushed halfway down her thighs and showed off those shapely legs that looked so damn good propped against his shoulders as he drove into her.

They'd been together for six days. In that time, he'd done his damnedest to make up for all the time together they'd lost. When they'd returned from Camp David to the White House, they'd had a brief argument about her living arrangements going forward. She'd actually thought she would go back to her apartment each night. Foolish woman. Of course she needed to keep it for appearance's sake, but she wasn't sleeping anywhere but beside him. He'd ended the argument by showing her just how soft and perfect for sex his presidential bed was.

He liked his new morning schedule. Wake at five thirty. Fuck Elizabeth. Six fifteen: shower with Elizabeth that would probably lead to fucking her again. Seven: breakfast with Elizabeth, and often with Gus and Roman. Seven thirty to midday: work. Noon: nooner with Elizabeth. Oh, and food…when they had time. Occasionally, he had to be flexible with lunches because he often played host to some congressional windbag or foreign dignitary, so he had to behave like a choir boy. Then, he often made do with a quickie in Elizabeth's office where he shoved his face in her pussy or she sucked him off. Afternoons were the worst because she seemed to think she had to work and he should do the same, but when the day ended at six thirty, they hit the sheets and didn't stop for more than a quick bite until they both fell asleep.

All in all, as long as no global skirmishes or natural disasters plagued him, it was a great schedule.

"Zack? Have you heard a word I've said?"

Nope, but he could guess what she was talking about. It was the only thing she'd talked about since they'd put their plan in motion. "The press is paying attention to the story about Joy and Roman in Capitol Scandals and you're worried."

When he'd put the gas pipeline on hold, he'd put the Russians on notice that he wouldn't make any rash decisions. Now, he was letting the air out of their balloon, so to speak.

The first thing they had done was take care of the worst of their problems.

"Yes," Elizabeth replied, standing in front of him, the Resolute desk between them. "Today it's just a whisper because apparently someone assassinated the head of a large South American drug cartel and all his important underlings. Strangely enough, it's the same man mentioned in the blackmailer's letter, the one who threatened to come after Connor and Lara."

"Well, now he can't, so problem solved." Zack didn't see an issue since Connor had worked fast and clean. In fact, he was already on his way back to the States. When he returned, they could start a soft roll-out of the second part of their plan. "And he used sustainably sourced bullets so Lara can't be too mad at him."

"What does that even mean?"

"I don't know. I made it up. Show me your breasts." He picked up the phone and dialed his new favorite number. "Freddy, I need a blackout in the Oval."

"Sure thing, Mr. President, and might I add I really like the bunker. I don't know what Sara is complaining about. I think it's awesome. And you're dark," Freddy said over the line.

Sometimes he worried letting Freddy squat in the bunker might mean he would become the phantom of the White House, but he wasn't about to tell the man to move out. Freddy had immediately figured out how to handle the CCTV that followed Zack around. It had saved him from making many a sex tape in the last few days. "Give it about twenty minutes, then turn it back on. And I'll make sure the juice boxes get resupplied."

Freddy seemed to survive on a steady supply of beef jerky and apple juice. He wouldn't want to be that man's doctor, but he was more than happy to have him shut off the cameras so he could seduce Elizabeth.

He set the phone back down but Elizabeth's gorgeous breasts were still secure behind her blouse.

"Zack, this is serious. You didn't mention that you would be assassinating people."

"He was a drug dealer also known for using slave labor to grow and harvest his product. I did the world a favor." He wasn't supposed to say that. "Or rather someone did. We can't possibly know who it was. Come sit on my lap."

She bit back a frustrated groan. "What else haven't you told me? I knew about leaking the Roman/Joy story, and I know Gabe and Everly are in Moscow now. Will anything else be coming around to smack me in the face?"

"Only if you get on your knees, baby." Getting her mouth on his cock would be an excellent way to start the afternoon. He had to meet with a group from the House this afternoon and listen to them harangue him about everything from infrastructure to world events. It would be boring as hell, and having the memory of Elizabeth's mouth on him would make it all bearable.

"You are incorrigible, Zack." She shook her head, but her lips curled up in the sweetest smile. "Is this what it's like to be a woman in the Perfect Gentlemen's inner circle? Always wondering what mischief y'all will cook up next?"

"Come here and I'll show you." He turned his chair so she could move in.

With a sigh, she skirted the desk and lowered herself to his lap. She cupped his cheeks. "I really can't resist you, even when I know I should."

She shouldn't ever resist him because he couldn't stand the thought of not having her. Now that she was in his bed and with him nearly twenty-four seven, he understood what a real partnership should be.

Except he was holding back from her. He wasn't telling her everything.

"There's no need to resist me. After all, I'm the president." He drew her down and kissed her, loving that moment when their lips met. He'd never been a big fan of kissing before, but now he realized he'd treated all his other sexual relationships like they were part of his job. With Joy it had been almost required in the beginning, a way to procreate the two point five kids he needed to look good. Not that he wouldn't have loved those kids, but it hadn't happened for them. When they'd realized it probably wouldn't, they'd stopped having sex altogether. And Zack hadn't missed it that much. He'd certainly never wanted Joy the way he craved Elizabeth. He could spend hours simply kissing her and letting his hands roam her body.

"I have so many good reasons to resist you," she said, laughing as he kissed her neck. "The staff is starting to gossip."

"They've gossiped about us for years." He couldn't care less. He'd had far worse things said about him. He would take gossip about sleeping with the most beautiful woman on the planet any day.

"But then, they were always wrong," she pointed out. "I have to think about how to handle the truth coming out so we get ahead of the story. There's about to be a lot of relationship drama surrounding your administration, and I would like to douse those flames before they start a wildfire."

She seemed determined to work, and Zack could only keep those cameras off for so long. He was going to have to multitask.

He got his hand on her knee and started working his way up. "You're the press expert. How would you play our relationship if you weren't in it?"

"Well, I would be pissed off for one thing," she admitted.

She made him laugh. So few people had ever been able to make him forget all of his responsibilities and simply enjoy the moment, but it was hard not to when she was around. "Pretend we're talking about someone else then. Not me, because I don't want you to ever see me with another woman again. Not even in your head. So I'm this dumpy politician who somehow has managed to snag the hottest chick in his administration. I'm single and a famous widower. How do you manage the press around that relationship?"

"Dumpy?" She shook her head, but he could see her thinking. It was good because it was likely distracting her from the fact that his fingers were inching closer and closer to her pussy. Once his hands reached nirvana, she would melt for him. She responded passionately to him each and every time he made love to her.

"I'm not vain. Proceed."

She relaxed against him, letting him pull up her skirt a bit. "I would advise the couple to go on a few low-key dates, ease the public into the situation. The politician in question is a beloved figure and respected, but it's been a long time since he had a relationship, temporary skanks aside. So as long as the woman is First Lady material, I think it would be fine."

She was thinking ahead. He liked that. "First Lady material?"

She'd thwarted his first inclination—get her pregnant so neither of them could dodge the issue of matrimony. It had almost worked for Mad. But if he needed to marry Elizabeth for the good press, then that was just what he'd have to do.

She stiffened in his arms. "I didn't mean it that way. I just meant if the woman is respectable, I don't think there would be much backlash."

He stopped and forced her chin up so she would look him in the eyes. "You're perfectly respectable. If it gets out that we're having an affair, it won't surprise too many people. I think my dating the way I have the last few weeks has done far more damage to my reputation than anything I might have done with you. I've heard certain tabloids have taken to calling me the Player President because they think I broke your heart. You're beloved, Elizabeth. Don't ever think otherwise."

The press adored her. She was quick, witty, easy to talk to, made press conferences lively, and never lied to the press. They greatly preferred her to him.

"I just don't want you to think I'm angling for a ring."

"I don't think that at all." But he had every intention of

giving her one. He'd already considered this. She made him happy. She couldn't betray him. It simply wasn't in her nature. "So you want to grab some coffee sometime?"

It would feel good not to have to sneak around. He could finally hold her hand in public without caring how it looked.

"Are you asking me on a date, Mr. President?" The haunted look in her eyes was gone. The happiness he saw there warmed him, encouraged him.

Damn, he was in deep. "I am, Ms. Matthews. But first, we've only got another ten minutes or so before those cameras come on."

She laughed but was interrupted by the door opening and Roman quickly shutting it. That was the good part. The bad part? Roman was on the wrong side of that door.

"Please tell me you haven't turned the Resolute desk into a sex surface," his chief of staff/best friend said with a fierce frown. "You do know there are cameras in here, right? Are you planning on having an X-rated section of your presidential library?"

He tried to keep hold of Elizabeth, but she was already struggling to her feet.

"Sorry." She straightened her skirt.

He turned on Roman, happy there was a desk between them or his insistent erection would likely be noted. "Hypocrite. I know you and Gus have sex on your desk all the time."

"But my desk wasn't a gift from Queen Victoria to Rutherford B. Hayes." Roman stalked into the space, nodding Elizabeth's way. "Have you had any calls about the article Lara published today?"

"A few. No one from the mainstream media yet, but a couple of Internet sites have sent inquiries." If it hadn't been for the light flush of her face, no one would know she'd almost gotten shoved on Queen Victoria's gift and taken hard and fast by the commander in chief.

His dick was pretty resolute about that happening soon, but it would have to wait. "She was just telling me she thinks you're going to have to do an interview."

"You and Gus," she corrected quickly. "Gus was one of Joy's best friends. The truth of the matter is, if Gus and the president aren't upset about it, I don't think the public can be. You need to keep being seen together. You and the president, as well."

There was a plan he could get behind. "You two can join us for our coffee date."

Roman's brow rose. "Coffee date? We have coffee here. Gus just had a cup. Should I send some?"

For a brilliant man, he could be obtuse. "It's a double date to get the public used to Elizabeth and I being together. She thinks we should start slowly, hence the double date and not an orgy. That comes later."

Roman grinned. "I would never let that happen. My fiancée has already run through a bunch of you assholes. I don't need for her to have more to compare and contrast. Sure, we'll join you. Anything to get the story out there so it can go away quickly."

"That's the plan," Elizabeth said. "I'll go back to my office and start thinking about an official statement."

"Elizabeth?" She was forgetting something, and he wouldn't have it. His whole life revolved around rules and protocols. This was one he'd put in place. "He's not the public."

She flushed again but moved around the desk and leaned closer. "I'll see you tonight."

She kissed him and he watched her go, her hips swaying. The door opened and closed. Then his world seemed to dim a little.

"Damn it, Zack, you are in too deep with that woman."

Zack stood, facing off with his best friend. "Her name

is Elizabeth and if you call her 'that woman' again, I'll fire you. Do I make myself plain?"

"You prove my point, Mr. President." The title was proof that Roman was irritated with him. He never referred to him as anything but Zack when they were alone. "I came here to give you an update on a couple of things. I talked to the VP and calmed him down."

"Shorn's pissed I'm keeping him out of the loop when it comes to the pipeline," Zack explained as he moved around to the couches decorating the office. One of them, he'd discovered, was a spectacular make-out spot. He didn't mention that to Roman, though. "He's been taking a lot of meetings. I'm worried he's making promises he can't keep."

"He's grumbling about us taking our time, but he seems more measured and rational since we spoke." Roman parked himself on the very spot where Zack had gotten an excellent blowjob the day before.

Zack sat across from him. "Have Dax and Holland come up with anything on him yet?"

The couple were investigating the vice president. The truth of the matter was, Wallace Shorn didn't want the pipeline built for environmental reasons. It was a massive undertaking, and if it happened there would be compromises along the way. Nothing new there. But Wally's record of concern for the environment was precisely why he'd been put on the ticket. Zack had needed some balance and found value in differing opinions. Simply because Shorn might do something the Russians wanted didn't mean he was in league with them, but Roman could be a paranoid bastard.

"Nothing yet, but they have to be careful. I can't imagine what would happen if the press found out we're tailing our own VP," Roman explained. "They're looking for any connections beyond the ones we already know. Your father approved of him, right?"

"Yes, he balanced out the ticket in several ways." He

couldn't help but remember Elizabeth had been on board with the plan. In fact, she'd been the first one to throw his name out.

"Holland wants a couple of days to watch him. But I came to talk to you about what's happening with Mad and Sara."

"Hopefully they're working it out." He wanted to go down and visit them, but he'd been especially busy...with Elizabeth. He hoped Mad found himself similarly occupied.

Roman winced. "Let's just say Mad is not sleeping in the bed. I went down there and he's apparently all about the couch for now. But I wasn't referring to their relationship. Mad and Sara have been working. They've found some things you should know about."

He didn't like the sound of that. After all, Mad and Sara had been poring over Joy's records. Gus had wanted the job, but she and Holland had been far too close to Joy. They'd been sorority sisters and friends. The idea that Joy had been anything less than the perfect political wife she'd seemed might crush Gus. Sara had never been close to Joy, and Joy had actively hated Mad, so they were the perfect duo to look at her records with impersonal eyes.

"What have they discovered?" Zack wasn't sure he wanted to know.

"We're having them look through all of the evidence we collected in England, along with Joy's calendars. So far, they haven't found anything new. If Joy visited your mother clandestinely, she somehow managed it without you knowing."

"How would she do that?" It wasn't as if Joy could have hopped in the car for a quick trip to England.

"She did take a couple of official trips to London. Would it have been that hard to sneak up north to the facility where your mother was being treated?"

"First, don't use that word. They didn't treat her. They

held her captive for my father so she couldn't talk and screw up my political career. It was a glorified prison for Constance." Zack found it hard to call her mom now. She'd never really been any sort of normal mother to him. Second, he didn't even know if she *was* his biological mother. Still, he hated how his father had all but discarded her in her later years.

Roman nodded but continued. "Point taken."

"And we're also speculating. We don't know if Joy's records are accurate. We know there's a chance the facility's have been tampered with."

But if Roman's supposition was right, Zack's sexless marriage had made it easy for Joy to be dishonest with him. He would never have had any reason to suspect that his wife wasn't precisely where she claimed she'd be. They had rarely called each other without a specific reason. Still, why would Joy have secretly visited his mother? And could she really have been the mysterious "family member" to check Constance out the night she'd died. It seemed unfathomable.

"What do you think Joy was guilty of?"

Roman glanced away, his eyes full of an old shame. "I don't know. Do you think I even want to accuse her of any wrongdoing? I loved Joy." He put a hand up, stopping the denial Zack was about to express. "No, I know now that I was always meant to be with Gus, and marrying Joy would have been a horrible mistake, but at the time I thought I loved her."

"Have you ever considered that you've spent your entire life backing me up?"

"What does that mean?"

"It means I wonder if deep down you didn't see how much I wanted Elizabeth, how miserable I was in that marriage to Joy, and you offered me a way out." He'd thought about it a lot after finding out the truth of Joy's death, contemplated that time over and over again in his head. Roman was ruthless, but so loyal he had no idea how he would have survived this without him.

"It felt right at the time." Roman's voice was softer than normal. "Strangely, nothing like what I feel with Gus. When I thought about having a life with Joy, I felt content."

"And with Gus?"

"I feel alive."

That was how he felt with Elizabeth. He felt fire and passion and life. He felt the weight of all his responsibilities float away because she wasn't a responsibility. She was a necessity. She was air in his lungs, blood in his veins. "Good. You deserve that. Now tell me the rest of it because I can see by the look in your eyes that you haven't laid the worst on me yet."

"You're the only person in the world who can read me," Roman admitted. "Well, Gus can for the most part, but she also puts the worst possible spin on every expression I have."

"Tell me."

Roman sighed. "One of the things Sara and Mad have uncovered while going through Joy's old notebooks is that she already had chosen her initiative and she'd found a group she wanted to work with."

Fuck. "I think I know, but tell me. We never discussed what her initiatives would be. She told me it would be premature and bad luck."

"She'd already decided. She was going to focus on women and girls' education in America and around the world."

Every single rock they turned over uncovered another shitty secret. "Are you telling me she'd planned to partner with Tavia Gordon's organization, the one that was a front for a Russian syndicate?"

"Yes. According to her planners she'd had several meetings with Tavia. And she wasn't the only one."

Another nail in the coffin. "Who else?"

"Liz went with her to at least one of those meetings, one of the early ones."

Zack tensed in denial. "Elizabeth went to a lot of meetings with Joy. She was running press for the campaign. If she thought Joy needed backup, she absolutely would have gone with her."

"But she hasn't mentioned this get-together to us."

"Do you remember every single person you ever met with in the last five years?"

"Yes."

Roman was a bastard. "Well, I don't. This proves nothing except that Elizabeth did her job."

"Don't blame me," Roman said, his jaw tight. "I hate telling you these things. I'm not the fucking grim reaper everyone thinks I am, but I can't be Suzy Sunshine. You need me to tell you the hard truths, and I'm not done with them yet. Did you know Liz was found in the Treaty Room by herself the day we brought her to Camp David?"

The Treaty Room was his private retreat. Some people called it the Man Cave, but it was where he did the majority of his work, especially if he put in hours on nights and weekends. Why would she be in there? There was a simple way to fix the problem. He would simply ask her.

When he stood, Roman got to his feet and blocked Zack's path. "You can't go to her with this, not unless you want to sit her down and truly interrogate her. This is not something you casually mention or, if she's guilty, she'll know we're onto her."

"How do you know she won't tell me the truth so we can be done with all this suspicion and bullshit?"

Roman shook his head. "It can't work that way. This is not merely about you, Zack. I hate to say it, but you don't get the freedom the average citizen has. When you make this decision, you're not making it as Zack Hayes. You're the president of the United States and you took an oath to serve the needs of the people first. This is precisely why I thought getting involved with Liz was a bad idea. When it comes to finding the truth, you can't treat her like your girlfriend."

Zack hated this—all of it. But Roman's questions still circled in his brain. Why would Elizabeth have been in his unofficial office? What would make her go there in the middle of the day?

"Where was my father at the time?"

Roman sighed. "Gus said she'd heard he'd wandered in there, but she didn't actually see him."

Zack smiled. "Good. Now I have one person I *can* ask."

Chapter Nine

"My phone has been blowing up all day about this Capitol Scandals article." Vanessa looked frazzled as Liz walked into the press office. She turned her screen Liz's way. "Have you seen this? It's ridiculous. Tell me we're suing the hell out of whoever runs this trashy rag."

So the story was already making the rounds. Liz had known it wouldn't stay a blip for long.

She headed for her office. "We're not suing anyone. I'll have a statement for the press in an hour or so."

"Do you know what they're saying?" Vanessa managed to make her shocked expression somehow look pouty.

"I've read the article." She didn't mention that she'd helped Lara write it.

"They're accusing the First Lady of having an affair."

"She was never the First Lady." Why had that come out sounding so defensive?

Vanessa reared back. In fact, she wasn't the only one who seemed surprised. Most of the office had turned their attention to the byplay between her and Vanessa. "She would have been. And she would have been a great First Lady. This article drags her through the mud."

"I'll have a discussion with the chief of staff about it and we'll proceed from there." She glanced around at the room, bringing them all into the conversation. "For now, if anyone asks, we don't respond to tabloid reporting. I know that we'll have to deal with it when the mainstream media get hold of the story, but until then, that's our line. No leaks, people."

She turned to head toward her office. Vanessa followed.

"And what about the other story that's going to break at some point?" Vanessa asked.

Liz had a million stories to worry about. "Which one?"

"The one where the president of the United States is sleeping with his press secretary." The brunette thrust a hand on her hip, her stare full of accusation. "Did you think you could keep that secret for long?"

With the way Zack was on top of her most of the time? No. "If that speculation hits the public, the president and I will decide how to handle it."

"You know, I'm shocked. Truly, I am. I knew you were close to him, but I didn't think you would behave this unprofessionally. You were his wife's friend."

"Joy Hayes has been gone for three years. The president is a single man, and as you know he's been on multiple dates with high-profile women recently. I don't appreciate your speculation about my relationship with him. Frankly, it's unprofessional for you to gossip in the office, especially to me. I don't want to hear another word about this. If that's a problem for you, Vanessa, the door is right there."

The younger woman's eyes widened. "I-I didn't mean it like that. I just...I heard the rumors. I thought you'd want to know because I looked up to you."

"Whatever relationship I have with the president is private and I won't discuss it. Nor do I want anyone else doing so in the office. Are we clear?"

"Yes." Vanessa had turned a nice shade of red. She gestured toward Liz's office. "You've got a visitor. He was very agitated, so I didn't want to leave him out here to disrupt everyone. He's in your office."

Liz raised a brow. "You let someone in my private office without my permission?"

That question seemed to stump her. "I-I thought... Well, we're supposed to squash rumors not feed into them, and that man could cause all sorts of rumors. You'll see what I mean. I'll be out here if you need me."

As Vanessa left, Liz fought the urge to charge after the woman and fire her, but she gritted her teeth, determined to get through the day without making rash, angry decisions. Besides, Vanessa had admired Joy, who had viewed herself as a mentor to the younger woman.

In fact, when she and Zack rolled out their relationship to the public, Liz knew she'd have to remember that, according to all polls, the American people had had a very favorable opinion of Joy. They had genuinely been horrified at her loss and mourned. She also couldn't forget that, besides being incredibly handsome, Zack was a beloved figure. No matter what happened, the press would always be fascinated with him. So once they went public, some women would view her as a social climber or worse. She would have to handle the accusations and the slurs with grace and aplomb.

Liz opened the door, ready to deal with whatever pesky reporter had an ax to grind. Instead, she stopped short at the sight of the man—not a reporter at all—standing by her desk.

Joy's father, Paul Harding, occupied her office, his hands shoved in the pockets of his slacks and wearing an angry glower. He was in his late sixties, still fit from years of training. His hair had gone a stark silver, which he kept neatly trimmed. His pale eyes reminded Liz so much of his daughter's.

He came to visit old Frank frequently. Joy's father and Zack's father had been friends forever; it was one reason their children had married. But today, Liz rued that Paul had been basically given open access to the White House because she knew exactly what story had brought him here.

"Hello, Paul."

"What the hell is going on, Liz? I got a call from a reporter wanting to know if my daughter cheated on her husband. Where is the White House's official response to this tripe? What is Zachary doing to quell it?"

Liz rounded her desk and sat with a sigh. "Why don't you have a seat, Paul?"

"I don't want a seat. I want to know why some tabloid is telling lies about my daughter, and you're not doing a damn thing about it. Joy was a good girl. She would never have cheated on Zack, and especially not with someone like Roman Calder."

"No one is saying Joy actually cheated on Zack. I believe what the article implies is that Joy and Roman were close emotionally."

Paul's mouth flattened in an angry line. "This trashy online tabloid said she planned to leave Zack if he lost the election."

"They were only married because of the election." It was time to get real with the man. Clearly, he wanted to play the ignorant, but she knew the truth. She'd bet he did too. "Their marriage wasn't a love match, Paul. You, Frank, and the other advisors carefully orchestrated it."

Paul Harding paced across her office. "Just because Joy married smart doesn't mean she didn't care about Zack. She was a good wife."

"No one is saying she wasn't." Though it would come up. Once social media ran with the story, Joy's reputation might get savaged, but Liz knew that treatment was waiting for her, too.

He braced his hands on the chair in front of her desk. "I want to talk to Zack."

"I'll call him and see if I can arrange a meeting."

"Why aren't you out there fighting this, Liz?" Paul's anger dissipated, leaving genuine confusion in its wake. "Why haven't you gone after this shit peddler? You would do it in a heartbeat if it was Zack's reputation on the line."

She couldn't tell the man the truth, that she'd helped to float the narrative so Zack could begin to defray a Russian blackmailer's threats. But she had to be as straight as possible with Paul because the story wasn't dying anytime soon. In fact, given their plans, it would likely get worse. "I'm not going after them because the story is true. We've recently found evidence that Joy and Roman planned to start dating after her divorce from Zack. She and Zack had discussed the situation and agreed that, if he lost the election, they would go their separate ways."

"No. I've never heard a word about this. Even if it's true, I don't care. She wouldn't have gone through with it. The pressure of the campaign simply got to her. You have to release a statement denying these allegations."

"Paul, the tabloid has copies of the electronic messages Joy and Roman sent each other. She was involved in an emotional affair with him. I think we can handle this delicate situation in a way that everyone will understand and forgive." In some ways, it might make Zack, Joy, and especially Roman, who wasn't particularly liked by the press, seem more human. "I'm going to handle this with kid gloves, I promise you. No one wants Joy to look like the bad guy."

His eyes narrowed. "But you'll have no problem painting her in that light if it helps Zack. You'll just throw my daughter to the sharks and not look back."

"I have no intention of allowing that to happen. Joy was loved by many."

"Tell me something. Who was Zack involved with? Because I don't believe for an instant Joy would have done this if she'd been getting the attention she needed and deserved from her husband. So I have to wonder if Zack wasn't having a...what did you call it? Emotional affair with another woman, probably someone close to him. Someone he saw every day. Who could that be?" He stroked his chin as if thinking hard. "Why isn't the media discussing that?"

Liz knew exactly what Paul was insinuating, but she and Zack had kept everything completely above board. Admittedly, they'd shared an attraction, but it had been completely unspoken until that lunch in Memphis before tragedy struck. Certainly they'd never sent one another emails or notes like Joy and Roman had clandestinely.

"The media isn't covering it because it didn't happen. Any other conversation you'd like to have on this subject should probably be between you and Zack." When it came to family matters, she couldn't speak for Zack. Paul was his former father-in-law, so Zack was best suited to handle the man and the delicate situation. "I know his schedule for this afternoon is tight. I can see if he has any time next week."

"By then it will be too late, won't it?" He backed up, shaking his head. "I can see what's happening now. He's planning on marrying again and he knows how beloved Joy was. If he can make her look bad, then people will sympathize with him and accept his new wife. I have theories of my own about who that could be. Don't expect me to play along."

"That sounds like a threat. I think you should remember who you're talking about."

"And I think you should remember why he's in this house right now. We all know he wouldn't be here if it hadn't been for my daughter. If you think for one second that I'll let him use her in death the same way he did in life, you're completely mistaken. You know what? I don't think I need to talk to Zack at all. You've always had his...ear. You tell him that if he doesn't deny this story, I'll release one of my own, and he won't like it."

Paul turned and stormed out of her office.

She leapt from her chair and headed straight for the Oval. As much as she hated to, she had to tell Zack about Paul's visit.

Ahead of her, the man's long, angry strides took him not toward the exit, but in a completely different direction. She followed, her every instinct flaring as he marched to the residential wing.

He stopped to talk to a security guard who checked his credentials. Then a man in scrubs came down the stairs and shook Paul's hand. Together, they walked back up.

Liz eased into the hall. "Hey, Jim. Is Paul Harding going to see Ambassador Hayes?"

"Yes. He's right on time," the sentry said, gesturing to the schedule on his laptop. "It's nice of him to visit since, according to the nurses, he's the only one besides the president who can get the ambassador to talk for any length of time. They have pleasant chats."

Paul visiting Frank Hayes was a fairly recent development. He'd been active in the campaign, but after Joy's death, he'd retreated to his California estate for a couple of years. Not too long ago he'd moved back to the DC area, saying it felt more like home.

"I'm glad to hear that." She forced a smile. "It's nice that someone can calm him down. I need to go up and grab a few things I left up there. I won't be long."

Jim's grin told her he wasn't unaware of where she'd been sleeping lately. "Of course, Ms. Matthews."

"Liz, please." She didn't love the formality so many

longtimers clung to.

"I don't think it will be Liz for long." He leaned over, his voice conspiratorially low. "You know we're not allowed to call the First Lady by her first name."

"That is not happening any time soon." She didn't even try to deny it. They couldn't exactly hide the fact that she had practically moved in. And then she winced as she remembered another tradition. "Tell me the staff hasn't started a betting pool."

His laugh let her know they had. "I've got my money on under six weeks because I know President Hayes and when he decides he wants something, he goes after it and gets it very quickly. Work fast, future FLOTUS, because my daughter starts college soon and I need cash."

"You're all horrible," she admonished with a smile. His gentle teasing was a balm to the hurt she'd felt after her run-in with Vanessa.

At least it seemed as if the general staff wasn't bothered at the thought of her having a relationship with their commander and chief. She winked his way and climbed the stairs.

How close could she get to Frank's room without anyone noticing? Heck, why was she bothering? Paul was just pissed off and looking for someone to take his frustration out on. She'd been convenient. Unless he'd come to see if Frank could tell him who the president slept with these days—good luck with Frank remembering anything beyond his own name—she didn't see how Paul's visit could be anything except their regularly scheduled get-together.

On the other hand, she didn't trust Paul in this mood and she didn't need him stirring the pot. Best to make sure he wasn't agitating the ailing man.

Liz turned down the hallway that led to Frank's rooms. If anyone asked, she would say she was checking on him.

She did it from time to time because it was hard for Zack to break free and see the older man...and because Zack and his father had a complicated relationship. Still, they both felt better knowing he was well taken care of.

She turned again, just in time to see the nurse walk across the hall and into the space he used for his breakroom, a soft drink in hand. He hummed as he opened the door and entered.

So the nurses left Paul alone with Frank. That was interesting. She crept further along the hallway. Frank had a suite of rooms, a bedroom, sitting room, small dining area, and a bathroom they'd converted to make it easy for him to shower. If the older men were back in his bedroom, she would have to sneak into the unit to hear them.

Liz took two steps in that direction, then noticed the nurse hadn't closed the breakroom door. She stopped herself inches shy of the nurse being able to spot her if he looked across the hall. Then she frowned, feeling foolish.

What the hell was she doing? She wasn't sneaky. She definitely wasn't a spy. If Paul caught her, god only knew what excuse she could give. Probably not a good one, and in his mood she didn't think it was smart to piss him off more.

Liz shook her head. She couldn't do this. So Paul was grief-ridden and bitter—who could blame him—and he might fire back at Zack in the press? It was nothing she couldn't handle. She had no right or reason to listen in on this conversation.

She turned around to head back down the hall—and ran smack into a wall of muscle.

"Elizabeth?" Zack cupped her arms, balancing her so she didn't stumble over.

Why did she feel like she'd been caught doing something wrong? "Sorry, I was...this is going to sound crazy, but Paul Harding showed up in my office. He was very upset about the Capitol Scandals story. He made some threats and stormed out, so I followed him."

"He's here, visiting my father?" Zack looked toward Frank's door. When she nodded, Zack frowned. "And you wanted to listen in to find out what they discussed?"

She winced. "Maybe it sounds crazy, but I wanted to make sure Paul wasn't stirring up trouble by either planting suggestions in your dad's head or trying to ask Frank for dirt about our relationship. But the nurse didn't close the breakroom door and he would have seen me walking by. I couldn't think of a good excuse for being up here, so I turned to leave. I wouldn't have followed him at all...except he said some things that worried me."

"Which means he was angry about the Joy and Roman story and threatened to expose you and me, right? We'll talk about it this evening." Zack started leading her away.

She nodded, following. "Paul was really furious that we're allowing Joy's good name to be smeared. As much as I hate to ask...I wonder if Freddy can find out if there's any surveillance equipment inside your father's suite. Just in case. I'd rather not be blindsided if Paul decides to spread gossip."

He kissed her and promised to look into it before sending her down the stairs that led to the first floor.

It wasn't until she'd gone that she realized she forgot to ask him why he'd been there himself.

* * * *

Mad stared down at row after row of photos displayed on the computer screen in front of him. He wasn't sure why Sara was scanning the pictures they'd found on Joy's laptop. Well, he understood the purpose. Maybe Joy had captured something—unwitting or not—that might help them end the Russian syndicate's blackmail threat. But he didn't think that was Sara's current focus as she stared at endless pictures of Zack and Joy's wedding.

Row after row of Zack in his tuxedo looking young and ready to take on the world, yet still oddly remote. He and Joy smiled gamely for the photographer, but Mad saw the disconnect between them, as if they'd been puppets, their strings being pulled by others.

Or maybe he thought that because he knew it was the truth.

"I remember that day well," he murmured.

Sara started and turned on him, her eyes narrowing. "Don't sneak up on me like that."

He set the mug of tea he'd made in front of her. "I didn't. First, I asked if you wanted sugar. Then I cursed as I tripped over the extension cord and nearly dropped the mug. Next, I kicked the coffee table because I was frustrated that it was in my way. Baby, a bull charging through a china shop would have been more subtle."

She sent him a sheepish glance as she picked up the mug. "Oh. I was lost in thought. I came across these pictures and couldn't forget how I felt that day."

He pulled up a chair and sat beside her, glancing at the image on the large monitor, one of him and Gabe. They each had a champagne glass in hand as they peered at the happy couple. "I hated that tuxedo. Uncomfortable as hell."

"You looked nice in it."

Mad turned to her, brow raised. "Did I?"

"All of you did," she clarified quickly. "Why didn't you like it?"

"It wasn't just the penguin suit. Zack's wedding was a big event, which would have been all right...except I didn't feel a lot of happiness from either the bride or groom. It was more like a show than a celebration of two lovers choosing to spend their lives together. And then Roman killed what little fun we had planned. You have no idea what he threatened to do to us if we, say, tied twenty-five of the largest neon-colored dildos to the back of the getaway limo."

She turned to him with an impish grin on her face. "Is that where those came from? Later that year, Mom asked me to go to Gabe's old room and grab a coat or something out of his closet. When I opened the door, they all fell on me."

Oh, Mad wished he'd seen that. "Well, we needed a place to stash those, and Gabe didn't trust me. I have no idea why."

He glanced back at the monitor, then took command of the mouse, scrolling up to what he liked to think of as the "before" shots. Photographers had been in both the groom's and bride's rooms, snapping photos of them getting ready and speaking tenderly to their friends and family. He pointed to a picture in the groom's room with all of them sitting around, Scotch glasses in hand. Frank Hayes glowered at them all as if they were ill-bred mongrels, not yet house trained, that his son had dragged home.

"The pictures don't show it, but Zack was miserable that day. Not because of Joy but because her parents ruled that wedding with an iron fist. He literally had no say in anything. They picked the cake, Joy's gown, and those horrifically uncomfortable tuxedoes. The wedding planner was some distant family member who yelled a lot and harped about how important the seating arrangement was. She was one bitter woman, let me tell you. But some of her assistants were, um…nice young ladies."

She rolled her eyes. "How many of them did you sleep with?"

His stupid mouth got him in trouble a lot. "It's hard to remember. Hey, you weren't exactly an angel, either. As I recall, you showed up to the wedding with that asshole you were dating who thought he was the shit because he was on that soap opera."

Her smile turned distinctly coy. "He came to Bond

Aeronautics because he had to learn how to fly for a movie he was in. But I taught him lots more that summer."

Her challenging expression told him she was waiting to see if he was a hypocrite. Sadly for Mad, he could be a big one, at least when it came to Sara.

"Last I heard he's now doing local furniture commercials in the Midwest. So sad for him."

She tsked at him and turned her attention back to the screen.

"Hey, I can't help it if I'm jealous. I pretty much hate every man who's ever touched you."

"If I had the same attitude, I'd have to hate half the women on the planet, including one of my best friends."

Damn it, he didn't want to fight or hash out a past they couldn't change. "I'm not saying this the right way. The truth is, I don't blame a single one of your former lovers for wanting you. God knows I understand how they must have felt to be with you. I only wish…" He shrugged. "I wish I could look back on my life and that I'd only known you."

"That's ridiculous, Mad. You started having sex when you were what? Thirteen?"

"Actually, I had just turned seventeen."

"Impossible."

"No, I'm serious. Gabe had been the stud of Creighton for over a year. Your brother plowed through them all—students, teachers… Pretty sure even some of our moms."

She scowled in denial. "He did not."

Mad quit that topic. No reason to disillusion her more. "Anyway, you probably knew my first time was with Gus. That was nice. But after that…the first girl I really wanted to be my girlfriend was a beautiful girl from our sister school. I got with her, and after we did the deed, which was over far sooner than I'd like to admit, she asked me when she could meet Zack."

Sara gasped. "Are you serious?"

"Even then, everyone knew how important Zack would be. I've had more than one woman use me to get to him. But that's not the point. I'm trying to explain that I wish I'd waited for you. And when I think about those other guys, I hate that they got to spend time with you that I didn't."

Something soft crossed her face, but she pressed her lips together, not saying a word.

Trying not to be disheartened, he turned back to the pictures, his gaze landing on one of Joy in her white gown, pale roses in hand as she allowed the assistants to fix her long lacy veil. It had taken three young women to get it just right.

Something was off about that picture. Mad couldn't quite figure it out, but that image bugged him for some reason.

"You were mighty busy with all those other women."

She was missing the point. "I would never have bothered with the vast majority of those women if you had said yes the first time I asked you out. That's the difference."

"I was sixteen."

He shrugged. "I would have happily walked away from any one of them to simply hold your hand."

She turned back to the screen, but not before he saw her expression turn thoughtful.

Mad hoped that meant something good. In the last few days, she'd proven incredibly mulish. She hadn't softened much. Oh, she'd been perfectly fine with him working beside her, talking to her about anything at all–except their relationship. If he brought that up, she would carefully stop whatever she'd been doing, escape into the bedroom, and shut him out. He had to take some solace that she hadn't done it this time, but he also wasn't going to push it. He'd said what he needed to say for now.

Baby steps. That was his new plan. By the time his

daughter was walking, maybe her mom would smile at him again.

Or maybe she would have found someone else without his shitty reputation who hadn't found himself ass deep in international espionage. Someone who would have concocted some clever way to keep them all together instead of immediately jumping off the nearest ledge into chaos.

Lately, he wondered if she was right about his decisions.

He shook off the introspection and resumed looking at the pictures, his gaze straying again to the image of Joy having her veil straightened. Her father was standing to the side, with Frank.

What was off with this snapshot?

"Gabe's wedding was far more reserved, and I think he liked it that way," she said, reaching again for the tea he'd brought her. "He didn't like Zack's wedding either. He thought it was more about the press than their devotion."

"What was it like, Gabe and Everly's wedding?"

Her lips curled up, but the smile seemed bittersweet. "Lovely and intimate. Only a few of us were there, all close friends and family. I won't go into details. You'd get bored."

"No. I want to hear everything. What did she wear?"

Sara turned. "Really?"

"She's my sister and he's...he was my best friend. I hate that I missed it. I was supposed to be his best man. We'd never talked about it or anything because we're guys and we don't plan weddings in our heads, but we both knew how it would go. Roman and Zack. Dax and Connor. Me and Gabe. And I missed it. I can't get that moment back. Those guys...they're the only family I have left. Hell, sometimes I think they were the only family I ever had."

She stood and lifted her mug. "All right, then. I'll tell you the whole story. Come to the kitchen though. I'm craving soup and I think there's some chicken noodle in the pantry. But first, you were planning on tying all those neon dildos to Zack's limo, right?"

Not only was Sara talking, she was joking with him. Humor and something even warmer lit her eyes again. That gave him hope in a way nothing else lately had. "After Roman's threat, I didn't dare. But I had this great idea to do a whole confetti-swap at the reception. Remember all those sparkly hearts they dropped on Zack and Joy during their first dance and how romantic everyone said that was? I was going to replace the hearts with penis-shaped glitter." When Sara didn't look amused, he sighed. "I can tell you don't think that's funny, but sometimes subtlety is called for. Imagine everyone smiling at how pretty the reception looked and how lovely the happy couple seemed in their confetti before the crowd realized they were covered in dicks."

Her laugh sent a wave of joy through him.

"You know, at some point I'll throw Gabe and Ev a beautiful anniversary party because I would love to see that," she vowed. "Now, we'll start with the dress. Getting Everly in a decent wedding gown was not an easy task. She wasn't remotely interested in designer. That girl is all about comfort."

She continued talking as she returned to the monitor. Mad followed, his stare drifting back to that niggling photo.

He would figure it out eventually. For now, he just wanted to hear Sara's story.

* * * *

From the doorway, Zack stared at the old man in his comfortable room. The hour was far later than he'd hoped, but then he'd gotten caught up in briefings about a skirmish of warring factions in the Middle East. So much war that had such far-reaching ramifications.

A butterfly flaps its wings...and oil prices go through the roof.

Sometimes he wished his father had wanted him to be an insurance salesman or something normal. Something where the fate of the freaking world didn't rest on his shoulders.

"He had a good day," the nurse was saying. "He always seems happier and more settled after Mr. Harding visits. These days, he seems to remember his friend better than almost anyone else."

Maybe that wasn't surprising since they'd been friends for decades. They'd definitely played a lot of golf together, and after the wedding, they'd been shoved together at every family function until Joy's death. "I'm glad. Can you tell me something? Has he been wandering around a lot lately?"

"Not as much as usual," he said. "Honestly, he's seemed tired lately. He's needed more medication than, say, a few weeks ago. Are you worried about him?"

No, he was trying to rationalize why Elizabeth had been in the Treaty Room shortly before they'd gone to Camp David. Yes, Gus had corroborated that Elizabeth had been told his father was wandering around upstairs, but Gus hadn't seen Frank in the room herself. Roman kept harping that Elizabeth could be in bed with the Russians, but Zack refused to believe that she would riffle through his papers without a reason.

But admittedly, she seemed to be in this part of the house an awful lot lately.

He shook it off. He refused to think the worst of her without proof. Elizabeth wasn't some spy, and she'd proven that today when she wouldn't even listen in on two old men.

And if she wasn't listening in? Roman had asked when he'd told his friend the story. *What if you caught her leaving a meeting? How can you know?*

He knew. His gut knew. His heart knew. He would not let Roman's paranoia wreck his happiness.

So why couldn't he silence that little voice whispering and poking at him?

"I was about to give him his nighttime meds," the nurse said. "They put him to sleep fairly quickly. Do you want me to hold off? I know you don't get much time with him."

He heard a hint of judgment in the man's tone, but Zack didn't come back with any of the logical excuses he could give. Nor did he explain to the man that his father had only ever spent time training him to be perfect, to make right all the wrongs the world had done to him by not giving him the political power he sought. He could say his father had never once thrown a baseball with him but had grounded him as a second grader for not making the top reading group. In fact, his father had locked him away with tutors, denying him playmates because his son should always be the best without question.

No one wanted to hear that now. When they looked at his father, they couldn't see the tyrant he'd been, or the unfeeling bastard who had driven his mother to the bottom of a bottle again and again. Nope, they saw a sick old man and his entitled son who ignored him.

"Yes, please. I'd like to spend a few moments with him alone."

The nurse backed off. "Of course, Mr. President. I'll be across the hall. Let me know when you're done. Or call out if you need me."

Because good old dad could be hard to handle. He used to only be abusive verbally, but the disease that had infected his mind turned him violent from time to time. "I will."

Without looking back, he entered his father's rooms and couldn't help but remember how it had felt to walk into his father's office as a child. He couldn't recall a time he'd ever been in his father's bedroom. His mother's from time to time, but not often. No, he'd been left to nannies, who had taken care of his personal needs. If he'd been summoned to see his father, it had always been in his overtly masculine office. He remembered how small he'd felt going in that office, even after he'd grown taller than his father.

Now he eased into a room filled with medical equipment and a man who seemed to have shrunken in on himself. Still, Zack felt oddly apprehensive entering the man's domain.

"Hello, Father."

The old man looked up, his eyes showing no recognition at all. "Who are you?"

He sank down on the couch opposite his father's lounger. Frank wore a set of royal blue pajamas that looked like they'd come straight out of the 50s. "I'm Zack. I'm your son."

What would his father say if he'd answered a different way? If he'd said he was Sergei? Would that register with him at all?

Zack watched his father carefully, looking for any sign that suggested his father was acting. Could he manage such a feat when he took all those medications? Zack had watched him swallow the pills before. He certainly paid for them every month, just as he paid for the nurses and doctors who took care of his father.

His father shook his head. "Zachary is fourteen years old. You can't be him. Did one of his ridiculous friends send you here? If I'd known he would fall in with that crowd, I would never have sent him to Creighton."

Well, dear old dad never had liked his friends. They were the one thing Zack had never relented to his father about. "I remember you cursing them all and telling me I wasn't allowed to go back there."

His father's head snapped up. "I enrolled you in a better

school, but you were rebellious. You said if I removed you from Creighton you wouldn't perform."

"I told you if you enrolled me in a new school I would tank every single class I had so I couldn't get into Yale. You locked me in my room at the start of the summer and refused to let me out. After a week, you took my books and my computer, and I wouldn't give in. The week after that, you took the sheets off my bed. I wouldn't give in. Then you fed me sandwiches and water twice a day until the fall term started. I still wouldn't give in."

It had been a long three months, but in the end, he'd gone back to Creighton and the subject of his friends hadn't come up again. He'd drawn a line in the sand and for the first time found out that he had power, too.

He was doing the same now with Elizabeth.

"Stubborn boy. Couldn't see what was best for you."

"I deserved to have a personal life. They were my first real friends. I certainly wasn't allowed to have any playmates when we lived in Russia." He needed to ease his father into the past or his memories could go wildly askew.

A ghost of a smile crossed his father's face. "Moscow. I didn't want to go, but there was power there. I wanted to stay and run for office again, but my father told me to go." He frowned suddenly, as though he'd lost his train of thought. "I was the ambassador."

"Yes, you were. We lived in Moscow for many years." Zack leaned forward. "Do you remember Nata?"

He used the nickname the household had used for his nanny, Natalia Kuilikov. When he closed his eyes, he could see the young woman she'd been. She'd taken care of him until he'd been sent back to the States for schooling. He preferred to remember her as young and vibrant, not as the corpse he'd seen months ago. Somewhere along the way, she'd come to America and been nearby, though he'd never known it.

"Where am I?" His father looked around, blinking as he tried to reorient.

Zack sighed. This was probably a fool's errand, but he still felt compelled to try. He'd known this wouldn't be easy. "You're in the White House. Where you always wanted to be."

Pleasure creased his face. "I ran for president."

He had. His father had been a congressman in his younger days and had made a run at the White House after a couple of terms. He'd run out of funds just after the Iowa caucus, but he'd gotten his ambassadorship by campaigning for the man who ultimately won, and he'd settled in there, vowing all the while that his son wouldn't make the same mistakes.

Instead, Zack had made all new ones.

"You did, but you ended up going to Russia instead."

"Why would I go to Russia? I don't know anyone there." He frowned and stared at his hands.

"You went to Russia because you were the ambassador," Zack prompted.

"My father wanted me to go to Russia. Connie wanted to go to England. But the old bastard threatened to cut off my money if I didn't do what he said. He insisted that it was my destiny. I don't want to go to Moscow. I don't think good things happen there. We should stay here. Connie and I should stay in the States so I can run again. I'll form a committee and raise money. I'll show my father. But we shouldn't go to Russia."

Now they were getting somewhere. "Why did Grandfather want you to go to Russia? The English post would have been far more prestigious."

"Nasty goat demanded I go, said I'd make a name for myself. It's cold in Moscow. Colder than here. I hated the cold, but he said it was best for me, that it would make me strong. Then the putz who won gave the English position to that other fool, and I had no choice."

"When did you meet Nata?"

His father shook his head. "Why is she screaming? Stop that screaming now. You're going to wake the household."

"Who was screaming?" His heart rate ticked up. His father had never talked about their time in Moscow. Ever. Even when he'd been perfectly sane, his only comment on his stint there was that it had been productive.

His father stood and pointed at something Zack couldn't see. "You. You bitch. What have you done? You've ruined everything."

The last words were screamed at some invisible being, his father's bile and vitriol rising to the surface. His legs were shaking and he looked in danger of falling over.

Zack stood and reached for him. "How did she ruin things? Who are you talking to?"

His father's hands trembled and his eyes went wide as he looked at Zack. "Why did she do it? Such a stupid woman. *She* was the problem. I should never have married her. I should have found someone smarter, someone less emotional. She's the reason we're here. God, there wasn't even any blood. It looked like a damn lifeless doll."

"What did Mother do?" Bile rose in Zack's throat but he forced it back down. He knew exactly what his mother thought she had done—accidentally killed a baby.

She thought she'd killed him.

"Who are you?"

The tension that had threatened to split the air only moments ago was gone in an instant. Zack felt his heart sink.

His mother had smothered a baby. Most likely, her baby. The real Zack Hayes.

The nurse rushed in, concern stretching across his face. "Mr. Hayes, you know you shouldn't be up. You can't stand or walk for more than a few minutes. What has you so upset?"

"Could you call for my son, young man? I need to talk to him about those boys. They're going to get him into trouble. I can't have it." His father's shoulders straightened, but his legs wobbled beneath him and he started to collapse.

The nurse eased him back into the chair. "Mr. President, he needs rest and his meds now. It's been a long day."

Zack couldn't agree more. It had been a very long day.

Moments later, he emerged into the hallway. His constant shadow, Thomas, was waiting for him.

He didn't say a word, merely walked away from his father, his parents' sins weighing on him with every single step. He turned down the hall that led to his private residence, though nothing in his life was truly private.

Had Natalia Kuilikov given her son so no one would ever know that Zachary Hayes had died as an infant? Was that why she'd been so kind to him as a boy? Why she'd held him in her arms and rocked him to sleep, always with a smile? Because she'd been his biological mother? Was that why Constance Hayes hadn't taken much interest in him? Hell, seemed barely able to look at him.

What the fuck did he do now?

His father's delusions didn't substantiate anything. That's what he was sure Roman would say.

But the Russians must have proof if they were coming after him. He should call Roman and Connor and tell them everything he knew. They had to find a way to do a DNA test. There had to be some distant cousin or relative they could exhume. Something.

"Good night, Mr. President," Thomas said. "I think you'll find Ms. Matthews has also retired for the evening."

Elizabeth.

He wouldn't call Roman or anyone else tonight. That could wait. Everything he needed was behind that door.

He walked through, pulling at his tie and tossing it aside, along with his jacket. He would burn off all of his anxiety and pent-up stress in her gorgeous body. He would throw her on the bed and not let her up until morning. Then he could start again tomorrow with a clear head.

Zack prowled through the residence, a hungry lion scenting his prey, but when he reached the bedroom, he froze.

Elizabeth was sitting up against the headboard, reading a book, her blonde hair piled on her head. She looked soft and sweet all tucked in right where she should be.

The need to brand himself on her faded as another need took its place.

She looked his way and her eyes lit up. "Hey. I was worried you were going to be at it all night. Is everything okay? Well, as okay as it's going to be, given that we're talking about the Middle East."

"Everything is perfectly normal—all fucked up," he quipped as he reached her side at the edge of the mattress.

She scrambled to her knees, her hands on his shoulders as she searched his face. "What's wrong?"

He pressed his forehead to hers and anchored his hands to her waist, breathing in her scent. This was what he needed, to be here alone with her. "What would you say if I wasn't Zack Hayes?"

She gasped and pulled back enough to cup his face in her palms and stare into his eyes as though she willed him to believe her. "I would say I love you."

"I love you, Elizabeth."

She smiled. "I love you, no matter who you are. No matter what comes next."

"If I step down?" It might be the easiest way to circumvent whatever the Russians had planned, though it felt easy and he worried that might be giving the syndicate exactly what they wanted.

"Then we can go to Paris," she whispered. "Like we planned."

He kissed her softly. This wasn't about burning stress and anger off. This was about building something new. It was about stepping out of the shadow of the past and forging a new future.

Zack lowered her to the bed and started the best part of his day.

Chapter Ten

Sara glanced at the clock the following day. Two o'clock in the afternoon. Not that she had any other means of telling the time. It wasn't as if she could check the position of the sun by looking out the window. The bunker had no windows. How many days had passed since she'd seen the sun? Breathed fresh air? It was starting to get to her. She had bunker fever.

She also had been way too close to the sexiest man in the world and having to constantly resist his touch fever. Yes, that was definitely starting to wear on her, too.

A fluttering sensation caught her attention and she placed a hand on her belly. Soon she would need bigger clothes because her daughter was growing. She wouldn't be able to hide behind large handbags or black clothes for much longer. People would start talking and she would have questions to answer.

Who is the father?

Well, Great Aunt Tilda, the father is a notorious playboy who died but magically came back from the dead, and I have no idea what I'm going to do because I love him...but I can't trust him.

That wouldn't raise more questions at all...

The real trouble was Mad wasn't going to conveniently fade into the background. Even if she asked him to.

With a sigh, she stood and stretched her back. Hours and hours of poring over historical records documenting Zack's family back for generations—and trying to ignore the pull toward Mad—were taking a toll.

"Would you like me to rub your back?" He glanced her way from the kitchen table where he'd set up a workstation of his own.

The first couple of days she'd let him rub her feet, but then she'd had a dream where he'd massaged her arches before those big hands had begun drifting up to her calf and skimming over her knees. Soon, he'd started rubbing her thighs, then brushing over her... Well, she'd woken up in a terrible state of need and thought seriously about finding Mad on the couch and inviting him back to bed with her.

Letting him close to her again would be a terrible mistake, so after that dream she'd stopped saying yes when he offered to touch her, even if he only meant a helpful massage.

How long would they be stuck in here together? How long could she possibly hold out? "No, I'm fine. I just need a nap."

He stared at her before his gaze strayed to her belly. "Are you okay? Is she okay?"

His hands weren't the only things threatening to rip through all her good sense. In the days they'd been stuck in this bunker together, he'd taken care of her in ways she wouldn't have thought were in Mad's nature. He'd always been good about seeing to her happiness and welfare when they'd been dating, but that had largely involved throwing around cash. Here, he'd done it all himself. He helped her cook and did the dishes afterward. He'd taken to doing the laundry and straightening up.

Domestic Mad was way more dangerous to her heart than the bad boy she'd fallen in love with. This Mad was one she could envision spending her life with.

"I'm fine, but scouring these records all day tires me out. And she's moving around a lot. I just need to put my feet up for a while." She ran a hand over the swell of her belly. "You're playing around in there, aren't you? Doing somersaults because you're my little gymnast."

"She's moving?" Mad stood, wearing a silent plea.

"She's always moved, but she's big enough now that I can really feel her." It had started a few weeks before, an odd fluttering in her abdomen that had become stronger in recent weeks. Recently, she'd even felt a kick or two. "I'll get back to reading in a while, then I'll make some dinner."

She walked to the small bedroom and sat on the edge of the mattress.

What the hell was she going to do when she and Mad could finally leave here? Something would happen soon, one way or another. Either Mad would be forced to go on the run again or they would all be free. Either way, she and Mad would be apart…and she would have to mourn him all over again.

"I miss our walks on the beach," she said to her daughter.

"You talk to her?" Mad stood in the doorway, looking honestly curious.

He was dressed casually in worn jeans and a T-shirt. Sara wasn't used to seeing him so dressed down. He'd always worn a suit for both work and play. Occasionally, when they'd been in New York, he'd bummed around in khakis and a dress shirt. But until now, the only time she'd ever seen him wear T-shirts was to go to the gym.

And when he wore nothing but a pair of athletic

shorts… He taunted her with his perfect chest and abs. Even in the bunker, he worked out every day without fail. And because they were in such close quarters, she couldn't really avoid watching him. She often wondered if her eyes bulged as he lifted the free weights Roman had sent down or did pull-ups on the bar attached to the bedroom doorframe. It was hypnotic, watching the controlled way he lifted his own weight up and lower it down slowly. It was arousing.

Who could have guessed being pregnant would make her crave sex so badly?

"I was alone for a long time after you…" He hadn't actually died, so she couldn't call it that anymore. "After you ripped my heart out and faked your death, so I started talking to her. We would take long walks on the beach and I would tell her about the world, about her family. I'm sure everyone in the Hamptons thought I'd lost my mind."

"I want to talk to her."

"What?"

He shrugged a shoulder. "You get to talk to her all the time. I want some time with her, too. You seem determined that we won't be a couple again, so she should get used to each of us having partial custody."

Talking about the notion of custody made Sara ill. She hadn't given that reality any thought because for so long, Mad had been "dead." Oh, god… Would they end up in court? Would her child be something they fought over?

Mad dropped to his knees in front of her, his eyes softening with sheer emotion. "Hey, don't worry. We'll work everything out, and I promise we won't need a lawyer to do it. I'm never going to fight you on this, and I trust that you won't keep our daughter from me."

"I wouldn't do that." She couldn't keep him out of their daughter's life if he wanted to be in it. This child deserved two loving parents, and if he could be that, she would never let her own problems with him interfere with their bond.

He nodded. "I know. So don't worry. No matter what happens, we're going to love her and respect each other. We made her together. We'll parent her the same way whether we're a couple or not."

Sara nodded, choking back emotion. Everything Mad said was logical, even reasonable. Of course they would make the best of this situation. But she'd be lying if she said it didn't make her sad to think about the two of them raising their daughter apart.

"So I think we should begin as we mean to go. I want equal time with her starting now."

What was he trying to say? "You want to talk to our daughter, too?"

"Yep. And I'd love to feel her moving. But I won't touch you, even for that, if you don't want me to."

She wished he would say something annoying or screw up in some way so she would have a good reason to lose her temper with him. Because as solicitous and charming as Mad was being now, she couldn't deny him. Somewhere along the way he'd figured out how to defuse her anger. "It's all right. I'm going to lie back. She moves a lot when I'm still. It's like I start to relax or drift off, and she decides it's play time."

His eyes lit up and he held out his hand to help her lie back. Once she'd settled, he climbed on the mattress beside her and reached out, seeming almost hesitant to lay his hand on her baby bump.

"You won't hurt her. I'm not fragile either." She took his hand and brought it to her belly. "You might have to wait for it. Like her mother, she doesn't perform on command."

"I remember a time when you did perform on command," he said, his tone going silky smooth, reminding her again just how sexy he could be. "When we were in Toronto for that conference—"

"No." She shot him a censuring stare to let him know they were not strolling down memory lane. "I thought you wanted to talk to our daughter, Mad, not seduce me."

His expression turned serious, and he caressed her belly as he settled comfortably beside her. "Have we decided on a name yet or am I just calling her Baby Girl?"

"We?"

He winced. "By *we* I mean you because I gave up all rights to name the baby what I would have when…how did you put it? I ripped your heart out and faked my own death."

He was definitely learning. "Excellent. No. We haven't decided. Dare I ask what name you would have selected if you hadn't done all those foolish things?"

"Hortense. It was my grandmother's name, and she made me promise to hand it down to my daughter if I ever had one. She said the world would have less problems if women were named properly. As if naming my daughter Hortense would somehow keep her from wet T-shirt contests and dancing on bars."

"You are not naming her Hortense."

"Well, I'm not now because I did all those other things. So when you really think about it, I kind of saved her from a childhood of teasing and misery."

She shook her head, noting his clever play. "Not working. Now talk to Baby Girl."

He fell silent for a moment and she closed her eyes against his stare, trying not to enjoy the feel of him pressed against her, his hand resting where their child grew.

"Hey, Baby Girl. I'm your dad. I know. I've been gone most of the time you've been baking in there, so I've missed a lot of stuff. But I thought about you every second of every day I was gone. You and your mom." He caressed her belly, and Sara tried not to be moved. "I'm going to level with you. I don't know how much I'm going to bring to the table here, kiddo. My dad was not the best parent and my mom mostly shopped her way through my childhood. So I don't know a ton about how to be a good dad, but I'm going to try. I'm sure there's a YouTube video or an app. Something. I promise I'll figure it out."

She opened her eyes. "Seriously?"

He frowned at her. "This is a private conversation between me and my daughter, please."

She rolled her eyes, then shut them again because it appeared he was serious.

"I also don't bring a ton of family. My parents are both gone, and I didn't have any siblings growing up. I had some friends and they were my family. I can tell you stories about your Uncle Gabe."

She scowled at him because she knew some of those stories herself.

Mad shrugged with all innocence. "Only the G-rated ones. I promise." He looked back at her belly. "Don't tell your mom. She worries I'll corrupt you, but you've already got my blood running through your veins. I fear for your teenaged years. Unless you take after your mom. Then I just fear because your mother is the most beautiful woman in the world. She's gorgeous and kind. And she's so smart, I had to hustle for years to even get her to look at me."

Not true. Sara had always looked at him.

When she was younger and Gabe would say he was bringing home a friend for the weekend, she'd always prayed it was Mad. Even at the age of ten, she'd had the worst crush on him. He'd been thirteen, and he'd been funny and patient with her even then. Every time she'd clapped eyes on him she'd sighed.

Once she'd turned sixteen, he'd started to notice her as a woman. Of course his reputation had been cemented by then. She had been smart enough to know he could break her heart.

And he had.

"She's the only woman I've ever loved, the only one I ever said *I love you* to. But that's going to change because I love you, Baby Girl. You're the only two women I'll ever say those three words to. I love you and I'll do everything I can to be here for you. I promise."

Her daughter fluttered, and Mad's eyes widened with wonder.

Sara couldn't help but smile. "That's her. She hears you."

He caressed her belly in return. "I hear you, too, Baby Girl."

Then Mad sighed as though he was completely content with the world. Despite being known as the world's most infamous playboy, he seemed totally happy just chilling and talking to his unborn child.

As the sound of his voice began to lull her to sleep, Sara realized she was happy, too.

* * * *

Zack shook the hand of the reporter and photographer, relieved to have this chore off his checklist without too much fuss.

"Thanks for being so flexible, Mr. President. And for taking the time." The photographer slung his bag over his shoulder.

"It was no trouble," Zack replied as Elizabeth stood nearby, giving the reporter a gracious smile as she shook his hand.

The light in the China Room was sunny and bright, almost golden. It practically gave Elizabeth a halo. She looked so pretty standing there. If this piece of publicity had taken place a few months down the line, she would have been in that picture with him, showing off the elegant china pattern she'd selected for his term in office. She'd picked it, of course, but she wasn't the First Lady so he'd been forced to stand beside the place setting alone as the press documented it for posterity. Instead, Elizabeth had stood back, carefully arranging everything, making sure this chore came off smoothly for him, exactly as she'd done for years.

As the reporter and photographer left with their escort, he thought about the mountain of work waiting for him in the Oval. Elizabeth probably had her own Everest of paperwork and emails on her desk back in the press office. But damn it, he didn't want to spend the afternoon apart from her.

Mad was so lucky. Oh, he was sure Sara wasn't making anything easy on him, but at least Mad got to spend every moment with the woman he loved. No one forced him to spend countless hours apart from her in order to listen to congressmen complain and senators bark. Mad didn't have to wait until after dark to hold her in his arms, feel his skin against hers.

He shouldn't either.

Zack joined Elizabeth, smiling now that they were alone. "What's your schedule like the rest of the day?"

"I've got to get ready for tomorrow's briefing. I haven't done one in a week, and the White House press pool is starting to circle like hungry sharks." She glanced around and made certain they were alone with the exception of Thomas. "I've also put out some feelers to narrow down who we'll trust to do Roman and Gus's interview. The *Times* picked up the story today. Tomorrow it will be all over the morning shows."

"I know. He does, too. We're ready."

"I don't think we are. I'm worried that Paul Harding will go to the press himself with his own version of the truth."

She'd mentioned Paul's threats, but Zack wasn't particularly worried about them. He wasn't sure what Paul could say that hadn't already been suggested, and they had a couple of excellent distractions if need be. He and Elizabeth dating would take over all the news cycles when they chose to come out of the shadows.

And at some point, Maddox Crawford's rising from the grave would send the press into a tizzy, and nothing else would occupy the news for a good long while. They had time and resources to deal with Paul.

He took Elizabeth's hand and headed for the hall. "Let's have lunch in the residence today."

Because he wanted to lay her out and make a meal of her.

"Zack, you're not taking this seriously enough." Her heels clicked across the floor as she hurried to keep pace with him. "He was genuinely angry. I think he meant everything he threatened. He's been out of the game for a while, but he still has connections. He'll use them against us if we don't handle this right."

Fine. She wanted to talk? He could do that. He stopped in the middle of the China Room and hauled her against his body, relishing the way her breasts flattened against his chest. "We're following your plan."

She was a bit breathless as she looked up at him. "And I still think it's a good plan, but I didn't think Joy's father would come at us this hard. I'm worried what he'll do."

He brushed back her hair and leaned over to kiss her forehead. "Stop worrying. We're going to follow your plan and everything will be fine. We're so close to being virtually bulletproof. A few more moves, and they won't be able to hurt us."

Elizabeth shook her head. "Don't be so cavalier. They can still come after you about shutting down the FAA report. And Gabe."

"Ah, but if they do we've got the best piece of evidence of all. Gabe can't have killed Mad and I can't have covered for him because Mad's not dead. See, soon they will have absolutely no more secrets to blackmail me with." Nothing...except his identity.

But he couldn't think about that now.

"Mr. President, a private, guided tour is about to walk through," Thomas said, gesturing to the hall.

Damn it. The place had been shut down for self-guided tours today, but apparently someone, likely a bigwig, had scheduled a private gig. They did them so rarely. It was pure bad luck to have one moving through.

Still, if Zack let Elizabeth go now, he wouldn't get her back until evening. That didn't suit him at all.

He scanned the room and found what he was looking for—a door. "Thank you for the heads-up, Thomas. We'll only be a few minutes."

"Zack?" Elizabeth sounded startled as he hauled her into the closet. It was perfect. Dark and quiet, and with plenty of room. "What are you doing?"

"I've been a good boy all day. I've done everything you've asked me to do. Kiss me." He fumbled on the wall for the light switch and turned it on. He wanted to see her.

Her eyes were wide. "You want me to kiss you? Here?"

"I'm the president of the United States and this is my house. I should explore it more thoroughly and often. This is a very nice closet, don't you think? Now kiss me."

"You know where that usually leads."

God, he hoped so.

Zack flashed her a winning smile. Elizabeth rolled her eyes, but he saw the moment she decided to capitulate. One second she was stiff. The next, she rose to her tiptoes and brushed her lips against his.

His entire body went hard, flashed hot. Every sense he possessed focused solely on her. The rest of the world fell away, and he was left with the best part of it.

He sank his hands in the silk of her hair and let himself

kiss her the way he always hungered to. He devoured her. No matter how many times he had Elizabeth, he always wanted more. This need was what made his friends stop what they were doing anytime their wives walked in the room. This was true passion. It made him feel young and vital and alive, maybe for the first time in his life.

He skimmed his palms down Elizabeth's curves, cursing the material between them, but he had to make do.

"Zack, if we're going to do this we should go to your room," she whispered.

"No time." He wanted her too badly to stop.

"But there's a tour coming through."

"Then you'll have to be very quiet, won't you? I know how hard it is for you not to shout out my name during orgasm, but you'll have to find a way to stay silent while I make you come."

"Zack…"

He stifled whatever protest she might have made with a long, slow kiss. He tangled his tongue with hers. She kissed him back, her hands splayed across his back. If he hadn't been wearing a suitcoat, he would have felt the drag of her nails on his skin.

When Elizabeth went wild, she didn't hold back. The morning after they'd first made love, she'd been horrified that she'd marked him, but he'd spent the whole day reveling in the slight scratches her nails had left on his skin. Each little pain reminded him that he was the man who had driven her past her usual reason and decorum. No one else.

The closet they found themselves in now was really more of a small workroom, likely where they stored china that wasn't on display. It had a nice, sturdy table that looked to be the perfect height. He picked her up, lifting her body against his. In two steps, he set her down right where he wanted her because he knew how to make her hot for him in quick order.

"What are you—"

"We've reached a particularly lovely section of the White House," a feminine voice said, proving that door between them wasn't soundproof.

Elizabeth gasped as he shoved her skirt up, wearing his most mischievous grin.

"Quiet," he whispered against her lips. "You can't make a sound—not a pant, not a whimper, not a moan—or they're going to wonder what's happening in here. Do you want to give those people a real backstage tour of what happens in the White House?"

"No." She breathed out, and in the low light, he saw her eyes flare with heat.

Zack hooked his fingers under the sides of her lacy underwear. "Lift up for me."

She did as he asked, raising her pelvis up so he could pull those panties right off her. He caressed the silky smooth skin of her long, shapely legs. He loved to kiss every inch of them as he worked his way up to his favorite part of her body.

The woman leading the tour went on about Lincoln's pattern, but Zack couldn't care less what was happening outside this small room.

"I could tell them what the real secret gem of this place is." He dropped to his knees and spread her legs. He could already smell her arousal, and it made his cock stiffen and ache. "There's one thing that can make the president do anything. We should explore that. Have I mentioned how much I love these shoes?"

She was wearing purple stilettos today. They elongated her legs, and the sharp, pointed toes did something for him. He couldn't explain why, but they were infinitely sexy.

"I'm glad you find me acceptable, Mr. President."

He could barely hear her, but the words sent a thrill through him. "Going to play it that way, huh? Fine. You're more than acceptable. You're stunning. Do you have any idea what these fuck-me shoes do to me? Do you know how much I love to see you in nothing?"

"I don't wear them for you. They're for me. They make me feel strong."

He needed to make something plain to her. Well, first he needed to kiss her knees and work his lips up her thighs because the spicy scent of her arousal was luring him exactly where he wanted to be. "You don't need a pair of shoes to be strong. You're incredibly smart and resilient, and you're every bit as gorgeous as I dreamed you to be. Do you have any idea how many nights I spent lying awake and thinking about you like this? Fuck the nights. I spent the days that way, too. It's very distracting to be in a meeting with the British prime minister and get a massive erection because you walked into the room. I don't want to merely fantasize anymore. I want to have you whenever I want you. If I want you in the middle of a meeting, I should be able to get up, find the nearest private space, and lay you out. I wouldn't let you up until I'm satisfied. Then maybe I'd be able to think straight for a little while. You ruin my concentration."

Because she was so fucking soft and perfect, and the rest of the world couldn't begin to compare to what he felt when he was with her. With Elizabeth, he didn't have to be in control every second. He didn't have to put on a bland face and compromise. She was the only place where he could simply be Zack Hayes.

Would he end up taking her down with him?

"Please, Zack." Her quiet plea jerked him from his dark thoughts, and he shoved them all aside in favor of the task at hand. He'd been right. The table was the perfect height. All he had to do was lean forward to be exactly where he wanted. He breathed hot on her pussy.

"Oh my god," she said.

"Is everyone okay?" The tour guide sounded startled, then she laughed. "I know it's very exciting, but let's keep it down so everyone can hear. If you'll look to your left, you'll see the lovely pattern commissioned for the Hayes administration. The president has excellent taste, as you can see."

"Yes, I do." He whispered the words against her sensitive flesh right before he dragged his tongue over her clitoris.

This was the real jewel of his White House, the one thing that got him up and moving every morning. Elizabeth was the reason he now woke up happy and prepared to face the most stressful job on the planet. She grounded him. He'd moved long past ambition and power. He wanted to be the man she looked up to, the one she needed and trusted.

He licked at her, loving the way she tasted, how readily she responded. She'd already been slick before he'd even touched her, as though she could hear his need in his voice and responded by making herself ready for his pleasure.

He pulled back slightly but teased her with his thumb, rubbing her clit in gentle circles. "Do you want more, Elizabeth?"

"You know I do. I want everything." She leaned back, balancing her palms against the table and giving him complete access to her body.

Elizabeth was the perfect erotic picture of wanton need.

Zack sprung to his feet because he wanted everything, too. Now. He couldn't withstand more than a couple of hours without her. He'd always thought of himself as strong, but his need for her made him so, so weak…

His fingers trembled as he tore into his belt buckle, then made quick work of his zipper. He'd had a lot of practice lately. Without any hesitation or fuss, he shoved his boxers and slacks down, not bothering to wince when the buckle hit the floor with a clang. He didn't care if everyone outside the door heard as long as no one bothered them.

Elizabeth's head had snapped up, her eyes shining in the dim light as she pushed herself off the table. "Not yet. Let's see how quiet you can be."

The challenge in her gaze had him biting back a groan as she dropped to her knees, skirt still bunched around her hips.

He adored the way she lost her ladylike demeanor when she got hot. Elizabeth was never polite in bed. She demanded her pleasure and gave it back to him tenfold.

As she wrapped her slender fingers around his cock and her grip tightened on him, his eyes nearly rolled into the back of his head. He bit back a groan.

"Not so easy, huh?" she whispered before that talented tongue of hers swiped across the head of his cock.

"No." Not easy at all since he wanted to shout out. Dizzying arousal and heat sizzled along his skin as he stared down, watching his erection disappear between her lips. Her hand worked the base as she stroked him with her tongue, and he nearly lost his mind.

His whole body was taut, ready to go off, but he held on to his willpower, wanting this to last as long as he could manage. It would be hours before he could hold her again. Still, he couldn't stop himself from sinking his hands into her hair and forcing her to take a little more.

Damn, she was a siren.

"I can be quiet, baby," he promised. "But the truth is I don't care who knows what we're doing. I've got this gorgeous, intelligent lady who comes behind me whenever I make a mistake and fixes things. How do you think she would fix it if I got caught fucking in the china closet in the middle of a work day? I think anyone who sees you would understand."

Her eyes flashed, but he sank deeper into her mouth, letting his head fall back as ecstasy climbed.

This was an excellent way to prevent any further arguments.

He closed his eyes and let himself sink into the moment. In the past, he sometimes worried he'd missed out. He hadn't fucked his way through half the female population like Mad and Gabe. He hadn't seen the world with the same freedom as Dax and Connor. He'd had to be disciplined, keep a tight rein on all of his desires. Sometimes he'd resented his friends for having all the personal freedom he hadn't, but it had been worth every sacrifice in the end because nothing in the world would ever feel as good as this woman now giving all of herself to him.

Just when he thought he couldn't feel any better, Elizabeth reached out and cupped his balls, cradling them in the warmth of her small hand.

Dear god, he couldn't take another second. If she sucked him deep one more time, he wouldn't be able to hold out, and he didn't want to come in her mouth. He wanted to be deep inside her. One with her.

He tugged gently on her hair as he heard the guide saying something about being treated to a Secret Service presence.

"They aren't normally securing the China Room," she said. "They usually stick close to the president, so this is a treat for you."

Elizabeth bit back a laugh as he hauled her upright and set her back on the table, then moved in between her legs. Let the tour group have their fun. It was time for theirs.

"I've got a treat for you." He gripped her luscious ass and started to work his way inside her. It didn't matter how many times he made love to Elizabeth, it always was a revelation. She was always tight and hot and perfect.

She always felt like home.

Elizabeth glanced toward the door, renewed hesitation and anxiety in her eyes.

He wasn't having that. "You keep your attention on me. Nothing else matters except us."

Her eyes softened, taking on that look that never failed to make him feel like he was ten feet tall. "Us."

He thrust in and held tight, fitting their mouths together. He didn't want an inch of distance between them. Instead, he stroked in and out of her with both his cock and his tongue.

Elizabeth wrapped her arms around him. Sure enough, he felt her nails dig in as she started to climb higher. Her breathing picked up, a sweet sound that would haunt him until his dying day.

He held her close as her whole body tensed just before she clamped down around him. Then, nails digging at his back, she gave her pleasure over to him and released.

Then it was his turn. He focused on her alone. It was like this with Elizabeth every single time. Heart chugging, blood pumping, veins sizzling as he climbed… Then he felt the orgasm roll over him, suffusing his body with energy and ecstasy. But in the end it was all about her. In that one moment, he was utterly connected to her. As he poured himself into her body, Zack knew he wasn't alone. As long as he had her, he never would be.

As he bucked into her, he knew damn well the table shook with the power of his thrusts. A breathy moan fell from her mouth, but she was too far gone to care. She moved her hips as though desperate to spend every last second of connection with him.

Moments later, he panted as he slumped against her and remained close for a long, calming moment, listening to the sound of her respiration and heartbeat starting to normalize.

"I don't know. Maybe someone is moving something heavy in that room. Now, if you'll come this way, I'll show you the library. There are some very interesting items to discuss there." The guide's voice started to fade away.

"That was close," Liz murmured, her hands smoothing back his hair.

He kissed her again. "No. Thomas would never have let them in. I promise."

She winced when he withdrew and stepped away. "I'm still trying to get used to the fact that Thomas is standing outside the door."

"He's always outside the door, baby." He tucked himself back into his slacks before she tempted him again. "Now go back to work. Don't you have responsibilities, Ms. Matthews?"

Her eyes narrowed as she hopped down and pulled at her skirt. "You mean besides taking a shower and finding new undies?"

She was so adorable when she was irritated.

He leaned over and kissed her on the bridge of her nose. "You do that. Hey, maybe I should join you."

She pushed at his chest, laughing. "You have an appointment with Roman. I'll see you tonight."

She opened the door, poking her head out.

"The coast is clear, Ms. Matthews. Well, mostly clear," Thomas said.

"What the hell?" Roman. His chief of staff had come looking for him.

Well, it wasn't like he hadn't found Roman in compromising positions before.

"Sorry. Zack and I, um…needed to talk about something private," she stammered. "I'll be in my office if anyone needs me."

Zack watched her practically run away.

"Really, Zack? In the China Room?" Roman braced his hands on his hips as he glared Zack's way. "Is nothing sacred?"

"It's my house."

"It's the people's house."

Zack shrugged. "Well, I'm occupying it, and that means I get to do fun stuff in it. I assure you presidents have had sex in the White House before. Lots of sex. Way more than me."

"Well, you're making up for it now. She forgot something. You might want to grab that or the staff will wonder who's been here." Roman pointed behind him.

A scrap of lace lay on the floor and Zack scooped it up, easing her panties into the pocket of his pants. He grinned, feeling lighter than he had. Perfectly content to go about his business for the rest of the day.

"Thanks for the save." He looked at his chief of staff, who still wore a frown. "So what's shoved up your ass this afternoon, and why hasn't Gus fixed that yet?"

Roman glowered. "I don't know that I like the new Zack."

He shrugged. It was also good to know he could shock his oldest friend from time to time. "Get used to it. Walk with me."

Roman fell into step beside him. "I need to talk to you."

"You always need to talk to me. We work together."

"Zack, I'm serious. I visited the bunker and talked to Mad. He and Sara have found some ties your grandfather had to some interesting people."

And just like that his good mood was blown. "The syndicate?"

Roman pressed his lips together. "You know your grandfather started out in the state senate."

Of course. "He represented Little Odessa in the beginning." It was an area also known as Brighton Beach, a working-class district. But his grandfather's family had decided it would be an easy way to get into state politics since they had Russian ancestors. "That's not a surprise."

"No, but Mad managed to find records of political donations to his campaign."

"God, tell me it wasn't Krylov."

"I wish I could," Roman replied. "Look, it's a whisper right now, nothing more. But it does suggest that they could have been applying this pressure to your family for a very long time. It also explains why your grandfather wanted your father to take that position in Moscow instead of the British post."

He'd told Roman all about the talk he'd had with his father. They'd made careful notes. Not careful enough for his chief of staff, who'd been upset that Zack hadn't come to him first. Roman would be even more upset if he knew he'd already told Elizabeth about the conversation. After he'd made love to her, he'd held her close and let out everything that had happened between himself and his father. He admitted how worried he was. She'd lain her head on his chest and promised she would be with him through anything that came their way.

He'd actually slept that night. It had been such a surprise to open his eyes when the alarm went off and feel so rested.

"Zack, nothing's changed, you know," Roman said quietly. "I hate to be the bad guy here, but we still have no idea if Liz is involved in this mess. She talked to Gus last night about putting off our interview and denying the story."

"Because she's worried about some threats Paul Harding made."

"Or she's gotten new orders."

"Why would she have laid out such a perfect plan for handling the threats against me if she was working with the enemy?" He was getting sick of Roman's constant suspicion. "You agreed to the plan. You thought it was brilliant."

"Yes," Roman agreed. "It was brilliant, and it's also an excellent way to quiet any worries that she might be working against us. How long was she alone with Paul?"

Here they went again. "I have no idea. I only know that what he said upset her."

"Did anyone else see or hear this conversation?"

"Of course not. Paul is too wily to threaten me in front of a group of people. Besides, he was already in her office when she got there."

"He felt comfortable enough to just wander into her office? She doesn't keep it locked? I find that interesting. She's got a lot of sensitive material in there." Roman's voice was a snake inside his head, rattling and slithering.

Elizabeth also had a lot of people come in and out of her office all day because they needed things from inside. She was smart. She wouldn't simply leave sensitive materials out in the open, and she would have her laptop locked down. "I wouldn't want Paul standing around and talking to the press staff. I'm fine with the fact he waited for her. Yes, I hear you. You don't trust her and you wish I would focus on my job. You've made that point abundantly clear, Roman. I'm getting bored by it."

"Do you think I want to disappoint you? I told you I hate being the bad guy, but damn it, you're not some salesman who might lose a couple of bucks if your girlfriend is trying to take your leads. You're the president and the whole country loses if you aren't vigilant."

He turned on his friend. "Do you think I don't know that?"

"I worry that you're distracted, Mr. President."

Anger thrummed through his system, a rage he could barely keep contained. All his life he'd waited for an ounce of fucking happiness. Now that he'd finally managed to find some, Roman was determined to shit all over it. But Zack bit back his attitude. Barely. Instead, he took a long breath and smoothed out his suit, well aware that a hallway wasn't the place to have this argument.

In fact, right now there was no good place to have it out

with Roman. He needed space. "I'll get back to work then."

Roman sighed. "Can we talk? Let's have lunch and discuss this."

So his best friend could drag Elizabeth through the mud some more? "I'll pass. After all, it's been pointed out to me that I don't work enough. I'll see you tonight when we get together with the others."

Roman called out his name, but Zack didn't turn around.

He simply kept walking to his office and never looked back.

Chapter Eleven

Liz stood outside the door to the Red Room and wondered briefly what Jackie Kennedy would have thought about the current connotations of "red room." This particular room of the White House had been decorated in scarlet shades since the Polk administration, and over the years luminaries like Louis Comfort Tiffany had been commissioned to renovate it. The stunning room was picture perfect, all done in crimsons and golds, with classic Empire-style furniture and drapes.

It was also where the women had gathered this evening. Liz hesitated to join them because she wasn't sure she really belonged.

"Is something wrong?" a soft voice asked from behind her. "Please tell me we're not getting kicked out. I've been cooped up in that bunker for a week, and it's driving me crazy. I can't go back yet."

Liz turned to find Sara Bond in the hallway. She looked elegant in her plain sheath with her hair pinned up, despite the fact that she wore very little makeup and the swell of her belly was no longer deniable.

What would it feel like to be pregnant? To be having Zack's child? Would it make her feel closer to him? Or would she simply be more worried about the future of their relationship?

Liz stepped back. "No, I was just thinking I should skip this party and get back to work. Go ahead. I know you ladies have a lot to catch up on."

"If by 'catching up' you mean everyone asking whether or not I've forgiven Mad, then I'm sure we do." Sara brushed back a tuft of hair that had escaped her twist. "Come with me. If you're feeling like you don't belong because your relationship with Zack is new, don't. In a lot of ways, you've been a couple for years. All of us have known you two would get together. It was only a matter of time. If anything, I'm the one who doesn't belong, but I had to get out of that bunker, especially when the guys all descended like well-dressed wolves. Everly escorted me up here since it's after hours and I'm not the one who's supposed to be dead."

The men were gathering down in the bunker so the staff didn't spot Mad. But as Sara pointed out, it wasn't a problem if anyone saw her, so Liz wasn't sure why Gabe's sister hadn't been allowed out of the bunker before now. "Did you ask why you've been locked up?"

Sara waved the question away. "Zack did that for Mad's sake. It's another one of his plots."

Of course. "I'll get you a room outside the bunker."

Sara paused, looking thoughtful for a moment. "Don't. It's been good for us. We're talking again and that will benefit our daughter."

"I'm happy to hear it." Gus approached, bottle of vodka in hand. "Head on in. We won't have long, and I want to make sure we exchange all the necessary information before the boys realize they shouldn't have insisted we stay out of their discussion. We need privacy, ladies, so we're serving ourselves tonight, but Lara is a surprisingly good bartender."

Sara sighed. "I wouldn't know. I'll go find my sad bottle of water."

Gus gave her a grin. "Well, I did have the chef send up food. We've got all kinds of delicious apps and a whole tray of macarons."

"You're a lifesaver, Gus," Sara said, pushing her way through the door.

Gus's grin turned down as she looked at Liz. "Please tell me you're not hesitating to spend time with us. We've been your friends for a long time. I know Everly and Lara are new to the group, but…"

"I'm not a wife or a fiancée. And I'm not pregnant with anyone's baby." In fact, Liz wasn't sure where she and Zack were heading. When they made love, she felt so close to him…but she also sensed some hesitation on his part. Despite being with her—and on her—all the time, he still had some barrier up between them. She couldn't pinpoint why.

"But you will be," Gus said with a congenial pat on the back. "And since you two are constantly getting busy, it probably won't be long before he slips up and gets you pregnant. Come on. Don't you want to know what's going on with the investigation? Trust me, the guys are downstairs right now, examining all the information they've collected, thinking they were so smart for leaving us delicate flowers out of the discussion. But I started planning this the minute I heard Everly was back."

Trust Gus to be one step ahead.

Liz followed her friend through the door because she did have a couple of questions. "Why would they leave us out? Gabe took Everly with him to Moscow, right?"

A nice blaze burned in the gorgeous fireplace and, sure

enough, a hearty buffet had been laid out. Since Liz had skipped dinner, she was grateful Gus had ordered enough for everyone.

At the sound of her name, Everly glanced up from her plate as she sat next to Holland on a couch that had probably been a gift from some past foreign leader. "Oh, he took me along but when it got the slightest bit dangerous, he started arguing that I should stay behind in the hotel room and do 'research.' I won that argument, by the way."

"Those men are downstairs doing what they always do," Holland explained with a wave of her hand. "Getting their stories straight. It's an old habit that needs to die hard."

"They used to do it as a way to stay out of trouble. Well, as much as possible." Sara stood at the buffet, a plate in her hand. "Now they do it in an attempt to keep all of you out of trouble. Their words, not mine."

Lara took the vodka from Gus and started pouring it into a shaker. "I'm used to it. Connor tells me most stuff, but I've decided to be serene about the whole killing thing. You have to love the whole man, and for me that means loving the fact that he's good at assassinations. He's promised me he only kills truly evil people and he uses very kind methods. Do you want a martini?"

Liz felt as if she could surely use one. "Please. Can someone explain how not talking to us keeps us out of trouble?"

Holland shook her head. "It doesn't, but they think it does. I assure you right now Dax assumes I'm on our sofa cuddled up with a book, and when he comes home later tonight, he'll give me whatever version of the truth they've decided on. It could be the actual truth if cooler heads prevail. Who knows?"

"Connor always wants to lay it out there," Everly continued. "Dax usually votes with him. The others …always a guess."

Lara gave her a serene smile. "I trust Connor to keep me in the loop. He takes care of the bad guys in a physical manner while I deal with them intellectually."

Gus poured herself a Scotch. "Lara and Connor have a deal, and she's never broken it. She didn't follow him on his recent jaunt to South America like some of us would have."

Sara sat, settling her plate on the table beside her. "Followed him? Why would you do that? He's a trained operative. And don't try to tell me he was some pencil pusher at Langley. We all knew he was a spy."

"I didn't," Lara said. "Not until someone told me. I was blinded by love."

"I would totally follow Dax," Holland argued. "If he was going into something dangerous and he tried to leave me behind, I would be on his ass in a heartbeat. He's been captaining a ship for years, not hunting down criminals and terrorists. And honestly, he's taken enough bullets that I question his ability. I think he's really the beauty in our relationship."

Everly leaned toward her. "That's what I say about Gabe. When was the last time my husband had to tackle a corporate spy, much less a real one? I did that a couple of months back, though it was more like I tripped over him because he wasn't very coordinated. Anyway, they know the situation we're dealing with is dangerous and they're doing their 'man feelings' circle thing and figuring out how much they risk telling us."

"But we can't go off on our own," Sara argued. "This is exactly why Mad claims he broke up with me and faked his own death. It's ridiculous."

"I agree that it was on the extreme side." Gus sat across from Sara. "But I understand how he thinks. He panicked that night because he's never had to deal with vicious threats, much less actual physical violence. It must have been hard for him. I remember almost losing Roman, and I would have done or said anything to stop it from happening."

"It's not the same," Sara said, then went quiet as she sat back.

"I guess I can't know, huh? I only know how it felt for me." Gus glanced Everly's way. "So what exactly did you and Gabe discover in Moscow?"

"That Russians are tight-lipped," she replied. "We couldn't get anyone to go on record, but we did learn there are several syndicates with close ties to the Kremlin, and yes, the Krylovs are one of them. We met with a member of a rival syndicate, someone higher up who Connor put us in touch with."

Sara's jaw dropped. "Gabe let you meet with a member of the Russian mob?"

Everly shrugged. "He didn't have much of a choice. And Dusan was surprisingly charming. Not once did he pull a gun on me. He's concerned about Krylov getting too much power. Apparently his group is more into oil than natural gas. Stealing it, that is."

"What did he have to say?" Liz took the martini Lara had concocted for her, gripping the cool glass like it was a lifeline.

In a way it was. She couldn't forget Zack's hollow expression when he'd come to her the night before. It still haunted her.

What would you say if I wasn't Zack Hayes?

He had to be. He was. No matter what came from this complicated tangle of political blackmail and espionage, he was exactly who she'd always thought he was.

"Dusan told me and Gabe that he'd asked some of the older men about the incident. None of them actually knew Natalia, but it was no secret the Kremlin often placed women—or men—in the households or hotel rooms of foreign dignitaries as assistants or domestic help. Often, the syndicates procured these people. We already know there's a connection between the Krylovs and Tavia Gordon's foundation, except back then, her mother was running the organization," Everly explained. "Those 'workers' were really captives and sex slaves used to spy or gain blackmail material on the men and women whose households they'd been placed in. Dusan wasn't at all surprised that we believe Frank had an affair with Natalia. Seducing him was likely her mission."

"But did she have a baby by him?" Lara asked.

That was one question they were all desperate to have the answer to.

Everly's lips thinned as though she knew what she had to say would disappoint everyone. "On the few records we were able to locate, the baby's father was listed as Natalia's husband, but who knows the truth? When we tried to track down people who had known her all those years ago to corroborate that possibility, we discovered they'd all died. Mysterious circumstances."

Liz winced. Another damn dead end. That would kill Zack.

"I'm sorry." Everly squeezed her hand. "I know it's maddening, but Dusan says he'll keep digging for us."

Awesome. The future of the country might depend on a Russian mobster.

"Not to add to the problems, but we've had another potential one arise." Liz hoped this was the right forum to talk about her concern. Zack hadn't acted like he cared much. In fact, he'd brushed her worries off entirely. "I'm wondering if we should pull the interview Gus and Roman are supposed to give this weekend because Joy's father showed up yesterday. He wasn't very happy about the way Lara's story made Joy look, and he threatened to fight back in the press."

"Before we get to that, let's talk about Joy." Gus's eyes

slid shut. When she opened them, Liz saw real pain there. "As much as I don't want to, I think we have to start looking objectively at everyone around us, even Joy. We don't have any proof that she was involved in anything, but what other young female family member could have taken Constance from that facility without someone alerting Frank Hayes?"

"But the woman who left with her that night was a blonde, according to the files," Holland argued.

"It's not hard to put on a wig." Gus sighed. "But I can't figure out why she would have procured Constance a rental and a bunch of booze and let the woman's addiction do the rest. I can't think of a single reason Joy would have wanted Constance dead."

Everly shrugged. "Maybe someone paid that nurse at the hospital to say it was a family member, but it wasn't?"

"Maybe." Gus sipped her drink. "We'll never know. But there's also the fact that Joy had decided to work with Tavia's foundation if she became FLOTUS."

"You can't think that makes her guilty of anything. Everyone thought the foundation was a good cause until they were exposed," Sara argued.

"True. And maybe I'm jumping at shadows now," Gus admitted. "Liz, did she ever say anything you found suspicious?"

She'd gone over those conversations a million times in her head. "No, but I have to be honest, I only accompanied Joy to a couple of those meetings with Tavia, and only because I wanted to make sure no one put pressure on Joy. She seemed so fragile most of the time. But I remember her telling me that if she became the First Lady, she wanted to concentrate on women and girls and gaining more opportunities for them."

"I wonder if she had any idea the foundation's mission was to find opportunities for those girls to get trafficked?" Gus mused. "I keep asking myself...if Joy was somehow involved in this mess, why? Why would she do it?"

Holland crossed the room to sit by Gus and take her hand. Of all the people here, those two had been closest to Joy. They'd been sorority sisters together. They'd remained close even after they'd pursued their own careers. "I don't know. And I don't even see how it's possible. I thought I knew her so well. But if—and it's a big if—Joy was a sleeper agent, she would have been well trained, and we met her when we were young and things like treason had never crossed our minds. So we can't blame ourselves for anything we might have missed."

"Still, she may have genuinely cared about you. There are complexities and nuances to every relationship," Liz pointed out.

"But if she was a sleeper, then she probably lied to us," Gus replied. "For years."

"Maybe. About some things." Lara seemed willing to embrace Liz's line of thought. "But then again, maybe this is moot. All the evidence is merely circumstantial. But what are the odds those coincidences mean anything? Joy was born in the States. She wasn't smuggled over from Russia. Why would she work for them?"

"That's a valid question," Gus said. "She didn't need the money, and she'd never done a blackmail-worthy act in her life. I think she was even a virgin when she and Zack married. So if she was a sleeper, she would have been indoctrinated by her parents."

"Paul Harding has always been wily and ambitious, which is another reason to be scared of whatever he's planning. He visits Frank, you know," Liz pointed out. "Regularly."

"Do you think it's possible he's plotting to use Zack's father in some scheme? Or…could they possibly be plotting together?" Gus looked shellshocked by that new and horrifying possibility, kind of like Liz felt. "I know Frank hasn't seemed capable of remembering what year it is for some time, but—"

"What if it's an act?" Liz finished her thought. "I caught him wandering into the Treaty Room recently. Zack likes to use it as his office away from the Oval. What if he's spying on Zack and has been for years?"

"Roman thinks someone is." Gus leapt to her feet and paced. "He won't talk to me about it, and that scares me. All right. We need to be smart about this. Someone needs to figure out if Frank's illness is real, and we damn straight need to know what Paul is up to."

"I'll start tracking Joy's father," Holland said. "I'm going to follow him wherever he goes for the next week or so."

"Excellent." This was what they needed. A plan. "I'll do the same with Frank. Gus and I are here all day long."

Gus sent her a conspiratorial wink. "We can shadow him *and* that head nurse of his. Frank gave us fits and acted up until all the others quit. But this guy seems to have the magic touch. How is that possible?"

Good question. Liz had wondered that herself. If Frank was spying on Zack, he would need someone to be his eyes and ears, someone everyone else would overlook, since Frank wasn't very mobile on his own.

"Connor and I are re-checking the Secret Service agents." Lara crossed her legs in a ladylike pose. "Freddy and I are also tracking some people on the Deep Web. I'll let you guys know if we find anything. Oh, and we discovered that the vice president does, in fact, have some past indiscretions that definitely make him vulnerable to blackmail. Do you remember the stories about his brother having a love child by his mistress years ago?"

"Yes, it showed up in oppo." Opposition research was a nasty but necessary part of life in politics. It referred to a candidate's team investigating the opposition for any nastiness that would help in a campaign. In this case, she'd run the same types of investigations on all of the men and women they'd considered for Zack's under ticket. Wallace Shorn had been clean; his brother...not so much. Ernest Shorn had a second family, one that hadn't included his wife. "But he hasn't been close to his brother in years. We didn't see how that could touch Wallace."

"A deeper dive seems to reveal a different story. Wally paid his 'estranged' brother half a million dollars right before he kicked off his campaign. Did you know that?" Lara asked, proving that despite her ethereal sweetness, she could find the dirt. "Even more digging suggests that Ernest was on a lengthy trip to Europe when the mistress's second child would have been conceived. That kid was only seven pounds when he was born, so there's no way she had an eleven-month pregnancy or something crazy. That most likely makes Ernest a liar."

Liz felt her whole body flush. Son of a bitch. "Wallace, too, it seems."

Lara nodded. "It looks like he's been paying Ernest to shoulder all the responsibility. Why else would he have paid another million and a half dollars since that first payment to a brother he's not even close to? And get this, Ernest is shacking up with the woman now. Left his wife and everything. He and the mistress are living quite well."

All on Wallace's dime because they were likely covering up for the VP. His wife's shoplifting addiction made more sense now, and was the least of Wallace's problems. "Damn it."

Sara eased down beside her and offered her a chicken wing. "Want one? Food makes everything better."

Liz picked it up and wished the spicy chicken could make all their problems go away.

"Eat up," Gus said, shaking off her pensiveness. "The men will sneak up here at some point and probably raid our buffet because none of them were smart enough to cater food. Now, Sara, let's talk about Mad."

The pregnant woman fell quiet.

Even though Gus meant well, Liz felt sorry for her. "I'll get you some dessert."

"Thanks."

Liz rose and fetched her a colorful selection of macaroons. Tonight, Sara had helped her to feel as if she belonged. Everyone had, in fact. Despite all their problems, Liz found herself smiling as she picked up another plate.

* * * *

Mad sat back in the tiny apartment that had somehow become more of a home to him than his elegant Manhattan mansion. Well, he no longer had the classy estate since it had burned down, but he'd never been as comfortable in that place as he was here.

Because of Sara.

The bunker accommodations were crowded now, since Freddy and all his friends had stuffed themselves into the small room. They'd collectively agreed that they couldn't risk him walking around the White House and potentially being seen. Of course, they also thought their wives were safely ensconced at their homes or hotel rooms, rather than a couple of floors above them plotting their own schemes.

How was he the only one who understood these women?

Mad thought about pointing out that Sara wasn't taking a walk or hanging out in the bedroom. But that would be tattling.

"So you trust this Russian mobster, Dusan?" Zack was dressed as casually as he ever did in a dress shirt and slacks, sans tie and suitcoat.

"About as far as I can throw him, but he has plenty of

reasons for not wanting Krylov to grab more power." Gabe relaxed against the back of the sofa between Connor and Dax.

His recent trip to Moscow was the reason for this meeting.

It was hard to believe that they used to get together simply because they were all friends. These days, they didn't talk about sports or work or their hookups. Not anymore. Now, they talked about who was gunning for them.

All in all, Mad would rather talk about basketball. And he wasn't even a fan.

"So we have to hope he'll find something useful." Roman paced the floor, something he'd been doing since he'd walked in a half hour earlier. "I hope you didn't promise him anything we can't deliver."

"I didn't promise you would deliver him anything at all," Gabe replied. "I promised him a hearty discount on a private jet. I was explicit about the fact that Zack would owe him nothing. Like I said, he's got his reasons for agreeing."

Zack nodded briefly before turning Connor's way. "You're absolutely certain you took care of your problem in South America?"

"If I were a surgeon, I would tell you that I cut out every bit of the cancer," Connor assured. "No one is left to come after me and my wife. Consider that you've got an all-clear from me. Now we only have to worry about you and Gabe after Roman survives his scandal."

Dax took a swig from the beer he'd brought down. They only had a sad six-pack to share since Mad had asked them not to bring down a lot of liquor because Sara couldn't drink. "What about Gus? Zack got Liz's sister a lawyer to help with that part of the blackmailer's scheme, but no one is talking about my sister. She's still got that tape out there."

Mad waved him off. "There are, like, ten tapes out

there. She went through a phase." He winced when Roman growled his way. "Sorry. I appear in none of them. By that point I was just a friend."

Glowering, Roman turned to reply to Dax. "Gus doesn't care about the tape. If this asshole wants to release it, she's ready. She says she's lost a couple of those suckers and would like them back, so whoever is behind this is actually doing her a favor."

Thank god for Gus. "So our only remaining worries are for Zack and Gabe. And the fact that I'm alive takes the teeth out of those threats. You're welcome."

"Your living state lets Gabe off for sure, but Zack still looks like he halted a federal investigation to cover your shenanigans," Roman pointed out.

"They weren't shenanigans, Mr. Calder." At least Freddy was willing to stick up for him. "If Mad hadn't done what he did, he would be dead by now. The Russians figured out he was investigating Tavia and her foundation. The beating was merely a warning. But he kept digging, so they planted the bomb to kill him."

At the grim reminder, the rest of the group tensed, every one of them looking his way.

"It was why we picked that day. Well, picked isn't the right word. More like they forced us to act," Mad explained.

"You were trying to tell me." Gabe paled. "That day at the restaurant, you were trying to tell me, and all I did was yell about the way you'd treated Sara. I wouldn't let you get a word in edgewise."

"I wanted to tell you, Gabe. But I couldn't. I just...I wanted to say good-bye. I didn't know what would happen, if I would ever come back, and it felt wrong to not see you one last time." Mad could still remember sitting in that restaurant in the Upper East Side. It had been the place their fathers went. The first time he and Gabe had gone alone, he'd felt like such an adult.

"That's why you left everything behind," Zack said solemnly. "I suppose calling me was the only way you could warn me."

He'd had so little time to figure out a plan—not to decide how to fake his death. Freddy and Matty had helped him work out the protocols and details weeks earlier, just in case. But it had been so surreal, driving to the airport and getting on that plane, knowing there was a bomb on board, and waiting until the right moment to jump, wondering all the while if he'd ever be able to return to the life—and friends—he'd always known.

Walking away when he'd been unable to warn his friends outright had been even tougher. But informing them would have put them all at risk much sooner.

"Yeah," Mad said finally. "I couldn't say more."

"Because you didn't know if I was involved." Zack held up a hand to stop Mad's forthcoming explanation. "Stop. We've discussed this. If I'd been in your place, I probably would have had the same questions. We're good, Mad."

He still hated that he'd questioned one of his oldest friends, that suspicion had ever come between them.

"Well, I'm back now, and once we put all of the grief behind us, we should have a party. A real one. Can we *please* do it up right? Because this, right here?" He gestured around the little room. "It's just sad."

The rest of the guys laughed, but Gabe was obviously still upset.

"I'm fine, man." Mad reassured his friend with a clap on the shoulder.

"No thanks to me," Gabe groused.

"That's not true. After you got your jealous head out of your ass, you took care of the two women in the world who mean the most to me. You made it easier for me to do the job I needed to do. Now let's finish this chat so we can join the women."

"Mad's right," Dax said. "I want to get back to Holland as soon as I can. I'm going to be tailing Paul Harding for days. I have to find a way to cover that up, and it will go over so much better if I spend some time with her first."

He honestly thought Holland was where he'd left her. Foolish man. And Mad would eat his shoes if Holland wasn't already planning her own surveillance.

"Has everyone read the report I sent detailing the dirt Lara dug up on Shorn?" Connor asked.

Roman's face twisted in distaste. Mad was sure his old pal would have worn the same expression if he'd caught his grandmother having sex. "How did that little asshole get two women to sleep with him? I don't even understand that."

"He did come from a lot of money," Zack mused. "That usually helps. But it doesn't matter. If Wallace Shorn lied and he's got a second family stashed away, he's got huge blackmail potential. It gives the Russians a way to shut that pipeline down even if I resign, so that potentially cuts off one of my exit strategies. Freddy, have you verified the other information Lara found?"

Freddy nodded. "Yes, Mr. President. I've managed to confirm everything, including our Russian friend's data. I'm getting into the nitty gritty on your family's connections."

"Check into Joy's family line," Mad requested. "I don't know if she was involved, but after prowling through her life the last few days, something tells me she might have been. I don't think she would have been making her own decisions though. Someone else was probably pulling the strings."

"*If* she was involved, absolutely. Joy wasn't a political animal, but she did insist on that last campaign push through the Midwest. I don't know why. I guess I never will." Roman had gone grim again. "But I have a hard time believing she would plan her own death."

"You haven't met true believers," Connor replied quietly. "Sometimes the brainwashing goes so deep, the operative ceases to care about anything but the mission."

"Or she didn't really understand the mission," Dax suggested. "Maybe she thought she would survive the shooting and the attempt would be enough to sway voters."

"Maybe," Mad allowed, but he'd thought of something else during the long hours he'd spent researching. "Or maybe we saw what they wanted us to see. Are we sure she's dead?"

The idea that Joy could be out there, waiting to show up at the worst possible moment, had haunted him. He knew exactly how easy it was to stage your own demise.

There was a moment of complete silence that made Mad wish he hadn't asked the question.

"She's dead," Zack said. "I assure you of that."

"None of us saw her body after that first night." Connor took up the inquiry. "Zack didn't actually leave his room until the day of the funeral."

Because he'd been so shocked and horrified. Upset. He hadn't gone to his election night party, hadn't delivered a traditional acceptance speech. Zack hadn't celebrated what he'd worked all his life to achieve because he'd been in mourning.

"I saw her." Roman finally stopped pacing. "I saw her body. I sat with her the night before the funeral, after the mortuary had finished prepping her. It was weird. I felt as if I couldn't leave her side. If she played a role in this Russian power grab, the syndicate was done with her. She'd served her purpose. Our correspondence, all her talk of the future...if she was in on the plot, she was damn good at hiding it. Or she was trying to get out."

"She didn't have to try," Zack said. "We had no chance of winning—until she was killed. If we'd lost, our marriage and my political career would have been over. She knew that. And maybe we'll never know if she was involved or what she was thinking before she died. Maybe we're pointing the finger at ghosts because we don't know who else to blame. Mad, you've been reading through her private notes. What do you think?"

"Everything she ever wrote felt well thought out and carefully stated. I can't even find an e-mail where she wasn't polite. She seems far too good to be true, but all my suspicions are just gut instinct," he admitted. "Unlike your current girl. Damn, man. Liz can take a dude down. By the way, is there a reason Freddy is monitoring Liz's mail?"

Zack tensed, but Roman seemed perfectly at ease. "Because she's close to Zack and it's my job to protect him. The order to kill the FAA investigation originated from a computer in her office."

"An office she doesn't keep locked because too many on her staff need access to it," Zack pointed out.

"Even if she did, I could easily get through one of those locks," Connor added.

Roman's expression turned thoughtful. "Liz is horrible with computers. How would she learn to route an e-mail to make it look as if it came from Zack?"

"I don't think she did," Zack said. "But someone wants us to believe that."

"She's got some odd logins," Freddy reported. "I'm looking into them now, but I'm not convinced one way or the other yet."

Freddy was never convinced of anything until it slapped him in the face—unless it was crazy conspiracy theories.

Mad leaned toward Zack. "You're right. It feels like someone wants to put a wall between you and Liz."

"How can they get a wall in there?" Roman teased. "He's always on top of her."

A hint of a smile curled up Zack's lips. "It's the best

way to make sure she stays out of trouble. Now, do we all have our list of questions and marching orders? Because I should go and do my job. I can't leave Elizabeth alone for too long."

Were they all so foolish? "You guys know that the ladies are somewhere in this building, gathered and plotting, right? Everly took Sara to one of the color rooms."

Roman froze. "I should have known Gus wasn't really working late."

Dax stood up with a sigh. "Oh, my sister is working. But if she's taken over a whole room, I bet she catered the thing."

Connor glanced at his phone. "According to my wife, they've set up a whole buffet and found more than a six-pack." When the others turned to stare at him, he shrugged. "What? I can't help it that I'm more modern than the rest of you. Lara and I don't do the sneaking around thing. If I sneak around, she does the same, and she's *so* much trouble. This is precisely why I said we should invite the ladies. Their plotting meetings always have a buffet and a full bar."

"Face it, gentlemen," Gabe said. "We screwed up. Sharing a six-pack doesn't cut it."

"I thought the brew was excellent," Freddy argued.

"Said the guy who lives in a cabin without indoor plumbing." Dax gave him the side-eye.

Everyone else laughed.

"Let's go join our women." Zack held a hand out, shaking Freddy's. "Thank you." He turned to Mad. "And thank you. I'll have Sara bring you down a plate. I'm sorry, but you have to—"

"Stay here so no one in the White House thinks they've seen a ghost. I know. It's fine."

"Hey, I'll hang with you for a while." Gabe sat down again. "Have my lovely wife walk back down with Sara, and make that two plates of whatever Gus ordered. And a bottle of Scotch. I know Gus has one of those."

Mad shook his head. "Gabe, you don't have—"

"I do. You're my best friend." Gabe settled in. "And if you're stuck in a bunker alone, I'll keep you company until Sara returns."

Smiling, Mad offered his best friend the last beer, satisfied that he wasn't alone anymore.

Chapter Twelve

Liz hurried to the elevator of the building she'd lived in since the week after Zack won the election. That time in her life had been such a flurry of activity, including Joy's funeral and the start of Zack's transition to power. At the bottom of her list had been finding a place to live, so when one of her assistants found this unit for lease, it had seemed good enough…mostly because she hadn't had time to look anymore. Now she wished she had searched a little more diligently. The unit and building were serviceable but lacked the amenities she'd been used to in the past. Still, it was close to the White House and within her budget.

Vaguely, she wondered how much longer she would need this place. Her lease was set to renew soon…

Refusing to wonder what the future held for her and Zack now, she pushed the button to call the elevator when her cell buzzed. Smiling, she slid her finger across the screen. "Hey, Gus."

"I just walked into your office and you aren't there. As I happen to know Zack is in a meeting with Roman, you're not underneath him, so how did you escape and can I join you? The interns are making me crazy, Vanessa especially. Can we fire her?"

Vanessa handled way too much for that. She could be touchy at times and they'd had their differences of opinion lately, but she was reliable and one of the most senior assistants in the press office. Vanessa had come on board when Zack had hired her toward the end of the campaign, and she'd saved Liz from drowning. She remained essential to keeping reporters off Liz. "We can't fire everyone who annoys you. We wouldn't have a staff left."

"True." Gus paused, telling Liz that Gus hadn't called to simply chat. "So...I talked to Roman after the party broke up last night."

After listening to her concerns about Paul Harding and the trouble he could cause for Zack, Gus had promised she would discuss the situation with her fiancé and they would decide together whether to move forward with the interview that weekend.

"What's the verdict?"

"Roman is adamant that we move forward. Zack agrees. And I'll be honest, I think we're too far down the road now to take an off-ramp. I know you're worried, but we've got this."

"And if Paul starts giving interviews? You know the things he could say about Zack."

"Of course I do. I'm engaged to a man who believes that not only is the glass half empty, but it's going to explode at any moment," Gus replied. "Trust me. Roman has gone over every terrible scenario Paul could contrive. None of them change the fact we still have to move forward. If Paul publicly implies that Zack was cheating on Joy, we deal with it. Or is the problem that you're afraid this public scrutiny might derail your relationship with Zack?"

That was only one of her worries. "No. What I'm truly

concerned about is that Paul might introduce the idea that Zack had his wife killed. Because think about it. Can Freddy really be the only one who's pieced together all the footage from those rallies?"

Liz hadn't seen Freddy's montage of assassination practices—and she didn't want to. She'd lived through the real thing. But Zack's description had been enough to haunt her.

"If Paul spouts that kind of garbage to the press, we'll handle that, too," Gus replied. "He has no proof because it's not true, so he'll probably come off sounding like a crazy man, and he won't win in the court of public opinion. And if worse comes to worst, we'll bring Paul in for questioning and leak to the press that he has strong Russian ties. I doubt he wants that kind of exposure, especially if he's involved with the syndicate. The truth is, we're playing a game of chess, Liz. This is merely another move in that game. How Paul reacts may tell us whether he's a pawn, a bishop, or a king."

"Okay." She couldn't fight all three of them. She simply had to brace for the worst. "I'll start strategizing how best to prepare the team without letting them know too much."

"The interview isn't for a few days. I've got press all over me, but I can handle it. Roman is struggling, but hey, the added stress is making for some lusty as hell sex. I'm counting it as a win."

Gus was the eternal optimist, but then she firmly believed she could bend the world to her will. Liz was more of a realist. "I'm glad some good is coming out of this mess. I'm heading up to my apartment to grab some fresh clothes. Maybe I should stay here for a while."

Because now that she thought about it, the likeliest scenario was Paul accusing Zack of adultery, and Liz knew the press would assume she'd been his mistress. It could cause a scandal that would hurt Zack both in the polls and in his reelection bid. If she pulled away now, they might change the perception or mitigate some of the damage.

"I don't think Zack will allow that. Get your clothes, then come back here. We'll have happy hour," Gus urged. "You and me. We'll order some pizza and put veggies on it so the guys won't touch it. If they come in, I'll start talking about my period. Vegetables and menses—the perfect combo to send the guys scrambling back to their man caves."

Liz wanted to demur. She really could use some time alone to decompress, but Gus would show up on her doorstep if she didn't return to the White House pronto. Not only that, Zack would have questions, too.

When the guys had emerged from the bunker to invade their party the evening before, she'd kept her distance because Zack had never been big on PDA, even around his friends. She'd been surprised when he'd taken her hand and tugged her onto his lap.

Was she, even subconsciously, putting off this interview because she was worried about their relationship? Did she think she might put Zack in a position to have to choose between her or the White House? They'd certainly been there before.

"I'll be back in about an hour," she promised Gus. "We can strategize then."

"I'll be waiting." From Gus, the promise sounded a little like a threat.

Liz ended the call, then strode onto the elevator, her thoughts already working on the problems ahead. She wasn't sure a good solution existed. This was exactly why pleasure and business didn't mix. She couldn't think logically about Zack. She loved him and had for far too long to pretend otherwise. It would be almost impossible to give him up now.

She would offer to step down, but what good would that do? There was no clear successor to her role. Even Vanessa, though very good, wasn't ready to helm the press office on her own. Chaos was the last thing the administration needed, especially now. In fact, the press was far more likely to speculate aloud if she suddenly stepped down. She would look guilty of something—probably being Zack's squeeze on the side.

The elevator dinged and then opened. Liz marched toward her door, determined to be positive. After all, she was surrounded by some of the smartest people in the world. Collectively, they would find a way out of this. They just needed a bit more time. Once they worked their way out of the blackmail, they would have more breathing room to decide how to proceed. Perhaps if Zack announced that he'd chosen not to run for a second term after all, that might unravel this tangle once and for all.

But Zack didn't want to step down.

As she slid her key into the front door and headed into her place for the first time in a week, she set her purse, phone, and keys on the bar while reviewing her mental checklist of items to pack. Clothes. Her hair supplies because Zack did not believe in conditioner. Did she have any lingerie or had she thrown it all out? She glanced briefly around the small vestibule that led to the living area and the kitchen she'd never once cooked in.

It was a bland apartment. It had come furnished. When she'd signed her lease, that had been a bonus. Now? Nothing about this place felt like home. It never had, despite the fact that she'd been looking forward to having a more permanent base camp after spending most of a decade running campaigns and being on the road.

A vision of a home with Zack floated through her head. He would want to be close to New York, so they would look in Connecticut for someplace with room to breathe, where the press wouldn't be all over them and they could sit together to have their morning coffee and watch the sunrise.

A place where they might raise a couple of kids.

It was way too soon to think about that, so she shoved the images aside and headed for her bedroom.

"Good evening, Ms. Matthews."

She froze, then whirled toward the unexpected voice with a gasp.

Oh my god. She wasn't alone.

A man sat on her sofa, leaning back casually as if he'd simply been waiting for a friend. But that deep Russian accent belied his seemingly relaxed nature and told her he wasn't even her garden-variety burglar or rapist.

Liz's heart revved. Suddenly, she feared she would appear on the news, this time because she was being carried out in a body bag.

"Who are you?" She managed to ask the question in an even tone, which was good because she was completely terrified.

How had this man gotten into her apartment? How long had he been waiting for her?

"Who am I?" The large, muscular man cocked an eyebrow as though pondering a philosophical issue. His dark hair might be graying at the temples, but that didn't make him look any less menacing. In fact, the scar marring his cheek bespoke his life of violence. "That is a very good question. Let us say I am a businessman. You received the package I left for you in London?"

Liz tried not to show her panic. How many steps to the door? Maybe she could run, grab her phone, and scream like hell. Hopefully someone would hear her and call the police. Except this building was notorious for being empty during the day. The whole tenant list was Washington insiders who worked far more than they were ever at home.

"I wouldn't run if I was you," the man said with a sigh.

"You never know who's lurking around these days. It can be very dangerous for a woman such as you. Besides, I am only here to talk. I thought it was long past time I made contact with one of the president's closest...friends. The last one I spoke with, he was not so lovely as you. I promise to treat you better than him."

Oh my god. She was standing in the same room with the man who'd beaten Mad half to death.

"You're Ivan Krylov."

His eyes were dark and serious, a predator studying his prey as he waved off her speculation. "Names, I find, are fairly useless in my business. If I disappear, another will take my place. Institutions, though, are forever. So don't think you can make this problem go away simply by getting rid of me, Ms. Matthews. This has been going on for far longer than you've been alive, and now that we have what we want, we will not let Zachary Hayes go simply because he does not wish to fulfill his destiny."

She felt her hands fist at her sides. She couldn't fight this man, not physically, and that made her feel so damn vulnerable. "It doesn't matter what you have on Zack. He won't do your bidding."

He considered her for a long moment. "That is a shame. I rather thought that would be his stance. That is why I am here, talking to his more reasonable half. Let me give you a history lesson of sorts. A long time ago, there were people—smart people—in the KGB who realized that your democracy was nothing but an illusion. It's a lovely mirage that allows the poor to believe they have some say in their lives while the real people in power manipulate matters for their benefit. Of course, they work quite hard to perpetrate the fantasy that voting is important, that America belongs to every citizen so you should all take care of it. You wouldn't destroy something that belongs to you, correct? It's quite a good scam, I think. If we had thought of this, perhaps we would have no revolution. But these men in Russia saw how tenuous your government's hold truly is and realized all we needed was a way in."

"Zack is not your way in."

"Oh, but he is," Krylov disagreed. "We thought perhaps his father would provide us the access we sought. His grandfather was a loyal man with roots going back to Moscow for generations. They did a good job of integrating here and building fruitful businesses, but he never forgot that he was Russian at heart. His grandfather knew that sometimes these things take time and patience. He built an empire, but his son was too impatient and weak to win the one prize we required."

The presidency. "Frank Hayes was working with you."

Those dark eyes stared through her. "Maybe he was...or maybe it is best to allow our targets to be as authentic as possible until such time as we find the need for them and the right tug on their leash. Until recently, Zachary did not realize there was a leash around his neck, did he? And now he is fighting it."

"He won't give in," Liz swore.

Krylov chuckled sanguinely. "That is why I am here, talking to someone practical. Someone capable of changing his mind. Maddox Crawford turned out to be more resilient than we expected. I suspect, despite his untimely and rather public death, that he is still around and causing me trouble. But you will not prove difficult, will you, pretty lady?"

"You underestimate me." Anger started to crowd out her fear. How dare he think he could come into her home and threaten her?

"But I do not underestimate your love for him. You do not wish to see him removed from office."

"I don't care if he's the president. If he stepped down tomorrow, I would still be by his side." But she also knew Zack wouldn't resign if he thought it would give the syndicate the upper hand they wanted. Still, she had no problems encouraging him to walk away if it meant saving him the stress and worry of being used as a Russian puppet.

"Step down? You misunderstand. This is not the only way to eliminate a problem." The Russian stood. "Ask Joy Hayes."

A chill iced Liz's veins, and she couldn't help but take a step back. "You killed her."

"I said no such thing. I worry, though. That family seems cursed. Death stalks them. So sad... Please let your president know that I will pray for his continued health and that perhaps next time we shall have more pleasant things to discuss. If the kind letter I sent to him in London isn't clear enough and he chooses to view it instead as a to-do list, rather than a friendly bargain, I will be forced to rethink my strategy. Perhaps even end this experiment."

"Kill him?" The question slipped past her numb lips.

"I put him where he is. I can take him out, too. This is the way of the world. I have bosses who want results. If I do not produce them, I will be the one with the future in question. So I must choose between me or President Hayes. And to me, that is no choice at all. I will try to make my point one last time before decisions must be made. The president is close to his friends, is he not? I suspect he is the reason Mr. Crawford has evaded capture for so long. He hasn't hidden the rest of them so well though. Tell him next time, it will not be the brakes that malfunction. It will be a bomb, and perhaps not in her car."

"What do you mean?"

"Your boyfriend will know. If he forces a next time, well, I will do what I have to do. Shut down the pipeline. After that, we shall discuss strengthening relations between our countries. We don't need all these sanctions, do we?"

Liz paled. "He'll never do it."

She already knew Zack would be stubborn.

"Then I will have to take care of the situation. The good news is, I have people in place to do my bidding. I hope the president can say the same. Tell him we are willing to die for our cause…or kill. Good-bye, Ms. Matthews. It was lovely to meet you. I think you will make an excellent First Lady should the president decide he wants to live."

She stepped back, not wanting to even risk touching the man as he sauntered out of her apartment, the door closing behind him with a quiet yet ominous click.

As Liz watched him go, her hands shook. The syndicate was willing to do everything Krylov had threatened. They would kill Zack.

Suddenly, she was right back in that moment when she heard the gun shots and chaos had erupted all around her. Back in that moment she'd realized how fragile they all were.

Liz forced herself to lock the door behind him, to test it and make sure it still worked, though it was obviously flimsy protection at best.

Her phone rang, a trilling sound she'd selected because it was soothing. Now, she jumped at the sound, barely managing to pick it up and swipe across the screen. "Hello?"

"Hey," Gus said, sounding out of breath as though she was on the move. "We might have to postpone happy hour. Holland's car malfunctioned. Weirdly, her brakes quit working. She's okay, but apparently it was a close call."

If she'd needed proof that her unexpected visitor was serious, she'd just gotten it.

Liz sank to her knees and she cried.

* * * *

Zack stripped off his tie and glanced at the clock. What was taking Elizabeth so long?

Roman opened the door to the Treaty Room and stepped inside. "Dax called. Holland's perfectly fine but she's pissed at her mechanic. She swears she took it in for a tune-up a month ago and they said nothing at all about a problem with the brakes."

After she and Dax had moved to DC, Holland bought a classic Mustang. They had been fighting about it ever since. He wanted her driving a car with every possible state-of-the-art safety feature, but she insisted that Mustang was her dream car. "Are they arguing about it again?"

"Dax was pretty spooked, but I bet she'll win in the end." Roman leaned on the desk with a sigh that portended bad news. "We need to talk about something else."

Zack didn't want to talk about anything right now. He wanted Elizabeth here, wanted to spend the evening pretending they were nothing more than an average couple winding down after a long day. But he didn't get to put things off. "What?"

"Shorn caught me a few minutes ago." Roman grimaced. "He wanted to know why he hadn't been invited to the meeting with the energy director about the pipeline."

Zack's stomach took a hard turn. That nonexistent meeting had been the litmus test Roman had devised for Elizabeth. He'd told her the information in confidence, never believing she wouldn't keep the "secret" between them. How the hell had Shorn found out?

Roman stared at him with grave eyes. "I'm sorry. I didn't want to be right about this."

"There could be another explanation."

"Like what? You asked Liz to keep it quiet. Maybe I could understand if Gus had asked me about the meeting, but Wally Shorn? Liz doesn't even like the man, so why would he know about a supposedly secret get-together to discuss the pipeline? Which begs the question, who else knows about it."

There must be some other explanation besides what Roman saw as the obvious. Maybe Liz had mentioned it to Gus, thinking she knew as well... Except Gus thought everything was a secret. For all that she could be mouthy, Gus could also be very tight-lipped. She certainly wouldn't tell the vice president anything she hadn't run past Roman. Of course, he'd thought the same thing of Elizabeth, too.

No. Zack refused to accept that Elizabeth was working with the Russians. It wasn't possible. There was another reason Shorn knew. Maybe she'd slipped and said something to someone in her office. Maybe Shorn was speculating. There had to be some explanation.

"Zack..." Roman began.

Anything Roman would have said was cut off by the door crashing open and Elizabeth rushing in, looking pale and shaken.

Zack stood, worry flaring through him. She did not look like a woman who'd had a casual trip to her old apartment. She looked like she'd seen a ghost. "What happened?"

Gus, who had followed her in, reached out to give Elizabeth a steadying hand. Roman frowned beside him.

"H-he was waiting for me," Elizabeth managed. "Inside my apartment."

Zack's heart threatened to stop. He should never have allowed Elizabeth to leave the safety of the White House without an escort. Hell, he should never have let her go at all. He should have sent someone to gather her things. "Who?"

"Ivan Krylov. A-at least I think so. He was sitting on my couch. I don't know how he got in. The door was locked. I used my key. I..." Her words were spilling out fast, just like her tears.

"Did he touch you? Did he hurt you?"

"No. But the things he said..." She pressed a hand to her chest. "The things he threatened... He told me he would make an example of one of us. This time, he said, it was the brakes, but next time would be a bomb. Is Holland okay? Gus said that her brakes suddenly failed?"

"Her brakes went out because the car is old," Roman said, reaching for his fiancée in spite of his reassurances. "That's what Dax said."

Elizabeth shook her head as she reached for him. "It was Krylov. He told me it was a message for you."

Zack bit back his own panic. He needed to get her calm or he might lose it, too.

He hauled her close, grateful when her arms encircled his neck and she began to relax.

"I'm going to get us some wine," Gus said, holding her fiancé's hand. "Why don't you come and help me?"

Roman frowned. "If there's one thing you don't need help doing, it's finding the liquor. I need to stay and hear everything that happened."

Gus groaned. "You're lucky you're so pretty. Liz already told me what happened, and I'll tell you while we let them have a moment alone."

"I would appreciate it." Zack pressed Elizabeth even closer, feeling a fine tremble wind through her body.

Roman let Gus lead him out.

He tilted Elizabeth's head up and smoothed back her hair. "Tell me everything that happened."

She nodded and seemed to calm. "I went to my apartment like I told you."

"Like you texted me," he corrected. If she'd faced him and said she'd planned to go home alone, he would never have allowed that. And he worried she was well aware of that. He would have sent a Secret Service agent with her, one of Thomas's trusted men. Was that the reason she'd texted him in the first place?

She ignored him and continued. "I went to my apartment and used the key to unlock the door and he was sitting there on my couch."

"Ivan Krylov, the head of the Krylov syndicate, was just hanging out?"

"I think it was him. He wouldn't say his name. I guessed, but he neither confirmed nor denied."

It didn't matter. She could ID him from a picture. They had a good-sized file on the head of the syndicate.

God, she'd walked into someplace she should have been safe and found herself alone with a killer. "Did he hurt you?"

She shook her head. "No. He just talked to me. Zack, he said a lot of nasty things, but the most important thing he said was that if you don't stop the pipeline, he's going to assassinate you, just like Freddy and Mad suspected."

She clung to him as she started to tell him everything.

And Zack held her, trying not to think about the fact that this was the second time she'd been the one to bring him the syndicate's message.

Chapter Thirteen

Zack's head was still reeling three hours later when all the guys, with the exception of Dax and Mad, crowded into the Treaty Room. Gus had taken the ladies out to visit Holland, though Dax's wife swore she was perfectly fine. Captain Awesome—a nickname that still got a grin out of Zack—had Holland on bedrest and was watching over her like a hawk.

"Have we heard anything from the mechanic?" Roman paced like a frustrated tiger.

"Yes." Connor sat at the desk, making notes. He'd either been on the phone or focused on his laptop for hours. "Someone fucked with her brakes. The guy spoke in technical terms I won't bore everyone with, but it definitely wasn't an accident."

Zack bit back nausea. They could have lost Holland. The danger had been real for quite some time, but it hit him again that someone was truly trying to hurt him—and they were willing to use his friends to do it.

Would one of them die because of him?

Roman cursed. "Tomorrow, we'll talk to Holland and find out where her car has been and who might have had access to it."

"I'm not sure it matters. According to Elizabeth, next time Krylov will use a bomb." Zack pushed aside his dark thoughts and tried to concentrate on the investigation. "Do we know anything useful about him or his whereabouts?"

"Krylov is definitely in the States," Connor confirmed. "I called a contact I still have at the Agency and they say he's been in the US for two weeks, but according to them he's been taking meetings in New York."

That meant nothing. It was easy to get to DC from the city. It wouldn't be hard at all for Krylov to hop on a train or even to drive down.

"How did he know when Liz would be home? After all, she hadn't been there for a while." Gabe asked. "Does he have ESP? Had he been sitting in her living room for days?"

Or had Elizabeth simply called him?

"He couldn't have waited for long." Connor turned the laptop in front of him, flashing surveillance pictures. "He was seen in Manhattan yesterday. The FBI had a couple of agents tracking him, but if he's in DC, then they lost him sometime between now and then. According to the agents, he's been in his hotel room all day, which they admitted they found odd. From what they say, he's very social when he's in the city."

"Or he's still in New York and Liz is lying to us." Roman always had to play devil's advocate. It was his calling in life.

"Why would she lie?" Gabe was the naïve one. He'd played corporate games for years, but those never had stakes as high as world domination.

"Because she's working with Krylov," Connor said. "Or at least that's what's going through Roman's head. And if it's going through Roman's, it's going to infect Zack's thoughts if it already hasn't."

Infect might not be the right word, but Zack was certainly being forced to consider the possibility that his beloved Elizabeth was a traitor. "What did you find out about the security at her apartment building?"

"The CCTV only covers the exterior entrances, front and back," Gabe explained. "The manager let me see today's footage. No Krylov or anyone who looks like him. But this guy is smart, right? Hasn't he been eluding the authorities and their surveillance for decades? Certainly, he could manage to avoid some rudimentary building cameras."

Obviously, Gabe was Team Elizabeth.

Zack frowned. "Did you show the manager Krylov's picture?"

Gabe's tight jaw told him the answer even before he said the words. "He said he'd never seen the man before. But again, that doesn't mean Krylov didn't find another way in. It also doesn't mean the manager remembered or that he's telling me the truth."

"Why would Krylov flash his mug all over Manhattan but avoid the cameras in DC?" Roman asked. "Why would he treat a visit to Liz's building differently than any other meeting?"

"Because he wants to fracture us," Connor supplied. "It's what I would do if I were running this op. If he's able to split Zack off from his closest allies, it leaves the president—his target—vulnerable. In Krylov's shoes, I wouldn't go straight after Roman, but I would have studied Zack's inner circle thoroughly, certainly well enough to know that Roman questions everything. So my goal would be to make Roman believe the woman Zack cares about is duplicitous. It's the most likely thing to cause trouble between the two of you."

"It's my damn job to question everything." Roman

glared Connor's way. "It's always been the way I protect us. Do you think I enjoy being the damn Eeyore of the group? Mad and Gabe were the partiers. Dax and Connor were always thinking about freaking sports, and Zack had a future. I had to be the one who watched our backs when it came to stuff like this."

"All I'm saying is, if I were Krylov, I would know that," Connor replied.

"Let me get this straight." Zack took charge of the meeting so it didn't drag on for hours. "Elizabeth told me Krylov was in her apartment this evening, but we have no proof. If he didn't waltz in through the front or back entrance, how would he have gotten into the building? And do we have any proof that he forced his way into Elizabeth's unit?"

"I didn't find anything to indicate that he'd picked the lock," Connor admitted. "Usually that kind of thing leaves trace evidence behind, but it also wouldn't be terribly hard to steal a key. The manager has a master, I'm sure. I would have gone after that."

"That doesn't change the fact that no one at all saw him," Roman maintained.

"Do we have any reason to think Freddy might have some Dark Web, back-door connection that could provide additional information?" Zack felt like he was grasping at straws.

Connor shook his head. "He's really been an asset to me in reverifying all the White House staffers and Secret Service agents. And with all due respect, that's more important than checking up on your girl's story right now. Liz's guilt…it's just a theory."

"It's a well thought-out suspicion," Roman corrected. "Don't you also think it's interesting that the two times the syndicate has directly sent a message to us, they've used Liz Matthews?"

That fact had been tormenting Zack for hours. "According to Elizabeth, the syndicate is merely a go-between for a faction of the Russian government. SVR runs the show now, but this plot was hatched by a bunch of KGB men back in my grandfather's day. They've been biding their time until they could get a Hayes in the White House."

Roman sighed. "And why would he have told her that? Why explain his whole plan to Liz? And not one of us?"

Zack knew the answer to that question. "Because I would tell any one of you to suck it up and stop worrying. I can't do that with her when she's afraid for me. That man terrorized her."

"Or she's incredibly smart and she's using your relationship to manipulate you into doing exactly what they want," Roman pointed out.

"What is that?" Gabe asked.

"She wants me to cancel the interview Roman and Gus were going to give about Roman's 'relationship' with Joy." And since Krylov's visit, Elizabeth had more ideas about how he should call off the dogs. "In fact, she wants me to deny the story altogether. She also asked me to put off any decision about the pipeline unless I'm willing to scrap the whole thing."

Actually, she'd pleaded tearfully with him, swearing that if he didn't do what Krylov wanted, the syndicate would kill Zack the same way they had Joy. She'd looked terrified. He'd had to hold her until she finally calmed.

Around Zack, the room had gone quiet, each of them seemingly lost in thought.

Was it possible Elizabeth was a Russian agent? God, he was an idiot. It wasn't merely possible; it was the explanation that made the most sense. He'd been trained all his life to think logically, to rationalize his way through a situation and come to the most reasonable conclusion. Now, he had to stop being a man, start being a president, and look at the hard facts.

One, Elizabeth had worked closely with Joy. In fact, Joy and her father had encouraged him to hire Elizabeth.

Two, the order to call off the FAA investigation had come from the press office, which Elizabeth ran.

Three, the initial blackmail threat had been delivered to Elizabeth's room in London, and the threat against her had neither been directed her way nor difficult to deal with.

Four, he'd given her—and her alone—information about the fake "secret" meeting that had somehow leaked out.

Five, now that they had found a way to minimize the threat of blackmail, Krylov had an unverifiable chat with Elizabeth—and no one else—and he magically said the perfect words to make her beg Zack to put himself and his presidency in a corner.

Damn it, if he denied the story about Joy and Roman he'd planted, not only would he look like a fool when the Russians released the evidence, he would be vulnerable to them again. They would continue to maneuver the situation in unpredictable ways to forward their game. Could they somehow manipulate matters to ensure Mad couldn't emerge from hiding, leaving both Zack and Gabe in the crosshairs?

Zack didn't doubt they had a solid-as-hell plan. He was tired of running blind, always two paces behind.

Of course he'd thought they had a good strategy themselves. But the moment he'd made a move, they had plunked the queen squarely in front of him. *His* queen. They were neatly forcing him into an untenable position, one he couldn't get out of without hurting her or someone he loved dying.

They'd been playing this decades-long game so cleverly. They'd placed Joy at his side. But when she'd been unable to manipulate him as needed because he'd never felt true passion for her, why wouldn't they have tried again with a different type of woman? After all, when they'd expended Joy to put him in the White House, they'd still had a woman on the inside, one poised to manipulate the president of the United States.

In Elizabeth, they might have found the perfect Mata Hari.

Or the Russians had another agent in place and were manipulating the situation to make her look like a major player, not the innocent pawn she was.

Zack's heart told him one thing. But logic told him which possibility was more likely.

"What do you want me to do?" Roman's voice cut through the silence.

"We should look deeper into Elizabeth's background." The words made him sick, but he forced himself to say them.

Connor's eyes went stony. "If that's what it takes."

He had to be the president now or his friends could lose their lives, wives, and futures. He didn't get to go to Elizabeth and plead for her love, beg her to tell him the truth and not be a traitor. He had to play the Russians' game the dirty way.

Zack stood. "It does. And Connor, I expect you to be thorough. And don't breathe a word of this to Lara."

"Oh, I won't tell my wife a thing because she would have my hide." Connor closed his laptop. "I'll head over to Dax's. I want to check on him and Holland. Then I'll get to work on trying to figure out if Liz is some kind of Russian plant."

But he sounded skeptical.

"I'm serious, Connor," Zack insisted. This was too important to simply let go.

"I will do my job, Mr. President," Connor vowed in a chilly tone.

"I'll head over with you." Gabe crossed the room to stand beside Connor, his keys in hand. "I'll drive. I need to pick up my wife." He turned to Zack. "Should I take Liz with us or are you going to send her back to her apartment?"

"Why would I do that?" He raised a brow.

Zack had zero intention of letting Elizabeth out of his sight. She always managed to find trouble when she was on her own. He couldn't allow her to cause more. And if he was wrong about her… Well, he had no intention of letting her get away.

More than once, Zack had asked himself what he would do if she proved to be a turncoat. He didn't have an answer. He wasn't sure he could ever turn her in and allow her to be taken away to a maximum-security federal penitentiary where he would never see her again. First, the scandal would be too great. Second…he didn't want to live without her. No, better to deal with her in his own way, and he couldn't do that if he put distance between them now.

"Earth to Zack?" Gabe called.

Zack zipped a sharp stare to his old friend. "Elizabeth will stay right where she's supposed to be. Nothing changes. We can't give anyone who's watching us the idea that anything is wrong. It's best to let them think that their plan is working."

"And you're not even going to ask Liz for her side of the story? I think that's a mistake," Gabe said.

"Have you thought about the fact that if I'm wrong, someone dies?" Zack asked. "I know you're all looking at me and Roman, thinking we're monsters for even questioning a woman we've always considered a friend. Hell, she's far more to me, and you know it. Unlike the rest of you, I can count the women I've slept with on one hand. When I was younger, I didn't get to be reckless or wild. I've always had to be careful. I'm not going to change at a moment when my mistakes could cost the people I love their lives, and that includes her. If she's involved, she could get hurt. If she's not, then she could suffer in an entirely different way. So judge me if you like, walk out of here and tell yourself I'm a cold asshole, but I'm going to find out everything I can so I'll have all the data possible before I decide how to proceed."

Connor held out a hand. "I'm sorry, Zack. I'll get you everything you need. We all care about her, but you know we've got your back."

"We do." Gabe joined Connor. "We'll back whatever play you come up with. I'll make sure Liz and Gus have an escort home."

They left, and Zack let out a long breath. At least his friends didn't hate him.

"It's going to be okay," Roman assured. "Go and sit for a while. I'll wait for the women."

Roman always knew when he needed time and space to decompress. "Thanks."

He walked out of the room and was immediately followed by a Secret Service agent Thomas trusted. Zack hurried to the residence because he needed quiet and silence. Solitude. So he could think…and worry.

God, he hoped he didn't have to mourn, too.

* * * *

Liz nodded at the Secret Service agent who stood outside the doorway to the residence and realized how happy she was to have him there. After the day she'd had, an armed guard no longer seemed like an inconvenience or a reminder that privacy was an illusion. It was a reassurance that Russian assholes wouldn't be lying in wait.

"Good evening, Ms. Matthews," he said, opening the door for her. "The president is waiting for you. I hope your evening was a pleasant one."

"Thank you." She didn't respond about her dreadful, futile evening. It wasn't as if she could dump everything on him.

Once she'd fled her apartment, she realized that she hadn't even retrieved her clothes. Instead, she'd grabbed all the personal belongings she'd set on the counter when she'd walked in, summoned a car, and headed around the corner to a busy coffee shop, where she could at least tell herself she had safety in numbers, to wait. Between there and the White House, she'd called Gus and told her about the entire encounter. Gus had listened, aghast. Then she'd suggested they send a couple of interns over to Liz's to get her clothes. But that seemed like a bad idea on a couple of fronts.

And Liz certainly never wanted to walk into that apartment again.

She sighed as the door closed behind her and she set her purse on the entry table beside Zack's wallet. He didn't have to carry one, but he liked to. Force of habit. He often talked about how he missed normal things, like having a set of keys in his pocket. He didn't drive anymore, but one day, they would do everyday things others took for granted again and it would be wonderful.

But Liz couldn't think about cars right now, not after what had happened to Holland tonight. Her friend was a bit sore but thankfully fine, though she'd declared Dax was being overly protective. The woman was far more worried about her car than hearing about the grimmer outcomes that had been possible.

Holland could have died.

Next time, the Russians would plant a bomb.

Next time, they might be targeting Zack.

The thought made her tremble, but she was determined to not break down again tonight. She'd done enough of that this afternoon.

Liz walked through the living room, back to their

bedroom. Zack hadn't been waiting with Roman, so she'd known he would retreat here. This was the only place where he could be alone, even if the solitude was mostly an illusion. Roman had said Zack had wanted some space, but she knew what he needed—someone to take care of him, to remind him that everything around him wasn't horrible.

He needed her. And god knew she needed him, too.

Liz found the bedroom empty, but she saw his suitcoat draped over the back of a chair. She picked it up and hung it in the closet, the sense of intimacy so sweet it brought tears to her eyes. This was what she'd wanted for years—to be close to him, to have a life with him. They couldn't lose that now, not when they seemed so close to having everything they'd dreamed of.

The sound of running water drifted from the bathroom, and she smelled Zack's soap. The sandalwood scent clung to Zack, and she loved the way it smelled on him.

The evening so far had been spent on worrying about the future, but they had tonight.

Liz stripped out of her clothes. After their rough day, being together would at least ensure it ended well. Having Zack working over her, stroking himself deep inside her, then wrapping his arms around her while they slept, would remind them of everything they were fighting for.

Tomorrow they would get up and again start fighting the mess that would still be waiting, but for these few hours before dawn, they could sink into each other and tune out the rest of the world entirely.

She walked into the bathroom, the steam from his shower caressing her skin. Making love tonight would be an act of intimacy, but also one of defiance. While she'd sat in Dax and Holland's living room, she'd thought about how she'd handled things this afternoon—without utter panic. She still believed they needed to back away from the Joy and Roman story, along with the pipeline, until they could collectively devise a better plan. But she hated the fact that she'd broken down. Zack needed her to be strong, to be by his side. Instead, she'd taken strength from him.

She stepped toward the natural stone shower and simply watched him for a sublime moment. He was the single most beautiful man she'd ever seen. No matter how many times she saw him naked, he still took her breath away. But this time seeing him also hurt her heart because his head was down, one strong arm braced against the shower wall as if he needed the support to hold him up. He had so much weight on his shoulders, and he couldn't give it to anyone else. The burden was his to bear, and he obviously felt every ounce of it tonight.

If she could take his mind off his troubles for even a second, she would do anything.

"Hey. Want some company?" She spoke in soft, low tones, not wanting to startle him.

He looked over his shoulder, eyes fastening on her. For a moment he stared, that hungry, predatory part of himself he always tried to hide more than visible in the way he watched her. It made her feel like prey, but the best kind, the loved kind. Her body heated in anticipation, and she could already feel her nipples hardening under his gaze.

Their lovemaking would be rough and fast. He would reach out for her and she wouldn't have another second to think. His mouth would fasten on hers as he pressed her against the wall of the shower. He wouldn't say a word. He would let his cock speak for him and give her what she needed. She was ready. In fact, she was always ready for him.

Then he blinked, and his expression disappeared, replaced with something polite and blank she often saw in meetings when he was listening to politicians complain. He stood upright and stepped out of the shower, leaving it on while he reached for a towel.

"I'm done. It's all yours." He wrapped the terrycloth around his waist and strode to the closet.

Liz stared after him, embarrassment flooding her system. "Zack, what's wrong?"

He didn't look up, merely dried himself off with short jerks over his body. "The list is long and varied."

A second before she'd felt perfectly happy in nothing but her own skin. Now she reached for a robe, wanting to cover up as quickly as possible. She wasn't going to hop in that shower by herself like nothing was happening. Maybe she'd read him wrong and he didn't need sex tonight. "Do you want to talk about it?"

He dropped the towel and started toward the bedroom without a backward glance. "I want to sleep, Elizabeth. I want to rest. I don't know if you remember this, but I have a job and it can be stressful."

Wow. She was surprised at how much his cold sarcasm hurt. She wasn't some delicate flower who wilted at the first sign of anger, but Zack was supposed to be her sanctuary.

What had happened between the time he'd held her while she cried and now?

Did he blame her? Was this a case of wanting to shoot the messenger for the news she'd carried?

She turned off the shower and followed him out. He didn't bother with pajamas. He stalked through the bedroom leaving every inch of his body on display. He pulled back the covers and climbed into bed, reaching up and turning off the lamp without looking her way.

Silvery moonlight illuminated the room, giving the whole world a ghostly glow. It might have been better to be plunged into darkness rather than see the dismissive way Zack turned over, giving her his back.

The silence between them felt overwhelming.

"Are you getting into bed or staying up for a while?" Zack didn't turn to regard her. "If you need to work, make sure you close the door behind you. I have an early morning meeting I'd like to be rested for."

She wanted to talk, needed to ask him what had gone wrong, but she'd been around Zack long enough to know what that flat tone meant. He was done and nothing would move him. He would talk when he wanted to, and all she would do was start a fight.

Maybe they both needed some space.

"I'll go back to my place for the night." But as she said the words, she knew she couldn't.

He sat up, and even in the dim light she could see his eyes narrow on her. "Where the Russian mobster visited you? You want to sleep in a place you know isn't safe?"

"You're right. I'll go to a hotel or stay with Gus. I don't want to bother you. I'll probably toss and turn all night and like you said, you need your sleep."

"If you leave, you'll take an escort," he insisted. "Do you want me to wake one of the Secret Service agents and let him know he'll have to stand outside of wherever it is you choose to sleep?"

"No. I'll find one of the other bedrooms around here. I don't need an agent standing outside the door if I stay close." She wasn't getting into bed with a man who obviously didn't want her there.

"What is this about?" he asked with a lengthy sigh that let her know he wasn't pleased with the conversation.

"I'm not stupid, Zack. I can read your body language, and I certainly know that tone you're using. I'm trying to be respectful because I know you're having a rough day, but I'm not a doormat. You made it clear you want to sleep and you don't want company. I'll go."

"I never said I wanted to kick you out of our bedroom."

"It's not *our* bedroom," she reminded. "It's yours and you have the right to have whoever you would like stay here."

He cursed under his breath. "I didn't want sex in the shower. That's all. I've got a lot on my mind."

She tried to calm the sinking feeling in her gut that something more was going on. "Then you could have told me that instead of giving me the cold shoulder."

"Please come to bed, Elizabeth."

She stood still for a moment, unsure what she should do. The last thing they needed tonight was a fight.

"I'm sorry I was irritated," he continued. "Will you please come to bed? I won't sleep well without you."

The words were sweet, but she still didn't like the way he said them. They weren't rude or snarky. But they weren't inviting or warm, either. It was as if he was forcing himself to say something he knew she wanted to hear.

Still, it had been a terrible day, and her leaving to sleep in another room wouldn't solve anything. In fact, it might only make this unexpected crack between them become something more like a rift.

"Fine. I'll get ready."

She made her way to the bathroom and forced herself to go through the motions of preparing for bed. Her mind whirled, crafting a million different excuses for his behavior. Zack was normally very thoughtful. She didn't usually get treated to the cold bastard part of the man, but it was inevitable that he would be in a funk and she would get the downdraft of it at some point. Maybe she shouldn't take it personally.

This was what it meant to be truly intimate with someone. She would put up with his crappy moods from time to time, just like he would deal with hers. This particular snit had come at a bad time, but he'd apologized. She had to accept that. If she walked back into the bedroom and fought with him, she would do nothing but pile on to their problems.

Besides, they would only sleep tonight. That much was

for sure. He was obviously not in the mood. Well, thanks to him, neither was she.

Liz stepped lightly back into the bedroom to find him sitting up in bed, his gaze steady on her. He pulled back the covers. Grateful that she'd put on pajamas, she dropped her robe and slid in beside him.

Despite his sour mood, she would still feel better sleeping next to him.

So why when he wrapped his arms around her and drew her close did his arms suddenly feel like a cage?

Chapter Fourteen

Sara glanced at the clock beside the bed. Almost midnight. She wasn't getting to sleep any time soon. Her brain simply would not shut down. She couldn't stop worrying about everything that had happened in the last few days.

And she couldn't stop thinking about Mad.

Sighing, she set her book on the nightstand because she'd spent the last hour staring at the page, unable to absorb the words in front of her.

It was time to face a few hard facts: Ivan Krylov was real and dangerous. It still shocked Sara that he'd been in Liz's apartment, terrifying the holy hell out of her, mere hours ago. The same Ivan Krylov who'd been in Mad's home the night before he'd broken up with her. After a simple chat with the Russian mobster, Liz had been ready to call off all her plans.

Rather like Maddox had done after being beaten nearly to death.

It wasn't that she hadn't believed him. She'd known full well that some Russian baddie wanted to use Zack and was willing to hurt any or all of his friends to do it. But she'd seen Liz's trembling, pale reaction to the fact this killer had broken into her apartment and tossed around nasty threats. Even normally unruffled Holland seemed a bit more shaken after her near brush with death than she wanted to let on.

What had Krylov's savage confrontation been like for Mad?

The glow from under her bedroom door let her know she wasn't the only one not sleeping.

How much longer would she wait to really hear the man she'd once claimed to love? She'd cut him off when he'd tried to tell her his story. Of course she'd listened to the basics, assuming she needed nothing more to comprehend the incident so she could logically and calmly pass judgment and decide that he should have been able to do the same.

But she'd behaved as though the visceral truth didn't matter, as though her love for Mad somehow entitled him to less of her understanding, not more.

They were going through something horrific. After today, the danger seemed so much more real. Sara fully grasped now that someone had been targeting Zack Hayes since birth, maneuvering him into place, then using his friends to bend him to their will. Mad had merely been one of those chess pieces.

How had Mad's beating at Krylov's hands felt? Painful, yes. But what had it been like for Mad, who had always been larger than life, to have suddenly felt so helpless?

She needed to know.

Sara rose and wrapped her robe around her. A quick glance in the mirror made her wince. She should probably wait until morning to see him. She wouldn't look so tired then. But need won out over vanity. It didn't matter if Mad saw her without makeup. He'd seen her bare face before.

Besides, they should have this conversation without any artifice between them.

She eased the door open and glanced to the couch, but he wasn't there. The sheets and blankets he carefully folded up each morning hadn't been spread over the cushions to prepare for his night's sleep. They were still in a neat pile. Mad sat at the kitchen table, frowning at his laptop.

"Still at it?" she murmured softly.

He glanced her way and stood, as though he couldn't stay seated while she was in the room. "Hey, yeah. I thought I'd go over a few things again, see if there's anything I missed. But I've studied everything about Frank's time at the embassy. Connor managed to find every paper the man ever signed, all the way down to toilet paper requisitions. It's the most boring crap I've ever read. I definitely don't see any smoking guns." He scoffed. "Why are you up? Are you hungry? I could make you a sandwich. Or some tea."

That seemed to be Mad's mission in life now, taking care of her. He'd done nothing but wait on her hand and foot since they'd gotten stuck here together.

When they'd first arrived, she'd been convinced he would annoy her. Instead, she'd rapidly grown to depend on having him near. He was an oddly peaceful presence. Every now and then the old Mad would emerge, with his frenetic energy and audacious humor. But he seemed more thoughtful now, as though some piece of Mad that had always been agitated was now at rest. She'd fallen for the old Mad...but she liked the new one even more. "I would rather you talk to me."

His face fell. "Sara, please give us more time. I know that—"

"Tell me what happened the night Ivan Krylov came to see you."

His brow furrowed as he made his way to the living room. "I've told you what happened. There's nothing more to say."

She sat and studied Mad. He looked tired, and she wondered what sleeping on this couch had cost him. "Help me truly understand what it was like for you that night. Walk me through everything so I grasp what made you think you had to take the drastic action you did."

He sank down on the opposite end of the couch, the tension in his body telling her how wary this conversation made him. "I've explained why."

Did he think she would use his words to build her walls even higher? What had she done to him in the last few days? They'd been companionable, but she knew she hadn't exactly been warm or understanding, even when he'd done everything possible to make her comfortable.

"You told me the facts. You didn't really tell me how you felt."

His jaw went tight. "I felt like I was going to die."

Maybe she needed to give him something first. She hadn't been easy on him, after all. She'd avoided talking about anything personal in a futile effort to contain her own feelings. Her aloofness hadn't exactly inspired him to open up.

"When I got your text, I was in my bedroom looking at myself in the mirror, trying to assure myself no one would be able to tell that I was pregnant." She bit her lip. "I thought maybe you would ask me to marry you that night. I was hoping, anyway."

He hesitated, his stony gaze fastened on the wall. "I was. I had the ring and a plan."

Her heart caught. "I didn't want you to ask me because you thought you had to."

Then again, what would have happened if he'd asked her sooner? If she'd had a ring on her finger and they'd already told all their friends and the tabloids had known, what would have become of her when Krylov came calling?

Mad chuckled, though there wasn't a lot of amusement to the sound. "I wanted to ask a lot sooner, but I honestly didn't think you would say yes before you got pregnant. The day you told me the test was positive, I kind of felt like I'd won the lottery."

How could he think that? Once they'd gotten together, her whole world had revolved around him. "But we were dating. We were exclusive."

He turned to her with a cynical glance. "We were fucking, Sara. I know when a woman is using me for sex, and in the beginning that's what it was."

Had it been? "I was always attracted to you. From the time my hormones kicked in, you were the be-all, end-all of men for me. I dated guys who looked like you. My mother joked that I had a type, but you were always the benchmark. So when I took the job at Crawford, I decided that if the opportunity arose, I would sleep with you. I intended to prove to myself that you couldn't be as good as I dreamed. Then I hoped I would actually be able to have a real relationship with a man."

"I turned out to be pretty damn good, huh? I'd had a lot of practice by then. You should have taken me on in the early days. I would have been easy to walk away from then."

There was the Mad she knew, the real self-deprecating human with the easy humor behind the gorgeous mask. "Somehow I doubt that, but yes, you turned out to be spectacular. That first night with you was a revelation. Finally, I knew what I'd been missing. I meant to tell you the next morning that we couldn't do it again. I was worried about my career. No, I was worried about you breaking my heart."

"I know. But I was smarter and I kissed you before you could say a word." His eyes lit with a warm intimacy as he remembered. "I suspected what was going through your head and I knew if I could get you underneath me again, you wouldn't be able to dismiss me so easily."

"That weekend turned into something meaningful." They'd been at a conference and they'd hooked up the night before they were supposed to fly back to New York. She'd thought she was so smart, that she could fuck him out of her system, then go home and get on with her life. Thanks to Mad's persistence and a freak storm, they'd stayed in bed for another two days, putting off travel in favor of exploring the intimacy between them.

"It meant the world to me."

She believed him. "I should never have accepted those texts from you at face value. I should have marched to your place that night and demanded to know what was going on. I was afraid. I was weak."

"No, baby. You weren't weak. I knew exactly what I needed to say to keep you at arm's length so I could protect you. Everything I said was designed to cause maximum damage. I hated being so vicious and cruel, but I was…panicked. I couldn't have you anywhere near me."

Now they were getting somewhere. "You were scared. Mad, tell me why. Exactly why."

He was quiet for a moment, and she almost called back her words. Did she really need him to rehash what must have been the worst moment of his life?

"At first I thought Krylov and his cohort would simply talk to me, threaten me." He couldn't seem to look directly at her as the words spilled from his mouth. "I thought I could bargain with them. After all, I made deals all the time."

"Why didn't you run?"

"Where? They confronted me in the back of my car, then took me into my house. They'd done their homework. They knew there was a good chance I would be alone. But I still thought I could worm out of whatever they intended…until they handcuffed me. Then I knew there was no way out. And I never imagined what they would do to me."

She swallowed, afraid for him. "Mad, you don't have to go on."

"No, you should know, but I have to warn you, I don't come out of this story looking so great." He clasped his hands in front of him and focused there. "Krylov talked a lot. I wish I remembered even half of what he said. Some of it might have been helpful, but the whole time he spoke, his 'friend' worked me over. That guy was a consummate professional; he didn't touch my face. Krylov told me I needed to be able to go out and be seen, pretend like everything was normal. The rest of me was fair game though."

"Oh my god."

He swallowed. "You think you understand pain, but you can't really until it becomes your whole world, until you can't see anything past it. That's when you realize how fragile you are, how delicate life is. It's startling when all sense of security is stripped in an instant, and you can't escape the fact that you're helpless to do anything except wait and see if you survive."

She closed the space between them, laying her hand over his. "Mad, I'm so sorry. I hate that it happened to you."

"They beat me for what felt like hours and hours. Krylov talked about what he would do to my friends if I didn't stop investigating the foundation. He talked about your brother in vivid detail, and let me tell you if you ever get nieces and nephews, you're welcome." Mad took a shaky breath. "I couldn't put you in the way of that kind of violence. But I hated myself for breaking."

"You didn't break." She squeezed his hand. "You can't think that. You survived."

"Oh, baby, you don't know… I broke horribly. I begged

them to stop. I told them they could have everything I owned. Honestly, I would have given it to them, but they weren't after my wealth. As the beating went on, I actually hoped I would die. I might have if Freddy hadn't shown up." He sucked in a regretful breath. "You asked me why I chose to end things with you the way I did, why I didn't choose something kinder or more logical. The reason is, after they'd shown me what a fucking coward I was, I hated myself. You deserved a better man, and I decided your life would improve without me."

His harsh self-assessment was like a knife through her heart. "You weren't a coward, Mad. You fought on. You didn't even stop investigating."

"It took me days to start poking around again," Mad admitted. "I assure you that first week I had no intention of doing anything but healing and getting on with my sad life without you by my side. I realized I didn't deserve your love, so I reverted to all my old ways because they were safe. But then I got angry. That's what pushed me through at first. Slowly, Freddy brought me into his group, and all I wanted was to fuck over Krylov. The deeper I got into the conspiracy, the more I realized this could affect us all. And then…I found a motivation far stronger than anger."

"Love." She now knew that Mad hadn't succumbed to some thirst for adventure or juvenile overreaction. He'd been shown he could be reduced to something so small and he'd tried to protect her the only way he thought possible—by distancing, by letting her go.

He nodded. "I had to do everything I could to protect my family. I would have done it even if it meant losing you all forever. I would do it again if it saves you and our baby. I would walk away and never look back if it meant you'd be alive at the end. I would rather you be happy with someone else than dead with me. That's what I realized. I love you enough to put you first."

Sara understood him now. She truly did, but he needed to know that he couldn't make those same choices again. "Do you love me enough to let me take the risk with you? I can't do this—you and me—if you'll leave again. I need you to put our family first. That means staying together. I promise I'll be careful, but none of this can work if we're not together."

Something like hope lit his eyes. "What are you saying?"

"I'm saying I love you and I'm tired of not being with you." The confession felt good, like a weight being lifted off her shoulders. "I've loved you since I was a kid. I'm never going to get you out of my heart, and I don't want to anymore. Do you know what I'd decided to name our daughter?"

"Not Hortense."

He always made her laugh.

"No, definitely not Hortense. Even when I was angry with you, when I thought you were dead, I knew I wanted you to be a part of her life." Sara squeezed his hand. "I'm naming her Madeline."

"Madeline." His lips curled up in a grateful, reverent smile as he placed a big hand on her belly. "It's perfect. I love you, Madeline."

She lay her hand over his, tangling their fingers together. "Will you take me to bed? I haven't slept well since the day you left me."

"I'll never leave you again." He turned and cupped her face. "I promise. No matter what happens now, I will put you first, even above my friends. You and Maddie are my whole world now, and there is nothing I want more than to take you to bed."

Then he stood and helped her to her feet. Seconds later, she found herself scooped up in his arms.

There was no place she would rather be.

* * * *

Mad carried Sara into the small bedroom with ease. Even pregnant, she seemed so delicate and light to him.

Being with her again, having this second chance, seemed like more than he deserved, but he was going to grab onto her with both hands and hold her close for as long as she let him.

"Be sure, baby," he whispered as he lowered her to the bed. "Because I don't know what I'll do if you change your mind."

It was a lie. He knew what he would do. He would call her every hour, sleep on her doorstep, say whatever he had to until she gave him another chance. He would show her that he could be a relentless bastard when it came to winning her back.

"I won't change my mind. Sometimes I feel like I was born loving you."

"I know I was born to love you." His life felt as if it had really begun the moment she'd opened her heart to him. He'd had every material comfort a human being could have, but Sara and their child were the most precious gifts he'd ever been given.

Gently, Mad laid her on the bed, his body electric with arousal. For months, he'd felt dead inside, but now his blood thrummed and his skin seemed to awaken—all because she was finally here with him, not merely in body but in spirit. In heart.

This was what it felt like to come home.

As he yanked the T-shirt over his head, wanting nothing between them, she sat on the edge of the bed and watched. Those big eyes of hers always got to him. No matter how many times they made love, he was always so stunned that she could look at him with trust and adoration shining there.

"Do you have any idea how beautiful you are to me?" He stroked her hair, letting his fingers tangle in all that silk. He'd missed her so much, more than he'd missed anything in his life. When they'd been apart, he'd felt as if he was missing the most important pieces of himself.

Her hands shook as she reached for him and skimmed her palms along his ribs. It took everything he had not to purr like a freaking cat. He'd forgotten exactly how good it felt when she touched him.

Her gaze skated over him appreciatively. "Wow. You were always gorgeous, but now you look even better."

"Hanging out with Freddy, there wasn't a lot to do besides investigating Russians and working out. He doesn't even have a TV. I learned my lesson. From now on, only living on the grid for me." He grinned. "But the workout regimen I'll keep up because I like it. And because I always want to look good for my woman."

Her whole body tensed with obvious anxiety. "Mad, I don't look the same as you remember. I've been sitting and staring at the beach, eating every one of my emotions for months. And the baby has changed my shape, too. I'm so different. You might not—"

"Don't finish that sentence, Sara Bond. I don't want to be mad at you right now. I don't have to see your body to know how beautiful you are. That's my baby growing inside you. I wish I'd been there for every little development. Let me touch you, kiss you, love you. I'll show you exactly how I feel about your body."

He helped her to her feet, then eased the robe she wore off her shoulders and tugged her gown over her head. How could she think for a single second he wouldn't want her? All the time they'd spent apart he'd thought of nothing but her. Of finding his way back to her.

She stood in front of him, silently awaiting his judgment.

"Oh, you have changed, baby. You're even more stunning now." He cupped her shoulders and caressed his way down her arms, staring at her breasts and the sweet bump that proved his baby was growing inside her. "If you have any questions about how much I want you, all you have to do is look down."

She did. When she met his gaze again, he saw soft mischief in her eyes. "You seem happy to see me, Maddox Crawford."

"Never in all my life have I been any happier to see someone." He leaned over and brushed his lips against her forehead. "I missed you, Sara. I missed you so, so much."

Tears gathered in her eyes. "You can't leave me like that anymore. I thought I'd never see you again. I thought you were lost to me."

The pain in her expression shot through him. How would he have felt if he'd thought she was dead? His heart almost stopped at the thought.

"Please, baby, forgive me. I guess...I thought you wouldn't care anymore since I'd torn you apart."

"Not care that you had died? How could you think that?"

He'd fooled himself into believing he would be the only one hurt. "Because I didn't care about me. I hated myself and I couldn't imagine you'd have even a spark of love left inside you. I prayed that someday I could come back and make everything up to you. I hoped you would eventually understand. But I never thought you would really mourn me."

"I couldn't hate you, Mad. I tried. I tried so hard. But I couldn't." She moved her hand to the gentle swell of her belly. "After all, I had her."

Their child. Madeline had kept Sara connected to him in ways he hadn't imagined. The baby had been a bond that couldn't be broken.

She was going to be such a spoiled kid. She wasn't even born and she already had her father wrapped around her little finger. Would she ever know how important she was? How she might have saved her parents?

"I will never fail you again. I promise you, Sara."

She shook her head. "It's not about failing because we all make mistakes. I made one in not listening and not forgiving you sooner. It's about doing everything together. Win or lose, Mad, we have to stand together. Always."

"I promise."

Mad finally did what he'd been longing to do for months, since the moment after the last time he'd done it. He kissed Sara. He wanted to kiss her constantly, needed his lips on hers, their bodies close. This was his true home, this woman.

He gave up on words and did what came naturally every time he was around Sara. He tangled himself around her and breathed her in, his flesh lighting up everywhere their bodies touched. He drew her close with a groan, feeling her nipples tighten against his chest. They were slightly larger, as were her breasts, but that wasn't what made her beautiful. She glowed with life, health, and love. That was all he wanted, Sara safe and by his side.

While he kissed her, he touched her, relearning her body. Slowly, reverently, he skimmed his palms down her back, tracing the delicate length of her spine and molding to the curves that led to her perfectly heart-shaped ass. His heart rate ticked up as he cupped her there and rocked his erection against her. He couldn't wait to get inside her, but that wasn't the most important act between them tonight. The mere fact that she was in his arms felt like victory. Telling her he still loved her would be everything.

"Mad, I want you so much. I've missed you more than you'll ever know."

Not half as much as he'd missed her. Every day without

Sara had felt like forever. "You know, I used to listen in on your brother's conversations in the office just so I might hear him say your name."

Her hands roamed his back greedily, as if she was restless for more, as if she was trying to touch every inch of his skin. "Really?"

He kissed his way from her lips to the soft column of her throat. "Yep. I suspect he'll get me back for that and I'll let him. In fact, I'll probably let the guys play every trick they want on me as long as we're still friends. We have to stick together, you know. Our kiddo is going to need playmates."

"Gabe will forgive you," she said. "And I don't think Maddie is going to be alone for long. Gabe and Everly are already talking about starting a family, and I know Connor and Lara are already trying. I fear a world where Gus and Roman procreate."

Because that child would be a force of nature, and he couldn't wait until they were all a gang of kids tormenting their parents. If they could just survive the trial ahead, they might have the family they'd always wanted—a big group of close-knit brothers in each other's lives, sharing everything that came their way. "We'll parent differently. We're not only going to stay together, we're going to *be* together. I won't send Maddie away to some boarding school."

"Of course we won't." She leaned in and kissed his cheek, his lips, his shoulder, then his chest. "Touch me, Mad. It's been so long since I felt anything but sorrow."

He eased her down to the bed. He wasn't sleeping on the couch tonight, and his back was grateful for that. But right now joy filled his heart and desire scorched his veins because if he got his way, he'd never have to sleep another night without Sara beside him again.

"No more sorrow," he vowed. "Let me make you feel

adored and cherished. Beloved."

He kissed her again, starting at her mouth and working his way down. He dragged his lips across her jaw and down her throat, over the curve of her shoulders, then slowly eased to her breasts. He couldn't stop staring at them. "Are they more sensitive? I don't want to hurt you. I've read that pregnancy at this stage can make even touching them painful for some women."

"You've been reading about pregnancy?" There was zero way to mistake the incredulity in her tone.

She didn't understand how badly he'd wanted to stay connected to her in any way he could. "I bought one of those what-to-expect books. I wanted to be with you, know what you were going through. It was the only way I could share the experience with you."

She paused, thoughtfully, then spoke in a soft voice. "They're sensitive, but not in the way you think. Do you have any idea how hard it's been going to bed every night knowing you were just steps away? Ever since I hit the second trimester, I've been aching. I need you, Mad."

"The book said that was normal, but I'm happy to help, baby." He cupped her breast, feeling it swell against his palm. He had to bring her pleasure first because he wasn't at all certain he would last more than a few seconds once he got inside her.

He lowered his head and licked at her nipple, loving the way she gasped and her entire body arched tautly at the touch of his tongue. If this was what she needed, he was her man. He would fetch her whatever food she craved, rub her feet, and serve her all the tea she could drink. And he would make love to her—as long and as often as she liked.

"You're so fucking soft. Smooth as silk." He stroked a thumb over her nipple.

"Yeah? You're not soft at all. Anywhere," she murmured.

No, he was not. His cock was hard as stone and aching for her. For months, he'd fantasized about touching Sara again. The reality of her was so much better.

Mad sucked her nipple into his mouth while he cupped the other breast. A low moan escaped her throat. He lavished her breasts with affection, then inched lower because that wasn't the only part of her he needed to taste.

He kissed his way down her body, nuzzling her belly and praising her body with his touch before shifting between her legs. He breathed in the scent of her arousal.

His heartbeat gonged loudly in his ears. Being this close to Sara after enduring so much time and distance between them thrilled and warmed him like nothing ever had. Nothing mattered except worshipping her so that she felt wanted. Desirable. Sexy. Utterly necessary to his sanity and the salvation of his soul.

More than anything, he wanted to connect with her. Be with her. Find the peace only she could give him.

"I dreamed of you the whole time I was away. You don't know how often I would pray I'd stay asleep because you felt so vividly real in my dreams, I could swear you were right here against me." With insistent thumbs, he parted her sex, then circled the little jewel of her clitoris, making her wriggle in his arms. "Tell me you're mine. I still can't believe you're really here with me."

"I'm yours," she promised on a gasp as she stared down her body. Their gazes met and fused. "And you're mine. Don't forget it, Maddox Crawford."

"There's my girl. It turns me on when you get demanding. You're always such a lady, and yet you're so strong. You know what you want and you have the prettiest way of demanding it," he purred against her. "I love it when you walk in a boardroom and prove wrong all those assholes who underestimated you because they think you're nothing more than a gorgeous princess. And fuck yes, I'm yours. All yours. I've always been yours. I want a life with you, baby. You, me, Maddie… I want us to run Crawford together, teach our daughter how to work hard, love hard, and rule her kingdom."

"Or you could stay home with Maddie and let me handle Crawford," she said with a curl of her lips. "I'm better at running a business than you."

He laughed. He could do the stay-at-home dad gig if he needed to. "You handling the board room…and me handling the CEO? Maybe. We'll see…"

He'd do his best to start showing her the life he wanted right now.

Mad lowered his mouth to her pussy and kissed her the way he'd been dying to—long, passionate, giving her as much pleasure as she could possibly take. He settled in, content for now to ignore the ache in his cock because making love to Sara was about far more than simply getting inside her. She deserved all his attention. She deserved to feel the most sublime ecstasy when he touched her, every time he touched her.

He laved her with affection, his tongue working her most sensitive spots while she writhed beneath him. He eased his fingers inside her, softly stroking her in and out, curling his fingers right where she needed his touch. She was going to be so tight and hot around his cock. He would feel every inch of her, be so connected to her. Make her scream.

Be one with her.

Sara had always been responsive, but it really didn't take long before her breaths roughened and soft pleas fell from her lips.

He wouldn't have it.

"Don't hold back on me. I know what you sound like in pleasure. Baby, these walls are soundproof. Make all the noise you want." He teased her clit, swollen with desire, by brushing a barely there thumb over the bud. He followed that with a slow stroke of his tongue.

Her body strained. Her fists clasped the sheets, pulling at them. She was the perfect picture of arousal. "I'm going to scream if you don't give me what I need."

"What's that? It's been so long... I might have forgotten," he teased because he wanted to hear her say it. Her desire was evident, but he'd spent so many long days and nights apart from her, all of them wondering if he would ever have the chance to touch her again, that he simply needed to hear her say it.

"Make me come."

Every sultry word from her mouth made his cock fill and throb. "Make you come, you said?"

"Yes." There was no pleading in her tone. She demanded. She knew what her rights were and she wouldn't accept anything less from him. It was one of the reasons he'd never been able to resist her. "Make me come, Maddox. Now."

"My pleasure." Inside her, he pressed his fingertips right where she ached most and rubbed her in torturous strokes while he covered her clitoris with his lips and sucked.

Seconds later, she screamed his name while her body bucked and worked against him, lifting to his mouth and demanding every bit of bliss he could give. Then she went over the edge, gripping onto his arms and holding him as if she'd never let go.

Sweet moments later, she drifted down with a satisfied sigh. Mad couldn't wait to join with Sara for a second longer.

He lifted himself away from her and rose to his knees, shoving his sweatpants down to free his cock.

Then he stared at her again, splayed out in front of him, all flushed cheeks and womanly curves, her body open and welcoming. She took his breath away.

He couldn't wait to watch her change day by day as their baby grew. He would take it all in, catalog every single difference, and make sure she understood how amazing she was. He would show her every day, in every way he could, how much joy and warmth she brought to his life.

"I love you." He shifted between her legs and held himself above her gently swelling belly to align his crest with her slick opening. Then he pressed inside her. Heat lit through him as he sank deeper. A groan tore from his chest. Somehow, he managed to stay in control. What was on his mind was far too important to wait, and she was too precious to wonder. "I want to marry you before the baby comes. I still have your ring."

She gripped his arms and drew him closer even as she wrapped her legs around him. "Yes."

It wasn't the proposal he'd planned, but they weren't the wide-eyed kids they'd been mere months before. It was probably silly that he'd considered himself a kid then. He was almost forty, damn it. But the man he'd been before? That Mad had been naïve. He'd planned a dramatic, epic proposal, guaranteed to be plastered across social media and talked about for years.

He'd needed that then. Now all he needed was Sara.

Mad stroked into her, finding a rhythm he'd craved for months. The connection went far beyond sex, beyond mere pleasure.

Staring into her eyes, he thrust deeper, wanting to lose himself in her and stay in this moment forever. But her need soon proved as great as his. When she tightened, digging her nails into his skin, and urged him on by rocking her body with his, Mad couldn't hold out a second longer.

Climax hit him, rocketing through his body until he imploded and was reborn a new man. Until he swore he couldn't see anything but her. Until he forgot everything but

Sara and this moment that began the rest of their lives.

His entire body heavy with gratification, he rolled to his side and pulled her close. Sara lay breathless, wrapped in his arms, nestling her head on his chest. This was what they'd found that first night, what had surprised him even more than the amazing sex. They just fit together in ways he hadn't imagined and couldn't live without.

"I want you to marry me this week," he said. "We can do it up big later, but I want to be good and married when our child comes, even if it's only in our hearts and in front of our friends. We'll know the truth."

"Yes." She smiled as though she couldn't agree more and she was right where she wanted to be.

And Mad knew he was finally home for good.

Chapter Fifteen

"Are you sure nothing's wrong?" Gus asked as they strode down the hallway toward the press room.

Liz wasn't sure of anything after the previous night. Her odd spat with Zack had ended when she climbed into bed with him for a fitful night of sleep. This morning, he'd been his usual smooth-as-silk self, awakening her with kisses and making love to her like nothing had happened the night before. Still, when he looked at her, she'd seen something in his eyes she didn't like, a distance she'd never seen, even when they hadn't been lovers. She tried to write it off as his funky mood or her imagination...but worry lingered.

"Everything is fine. Well, as fine as it can be, given what's going on." She stopped because if they wanted to finish this conversation in private, they couldn't get any closer to Vanessa, who waited steps away with a bottle of water and her notes for the weekly press briefing.

"I meant between you and Zack. He and Roman are scheming. I had a long talk with my fiancé last night, but I couldn't get him to budge. He's claiming Chinese wall privilege, the bastard."

Only two lawyers would use that term in their romance, referring to the ethical division that kept their respective jobs separate from their personal lives. Basically, Roman had refused to tell his bride-to-be anything he and Zack exchanged. No doubt that made Gus crazy.

"He's right, you know. He can't tell you or Zack won't be able to be open and honest with him."

Gus's eyes rolled. "Ethics suck. They're up to something. I know it."

Liz wasn't sure what Roman would be up to besides his job, which entailed listening to Zack and advising him. "Is he worried about Krylov being in town?"

Gus shook her head. "No. They've got a security firm, someone Connor knows from his CIA days, tracking him now. They say he's already back in New York. Well, what they say is he's in New York and they can't figure out how he left. Apparently they don't have any footage of him ever exiting the hotel, much less stepping foot in DC."

"He's a mobster. I'm sure he's had plenty of practice eluding cameras and agents."

That's what was bugging her. She and Zack hadn't talked about the incident with Krylov at all this morning. After he'd made love to her, he'd dressed in sweats and his running shoes, then told her he would see her later. She would have thought Zack had put the whole thing out of his mind except he'd made her promise she wouldn't leave the White House without an escort.

"Well, all I know is the guys have gone into hyper alpha-protective-asshole mode. All of them. When I told Roman I intended to go to your place and pick up some clothes for you, he had a hissy. Have you ever seen a six-foot, three-inch wall of muscle have a hissy? It's a sight…" Gus sighed. "Apparently Connor will be selecting your wardrobe for the next week. I tried to take care of it for you but was told in no uncertain terms that he can handle shoving clothes in a suitcase. He's going to get all the wrong shoes and probably forget your undies. I'll apologize in advance for his fashion ignorance."

Liz cringed at the thought of Connor rifling through her underwear drawer, but she acknowledged the reasoning behind it. "It's all right. They're worried. I didn't really want to go back there in the first place, but now it's a no. You probably shouldn't go, either."

"Hmm. So, I'm told the press is like a school of hungry sharks today." Gus nodded toward the room where the briefings took place. "Don't give them any chum. Put on a happy face, pretend like the world isn't falling apart, and do what you do best. Once this is over with, we have a wedding to plan—and we've got to be quiet and fast about it."

A genuine smile curled up Liz's lips. Clearly, something good had come from last night because when she'd gone to the bunker to have morning coffee with Sara, she'd found a very cozy couple ready to tie the knot. "I'm so happy for them, but have we considered the fact that Mad's death certificate has been filed? Officially, he's dead. I'm not sure how we make their marriage legal."

Gus brushed those details aside. "We don't, at least not yet. The ceremony is for the two of them. Mostly, I think Mad wants a ring on her finger in case anything goes poorly. As soon as we can, we'll get all the paperwork done and make it right. But this gives us an excuse to celebrate, and we all need that right now."

"I think we can plan a serviceable wedding in a couple of days. They're getting married in a bunker—a place where many a war was launched—so the ambiance will be…interesting. Have you considered it for your own ceremony?"

Gus laughed, the sound booming in the quiet of the hall. "Wouldn't it be fitting? Roman and I are in a constant state of trying to figure out what the other is plotting. It keeps us both on our toes. Come on. It's go time. I'm going to try to blend in at the back and sneak out before they can surround me. Be on your toes because you know someone will ask about the Capitol Scandals story. And now that our interview has been postponed, the questions are likely to start."

That news jarred Liz. "I thought the guys were insisting that you two go through with it."

Gus gave her a friendly pat on the shoulder. "I told Roman that until you were comfortable with it, he could do that interview all on his own. He knows damn well it doesn't work without me. He's looking out for Zack. Someone needs to do the same for you. Let me know if you need anything."

God, she loved Gus. Liz had no idea what she would do without her. "Thank you."

As they started down the hall again, Vanessa looked at her watch as they approached. "You're cutting it close today. Here's the briefing. I typed it up from your notes."

"Thank you." She took the papers and the water bottle.

"You had a call from Mr. Harding this morning," Vanessa said, following her to the door.

The last person she needed now was Paul. "I think Zack should handle that one."

After all, he wasn't listening to her counsel about how dangerous Joy's father could be to Zack's reputation. Maybe if he talked to his former father-in-law himself, he would grasp the gravity of Paul's threats.

A single intensely judgmental brow rose over Vanessa's eyes. "I'll let Mr. Harding know you aren't interested in dealing with him."

Liz scowled at the woman. "Do you have something to say?"

The younger woman shrugged. "The man lost his

daughter publicly and violently. You were supposedly friends with her. It seems harsh for you to just dismiss him."

"Well, this is a family matter best handled by family, which I am not. So until you know the whole story, maybe you shouldn't form opinions." Liz dragged in a bracing breath and stopped. Vanessa's assessment didn't matter. She couldn't know the whole story. "I'll call Mr. Harding when I'm done here and see if I can connect him with the president. Thank you for letting me know."

Without waiting for Vanessa's reply, she threw open the door and forced herself to step behind the podium with a smile plastered on her face. As she addressed the press, the chaos began.

Twenty minutes in, Liz nodded at the reporter in the front row. "Candace."

The woman in the professional red power suit stood. "Does the president have any response to the story printed on the Capitol Scandals website about the affair his chief of staff allegedly had with his wife prior to her death?"

She glanced to the back of the White House briefing room and found Gus standing there. She gave Liz a shrug as if to say *you knew that was coming.*

"The president chooses not to respond to tabloids." It was the simplest answer. And it was the truth.

"The *New York Times* will be publishing a story tomorrow corroborating much of what Capitol Scandals reported," Candace insisted.

"I will ask the president if he wishes to respond after he's read the article. Bob?"

Bob Hewitt, from one of the largest cable news networks, stood. "This is about the natural gas pipeline project. The original timeline for an announcement has passed without a single word from the White House about its status. Are there any new developments?"

They had originally planned to announce the project in London a few weeks ago. That would have launched the major platform for his second term. But the Russians' blackmail threats had changed all of their plans. "As you know when attempting a project as technologically advanced as a transatlantic natural gas pipeline, many factors and issues must be considered. We have to take into account not only whether the project is viable, but also what effects it will have on the environment and the people affected by its building and maintenance. For all those reasons, the president wants to move cautiously and will keep everyone updated as to the project's current status."

Suddenly, every member of the room collectively bounced out of their seats. Liz quickly realized she was no longer the center of their attention.

She glanced over her shoulder to see Zack walking into the press room via the private entrance she'd used. He headed straight for the podium. Roman followed, looking big and grim in his tailored suit, like a fashionable reaper.

Anxiety churned Liz's stomach. Was this the scheme Gus feared they were plotting and planning? Liz glanced across the room, and sure enough Gus was glaring at her fiancé. He stared right back in a silent battle of wills.

"Ms. Matthews, if I could have the floor, please." Zack was solicitous, his face a polite blank.

She was not looking into the face of her lover, but an inscrutable stranger.

"What's going on?" The question slipped out.

"If you'll move out of the way, I'll tell you."

His words doused her like a frigid shower. He'd cut her entirely out of the decision-making process and would tell her whatever he'd decided when he told the press. Before he said another word, Liz already knew that whatever he uttered next would change things between them.

She stepped back. "I wouldn't dream of standing in your way."

His eyes gave away nothing as he climbed up to the podium, but the smile on his lips was the practiced expression of a career politician, nothing real.

Liz joined Roman a few paces away. "What's going on?"

"Zack is tired of waiting, and I agree," Roman said enigmatically.

"Waiting for what?" she whispered.

"Everyone, settle down." Zack raised a hand as he turned on the charm and ignored questions shouted his way. The crowd seemed to calm. "I wanted to make a few things plain about the pipeline. This was a project conceived by my predecessor, and it's one I believe in. We've done the work. As much as we can, we know both the positive and negative impacts this project could potentially have. So, with great enthusiasm I announce that we're moving forward. I've got a group of the world's smartest engineers meeting to plan the launch of a transatlantic pipeline that will bring American energy to the rest of the world. It will lower costs for our neighbors by introducing competition where there is none, and it will provide jobs for this country. I'll have a more formal announcement and documentation available this afternoon. My press secretary will be more than happy to distribute it to you when it's available."

Liz stared at him, her whole body going cold. He'd just put a massive target on his back and he hadn't once mentioned that he was even considering it.

"How could he do this?" she murmured to Roman. "After what happened to Holland..."

"He did it because of what happened to Holland. Now they have to make a move, and we can get this over with," Roman explained, his eyes steely. "Now they'll know we won't be cowed and maybe find someone else to push around. Don't worry, Liz. He's determined to protect you."

"He's not protecting himself," she sputtered.

"If you can't hold it together, you should leave. They're watching," Roman said.

They were. Most eyes were on the president, but she could see a few reporters staring her way, their gazes razor sharp, like predators sensing a good meal.

She forced a passive smile on her face, so she didn't give them anything that made the administration look less than one-hundred-percent in sync. No infighting. That had been their motto from day one. Of course they'd also promised to trust one another. Zack had never kept any job-affecting decision from her, so she'd always walked up to the podium with perfect confidence and the total trust of the pool of reporters who covered the White House.

Until today.

Now, she forced herself to stand serenely and look at Zack as if this had always been the plan and she was happy to serve.

Her heart thundered in her chest as Zack waved and brought the briefing to a close. He turned, ignoring the reporters who again leapt to their feet, shouting questions as he left the room. Liz fell into step behind him, Roman at her side.

Zack turned the minute they were safely out of the press room and in the hallway. "I'll have those documents to you in a few hours. They shouldn't expect anything before five. Let me know if you have any other questions."

Oh, she had plenty of questions. "How could you ambush me like that?"

He took her by the elbow and drew her away from the others. She hadn't even noticed Vanessa hanging around, but Zack obviously had. "I didn't ambush you. The plan changed very recently, and I thought I should brief the press."

"You could have mentioned it to me."

"It was on a need-to-know basis, and until now you didn't need to know," Zack replied without an ounce of emotion. "You are my press secretary, not an advisor on this project. And you know there are things I can't tell you. You've always known that."

"I still don't understand why you hijacked the press conference and dropped this bomb with zero notice."

Frustration showed in the way his jaw tightened, in the set of his shoulders. "How I what? I proceeded with a project that we all agree is important. That's all."

She kept her voice low but couldn't entirely hide her panic. "You're acting like this announcement was no big deal, but you and I both know this could get you killed."

"I've thought a lot about this," he replied with a long sigh. "I don't have any public appearances, so if they're going to try to assassinate me, they'll have to know my schedule. Roman and I discussed changing it up every day. I won't be easy to find, and Thomas is on alert. Connor will also stick close for a couple of weeks."

"Close enough to stop a bullet? Because that's what he might have to do."

He cupped her shoulders and forced her to look up at him. "Elizabeth, I can't give in to blackmail. I have to move forward. I've got two choices at this point. I can move on and deal with whatever happens, or I can step down and allow them to work their worst on my VP, who you know is deeply vulnerable to blackmail. Which one would you have me do?"

She understood his impulse. Zack wasn't a man used to being anything less than totally in control, but the Russians were serious. They'd killed before and they wouldn't hesitate to do so again. "The one that makes you safe."

"Then you picked the wrong man and we should have a long talk about our relationship."

Frustration welled. "Zack, I'm just worried about you. If we had more time to think about this, to plan something—"

"But we don't. Sometimes you have to force a fight out into the open in order to win it. I know what I'm doing. The question is, are you willing to stand with me or do you want to call it quits?" He loomed over her. "If you're worried about your own safety, then I think you should hand over the press office to Gus and I'll put you in protective custody. I know it doesn't feel fair, but if you're not completely with me, I'll have to insist you stay in a safe house until this is over."

She felt the blood leave her face. "You want me to leave?"

He shook his head. "I'm giving you all your options. You might not want to risk staying with me since you don't agree with my plans and you're worried it's unsafe."

"I didn't know about your plans until two minutes ago," she argued with a shake of her head. "You didn't bother to bring me into any of your decisions and announced what was happening before I got any say. I thought we were a team."

"We are, but you've always known who I am and that I won't let you make decisions for me." Zack's voice had gone rough, the first sign that he was emotional at all.

"You can't include me, even when the decision affects me? When it means our friends could be targeted?"

"Elizabeth, I have more to think about than merely our friends. Of all the people in the world, I would think you could understand that. I am the president. I don't get to be selfish. I have to do what's best for this country or get the fuck out of the way and hand the job over to someone who will," Zack swore. "If I step down now, Wallace Shorn takes the White House. Then nothing will stop them. So what would you have me do? If I give in on this, they'll want more. Should I give them our nuclear codes so you won't be afraid?"

"That's not at all what I said and it's certainly not fair."

"None of this is fair, and you arguing is only making it worse for me," he pointed out, his jaw tight. "I'm trying so hard not to fail, to do the right thing, and you're working against me."

"How can you say that? I'm only asking you to be more cautious."

"And that's impossible." He stepped back. "I can't have this fight now. I'm supposed to be in a meeting in ten minutes. Following that, I have a call with the French president."

She gathered herself with a breath. "I can feel you pulling away from me and I don't know what to do. Would you prefer I step down and let Gus run things for you?"

"You'll go in a safe house."

"Zack, I'm asking you what you want. I don't understand what's going on between us, so you'll have to tell me flat out. Would you like me to leave? I'll go into the safe house if that makes things easier on you. I can be ready this afternoon, and you won't have to see me again."

He stared at her, expressionless. "That's very martyr-like of you."

"I'm not being a martyr. I simply don't want to stay with a man who doesn't want me anymore. I guess the chase was the excitement for you. The reality of living with me doesn't seem to have met your expectations."

"Elizabeth, I am trying not to fail my country."

Liz scanned his face and did her best to see things his way. How much was this plot costing him? To her, he was behaving like a complete asshole, but the fate of the free world really was in his hands. She was caught between being selfish on behalf of the man she loved and potentially playing his doormat and fool. "I'm not trying to come between you and your duty, Zack. I don't understand this distance between us and I don't want to overstay my welcome. Tell me what you want from me."

He said nothing for a long moment. Liz was terrified that he would turn and walk away from her, maybe for good. Then he bowed his head, almost as if it was too heavy to hold up, in addition to all the weight of his responsibility. "I want you to be waiting for me after work. I want us to be normal. I want to be able to concentrate on loving the woman I've sought for years without all the rest of this shit hanging over our heads."

Liz felt her heart soften immediately and she reached for his hand. "I'm sorry. I'll back off. After I distribute the pipeline documents you send me, I'll be waiting for you this evening. We'll shut the door and we'll only talk about happy things, like how we're going to make a wedding for a billionaire happen in a day and a half without actually spending any of his money."

Liz forced a smile, willing to say almost anything to replace that hollow look in his eyes, to get back to the loving warmth they'd shared before Krylov had invaded her apartment and turned everything upside down. Was he still reeling from that incident? Zack played things very close to the vest, but his emotions also ran deep.

His lips curled up ever so slightly. "Technically, Mad is broke since he's legally dead. Make Gabe pay for the nuptials. He inherited everything, according to Mad's will. Besides, his sister is the bride, and her family is supposed to pay."

"I'll be sure to point that out to him." She sent Zack a tentative smile.

How much was the strain of this Russian conspiracy weighing on him?

She started to walk away, but he wrapped his long fingers around her arm and tugged her back to him. "I really am trying. I won't let you get hurt. No matter what happens. I promise. Even if things seem to go sideways, I won't let anything bad happen to you."

Liz felt like he was trying to tell her something, but she didn't understand his message. Or maybe she was reading too much into his speech. "I know, and I'll do my best to protect you, too."

He hesitated, stared into her eyes. Gaging her sincerity? Then he blinked, and the look was gone. Before she could ask, he pulled her in and kissed her swiftly. "I'll see you tonight."

He stepped away to join Roman, who looked over his shoulder at her before they left.

She swore she saw suspicion in the chief of staff's eyes. *What on earth…?*

"I told you they were plotting," Gus complained as she joined Liz. "Damn it. Let's get back to the office. Apparently, we have a lot of work to do. Those bastards could have given us a freaking heads-up. And you know they won't let us go anywhere now."

Liz couldn't disagree. Zack and his right-hand man were definitely plotting. Why did she suddenly have the feeling they might be plotting against her?

* * * *

Zack couldn't get her expression out of his head.

I thought we were a team.

He hadn't seen betrayal on her face. That he might have been able to take. Instead, he had seen sorrow. He'd made her and her feelings seem insignificant. The moment he'd realized that, he'd expended all his willpower to stop himself from dragging her into his arms and begging her forgiveness. But he couldn't. That wasn't part of the plan.

"I think that went surprisingly well." Connor had been

waiting in the Oval when they'd returned. He'd been a part of the early morning session hammering out the shift in their strategy for dealing with the blackmailers. Gabe and Dax had also been in on the move, which included getting Holland and Everly ready to move into the White House. Temporarily, he hoped.

Yesterday had proven they had to speed up this global game of chicken if they wanted to have any shot at winning.

"I don't know about that." Zack had projected cool and calm in front of the press, but inside he was so fucking angry he could barely see straight. Angry at the Russians and his own forefathers, who had apparently dragged him into this shitshow. Angry with Elizabeth for her seeming betrayal. Angry—so damn angry—at himself for wanting to believe her...and not quite being able to. In all his life, only his closest circle of longtime friends had never betrayed him.

Would Elizabeth be the first?

"I know that was rough, but you had to do it." Roman's voice brought him out of his thoughts.

"Did I? I couldn't have talked to her beforehand? Given her even a five-minute heads-up that we'd decided to completely change the game? Or how about simply sitting her down, showing her the evidence we have against her, and asking her flat out for an explanation?"

Roman sank into the chair across from him with a sigh. "You know why that's a bad idea."

Because if she was working with the Russians, Zack's element of surprise would be blown.

"I hate to admit it, but in this case Roman is right." Connor paced the Oval Office.

"Thank you." Roman waved a hand, looking relieved that someone backed him up.

Connor stopped, sending Roman a glare that could freeze fire. "Not because I'm saying Liz is an operative.

And consider that if she even gets a hint that Zack thinks she's working with the enemy, she'll do something stupid like run off on her own, either to lick her wounds or to prove her innocence."

"And if she *is* working for them, worse things than her telling them all our secrets could happen," Roman shot back. "Do you think I'm such an asshole that I've given zero consideration to her welfare? I don't know why she's behaving this way or allowing herself to be manipulated into it, but have either of you thought about what happens if she's no longer of value to the Russians? Hear me out. They killed Joy. We're absolutely certain of that. They probably killed her because she was worth more to them dead than alive. They'd already determined she couldn't manipulate Zack the way they'd hoped a wife could, so they waited for a moment her martyrdom would have maximum impact and pulled the trigger. But they probably knew a few years into the marriage that Joy had no sway over Zack, so they came up with a plan B and moved Liz into place."

"We don't know that." Zack hated how certain Roman always sounded when he talked about Elizabeth working for the enemy. He knew Roman always operated from his convictions, and it had served them well over the years. Today, it rankled.

"We do know that these men will discard her if they think for a second she's outlived her usefulness, whether or not she understands she was ever their tool." Roman seemingly tempered his words. He'd always been good at reading Zack's cues and adjusting. It was one of the reasons they worked so well together. "This is the best play. It protects her, too."

Connor shrugged slightly. "It will tell us quickly how they'll respond if we refuse to play along. We have to be ready for almost anything. I'm moving in this afternoon. Lara's already picked out a bedroom."

They'd decided to move everyone into the White House for the time being. If anyone asked, they would give some excuse about the preparations for Roman and Gus's wedding. It wasn't as if Zack hadn't had guests before. He was a bachelor, so the staff was used to him having his friends stay for the company. Now, though, they all had wives or fiancées.

Would Elizabeth be around a year from now? How about six months? He'd meant what he'd said to her. No matter what happened, he would protect her. He would never allow her to be hurt or arrested.

He might have to question her at some point, though. Intelligence and surveillance both indicated that Krylov had never left his hotel yesterday. This morning, he'd been walking around New York as though nothing at all had happened. When the feds had brought him in for questioning, he'd claimed he'd spent the entire day in his hotel room, sick after eating bad sushi the night before. They'd been forced to let him go. For now.

If that was true and Elizabeth wasn't working for the Russians, why would she lie?

Zack couldn't think of a single reason.

Suddenly, Roman clapped him on the shoulder. "Don't lose faith now. I know that was a pretty intense conversation you and Liz were having in the hallway. If she's innocent, she'll get over it."

Easy for Roman to say. He didn't have to sleep next to her.

"How did she take the sudden turnaround?" Connor asked.

"It wasn't a turnaround. I never intended to shut the pipeline down forever. It's a good project." Zack hated being forced to wait and see what the other side would do, when the other shoe would fall. "She was surprised I hadn't told her. I'm sure she wasn't thrilled that I made it look like she was on the outside before I took over her briefing. She's not the only one. Gus was giving me the glare. I could feel it from across the room."

Roman winced. "I'm not looking forward to facing her tonight. Sometimes I'm worried she'll manage to find a way to shoot lasers out of her eyes and deball me. She wants kids, though. That might save me."

"I'll talk to them both," Connor offered. "I'll explain it from an intelligence perspective. After what happened last night, we had to come back with a strong counter move or we seemed weak."

Zack peered at Connor, who'd been in this business for a very long time. "Do you think she's working with Krylov? I know we've talked about this, but now we have more evidence and I want to hear your perspective again."

Connor ran a hand over his short hair, the gesture looking deeply frustrated. "Obviously the evidence points that way. If she's innocent, then the fact that they've communicated through Liz both times is definitely an odd coincidence."

Connor didn't believe in coincidences. And he would have sucked as a politician.

"They communicated with Mad." Zack stubbornly looked for any way around Connor's logic.

"No, they beat the shit out of Mad, while Liz emerged from both of her encounters without a single hair out of place," Roman pointed out. "Everything seems to flow through Liz, and I would love to know why she was in the Treaty Room the day we left for Camp David. And she spends time with your father. Think about that."

"She checks on him for me because she knows I hate being in the same room with the old bastard." Zack knew he should be a better person. His father was sick now, but he couldn't see an invalid sitting there, just the tyrant who had pushed and pushed and pushed.

"Or she has an ulterior motive for talking to him, and Frank isn't as mentally gone as we think," Roman countered.

"I'm looking into his doctors." Connor started pacing again. "Who picked these specialists?"

"Joy handled it in the beginning. And then, when we were in the middle of the campaign, Elizabeth took over those visits." He'd been depending on Elizabeth for a long time. Both he and Joy had.

The sad truth was he'd taken Joy's advice a lot of the time. She'd been his friend, a partner as much as Roman had been. They hadn't been in love, but they'd had a shared goal and she'd been smart, competent, and quietly ambitious. Joy had been by his side when he'd won the senatorial seat on his first try, her steady head leading the parts of the campaign he hadn't enjoyed or understood.

There was a hard knock on his door, then Thomas stepped inside.

"Mr. President, the vice president would like a moment of your time." Thomas's expression was the same stoic blank he always wore. "He's rather insistent."

Zack stifled a groan. He should have known this would happen. "I don't suppose I can put him off."

Thomas shrugged a single broad shoulder. "I can absolutely explain the situation to him in vivid detail, sir."

That might be fun to watch, but it would only cause more trouble down the line.

Zack shook his head. "Let him in. I might as well get it over with."

He stood, walking to the desk that dominated the Oval Office. The Resolute desk. It was fitting for him to sit behind it now as he faced down a man who'd never liked him.

Wallace stormed in. The man had taken the VP slot because he'd known he had nowhere else to go. The campaign had almost certainly been the last time he would be able to credibly run. It had made them wary partners.

"What can I do for you, Wallace?"

"You can tell me what the fuck is going on." He glared, taking in the men in the room with a frown, then pointed at Connor. "You should leave. I need a moment alone with the president."

Connor simply sat on the couch, bracing his ankle over the opposite knee in a casual manner that did nothing to disguise his predatory nature. "But I'm so comfortable here."

"You think I don't know who you are?" Shorn said. "I might have to put up with Calder's ever-looming presence, but you're not a part of this administration."

"I assure you Mr. Sparks is, in fact, a trusted member of my administration, and he has all the security clearance he needs. You should feel free to say anything around him."

"What? He's nothing but your old drinking buddy," Shorn said scornfully.

"Oh, the president and I haven't merely imbibed together," Connor replied. "We've also handled problems together. In fact, that's my function."

Shorn scowled. "No, that's Calder's."

"Roman handles the legal issues. I make things disappear." Connor sent him a wolf's smile.

"Are you threatening me?"

Zack sighed. "Mr. Vice President, could you please tell me why you're here or get the hell out of my office?"

Shorn turned back to him, lips pursed. "What's going on? One minute we're moving on the pipeline. The next we're not. Now it's back on. I'm going to get a crick in my neck from watching you play ping pong with one of the administration's most important projects. And my environmental contacts aren't sure the EPA's findings are real. You could have a shit ton of lawsuits on your hands with this one, yet you don't bother to inform anyone in this administration what you're doing. I watched that press briefing." He scoffed. "You didn't even tell your girlfriend. You made her look like a fool, you know. At least now she understands what it means to be around President Zack Hayes."

"That's enough," Roman barked.

"No, please let him tell me what a son of a bitch I am." Zack sat back.

Shorn faced off with him, eyes narrowed. "You think you're so smart, but I see through you. Something funny is going on here."

"And what is that?"

He scanned the room before his stare landed on Zack again. "Something happened in England. You were supposed to make the announcement about the pipeline then. You were on a huge stage. It would have made world headlines. Yet you slammed on the brakes and refused to answer questions about it. Now you waltz into an everyday press briefing and announce the start of the pipeline like you're announcing an upcoming summit. This project changes the face of the world economy, and you're treating it like it's a science fair project. Why is that, Mr. President?"

No one had ever said Shorn was an idiot. "I thought people would want to know my plans now that I've studied the final EPA evaluation. Since that's accomplished, I'm comfortable announcing the decision I've made."

"This is the project your presidency will be judged on. You're one of the most careful bastards I've ever met, and yet Elizabeth Matthews had no idea what was going on. I don't think Augustine Spencer did either. That makes me think you and Calder are up to something. Oh, and Sparks, too. I know his reputation and his line of work." Shorn backed away. "Don't think you fool me. Someone is poking around my background and my private life. Are you going to try some dirty tricks to force me off the reelection ticket? You think you can use my base to get elected the first time, and now that the pipeline is off the ground, you can get rid of me?"

"Who's looking into you?" Zack was well aware that Roman and Connor had just tensed.

Shorn rolled his eyes. "Like you don't know someone was out at my brother's place asking questions."

"Your brother's place?" Zack asked pointedly. If Connor had nothing to do with that, he was deeply concerned.

"Yes," he insisted. "My brother has a mistress. I'm sure you know that. But I find it curious that as we're approaching the election cycle, now some very unsavory characters are asking questions. It won't work, Hayes. I won't step down. I won't allow you to bully me. Before you try, you should think about the dirt I have on you."

He turned on his overly expensive loafers and strode out.

Zack glanced Connor's way and knew he didn't even have to ask the question.

Connor held his hands up. "It wasn't one of my guys. I think we're pretty comfortable with the fact that those kids are Shorn's."

"Who else but the Russians would be poking into his business?" Zack asked.

Roman shrugged. "Are we sure it's them? He's trying to keep the pipeline going."

"And I assure you he'll change his mind if he's sitting behind this desk and gets threatened with losing it." Zack had no doubt about that. "It's why they were okay with me picking Shorn. They knew he was vulnerable."

"I'll send someone to try to figure out what they're doing." Connor had his phone in hand. "Although I think we know. Don't worry about this, Zack. We stay the course. We're handling it the right way."

"We hope," Roman said under his breath.

"Have a little faith, huh? I'll go do some homework and let you know where we stand." Connor rose and left him alone with his closest friend.

The noose was tightening. Zack could feel it.

"Are you sure we should expend the time and energy to let Sara and Mad get married now?" Roman asked. "I can talk to him. Surely he'll understand that now isn't the time for distractions. I'm honestly thinking about talking to Gus about delaying our own wedding, and that's still months away."

"Let them be, Roman, and you delay your wedding at your own peril. I don't think Gus likes kids enough to leave your balls on your body if you do that." Zack turned and looked out the window. It was a beautiful day. He'd love to spend it by taking Elizabeth's hand and walking through the Rose Garden just to enjoy the sunshine with her.

He wouldn't be doing that anytime soon. He would be in hiding, protecting himself. Keeping his emotional distance from her until he knew whether she wore a white hat or an ushanka.

"Are you sure?" Roman asked.

He didn't want his friends miserable because his situation was tenuous and dangerous. "I'm sure. Let them have some happiness."

Because tomorrow wasn't guaranteed. Not to anyone, and definitely not to him.

Chapter Sixteen

"Have I told you how beautiful you look? That bastard best friend of mine doesn't deserve you." Gabe slipped into the bunker unit the ladies had somehow managed to turn into a gorgeous bridal suite.

Sara smiled up at her brother, savoring the sense of peace that came with knowing she was finally going to marry the right man at the right time. But she was also happy that Gabe had come to let her know that all the arrangements for their midnight ceremony were finally in place.

"You might have mentioned your opinion that Mad is somehow unworthy despite being your best friend several times, but I'm happy to hear that I look beautiful on my wedding day." Especially since she didn't want to just feel pregnant. She wanted to feel like a bride.

"Let me see you." Gabe made a spinning motion with his finger.

With a laugh, she twirled around so her brother had a good look at the gorgeous beaded Zuhair Murad that Gus and Holland had managed to not only find, but have tailored in less than twelve hours. Sara was afraid to ask her bridesmaids how much it had cost or how many favors they'd had to trade in. They'd said it was their gift to her. To Sara, it was both perfect and priceless.

Gabe took her hand. "Stunning. You make a gorgeous bride, and I wish we were back in New York so everyone could see you. I wish Mom and Dad were alive to see you now."

They'd had an odd family dynamic. Their father had worked constantly, and Mother had been far more concerned with her social life and her charitable works than her children. Still, it had hardly been a rough childhood. She'd known her parents loved her. They'd merely led separate lives.

"I do, too, but Mad and I don't intend to raise Maddie the way we were raised."

"Maddie, huh? You know you're asking for trouble with that name." He grinned before he sobered. "Actually, Everly and I have had the same conversation. No nannies for us."

"Oh, are you getting rid of the maid, too?" Sara loved teasing her brother, and it felt good to be able to joke again. To be so incredibly happy.

"Never. Everly would give me up before she let Gwen go." He shuddered slightly. "I'll never learn how to clean, especially to Everly's high standards, so I'm better off not trying."

"I agree. The maid stays, and unless Mad learns how to do more than scramble eggs, we might need a chef, but we're going to raise this baby ourselves until she's an adult. And she's going to need cousins, so get busy."

A grin lit her brother's face. "We're working on it." He glanced around the normally utilitarian room, and Sara was again astounded by how the women had transformed the place with lush furnishings and carpets. A hearty tea service with accompanying snacks rested on a nearby table. Everywhere, evidence of the bridal party primping and polishing in preparation for her big day was visible. "The ladies can work some serious magic. I'm sorry we're doing this so late and so secretively. You should be able to walk out to the Rose Garden in the middle of the loveliest spring day. Or we should be doing this at Loyola."

She wrinkled her nose at the thought of getting married in that church. "Where we held Mad's funeral? No, thank you. I'm just happy we'll get to be outside in the moonlight."

"Are you sure you don't want to wait?" Gabe asked.

Sara had never been more sure of anything in her life. "I want to marry the man I love, and I can't wait until he's officially back from the dead. I know you guys think you're close to cracking this thing, so maybe this feels unnecessarily rushed to you. But we're controlling the one thing we can. I want to give Mad the knowledge that I'm his wife. I need to know he's my husband. And we've agreed that anything that happens after tonight, we face together. Now walk me up to the residence. I want to get to the honeymoon part."

Gabe winced. "I did not need to hear that."

She shrugged and picked up the lovely bouquet Lara had brought for her. "Well, I didn't want to hear your honeymoon either, but guess who decided to spend their first week as man and wife in the Hamptons? In the room beside mine? Yep, you and Ev. You should be happy you get to sleep upstairs, far from Mad and me. Because we're going to make some noise tonight."

Her very elegant brother made a retching sound, then offered her a hand. "They've already disguised Mad and sneaked him up to the residence. All the ladies are in place. We're just waiting on you."

It was almost midnight. They'd selected the time to

avoid staff and reporters. Connor and Dax had made certain they could walk to the residence without eyes on them. Freddy had even arranged a short window of surveillance blackout. Once they were in place, the wedding party would be alone without any eyes on them. Thomas would monitor the door to ensure it stayed that way.

Sara was thrilled that her whole family was together for her and Mad's big day.

As she and her brother walked up the stairs, the heels Gus had brought her clicked along the marble. She was happy for Gabe's steady hand because it had been months since she'd walked in any shoe that wasn't flat.

When they got to the residence, the women flocked over and buzzed around her, making sure her hair, makeup, dress, and veil all looked perfect.

"I'm grabbing the wireless speaker," Holland proclaimed, hurrying by. "Just another minute and we'll be ready. Don't leave the living room. We don't want Mad to see you until we're ready."

"The guys are on the balcony and I promise they're all wearing their best," Lara said, carrying the smaller bouquets the bridesmaids would hold as she made her way outside.

"Wait up," Gabe called to Connor's wife. "I need to make sure Mad is ready. And if he's misbehaving, Sara, I'll throw him off the balcony." He winked and departed.

"I forced Roman into a tux." Gus looked tall and beautiful in her elegant sheath. "He actually thought he might get away with wearing something casual since we're getting married in Hawaii. Not happening. We're going formal all the way. I did not wait this long to get married only to have him show up in shorts and a T-shirt."

Given the fact that less than two weeks ago Sara had believed Mad was lost to her forever, she would take him now wearing a speedo and a pink wig. "Thank you for making tonight so lovely for us."

"We did the best we could with the time and resources we had," Liz assured.

Sara took her hands. "It's perfect. Please don't worry that I feel like I'm getting the shaft with this quickie clandestine wedding. I don't. I'm overjoyed. But Gus, word of warning: all those men have been so circumspect for the last few months. They're going to cut loose at some point. Think about it."

Gus's eyes went wide as the implication obviously hit her. "We've had three Perfect Gentlemen weddings, and not a single one of them have been marked with crazy pranks because we've had this thing hanging over our heads. Once everything is back to normal, they will revert to form and focus all their attention on my wedding. Shit."

"And I have it on the highest authority there will be neon dildos," Sara said with a grin. "Many of them. I won't even go into Mad's thoughts about what he can do to your wedding cake."

Laughter rang through the room, Everly sounding the loudest as she headed outside. "I'm so excited about your wedding, Gus. It's going to be amazing. And Sara is right, probably crazy."

"I will murder all of them," Gus swore as she strode toward the balcony like a woman on a mission. "I'll see you outside. I have some ground rules to set with those men."

Everly followed, waving her off. "Why? The guys will agree to everything you say...and there will still be dildos at that wedding. I can't wait! I haven't seen a real Perfect Gentlemen shindig yet, and they only have two more weddings to get it right."

Suddenly, Sara found herself alone with Liz. "You know you should get nervous, too. There's nothing the guys like more than to tease Zack. They had to have a decoy limo for his first wedding because everyone was afraid of what Mad and the others would do to it."

Liz's smile didn't come close to reaching her eyes. "I'd heard that."

"Are you okay? You've been quiet all afternoon."

"Fine," she replied. "Just work stuff."

"Your work stuff also involves boyfriend stuff. That's got to be incredibly complex. I can't imagine what Zack is going through right now. He has to be a giant ball of stress."

"You could say that." Liz looked lovely in her lavender dress, her blonde hair piled artfully on her head and threaded through with white flowers.

"You two picked a difficult time to finally start your relationship."

"I don't know that we have one. I think I'm a convenient sexual outlet for him," Liz admitted, then shook her head. "I'm so sorry. I don't want to ruin your wedding with my whining."

"You're not. Like I said, this is a very difficult time for us all, but you and Zack more than anyone else. I don't think you should make any decisions until we're on the other side of this cluster."

"I may not get that choice." Liz drew in a long, calming breath. "You know, I always thought we would make time to be together after his first term. But now…"

"Liz, I know Zack. I'm not as close to him as my brother, but I've watched him over the years. Even as a kid he had this gravity to him, like he knew the sort of weighty responsibility coming his way. He was always so serious. We all knew exactly what his marriage to Joy was, and I never thought it would work, even though everyone seemed to adore her. She wasn't the right woman for him."

"But she was in a lot of ways," Liz argued. "She was the perfect political wife. She let him have his career and built her whole world around supporting that ambition. He's used to that. I'm something different."

"Yes, but you're much better for him. You push him."

"I don't know that he wants to be pushed, especially now. I think that might be our problem. I can't be the woman he needs. When I try to give him space, he insists on having me with him. But when I'm close, he doesn't seem to want me at all."

"He doesn't like being away from you, but he has a lot on his mind," Sara softly explained. "He's in a bad position, Liz. There are things he can't tell you, pressures that weigh on him."

"He's always had those, and I've never asked him to tell me anything classified. I can't explain, but whatever's happening now is something totally new. He's shutting me out of conversations and decisions he never has before and I don't understand why."

"I don't know, either. And I know that must hurt, but I hope you'll give him more time. He wouldn't use you. Zack Hayes is one of the most honorable men I've ever met. If he's acting like a douche, there's an underlying reason."

Liz sniffled, and Sara's heart went out to her. "I'm trying to be patient and stay calm."

"I hope you can be because Zack might have married Joy, but I never once saw him smile until he met you. When you first joined the team, Gus and I were worried because it was so obvious that he lit up when you walked into a room, and it wasn't simply about sexual chemistry. You two flowed and worked together like magic or something. Gus says the same thing. I think that's because you challenge Zack to be more than a politician. You've made him want something beyond this job. I've been worried for years about what happens to Zack when his presidency is over. How does anyone go on after they've already accomplished the one massive feat they've driven toward their whole life? Then I saw the two of you together, and I knew that Zack had a new dream. He's probably running for reelection because it's the right thing to do and because it safeguards us all, but I guarantee he's marking time until the moment he can have a normal life. You gave him that drive. He wants all of that because he wants it with you."

Stark pain crossed Liz's face. "I don't know about that."

"I do. He's never been in love before. Imagine what it must be like to be the most powerful man in the world and to be figuring out during the worst crisis of your life what it means to truly love someone."

"You've got a point." Liz nodded thoughtfully. "And he's facing his own vulnerability at the same time."

"That can't be easy. He probably doesn't even realize he's processing so many heavy things at once. They're all wrapped together in his brain," Sara said. "He's never been this vulnerable before—either professionally or personally. He's never had to think about his relationships because they didn't affect his heart. He's in deep with you and he's floundering. I should know."

"Because that's how Mad was in the beginning?"

"No, because I was Zack. I was terrified that Mad would break my heart and make me look like a fool. I know that's not exactly what's going on here, but the feelings are similar. I kept my distance from Mad for years. I sometimes wonder what would have happened if Mad had kept trying to get through to me when we were younger. Although that would have made him a little stalkery, so I guess things happen when they're supposed to. But Zack needs you."

"You really loved Mad all these years?"

Sara sighed happily. "I did and I was too afraid to even give him a try. Zack is doing his best to give you himself now. He simply needs time to open up and learn how. Just because he's got a genius-level IQ doesn't mean he's smart about everything."

Holland strode in, the wireless speaker in her hands. "We're ready."

Gabe stepped back into the room, followed by the rest of her lovely bridesmaids, the women who had made this beautiful wedding a reality.

She couldn't ask for better friends.

Dax's wife hit the button, and Pachelbel's "Canon in D" started playing through the residence. Her brother held out his arm. "Ready?"

"I'm still not sure how all this is going to work," Sara muttered. "We didn't exactly have a rehearsal, and you're also Mad's best man."

"I'm your brother first," Gabe said. "And I'm so proud of you. We got this. Now let's get you married so we can tie the knot on this family circle."

Sara nodded and took a deep breath, then walked toward her future.

* * * *

Mad stared at his wife across the crowded room, a deep sense of satisfaction coursing through his veins. Sara was finally his. She'd said I do and everything. Oh, she'd refused to take the lie detector test Freddy had suggested would make a great addition to their wedding vows, but other than that, the whole thing had gone off without a hitch.

They'd stood on the Truman Balcony, illuminated by twinkle lights Liz and Lara had spent hours setting up, and promised to love, honor, and cherish each other until death parted them. Screw that. He would love her long after death.

Now Sara Crawford stood in her gorgeous dress, looking like a sexy, beautiful angel he was going to make glorious, filthy love to very soon.

She glanced his way with a secretive smile that let him know he was on her mind, too.

Roman approached, clapping a hand on his shoulder and breaking into his X-rated thoughts. "How are you doing, married man?"

Dax strolled up, too, a beer in his hand. "Who would have guessed Maddox Crawford would take the plunge?"

He glanced toward the balcony where Zack lingered, his back to the room. "Oddly enough, Zack did. I think he was the only one who saw how crazy I was about Sara."

"Oh, we saw it," Roman allowed. "Everyone except Gabe, who didn't want to."

"I know from experience that it's weird when it's your sister." Dax frowned at them both.

The guy ought to know since he was well aware they'd both slept with Gus. Though in Mad's case it had first been about youthful lust. Comfort had followed a few years later. Since then, Gus had been his emotional sounding board and a very good friend.

"I don't know." Mad shrugged. "I don't mind that Gabe married my sister. They're happy."

"But you don't remember Everly as a child." Dax looked over to the women, now drinking wine and surrounding the small cake they'd brought in. Sara held her bottle of water and glowed with happiness.

Dax's expression softened as he looked at Gus. "You didn't grow up in your sister's shadow. She was my hero when I was a kid. I kind of thought of her as pure."

Mad nearly spit out the beer he'd just taken a sip of.

Roman laughed.

Dax rolled his eyes. "Okay, I thought that when I was ten. I also thought my mom and dad shared a bedroom to save money."

Roman chuckled, but his humor faded as he caught sight of Zack by himself. Mad watched as Roman turned, scanning the room for someone. When his gaze landed on Liz, standing in the back and slightly away from the other women, Mad knew there was trouble.

"Is he okay?" Mad nodded toward the balcony. "I

noticed he and Liz didn't seem terrifically cozy tonight. She doesn't look much happier than he does."

Dax and Roman shared a look.

Clearly, they knew something he didn't, and they hadn't planned on telling him. Thank goodness he grasped Perfect Gentlemen-style stares and facial ticks. This language all their own was something they'd perfected during long decades of friendship. It was all about watching for the little tells.

He and Gabe had used it often when deciding if one of the other guys had imbibed enough booze to need saving from starring in his own personal re-enactment of *The Hangover*. Often Dax and Connor used it when deciding whether or not someone was a threat. For Roman and Zack, it had always been about politics, at least until tonight.

Dax's eyes narrowed slightly. *Well, he's freaking Mad. I know he's been dead and all, but he's still our brother. Should he be in on this?*

Roman's eyes rolled back a bit, but not in full-on annoyance. *He doesn't need to know everything because I'm the douchebag godfather of this group and I like keeping a million and one secrets.*

Okay, that might be a loose translation.

Dax responded with a slight huff. *He might be able to help.*

Roman studied Mad, then followed with a shake of his head. *Are you forgetting? He's Mad. If I need help finding cocaine in a church on Sunday during a sermon on the sins of decadence, I'll call Mad. Otherwise...*

Dax's eyes narrowed. *You caused this problem.*

Mad joined the silent conversation with a nod. Roman could be an absolute bastard, and his dickishness often rubbed off on Zack. Always had.

Still, the whole thing made him frown. Dax and Roman had disagreed before, sure. The question was, what were they disagreeing about now? It obviously had to do with Liz.

"Zack's got a lot on his mind," Roman finally said in a lame attempt to dismiss the topic.

But Zack wasn't the only one who looked tense. Liz also seemed on edge.

Given what they were going through, the stress didn't surprise Mad. What did, though, was that they weren't tense together anymore. They weren't staying close to give or receive support. The distance between them now told Mad they were no longer boinking like crazy as a way to relieve the tension and reaffirm their bond. No, Zack was physically putting distance between them, and he had all night long.

Fuck.

He leaned in so only Roman and Dax could hear. "You honestly believe Liz is some kind of Russian errand girl and you're pushing your suspicion off on Zack, who just wants to enjoy sex for the first time in years. He should be relaxed, man. His balls have been beyond full for, like, a decade. And now, he's got a woman he adores who probably cured those oh-so-blue balls. That's gotta be good for him. I know because I went without for a couple of months and I thought I was going to explode. Why can't you let him have a win?"

Roman's eyes rolled fully now. "Because I'm the bad guy, Mad. I'm the asshole coming between perfect angel Zack and his chosen goddess of love, who also might be trying to set him up for treason. I know *you* can follow your gut, which, by the way, told you to fake your own death and live with Crazy Freddy and use outdoor toilets for months, but I have to look at the evidence and reach a logical conclusion. The rest of you get to be crazy. Zack and I don't."

Mad figured he was maturing because some of what Roman said actually made sense. Roman and Zack had always been the steadying influences of the group while he and Gabe had been the young, crazy, rich morons who had followed their wildest impulses because they knew Roman and Zack would be there if their shenanigans all went to hell.

But that had been when their biggest worry was getting kicked out of school. Now the fate of the free world lay on their shoulders. "I get that, and you're not an asshole. Well, you're not always an asshole and probably not about this, but I've been working on this very case for longer than you, and I think the Russians know exactly what they're doing."

"You think they're manipulating Liz, but she's unaware of it?" Roman asked. "That's crossed my mind, but you can't deny she's a smart woman. I struggle with the idea she's got no idea her strings are being pulled like a puppet's."

"She's a smart woman, yeah...who's crazy in love with a man." Mad knew a little about being so in love he couldn't see straight. "I know what you think and I can guess why you think it, but if you cost him the only woman he's ever loved, I don't know how your friendship will come back from that. I don't know how he'll come back."

"That's what I've been worried about," Dax concurred.

When Roman sighed heavily, Mad clapped him on the back. "I get it. But how about this: you be the voice of logic and reason, and I'll be cheering on the good vibes and awesome sex—basically anything that might help him save his sanity. Zack needs to hear both sides."

"I'm worried he'll throw caution to the wind and make a move he shouldn't." When Mad would have objected, Roman raised his hands in surrender. "But I see your point about balance. I still have to tell him what I think."

"Duh. Isn't your official title here devil's advocate?"

Roman sent him an acidic smirk. "Look, I like Liz. I don't want any of this to be true, and I admit I've worried what happens if I'm wrong."

Roman could lose Zack as a friend. Or Zack could lose his life.

Mad knew his president didn't need his advice much, but his friend did. And sometimes even the idiot of a group had a decent perspective.

He winked Sara's way and strode out to the balcony. In the distance the Washington Monument glowed like a jewel against the velvety night. All in all, it was a majestic view, but the man who got to look at it every night seemed beyond weary.

"Hey, do you want us to get out of your bedroom? You probably have some kind of party in the morning, right? Isn't that what you do?"

Zack turned, leaning against the wrought iron of the balcony, wearing a wisp of a smile. "I wish. I'm afraid my version of parties these days are more like diplomatic gatherings. I really miss keggers."

They had thrown some doozies in college. How could that time seem so far away now? Sometimes it felt like they'd been kids five minutes ago. Others, he was sure that had been another lifetime. "When all this is over, we'll have to throw a blowout. Personally I'm hoping we've wrapped this up by the time Roman and Gus's wedding takes place because I've got a bunch of glittery dildos I'm dying to break out."

Zack laughed, the sound echoing. "That is definitely something to look forward to, regardless of what Gus says."

Mad glanced inside. Sure enough Liz watched Zack, her eyes looking hollow and haunted. "Is there a reason you're not hanging out with your girl? You know I've got plans for your wedding, too, and I made mistakes with the last one. I'll be ready when you do it again."

The smile on Zack's face died quickly. "That's not happening anytime soon."

"Why? You're in love with her, right? If you're not

sure, I can take a poll if you like."

"Asshole," Zack tossed back affectionately. "Of course I love her, but there are mitigating circumstances."

Mad wasn't letting Zack off so easily. "I would ask, but Roman has already told me without really telling me that he's got you questioning every move Liz makes. I get that you have to be cautious because of your position."

"Yes. And I've even been questioning whether she's the first woman to fool me," Zack admitted, his voice rough. "I can't fathom Joy working against me. And maybe now I'm overreacting to the fact that the final stops on the campaign were those she insisted on and that she happened to be in Europe when a 'family member' checked my mother out of her mental ward and made sure she died."

"Don't forget that Joy considered working with Tavia for her FLOTUS initiative," Mad added. "And she kinda-sorta had an affair with your best friend."

"That, too." Zack acknowledged with a nod. "But none of that proves she was a Russian operative. It's so easy to jump at shadows..."

"For sure." Though Mad suspected Joy had been some sort of spy. Liz...not so much. "But I know Joy never loved you the way Liz does. It's precious, man. Don't throw it away without a lot of thought and consideration. You may never get it back."

Zack began to pace. "Where are you going with his? Has ten minutes of marriage turned you into some kind of expert?"

"No, but weeks of actually thinking every moment might be my last has given me a different perspective on things. I know I've always been the group's party boy, but I was watching you guys, too. Sure, you were often a Smurf, but that was only during my LSD phase. And you were still a mighty intellectual Smurf."

Zack sent him the censuring stare he'd perfected by

leveling it on Mad every time he'd behaved like a dumbass. Zack probably used it these days to make other world leaders fall in line. "Your point, Mad?"

The good news was, unlike days gone by, he actually had one that didn't involve a beer bong. "If you don't at least try to believe in Liz, you're going to screw things up with her, maybe forever."

"I assure you, I have tried." There was a wealth of weariness in Zack's tone.

"But I know what's going through your head."

"Oh? How can you?"

"Because I spent months after that beating Krylov gave me wondering if one of my best friends in the world was a Russian plant. I let the shit they did and the venom they spewed get to me. I gave them what they wanted. We know they've been trying to separate you from your friends for a long time. I think they're figuring out that's easier said than done."

"Maybe you're right. It wouldn't be the first time someone learned that lesson the hard way. My father tried to force me to cut you out of my life back in our Creighton days. I refused. It was the only time I ever won in a battle of wills with him."

"Exactly. I think the Russians have figured out how important the guys and I are to you. I think they assumed I would be so scared after Krylov's beating that I would run to the others and tell them what the bastard had said."

"That I was a willing participant in his Russia-first schemes?"

"Yes.

"Why didn't you? Why didn't you go to Gabe?" Zack asked.

Mad had thought about it. In those first long days, he'd considered every avenue. And chosen the only one he could live with. "Because despite being scared and confused, I couldn't accuse you. I didn't even want to ask the question. I couldn't let them consider such a shitty accusation when I had zero proof. As time went by and I found some power in investigating, I realized that I trusted you, proof or no, and I didn't want to live in a world where Zack Hayes betrayed his country."

"That's naïve of you."

"Is it? Have you ever wanted something so much that you couldn't take no for an answer? That's where I was. I was willing to tell the universe to fuck off. In this case I was determined to control my perspective and my reality, and guess what? I was right. Since I didn't blab to Gabe or the others and turn them against you, I think the Russians figured out that we're tight and decided to come after the person they hoped would be the weak link. They went after Liz."

Zack grimaced. "All the evidence is against her."

"And they're preying on Roman's role in both your administration and your friendship," Mad countered. "Think about it. Whatever 'proof' Roman has collected looks bad. Why wouldn't they want it to? Evidence, I've discovered, is all about perspective. Freddy is absolutely a crazy person, but he's taught me a lot about how to look at what's in front of me and question it. I think you're seeing what they want you to see."

"I don't know what to think," Zack admitted. "All of my life I've known precisely what moves to make. This...I don't know."

"Don't stop trying to figure it out. You will. I believe that. You don't have to make a decision tonight, but pushing Liz away isn't going to make things any better or easier for you."

Zack sighed. "Even if she turns out to be a traitor, I don't know that I can let her go."

That was a good sign. "Then don't. Talk to her. Tell her

what you're worried about. This whole thing might be cleared up with a single conversation."

"Or I could be handing her exactly what the Russians need to undo me. Mad, if this were just about me and Liz, we would have had this conversation a long time ago, but it's never been about only the two of us. I can't be some romantic hero who takes a leap of faith to get his girl because if I make a mistake, the world really could fall apart. If I fuck up and let them in, the damage they could do to this country would be unimaginable. And irreparable."

But Zack was forgetting something Mad knew quite well. "You will have to go with your gut at some point in time. You can't always sit back and wait this thing out. That's why you pulled that surprise announcement in the press room. You're gambling that going forward with the pipeline will force their hand."

"Yes, I am," Zack confirmed.

"See, you took a chance on that. Now take one on her. For as long as she's been by your side and worked hard to make your vision of this America a reality, doesn't she deserve some consideration? You're here because a whole lot of people in this country trust you. I know you think you have to sacrifice your own happiness, but you don't. Take that leap of faith, man. You'll find a lot of people will happily go over the edge with you."

Zack paused, then held out his hand. "I'll think about it."

Mad shook it. "Good. Now I'm going to go cut the cake so I can get busy with my bride."

"You know you'll have to have a big bash when everything settles down." Zack started to follow him inside. "A huge reception...where we will probably misbehave."

That was more like it. "I look forward to that."

Mad joined his wife and smiled when Zack parked himself beside Liz, bracing his hand on the small of her back. She seemed to relax at his touch and sent him a tenuous smile.

Sidling up to Sara, he kissed her temple. "I might need to consider a new career because I make a pretty damn good cupid."

His wife laughed and handed him the knife. "You ready to cut the cake, cherub?"

Mad glanced over at the dessert the ladies had managed to acquire for the occasion. It was simple and utterly elegant. "Sure."

"Hey, did we forget to mention there's a groom's cake?" Gabe pulled a domed silver lid off a nearby tray.

The sight his best friend revealed made Mad laugh because it was a large purple penis complete with a metric shit ton of glitter.

At least some things never changed.

Chapter Seventeen

Zack strode down the hall the next morning feeling cautiously optimistic. Four full days had passed since he'd announced his intention to move forward with the pipeline. Things had been surprisingly quiet. He'd spent most of that time in meetings with European leaders answering questions about how they could participate or hearing their vows to never allow it to touch their shores. One country who hadn't said a damn thing? Russia. The Russian president had released a brief statement that he was looking into the legalities of the project, but not once had he accused the US president of being a fraud.

Of course Zack doubted that was the end of Russian interference in his administration. They hadn't played this game for forty years to simply give up, but maybe he had finally found a maneuver that put them in a corner for a while. All in all, things were looking up.

He stopped in front of the press office and glanced back at Thomas, who looked somehow uncomfortable whenever he wasn't in his perfectly pressed suit. Today the agent was ready for a jog in standard gray sweatpants and a black T-shirt.

Zack had decided to take a calculated risk and—gasp—indulge in an outdoor run. The day was beautiful, and he was tired of being cooped up inside. Yes, he knew the risks, but he also knew Secret Service would surround and monitor him and Roman.

Oh, for the days when they'd jogged through Central Park and no one had given a damn.

"Hello, Mr. President. You're looking very fit." An attractive young brunette who'd hit on him before gave him a thorough once-over. Vanessa. She'd been around since the campaign. He'd never told Elizabeth that the woman had offered to take care of his personal needs on more than one occasion, but maybe he should.

He ignored her innuendo. "Good morning. Is Ms. Matthews here?"

"She's around somewhere," Vanessa offered with a dismissive wave. "But she's not the only one who can help. I know what goes on here, so I can take care of you, too."

"I would rather wait for Ms. Matthews. Since she's the most senior member of this staff, I know she'll be able to assist me." He respected the chain of command. And he wanted to talk to his girlfriend.

"I've been around almost as long as she has. Have you considered that other longtime staffers would love a chance to help you, sir?" Vanessa smiled in a gesture nothing less than flirty. "You might find new positions...on the issues."

Thomas cleared his throat, reminding Zack that he could take down petite problems full of hair spray and sass as efficiently as he could an assassin. Luckily he didn't have to give the order since Elizabeth stepped out of her office a moment later.

As always, his breath caught at the sight of her. Today, she wore a white shirt and slacks that molded to her every curve, her blonde hair loose and flowing past her shoulders. She'd been up and out of bed before him, preparing for what was sure to be a long press briefing, which he'd promised not to show up for.

Zack couldn't deny that he'd made her job difficult lately. She was having to prove to the press corps that she still had the president's trust, and he wasn't sure how to facilitate that. Walking in and taking over the press conference had launched his counterattack against the Russian menace, but he hadn't thought in advance about how it would affect her credibility. And he'd also found other ways to complicate her job.

She'd had to get up early because he'd kept her from working the night before. He'd made love to her—he hadn't been able to stop himself—but then he'd talked to her. Really talked to her. Not about Roman's suspicions or his resulting worries. He couldn't have that conversation with her yet. Once he had more facts, maybe talked to Paul Harding and hopefully pried some information out of him, he would sit Elizabeth down and explain why some of her actions had raised red flags. It would be an interrogation, but a gentle one.

The one he intended to have with Paul Harding this afternoon would be less so.

Zack didn't want to sully Joy's memory, but there were too many question marks about her behavior. Once he spoke to his father-in-law and assured him that he didn't intend to smear Joy's name through the press, maybe Paul would be forthcoming about the reasons his daughter had insisted on those last few appearances in the Midwest. And why she'd considered partnering with Tavia's organization. After all, Joy had done very little without her father's direction, even take a husband. And if Paul was willing to chat about his visits with his father, as well as Frank's lucidity or lack thereof, that would be a bonus.

"Hey." Elizabeth strode over, looking him up and down. "Going to hit the gym?"

"Going for a jog," he corrected. "I need some fresh air."

Her eyes widened and her voice dropped. *"Outside?* That's not a good idea."

He'd known she wouldn't approve. She seemed terrified about him leaving the White House now, but he couldn't serve the rest of his presidency inside these four walls and he refused to live in fear.

Zack pulled her to a quieter corner of the bustling press office. "Roman is coming with me, and we're only going to the south lawn. I'll be surrounded by Secret Service agents. It's been quiet. Connor hasn't heard a whisper on the Dark Web."

Since the pipeline announcement, the former CIA agent had been monitoring all the nasty corners of the web for any talk about professionals offing a high-profile figure.

She'd paled. "I know it's been quiet, but that doesn't mean anything. It's only been a few days. Don't be reckless."

He smiled because he didn't want to fuel office gossip and he wasn't arguing with her about this. "Stop worrying. We'll be fine. I'll see you at six. We need to talk then because the staff is definitely gossiping about us. It's only a matter of time before someone tips the press off and they run with the story. We need to set up a date and go public so we can control the narrative."

She nodded, but he saw the worry in her eyes. "Be careful."

"You ready or are we going to let ourselves go now that we've hit old age?" Roman joked from the doorway, wearing running shorts, a Yale T-shirt, and athletic shoes instead of his usual loafers. "Maybe you're giving up, but I'm getting married soon. I have to fit into the tux Gus picked out or she might change her mind."

Zack gave Liz one last glance. He wished he could kiss her. Hell, he wished he didn't have to care that eyes were on them all the time. First, he needed to ask her those few delicate questions so she could hopefully lay all the suspicions to rest before they went public. For now, he simply nodded her way, then turned and left. If all went well tonight, he would kiss her all he liked in the very near future.

"Do you realize that brunette was making doe eyes at you?" Roman asked as they strode down the hall toward the south lawn and the bright morning sun.

"You mean Vanessa?" Sometimes Zack thought his best friend had been born without a single polite gene. Roman sucked at remembering people he'd decided didn't matter. "She's worked with Elizabeth for the last three plus years, and you can't remember her name?"

"I know her name. I just don't like the way she looks at you," Roman admitted. "Does Liz know that woman is giving you fangirl eyes?"

"What the hell are fangirl eyes?"

They reached the exit and Roman pushed his way outside. "Aren't you up on the latest lingo? Come on, Thomas. You've got two kids. Surely you know all the fresh, hip stuff."

"I don't believe there is anything hip or fresh about fangirl. Been around a long time." Thomas's face never changed expression as he slid a pair of mirrored aviators over his eyes. "But what I believe Mr. Calder is trying to say is, girl got it bad for you, sir. However, I also think girl likes to cause trouble."

Zack pointed the observant agent's way. "Exactly. Vanessa has hit on me a couple of times, even when I was married. That makes her a mean girl, too. See, I know some of the new lingo."

"Not even close, sir." Thomas kept pace beside them,

constantly assessing their surroundings.

Oh, well. When his time in office was done, maybe he would learn some slang. Or maybe he would continue his old-man ways and let his kids make fun of him.

His kids. The thought almost stopped him where he stood.

When it seemed Joy couldn't have children, he'd let that particular hope go. But lately, he'd been thinking again about procreating. He didn't have a biological clock, per se, but he felt the pressure of time just the same. Mad was about to have a kid, and the rest of his friends wouldn't be far behind. If he wanted a player in that crazy group, he and Elizabeth needed to get moving.

"You ready for this afternoon?" Roman asked, starting down the jogging path.

Was anyone ever truly ready to confront their father-in-law about a deeply uncomfortable topic? "As ready as I can be."

"Connor is down in PEOC, preparing a room right now," Roman advised as they started to run.

"Will that send the wrong message to Paul? It's supposed to be a friendly chat."

"We'll couch it as a place where we can have the utmost privacy. So he can air his grievances as loudly as he'd like." Roman rolled his eyes. "And neither of you will have to deal with quite so many prying eyes and wagging tongues. It'll work."

"If you say so."

His chief of staff nodded. "Thomas will clear out all unneeded personnel and Freddy will observe behind two-way glass. He's pushing for that lie detector—the one he's souped up—but I told him no. I'll be there, too, to make sure everything is done in a purely above-board fashion and that Freddy doesn't get out of hand. But you should know, if Paul says anything incriminating, we can't hold him without bringing in the Justice Department."

"Jesus, you think everyone is guilty of something. I'm shocked you don't suspect me."

"Should I?" Roman returned, deadpan.

"I'm only going to ask Paul a few questions, see where it leads." Zack was aware he'd put this off for too long. Now he needed whatever answers he could get.

"Did you know Liz has been talking to him?" Roman asked.

Zack focused on the green lawn ahead, his heart rate starting to tick up. "She's been trying to soothe his ruffled feathers about the public rumors of your relationship with Joy so I don't have to deal with him. He thinks we're dragging her name through the mud posthumously. If someone hadn't talked to him, he would have gone to the press. We don't need that."

A pair of Secret Service agents jogged in front of them, giving him and Roman both some space and protection. Two more kept pace behind them while Thomas and Mike, another long-term agent, flanked them. He was never alone—except at night when he finally got to wrap himself around Elizabeth.

Zack picked up the pace, and Roman matched him. He wished he could sprint for a nice long distance without having to turn around, but he was stuck here on the lawn, especially until the Russian threat was over.

"If he doesn't give us anything to look into, we'll have to let him go," Roman said. "Then I worry he'll talk to Liz. I'd rather leave her out of these discussions until we have something firmer."

In other words, he didn't want to bring Liz in until he could prove everything he accused her of.

"Roman, I'm telling her everything tonight. I know what you're going to say because I've already heard it. But that's the end of the conversation." It was time to change the subject. "Have you heard from Connor this morning? He told me he had an update and that he'd fill me in soon."

The good news about taking a stand while they worked out was Roman's inability to pin him with that steely, disapproving stare of his. "He told me his Russian connection found some information we might find interesting. He didn't sound like it was a bad thing."

That was all they could say around the others. Connor was looking for any hospital records—footprints, blood type, other test results—anything that might tell them whether Zack was the baby Natalia had given birth to.

"I know you don't want to hear this, but you need to slow down with Liz." Roman didn't seem to think talking about his personal life fell under the same protocols as the case.

"I haven't sped up." They were right where they'd been since he'd first touched her at Camp David. He was wary, and she was confused. If she was acting, she was damn good. More and more he suspected he was missing some big picture that was right in front of his face.

"You're talking about going out on a date and revealing your relationship to the press. I think that's a bad idea at this stage."

"Well, I'll tell you something worse." The idea had been pinging around Zack's brain a lot lately. "I think I'm going to marry her in the next week or so and present the whole thing as a fait accompli. Then there's not much anyone can do about it."

And he couldn't be forced to testify against his wife if it came to that.

Not that Zack would ever allow a case against her to go that far.

"You have got to be kidding me." Roman stopped in the middle of the lawn. "You can't."

Zack sighed and stopped, too, forcing all the agents to

change course. "I can. I have very good reasons, including the fact that it could deflect a lot of the scrutiny that's on you right now."

"I'll handle the story about Joy without you resorting to such drastic measures."

Zack dismissed him and started running again. They were not having this out right now. If Roman wanted to debate, they would do it alone, back in the White House. But his chief of staff would find him an immovable mountain on this topic. He was tired of keeping Elizabeth at arm's length, based on little more than circumstantial evidence, innuendo, and Roman's suspicions.

Determined not to let Roman get to him, Zack turned his thoughts to whatever Connor's contact had found. God, he hoped it would help put an end to all the torture about his true identity. Not knowing was a bitch. Or he hoped they'd found solid proof of the conspirators' names and locations. Then he could breathe a sigh of relief and turn everything over to the Justice Department.

If he could trust them...

Paranoia was insidious. It threatened to choke him until he couldn't breathe. If he wanted to survive, he had to let it go. When he got Elizabeth in his arms tonight, he would tell her everything. He would ask for explanations and try to put his faith in her.

"Seriously, don't do this. It's not a problem you have to handle alone," Roman said, falling in beside him again. "I'm here."

"You're not the one who's got trust issues with the woman you love."

Zack wondered if he was looking at this all wrong. Maybe believing really was as easy as Mad suggested. Perhaps all he had to do was decide that the world would go his way and not give in until he got what he wanted.

"Down, now!"

Zack heard Thomas's shout an instant before someone tackled him from behind. He hit the ground hard, heart pounding. For a moment he couldn't breathe. Then he heard a crack-boom across the lawn and chaos reigned.

* * * *

"I've got a list of the questions the reporter will be allowed to ask." Liz set down a thick stack of papers, the end product of hours of negotiations with the network Roman and Gus would grant their exclusive interview to. "If she deviates from the list, don't comment. But I think she'll comply with the rules of engagement. She's ambitious but fair."

Zack intended to talk to her, too, explain his relationship with his wife briefly and swear publicly that no bad blood brewed between him and his chief of staff. Liz had advised him against the move, but he'd insisted.

Foolish man. He was being as reckless with this interview as he was with this morning's run. Worrying about him was starting to become her second job. She hated the fact that he'd chosen to put himself at risk. The Secret Service couldn't possibly check every surrounding tree and building.

On the other hand, she understood that he couldn't remain inside the White House every day for the rest of his presidency.

"You okay?" Gus ignored the papers and stood. "You look a little pale. Did you have breakfast this morning?"

She hadn't been eating anything but dinner for the last couple of days, and only then because Zack nagged her about it. Something had to give and soon. The tension was killing her. She couldn't sleep because every time she closed her eyes, she was back in her apartment with Krylov. Zack walked in, and the Russian pulled a gun and shot him.

"I had some coffee."

The last couple of days she'd been running on caffeine and willpower.

"Is Zack still being an asshole?"

"No. He's been wonderful since the wedding. I think whatever Mad said to him that night helped, but the cabin fever is getting to all of us. When Everly finds out Zack and Roman are outside jogging and she's not even allowed a simple trip to Neiman's, she's going to flip."

Gus waved the worry off. "Hey, if Everly wants to jog around the grounds, I'll find a detail to go with her. We're all welcome to do that as long as we take a bodyguard with us."

"How can you be so sanguine about this?" Gus was usually the first one to rail against restrictions, not agree with them.

"I grew up with a Southern momma, a Navy admiral for a father, and an alpha male brother. And don't get me started on Roman. I'm used to overly protective types. Besides, I don't mind staying in. I think I'm getting old. I've gotten to where I prefer books over bars."

Liz had always preferred them, but her nights in lately hadn't been relaxing. Well, except for the hours Zack's magical touch took her out of her head. When he made love to her, she forgot everything else. "Well, I'm looking forward to the trip overseas next month. I never thought I would consider a trip to the G7 Summit a vacation."

"Anything has got to be better than sitting around waiting for a bomb to go off." Gus stared down at the contract. "These look good, but Roman will want to go over them with a fine-tooth comb. I'm sure he'll demand a bunch of changes for the hell of it." Her gaze climbed up, and she studied Liz intently. "I'm worried my fiancé has it in his head that someone close to Zack is working with the enemy."

Liz glanced back, making sure the door was closed before sinking into the chair across from Gus. "Did they find anything while they were going through the personnel files?"

Not being able to be a part of the investigation was wearing on Liz. But she and Zack couldn't stop running the country to focus on their hush-hush inquiry. Too many questions would arise. So they were forced to rely on the rest of the group for answers.

Gus hesitated. "They've identified a couple of people they're unsure about."

Liz had worked with Gus long enough to read her cues. "What are you not telling me?"

Gus knotted her hands together as though trying to stop a nervous tic. "Can you think of a reason my incredibly suspicious ass of a fiancé would be investigating you?"

"Me? Roman is investigating me?"

"One of the private investigators he often uses sent him a report yesterday. I caught a glimpse, and it was pretty much a rundown of your whole life. Birth certificate. College transcripts. Validation of your résumé. I believe he talked to a couple of your childhood and college friends. Why would Roman do that?"

Liz felt her stomach flip over. "I don't know. Is he looking into all of us? Or everyone who hasn't been around since y'all were kids? I mean, it makes sense to vet the girlfriend of the president, though I went through all of this when I was hired. I've worked tirelessly for Zack for years."

"Yes, they did a full background check. Even I went through the process when I came on board." Gus drummed her nails against the top of her desk, a sure sign her mind was churning.

"So...I don't understand."

"I'm starting to think the guys don't trust you, and that worries me. Liz, are you working with the bad guys?"

"Are you kidding me? Of course not. That's ridiculous! I'm going to kick Roman's ass."

"Excellent." Gus smiled, obviously relieved. "He's way too deep into his own paranoia. Let's all have dinner tonight and drag this shit into the light. We can have a good old-fashioned screaming match and get it over with."

At least Zack didn't feel that way, although she could easily see how Roman's suspicious nature might influence him.

Wait. What if the tension she'd been feeling from him lately stemmed from more than their current conundrum? What if he was worried Roman's suspicions were true?

"Hey, don't frown. And don't worry. This is what Roman does. He's not an optimist. Where other people see sunshine, he sees melanoma." Gus leaned closer. "Sometimes it's cute. Sometimes it makes me want to strangle him."

Liz was gathering a comeback when someone knocked on the door, then shoved it open.

Gus sighed at the sight of the woman in the doorway. "Yes, Vanessa. Please come in."

"Something's happening." She glanced behind her. "Turn on the news."

Liz followed Vanessa's gaze. Sure enough, the whole office was buzzing. She stood, worry flooding her veins. "What?"

Gus reached for the remote on her desk and clicked it. The television monitor on the opposite wall flickered on. A noted news anchor's face filled the screen.

"I think it's the president." Vanessa clutched her phone. "What should we do? We're already getting calls."

"Oh my god," Gus breathed, going pale.

Liz's heart stopped when she heard what the news anchor was saying.

"We don't have details yet, but we're getting multiple

reports of an assassination attempt on President Zachary Hayes."

Liz did her best to tamp down her panic as she strode out of her office and into the main hub of press relations at the White House. Everyone started shouting questions her way. She didn't hear any of them because her whole being was focused on one thing—getting to Zack. Work wasn't registering in that moment. She wasn't a press secretary; she was a woman in love, desperate to know if her lover was alive.

"I'll come with you." Gus took her hand. "Roman was with him, right? Where were they going?"

The world seemed to slow even as her thoughts raced. Liz forced herself to focus on Gus because if she didn't, she would lose her mind. Where was Zack now? Was he even still alive?

Suddenly, she felt transported back to that awful evening in Memphis, standing in the auditorium and hearing the crack of the bullet, feeling the ground shift as the crowd sprinted for the exits. And seeing the blood. So much blood...

"They were on the south lawn," Liz managed to eke out. "Jogging. He and Roman wanted to be outside."

"I'm going to kill that man myself." The second the words passed Gus's lips, she paled. "I'm sorry, Liz. I didn't mean it."

"It's fine." All that mattered was Zack.

She squeezed Gus's hand, then started to plow through the small crowd staring at the monitors all around the press office. Every single news channel was covering this story.

Liz refused to wait around for cable news to tell her what had happened. She was going to find Zack herself.

In the distance, she heard sirens. Her stomach plummeted with dread, and she sent up a silent prayer that Zack would be all right. She couldn't lose him. She couldn't, not when they'd finally found each other and were getting so close to the life they'd both dreamed of, to the family they wanted.

She was nearly to the doors when they crashed open. Two men in dark suits strode in. Secret Service.

"What's happening?" Gus demanded immediately of the one who looked like he was in charge. "Where are they now?"

There was no question who "they" were. If Zack had been hit, Roman would have stayed with him, accompanied him to the hospital.

The agent touched a Bluetooth device attached to his ear and ignored her questions entirely, instead replying to whoever was speaking in his ear. "Yes, sir. I've sent a team to secure the vice president. I'm bringing Ms. Matthews down. Yes, sir. I'll let her know."

The icy-eyed agent grabbed her arm.

"What's happening?" Liz could barely contain her panic.

"I'm here to escort you downstairs, Ms. Matthews," he replied. "I have orders to take you to a secure location. Ms. Spencer, Mr. Calder would like you to stay in your office and wait for his call. He's uninjured."

"I'll go with Liz," Gus offered.

The second of the two agents stepped in front of her, coming between the women. "I'm sorry, Ms. Spencer. We have our orders."

Liz looked back, pure terror in her veins. Why would they leave Gus behind...unless Zack wasn't okay? Tears pooled in her eyes and she all but ran, trying to hurry the agent to Zack's side. Behind her, the world was erupting as the other agent moved everyone else into the press room.

"What hospital is the president at?" she asked, her voice shaking.

"Come with me, ma'am." He opened the door that led

to the hallway, then she found herself in an elevator.

Please don't let him be dead. Please. Let him be alive.
They could face anything if he just lived through this.

The elevator doors closed. Liz shut her eyes and tried to dredge up her inner strength. The world suddenly seemed so quiet it was stark, tense. Somehow, she had to stay calm. She couldn't lose it when Zack might need her.

What would she do if he was gone? If someone had managed to extinguish his life? She couldn't even consider it. He was alive. She would be by his side and holding his hand when he woke up. She would never complain about anything ever again if the universe gave her back the man she loved.

Finally, the elevator doors opened and she blinked. She wasn't in the garage she'd thought they were taking her to. They weren't anywhere near the underground parking.

They were in PEOC.

Were they taking her to see Mad and Sara? But that didn't make sense…

Cautiously, she stepped out and looked right. Her heart surged and pumped to life again because Zack was standing there, Thomas and Roman flanking him. His T-shirt was torn and his hair was a mess but he was thankfully, blessedly alive.

"Oh, Zack." She wept freely now and started to dash toward him.

The Secret Service agent clamped a hard grip around her elbow and hauled her back. She gaped at him, and reached out for Zack.

The chilly look in his eyes froze her where she stood. She'd never seen him look so cold, as if she meant less than a speck on his shoe. Like he could look through her and not feel a thing.

"Zack?" she whispered, his name a question and a prayer on her lips.

He ignored her, gesturing to a hallway on his right. "Please take her to the second interrogation room. Thank you."

"Interrogation?" she screeched. "Zack, what is going on?"

The agent began to drag her away from Zack.

Stunned, horrified, she glanced at the man she'd poured her heart and her life into. What the hell was happening? His face told her nothing.

Then her shoe slid on the slick tile and she started to fall. Strong arms wound around her before she could hit the floor, and she found herself swept up. Zack. He'd caught her, but he didn't look at all happy with this turn of events. In fact, his jaw was tight as he secured her against his chest. She could see where he'd suffered a minor abrasion, and she wanted to reach up and soothe him, but everything about his demeanor told her she'd better not dare.

"What's happening?" she breathed.

"Someone tried to assassinate me, sweetheart," he said, starting down the hallway.

"I know. I heard on the news. I was so worried and—"

"And you were the only one who knew where Roman and I planned to take our morning run. I'm afraid your time is up."

How could he talk to her in that arctic tone? Surely, he wasn't implying that she'd had anything to do with the attempt on his life. "My time? Zack, I didn't tell anyone. I would *never* do that. I didn't want you to go outside at all."

He said nothing, merely walked until Thomas opened a door. Zack entered and set her inside. The room was utilitarian, with only a metal table and a couple of chairs.

He set her on her feet and stepped away like she was a viper he suspected would attack at any moment. "We have some questions. I think it's best if Roman handles you. We already know I can't think straight when you're around."

This couldn't be happening. It must be some kind of nightmare. "Zack, don't do this. I would never hurt you. I love you."

"I don't expect you to admit anything to me. After all, you've got me whipped, so why stop lying now?"

"What? Lying?" She stared in open-mouthed horror.

"Think carefully about how you proceed." He stepped to the door. "Tell Roman the truth. Tell him everything you've done and what else your 'friends' are planning. Then you and I will talk. But if you don't tell Roman everything you know, I'll have to bring in someone else. You won't like the someone else. Make this easy on yourself, Elizabeth."

He thought she was capable of hurting him? Yes. He thought she was working with the Russians, so he also thought she was capable of treason.

She shuddered. "You can't honestly believe I'm some sort of spy. Zack, I know someone made an attempt on your life, and I was the last person you talked to, but whatever Roman thinks about my loyalties, he's wrong."

"It's not just Roman. I was suspicious of you long before now. Today merely clarified your guilt for me." He turned away.

The watchful Secret Service agent stood right by the door. Making sure she didn't get another chance to speak to the president. No, making sure she didn't get another chance to hurt him.

This was beyond surreal.

"You slept with me when you thought I was working against you?"

He'd made love to her like a man who couldn't get enough. He'd held her like he loved her. They'd been sharing a bed for two weeks and sharing their lives for far longer than that. She'd practically been a wife to him, and he hadn't given her the benefit of the doubt. He hadn't even done her the courtesy of telling her why he suspected her. Instead, he'd brought her to a secret site to be interrogated. He was locking her in a room and not letting her out until she gave him some sort of a confession.

"You know what they say," Zack began. "Keep your friends close and your enemies closer. I couldn't have gotten closer to you if I tried."

In that moment, all the cherished memories of the two of them she'd stored lovingly in her memory turned to ash.

He didn't love her. He never had.

With tears falling, she watched as he slammed the door between them and the lock slid into place.

Chapter Eighteen

Zack stood outside the interrogation room and tried hard to quell his need to punch something.

He glanced down at the monitors that showed the two small rooms. Elizabeth was in there. He'd said terrible things to her, sicced Roman on her, and locked her inside.

"Zack, we have a sniper suspect in custody." Connor strode up to him. "I want your authorization to speak to him. He's a Russian national and, according to my sources, he's got connections to the syndicate. We might finally have Krylov's balls in a vise if we can get this guy to talk, but I have to move fast. Krylov is in the US now, but if he thinks we can shut this plot down and expose him, he'll head straight for Moscow. And we'll never be able to touch him again."

"Arrogant bastard," Roman said, joining them after changing back into his standard suit and tie. He looked immaculate, not like a guy who had been inches from an assassination attempt less than an hour ago. "We can't let him get away with this, and I'm sure he believes he will."

"Why shouldn't he? He's gotten away with it for years. The whole Russian apparatus has," Connor pointed out. "No doubt he's hoping we'll be too busy trying to protect Zack to bother with him and his comrades."

"We have to put a stop to this, once and for all." Zack reached that decision as he'd locked the door and walked away from Elizabeth. This ended. Now. He wouldn't put any of his family through another day of this. It wouldn't rule him anymore. "And if we can't get Krylov and his whole ring, I'm going to talk to the attorney general in the morning. If I have to, I'll step down. I'll even go to fucking jail, but I'm not letting them win."

"I don't think that's a good idea," Roman argued.

Connor stopped him with a raised hand. "Before you do anything, let me talk to the assassin. Even if he doesn't confess, there's a good chance we'll be able to tie him back to the syndicate. It's not a smoking gun, but it will help corroborate our story if the Justice Department and the press get involved."

"Okay." Zack nodded. "While you're at it, have some of your boys round up Krylov in New York and question him."

"Will do. Now that they've tried to assassinate you, he's likely to make a mad dash to the airport."

"Even though he has no idea whether I'm dead or alive?" Zack turned to Roman. "We haven't given Gus any instructions on a statement for the press, right?"

His chief of staff confirmed with a shake of his head. "I called Gus and told her to say 'no comment' until we decided on our next move. Connor, find out from this asshole how he knew where Zack and I would be jogging." Roman stared down at the monitors displaying Elizabeth and Paul Harding in their respective interrogation rooms.

They'd brought Joy's father in thirty minutes earlier. Paul sat staring at the door, utterly still. Eerily still. He'd asked no questions, hadn't questioned the agents sent to bring him in.

Elizabeth, on the other hand, hadn't stopped moving. She also hadn't stopped crying, but at some point her tears seemed to have morphed from sorrowful to furious. With him.

Well, he was furious with her, too...but that didn't mean he wouldn't still do his damnedest to protect her. And he would have to. After today, Zack didn't see a way not to believe Elizabeth had set him up to die. She was the only one who'd known where he and Roman would be taking their morning run. The Secret Service would have caught anyone from inside the White House following them out to the lawn, so it wasn't a dirty staffer or agent. But Elizabeth had had plenty of time to contact her Russian handler with his location, presumably to trigger the assassin they must have stationed near the White House.

"The police only found the shooter because he had a freak accident and fell out of the tree he'd set his sniper nest in. He hit his head on the sidewalk and was found unconscious." Connor grinned. "He's awake now. Time for me to play."

"Don't get cocky. Remember, we thought we had the right guy when Joy was shot." Zack could still remember how he'd felt when he'd heard the man who'd killed Joy was dead. Now he knew that man had been a patsy.

"I feel good about this one."

Thomas, who had been standing in the corner on his phone, joined the group. "I've just received confirmation that the caliber of bullet fragments CSI dug out of the tree is .308. That matches the caliber of the assassin's weapon."

"Bingo." Connor looked happy. "I mean, we'll have to run ballistics to make sure that bullet came from his weapon, but I like our odds. Plus, the police said they found a backpack and lots of fun sniper toys, so they think he's been sticking close to the White House for a while."

Just waiting for someone to call him and tell him to off the president of the United States.

"Likely so." Thomas said. "It's amazing that bullet went clean through Mike's arm without blowing it off."

Zack listened with half an ear. All this talk of bullets and violence and intent to kill. And god, he couldn't stop thinking about Elizabeth, about forgiving her. She might have sent an assassin to ensure his death, and he was foolishly thinking about how he could possibly keep her. He was a masochist.

"Did the shooter have a cell phone?" When Connor nodded, Zack continued. "I want to know who he's been talking to. I want that number."

"You must know it was a burner phone, and I'm sure we'll find out the call came from another burner. This guy falling out of the tree was a fluke. The truth is, these guys are never sloppy. But we can figure out roughly where the call originated from. So do I have authority to take over his questioning?" Connor's whole body was tense as though he was already in work mode.

Zack nodded, almost feeling sorry for the bastard. "Go, and call when you have any information at all. I want to know who tipped him off."

Connor nodded, clapped him on the shoulder, and left once again to do his country's dirty work.

"Gus is going to kill me, you know." Roman looked grim as he stared down at the monitors. "Dax and Gabe are in Elizabeth's office searching it right now, finding out if she had anything incriminating stored there. They'll do the same at her apartment when they're through with her office. Are you going to wait for Connor or start interrogating now?"

"We can't wait," Zack said grimly. "Talk to her. Find out if she's been trying to protect someone, if she was blackmailed into this." Nothing else made sense. She loved him; Zack believed that. Or he wanted to. Then again, it was possible he'd been colossally fooled before.

Was he making a mistake in second-guessing her loyalty? But how could he not ask critical questions?

Zack hardened his resolve. He had a right to get to the bottom of her actions. Of her likely perfidy. There were simply too many coincidences for her to be anything but guilty.

"I'll handle Liz," Roman promised. "Be careful with Paul. We have no idea what he's capable of."

Was Roman doing his paranoid thing again or was he right?

"Actually, Freddy and I have some questions for Mr. Harding, too." Mad stood in the doorway. "That is, if you don't mind."

"You're supposed to be dead," Roman reminded.

"After what happened today, I'm not going to hide while those bastards are taking shots at my friends."

Zack shook his head. "We may need the element of surprise later." And no one knew the case like Freddy. "Send your crazy friend with me."

Mad shrugged. "If that's what you want..." Then he glanced down at the monitors and winced when he saw Elizabeth. "Damn it, Zack. Seriously?"

Roman didn't let him reply. "She was the only one who knew where we planned to jog this morning."

"Hello, the Secret Service knew," Mad pointed out. "We're already aware of at least two agents in the past who were compromised. Who's to say there aren't more? Connor and Freddy still haven't finished vetting everyone."

"Out of an abundance of caution, we have to look into every possible suspect. There's no way we can't ask her." Roman sighed as if he was not looking forward to this task. "I'm going to grab a stiff cup of coffee and get started. Be careful, Zack."

Mad shook his head Zack's way. "If you throw her in jail, there's no coming back from this."

"She's not in jail." Of course she wouldn't be allowed to leave either. What would she do the second he unlocked the door? He had to look at all the evidence and make his best judgment call. What if she'd had a good reason for calling an assassin down on his head?

What the hell would constitute a good reason?

Misery swamped him. He wasn't even angry anymore. In those first few moments when he'd realized she must be guilty, rage had thrummed through his veins. He'd wanted to walk right into her office, confront her...and he wasn't sure what he would have done to her then.

His first impulse had faded as he'd been bodily hauled to safety, his movements restricted. In those moments, he hadn't been Zack Hayes, an American citizen born with inalienable rights. He'd been the president, property of the American people. No amount of arguing would change the fact that he had no right to be simply a man in love. He'd wanted to go to her, force her to explain. And he hadn't been allowed to.

That's when his rage had morphed into sorrow. She'd just called an assassin to snuff him out, and he was still pathetically in love with her.

"Zack, go in there and talk to her. You could have died, so you totally have a right to your suspicions. But get her side of the story first." Who would have guessed that Maddox Crawford would play angel to Roman's obvious devil? That he would be the champion of true love? "Liz will understand. She's a smart woman who gets the pressure you've been under."

"I have to talk to Paul." Zack didn't trust himself to be alone with Elizabeth, even with cameras rolling. As far as he could see that interrogation ended one of two ways:

either he hurt her more or fell right back into her trap. He turned to Roman. "Go. Find out why she's done this."

"Actually, Zack wants to know *if* she's done this," Mad cautioned. "Treat her like the friend she is. Or better yet, I'll do it."

Mad might be onto something. "Go with Roman and figure out what's going on."

Hopefully, they would balance one another.

"You got it." Mad grinned.

Roman just sighed.

"And I'll take Freddy with me. Do we know where he's hiding?"

"I'm here," a disembodied voice from above said.

Suddenly, Zack found himself right back under Thomas, and three Secret Service agents all trained their firearms at the ceiling.

"Don't shoot him." The phantom of the White House was at work again, and Zack vowed to add a new line in the budget for completely redoing all the ductwork in the White House to ensure no crazy people could use them to sneak around in the future. "He's a friendly."

Thomas let him up, still wearing his usual stoic expression. One of the other agents kept his gun trained as Freddy popped the vent and wiggled out.

"I can give you the name of a guy who will secure the whole system, Mr. President." Freddy held up his hands to show he wasn't carrying.

They frisked him anyway.

"Dare I ask why you aren't in the very nice room I assigned you to?" Roman asked.

Freddy shrugged. "It was a cage, man. Been there, done that. Never again. Besides, the security guard down here watches TV at night and he's doing a great binge of *Star Trek: The Next Generation*. I couldn't miss that. If you could tell him to turn up the volume, though, that would be helpful."

Zack made a mental note to have someone talk to the guard who apparently didn't realize he was being spied on. He turned to Freddy. "What do you know about Paul Harding?"

A feral grin lit Freddy's face. "Enough to suspect he's been working for the Russians since he was a kid. I've really been looking at him the last few days, and I'm almost positive. Do I really get to question a suspect?"

"I'm in charge." He needed to make that very clear.

Freddy gave him a jaunty salute. "I'm happy to play the perky sidekick."

More like the insane sidekick. He turned to Mad and Roman. "Get me answers."

Then Zack forced himself to turn away and focus on the job at hand. His father-in-law knew something and he was going to find out what.

* * * *

Zack stepped inside the utilitarian room and Paul Harding's pale eyes shifted toward him. It was the first movement he'd seen from the man in the hour since he'd been brought in.

"Hello, Zachary. Might I ask why I was dragged from my home on such a nice day?" There was no deep indignation in his manner, merely curiosity.

Zack took the seat opposite, allowing Freddy to pace, which he seemed compelled to do anyway. Thomas, as always, remained his shadow.

"I'd like to ask you a few questions."

"I would like the same courtesy, Zachary." Paul placed his hands on the table and leaned in. One of them was cuffed to the bar that ran along the side of the table. "*Kak, po-tvoemy, mozhno izbezhat svoyu sudbu?*" His Russian accent sounded as perfect as his bland American one.

How do you think to avoid your fate?

Zack's stomach knotted. He swallowed down his shock. "You're not even going to try to deny your guilt?"

"No, because he knows we have him," Freddy said, sounding far more serious than Zack had ever heard him. The military intelligence officer in him was ingrained deep and had taken over. "It's actually not surprising. They're moving the operation to the next level, very likely because of your pipeline announcement the other day. Are you acting as the primary contact between the Russians and the administration now, Mr. Harding?"

"Well, since President Hayes has proven to be uncompromising so far, it's become necessary to make contact," he said. "Clearly, I no longer have influence over him in any valuable way, so I'm being put to other uses. However, I will not be your contact in the future. I am merely a messenger."

God, it was all fucking true. Everything they'd been investigating and suspecting, the people hiding in the shadows, intending to control him or kill him…all of it was true. He'd been surrounded by wolves for years. "So your next move was to have me killed."

A single shoulder shrugged. "Which has proven ineffective as well. I told them it would be better to poison you and implicate one of your friends. They argued that poisoning is more difficult than a bullet and harder to pin on someone. And unfortunately, I no longer have the kind of close contact with you that allowed me to properly doctor your food."

The fact that his once kindly father-in-law was calmly discussing how best to kill him struck him squarely in the gut. He'd gone on fishing trips with this man, opened up to him about the fact he and Joy had tried to have children. Never once had he seen even a hint of the predator under Paul's surface.

"When did SVR recruit you?" Freddy took up the questioning, seeming to understand that Zack needed a moment.

The expression on Paul's face was like nothing Zack had ever seen. His mask had fallen away, finally revealing the real man. Cruel. Superior. Sure of his place in the world. "Please. They are nothing but a cover for the KGB. Don't think for a moment they aren't the same. You can't change something like the KGB."

"Your parents were planted by the KGB," Freddy said. "I've been studying you. Your parents immigrated from Canada, but I would bet they were born in the USSR."

Paul cocked a brow, a silent nod to Freddy's cleverness. "You are the first to realize this. My parents were smart."

"Mr. President, have you heard of a program called 'the illegals'?" Freddy asked.

Paul rolled his eyes. "We had nothing to do with those idiots."

Zack shook his head and waited for Freddy to clue him in.

"The US Department of Justice started tracking a group of sleeper agents years ago that ended in the arrests of ten operatives, many whom had been living in the US for decades and had children born in the US. Mr. Harding's group was a precursor to that particular program. His father and mother came to the US under forged Canadian documents. It was simpler to arrange such things in 1957. Paul was fifteen then. His father was a nuclear engineer. His knowledge would have been deemed valuable. It would have been easy for them to get a work visa and a job, especially since he was a family man."

"I was trained alongside my parents," Paul explained. "Even at a young age, I knew about the corruption of your system. America is the whining child of the world. We were a small, but well-trained group. We were tasked with building a home and a life in the United States. My father sent information back to Mother Russia about your government programs for years. I did the same in the military. After I graduated at the top of my class in high school, getting admitted into the Naval Academy was simple. Excelling was even easier. After all, I was disciplined. I was working toward something monumental while my pathetic classmates cared only for drinking and making idiots of themselves. I fought in Vietnam, and came back a great American hero." He sneered. "I was always helping my comrades on the other side, and no one ever suspected."

Zack's head reeled. Dear god. How many like Paul were out there? "That's treason. You deserve everything that's coming for you. Our past relations won't save you. I won't keep quiet, not after you actively aided the enemy in a time of war."

"I was the enemy, boy. I always have been."

Clearly, and the implications were staggering.

Freddy simply looked on. "Your parents never went back to Russia. They lived here until they passed."

"My parents were true patriots. They showed me how to be loyal to my country, my people, no matter where I lived. I didn't have to be in Russia to love it. That is what none of you understand. When my naval career brought me to loftier heights, we realized that we had an opportunity to use my skills and contacts for a greater purpose than I had previously imagined."

To elect him to become a puppet for Russia. Zack could hardly fathom it.

"How much of this did Joy know?"

"Most everything." He smiled, and Zack gaped, feeling sick. "My daughter was a true Russian asset. Her mother and I raised her to always serve the land of her heart," he said with the aura of a true believer. "She did so admirably because she knew her duty and embraced it."

"Did she set herself up to die?"

For a tiny instant, Paul looked downcast. "No. When it became clear you would not win the election otherwise, she became my gift to my people, an unfortunate sacrifice I made for Russia's greater good." Paul settled back. "After all, one cannot have victory without sacrifice, so I proudly made mine. We all must. It's what entitled Americans like you don't understand. You think you can have everything without paying a price. Without getting blood on your hands. But blood reminds us what is at stake."

Zack sat back, swallowing down rising bile. Shock didn't begin to cover how he felt.

Had Joy taken instructions from her handlers, thinking she merely had to get through the last days of the campaign before she could be free, never knowing her own parents were helping to sacrifice her for the cause? Had she realized what had happened, the way her mother and father had betrayed her, as the bullet tore through her chest?

"So you weren't involved directly with the Hayes family in the beginning?" Thank god Freddy was capable of viewing this as an intellectual exercise. "Did you know Zack Hayes's grandfather was a Russian asset?"

Paul shook his head. "They chose to handle him differently because he was always destined for this cause. I later fell into it."

Based on what Zack knew, that made sense. "What do you know about Natalia Kuilikov?"

"Bah, she was nothing but a tool, and an ineffective one at that. She was a weak woman who cared too much. They did not break her properly."

"She cared about *me*." Zack remembered how kind Nata had been.

"The stupid woman was supposed to raise you right, help you understand your loyalties. But she became

...difficult. So you were sent away to that boarding school. It was important that your education look thorough and proper, that you made the right connections," Paul explained.

"So my parents weren't involved in this giant scheme? They certainly didn't raise me the way you did Joy."

For the first time, Paul played coy. "You see, the CIA is quite intelligent. They have ways of finding our connections. So we had to ensure that your father had no idea where his father's loyalties truly lie. Unfortunately, he proved...unsuitable for our needs."

So the Russians had sought to compromise his father, help install him as president of the United States, and use him for their own ends. But when he'd been unable to win the primary, they'd shifted to another plan. They'd looked to the future. Zack.

"What you're saying is that you wanted an asset who could be vetted and would have absolutely no problem passing a lie detector test," Freddy mused. "Or any test since a good agent can get the truth out in other ways. But you knew that, so you avoided that possibility. After all, an asset can't fail such an indicator if he doesn't know he's an asset until it's too late."

"Frank Hayes was weak, and they thought it best that he not know his part of the plot until he could no longer escape," Paul confirmed. "For the same reasons, we would have preferred Zachary never knew he was being manipulated. If he had been strong enough to win the election on his own, my Joy would have made sure the right people were advising him."

The right people? Did that include Liz? Maybe...but maybe not. His father had hired her. At Paul's behest? On the orders of someone higher up in the old KGB structure? Or simply because her predecessor had been ineffectual at getting him positive press and she'd been damn good at her job? He wasn't sure since Joy had taken the burden of finding the right people for the right job off his shoulders during the campaign.

Of course she had. She'd been instructed to. And it certainly wouldn't surprise him if some of the people Joy had hired were still in their roles to this day.

That realization terrified him. The wolves could be anywhere, everywhere.

"Thomas, please go inform Mr. Calder that my late wife was working with the enemy."

"Sir—"

"I know you're not supposed to leave me, but Mr. Harding is an old man handcuffed to a table. I've survived one bullet today. I doubt there's much else he can do to me." When the agent still hesitated, Zack got stubborn. "I'm ordering you to. And I've got Freddy here to help me."

Thomas sighed as if he didn't like it at all, but he complied. "I'll be back shortly."

As he left, Zack sat back and tried to process everything Paul had hurled his way.

Joy had been a traitor. The woman he'd sought to make First Lady had been a Russian asset. Wow. Just…wow. Even as so many pieces of the puzzle began to snap into place, Zack thought of a thousand other questions. Why the emotional affair with Roman? What purpose would that have served to the Russians? To compromise his best friend? Possibly, but Roman was the one person he'd ever seen Joy be passionate about. Was it possible that she'd followed her heart that once? Had she changed her mind and shifted her loyalties, never knowing her end was near?

How much of her life had been dictated since the moment she was born? And what kind of relief had she felt when she'd thought she might escape? Zack could still remember the peace on her face when they'd realized he wasn't going to win the election. At first he'd thought Joy was merely being a supportive wife. Now he wondered if she'd seen losing as her one-way ticket out of a life she'd no longer wanted.

What would it be like to have spent a lifetime in service of those others whose sole intention was to use you?

"I suppose I never found the 'right people' in your eyes. My father sent me to Creighton because you thought a school with such a rigorous reputation would make me easier to mold. You didn't count on me finding a group of friends, did you?" Creighton had been isolating in the beginning. He'd spent the first half of a semester talking to no one until the mouthiest bad boy in the class sat down next to him and started talking. Maddox. He'd been the one to bring them all together. He hadn't had any idea how his need to form a family would change their lives forever. "It might have worked if I hadn't found my friends."

"We expected all of you to drift apart as you got older. Most people do. We waited for you to get involved in your lives and careers, find other interests and people. Mr. Calder, we knew would stay around, but we thought he would be easy to deal with, especially when it seemed clear that Joy would have more success manipulating him than you. A physical affair between the two of them would have made him vulnerable."

But Roman had never crossed that line.

Zack saw their plans now. They'd put him in the presidency, then waited until they'd been ready to use him. He was supposed to have been their frog in a pot. If they'd dropped him into scalding water, he would have leapt out. But by slowly turning up the heat, they had been hoping to boil him before he realized it was too late to escape.

"Instead, none of us drifted apart," Zack pointed out.

One person had held them together. He'd done it by showing up at the most inopportune times and slyly convincing them to party. But now, Zack saw clearly that had been Mad's way of holding his family together. He feared he would have done exactly what the Russians had expected without Mad Crawford to save the day. Even his death, sharing their grief, had held his band of brothers together. Everyone had underestimated Mad at every turn, even him.

"You did not. I didn't see this as a problem, though. I believed your friends would be excellent tools to wield against you," Paul explained.

"Hence the blackmail letter. Who delivered that to Ms. Matthews's suite in London?"

Paul shrugged. "I am not privy to trivial details. I merely know the matter was handled poorly."

A dead end, damn it. Zack raked a hand through his hair. No clue if or how involved Elizabeth might be.

That moment, Thomas stepped back into the room with a somber nod. It was done. Roman now knew that the woman he'd once thought he loved had been a traitor. Zack hated that he'd had to break it to Roman this way, but if it helped him at all in questioning Elizabeth…

Freddy jumped in with a narrow-eyed stare at Paul. "Why did you single out Maddox Crawford? I know he was getting close to discovering that Tavia Gordon's foundation was a front for trafficking, but if you were willing to give up your own daughter, why not give up Tavia?"

"That was out of my hands. Some of us believed we should have killed Mr. Crawford. I took the man seriously, if only because I knew Zachary would. My partners disagreed. They believed that, if properly motivated, he could be persuaded to see our side."

"I honestly thought I was going to find a corpse when I got to Mad's apartment that night," Freddy admitted.

Thank god Freddy hadn't. "I assure you, you would never have been able to turn Maddox Crawford into a Russian asset."

"Which is precisely why I wanted him dead. They thought he would break because he was a ridiculous, entitled playboy. I thought that his death would prove to you that our demands could not be ignored. The main handler chose a softer touch, but I knew you needed a hammer. And it is coming for you," Paul promised.

"Who is Sergei?" Zack asked the question he'd been desperate to know the answer to for months. Sergei must be the hammer Paul meant.

A nasty smile lit Paul's face. "You think it's you, don't you? Perhaps it is. Perhaps you are not who you believe yourself to be. It's what children forget. You are who your father made you to be. You cannot change that, and you must pay because he sinned."

"I know he did, but I will not make reparations for that. I am Zack Hayes. I don't give a damn who gave birth to me. That was nothing more than a trick of biology. If I was born to Natalia Kuilikov, it doesn't matter."

That truth finally hit him. The man sitting across the table had no power over him unless Zack gave it to him. He'd spent so much time panicking at the need to save his friends and his reputation while ensuring the Russians didn't have a backup plan that he hadn't fully considered that simple fact.

"I assure you the voting public will care very much."

"Then I'll step down, but as I do I'll drag every one of you traitorous bastards down with me." Maybe that's what he should have done the moment he'd received that blackmail letter. He'd hesitated because of Elizabeth. He hadn't wanted to bring anyone else into the investigation in case she was involved. He'd been trying to protect her. Same with Gabe, who'd also looked potentially guilty because of the FAA investigation into Mad's death.

Paul scoffed. "You cannot escape your past. Or your destiny. I am hardly the only one involved in this plan. I assure you, there are more of us. Many more. We're right here in your White House. We're waiting. You will do what we want or we will destroy everything and everyone you care about. If you need proof of our power over you, you will soon have it. And the price for your rebellion thus far will be steeper than you ever imagined. You cannot be rid of us. Not ever."

Zack's heart stopped. "What price?"

Paul merely curled his lips into the smile of a satisfied snake.

"What price?" he growled.

"You are easy, Zachary. You think those friends of yours make you strong, but every one of them is merely another weak link. I'm here to make you understand. And now I have done so. Call it the final act of a patriot. Cancel the pipeline or you'll mourn more of your friends."

Suddenly, Paul's face went pale and his hand began to shake.

"That's where you're wrong," Zack replied, studying his unexpected nemesis. Paul seemed to be in physical distress. Or maybe it was an act, like everything else about the man. The important thing was, Connor and the guys from Justice could hold him, question him more. But Zack refused for a second to let Paul think they'd won a thing. "Mad is alive. I don't have to mourn anything but my idiocy where you're concerned."

Paul staggered and paled further. Zack watched as the older man bucked, then a drop of blood dripped from his mouth. "I don't mean Maddox. I suspected he survived his 'crash.' There was a reason the FAA investigation was halted. But you have other friends. You see, the agents who picked me up were kind enough to allow an old man his coffee. My people have perfected some excellent new poisons. They work over the course of a few hours. My time is almost up. How will you handle that, Mr. President? I assure you no one has seen this poison yet. They won't be able to save either of us."

"Either?" Zack could hardly breathe. "What do you mean?"

Thomas stepped in front of him. "Don't get close, sir. We don't know what we're dealing with."

More blood spat from his mouth and he'd turned an ashy gray color. "Another of my country's inventions. Odorless. Tasteless. Quick but not too fast. I sincerely hope your whore enjoyed her coffee this morning. If you don't play the game properly, more will follow. This is my final message."

Paul's head fell forward and he slumped in his seat. In that moment, Zack knew precisely what real terror was.

Elizabeth.

He'd been such a fool. She loved him. He'd put her in a cell and failed to realize that the wolves around him would circle her the moment he pushed her away.

For his stupidity, he might have to put her in a coffin.

Without looking back, he dashed out the door, Thomas hot on his heels. Zack could only pray that somehow, someway he could save her.

* * * *

Liz was trying to pull herself together when the door burst open and Roman strode in, wearing his slick suit, carrying a thick file folder, and looking frightfully grim.

She gaped. Zack had sent his attack dog in after her rather than facing her himself? He'd nearly died and he hadn't needed to see her, hadn't wanted to hold her. No. He'd suspected she'd somehow been responsible for the attempt on his life and sicced Roman on her.

Mad followed, still in his pajama pants and a wrinkled T-shirt, looking like he'd rolled out of bed for this interrogation.

Roman frowned. "Liz—"

"Tell me exactly what I'm being accused of, you massive asshole. I'm never going to forgive you for this, by the way. Have you thought these ridiculous accusations through for even two fucking seconds? How long have you known me?"

He seemed slightly taken aback by her aggression, but he smoothed his expression as he set the file folder on the table and squared off with her. "I knew Joy, too. I knew her very well. And as it turns out, she was a Russian operative. Her father just told Zack that five minutes ago. So it doesn't matter how well I think I know you."

Liz felt her eyes go wide. Seriously?

But now that he said it, she felt stupid for not embracing that possibility sooner. She'd had her head in the clouds and hadn't seen the real threat in their midst. Joy. Joy had been in charge of so many facets of the campaign and Zack's life. Joy had been the ghost who'd kept her apart from Zack for years. Now she was the lie that could tear them in two for good. Liz had to handle this cross-examination well or risk losing everything.

"And that's on you, pal," Mad cut in. "Hey, Liz. You hungry? Sara made sandwiches. She could bring them down. Or booze." He looked at Roman. "Man, we could probably use some booze."

Roman glared his way. "I did not want you in here. You're sitting next to me because Zack asked me to include you. I can toss you out on your ass."

If that threat worried Mad, he didn't show it. "I'm here so Zack has a shot at coming out of this with his family intact. You're just going to ask Liz a whole bunch of questions you won't believe her answers to because she doesn't have definitive proof. But at some point the evidence she needs will pop up, and you'll have to live with the fact that you cost Zack the love of his life because you can't trust anyone. It sucks that Joy betrayed everyone. But you're taking it personally by taking it out on Liz. You need to stop."

Okay, Mad could stay.

Liz drew in a bracing breath. "I am not Joy, Roman."

"While Zack and Roman were jogging earlier today, someone took a shot at him," Mad explained. "Thomas managed to cover him, but one of the other Secret Service agents was hit in the arm. They've caught the man they believe is the shooter and Connor is talking to the Russian now at the police station."

"Are you planning on telling her everything?" Roman asked with a huff.

She turned a glare on Roman because he didn't get to have it both ways. "Well, according to you I should already know everything, shouldn't I? Since apparently I'm the one who set Zack up to die."

That was why she was here. They thought she'd sold Zack out. Now that she looked back, she could easily see that they'd suspected her for a while.

Her heart felt heavy in her chest. He'd suspected she was working with the Russians when he'd slept with her. What had he said? He kept his friends close and his enemies closer. Somewhere along the way she'd become his enemy, and only then had he taken her to bed. He didn't love her. He'd merely placated and used her.

She forced herself to pull the chair back and sit because their accusations were serious. Zack had abandoned her. She loved Gus like a sister, but in the end her very dear friend would stick with her fiancée. Liz was completely alone. Sure Mad was trying to help, but the Perfect Gentlemen would close ranks around Zack, and she would be outside their circle. It was past time to start protecting herself.

"I would like a lawyer."

"You don't need a lawyer." Mad pulled out his own chair and sat. "You need patience because this thing is going to settle out and Roman is going to see he's being a butthead."

"Is that a technical term?" Roman asked, shooting Mad a dirty look.

"Absolutely, Counselor." Mad attempted a smile as he leaned in, his voice conspiratorially low. "That's what we call him when he gets a stick up his butt about something, just like we have since we were kids. You have to understand that Roman feeds all of Zack's worst impulses."

"Could we stop psychoanalyzing me and focus?" Roman turned his attention back to her. "You're not under arrest. I have some simple questions, Liz. If you'll cooperate, I believe the president will work with you."

"What he's trying to say is Zack is absolutely sick at heart about this and he doesn't know what to do. He's crazy in love with you, but he's suspected Joy for a while, and finding out that she was in on the Russian conspiracy won't improve this situation for him at all," Mad explained.

Oh, Zack had been smart to send Mad in here. "I'm not Joy."

"I know that," Mad promised. "And deep down Zack knows it, too. He just needs time to get over his shock. And you have to forgive Roman. He's, like, ninety-nine percent cynicism. He was born that way. Once he has some proof, he'll be right back to being our lovable grouch."

She studied Roman. He *was* one of the most cynical humans she'd ever met. And she'd rather not play his game, but she didn't have a choice. "Ask your questions, Roman."

"How did you meet Joy?" Roman looked relieved to get down to business.

Her heart felt hollow as she answered. "You know I met her through Frank Hayes, the same way I met Zack. I had worked on a couple of other senatorial campaigns by then. As I understand it, Joy didn't get along with Zack's previous media consultant, and you didn't like him, either."

"He was old school," Roman admitted. "He didn't understand social media. His ways worked once upon a time, but I knew we needed a fresh voice, especially for the presidential election. I'm not great on camera, not the way you are. I liked the idea of bringing a woman onto the team. I thought it would make Zack look more inclusive."

She didn't take that statement poorly. Since Roman was a blunt instrument, he had very little tact. She'd always been more subtle. It was why Zack had needed both of them for that campaign. "I took the initial meeting with Frank and instantly disliked him. I didn't think there was any way I would accept the job if he offered it to me, but then I met Zack and I very quickly changed my mind. I even got along with Joy. But I hadn't met her or anyone else from the campaign before that day. I don't remember the exact day of our meeting. I think it was a Friday. I have years' worth of calendar data. I could check it if you want me to."

"What did you know about the Women and Girls Education Foundation?" Roman asked.

"I certainly didn't know it was responsible for trafficking women," she replied. "I went to a couple of meetings with Joy since she was considering partnering with them if she became First Lady. If I met Tavia Gordon, I don't recall."

"Are you aware that the e-mail that called off the FAA investigation into the crash that supposedly killed Mad originated from your office?"

Roman's question made her heart stop. "No. Are you sure? It wasn't me. Roman, it couldn't have been. I don't have the power to call off an FAA investigation."

"Well, someone on your team is tricky enough with our network and knew how to make that directive look as if it came from the Oval, but we've traced the message back to your office."

"And you didn't tell me?" Someone had been using her computer, setting her up and doing god only knew what else, and no one had bothered to mention it to her?

"Normally, you don't tell a suspect that you're on to their bad deeds," Roman replied. "It tends to hurt the investigation. I'll be honest with you, Liz. I believe you should have been isolated until we figured out your status. One way or another, the choices you've made have caused Zack a great deal of trouble."

"Wow." Mad sat back. "I don't even know how to save you from yourself, man."

Liz stood, glaring Roman's way. "Are you kidding me? My choices? How about the choices you've made, Calder? You chose to withhold vital information from me."

"We didn't know if we could trust you."

And they still didn't. "Then fire me. I believe during this process I offered to step down about ten times. I meant it. I was ready to quit. I still am."

"I would have happily accepted your resignation. I thought it was a good idea, in fact."

"Oh, I see. Zack wanted to torture me. He decided it would be more fun if he put me through the wringer before he tossed me aside. Tell me something, Mr. Calder, were we ever friends? I've worked beside you for years. I've sweated blood for this administration. I've acted as the First Lady without ever expecting a thing from either one of you, and you couldn't be troubled to ask me a few simple questions or give me the benefit of the doubt?"

"I've told you my reasons."

"Then tell me something else, and you really think before answering me. If you'd had even a hint that Joy was guilty all those years ago, would you have done this to her? Would you have allowed your best friend to use her sexually, to debase her with no thought to her feelings, so you could keep her close while you figured out if she's evil? Or would you have gone to her? Would you have asked the questions because Joy was kind and sweet, and if she was doing something she shouldn't, there must have been a good reason?"

Roman sat back, the color leaving his face. "He didn't use you."

"I assure you I feel very much used. Answer the question."

"I didn't..." He shook his head and sighed. "Damn it, yes. I would have asked her."

She'd known that. And he hadn't given her the same courtesy. "Because she was soft and compliant and never once challenged you. That was how she got you. She played the damsel in distress, and you always rode in to save her day. I never played you. I have always fought for what I believed in. I've crusaded beside you and Zack for what you two believed in. Trust me, I knew exactly how to play you, Calder, and I never did. So fuck you. If you had treated me with any kind of respect, I would have solved this by now because there are really only two people who have access to my office. Your future wife and Vanessa Jones. Without even talking to Gus, I have no trouble believing she's completely innocent. Vanessa, not so much. See, I just solved your damn mystery in two seconds. Now unless you're arresting me, I quit."

Mad shook his head as though trying to process something. "Vanessa Jones? Wait. I know that name. Why do I know that name?"

"Liz, please sit down. We aren't finished," Roman said, but he sounded far less certain than he had before.

She glared at him. "Oh, we are. I gave that man my everything and this is how y'all treat me. Arrest me or let me go because I'm not playing games with you anymore."

Roman slammed his fist on the table, making it shake.

"It's not a fucking game. It's real, and Zack could have died today. Hell, I could have. I felt that bullet hit the Secret Service agent who covered me. I had to change clothes because mine were covered in blood. So I fully understand this is not a game."

Her stomach turned at his words, but she couldn't back down now. "I get that you're scared. I am, too. And I understand that I was the only person Zack told where you two planned to run, but Vanessa was standing two feet away. She could easily have heard our conversation. Or the sniper could have been lying in wait because you and Zack have long-standing habits and it was only a matter of time before you returned to them."

"When did Vanessa join the staff? How old is she?" Mad's questions cut into the tension.

Roman frowned. "She was a volunteer during the campaign if I remember correctly. She's fairly young."

"She's in her mid-twenties now." Liz took a deep breath, trying to banish the rage burning through her as everything hit her like a ton of bricks. But she had to keep herself together. They had a conspiracy to uncover and it was deadly as hell. "Look, I'm angry with Zack right now. So angry. But I would never want him dead."

But that had almost happened today. Someone had taken a shot at him and barely missed.

Liz teared up again.

"Are you okay?" Roman's eyes were hooded as he looked at her.

"No, but it doesn't matter." She was furious and heartsick and nauseous. Her whole world had been obliterated by Roman Calder, but she still needed to find a way to make him understand. She turned back to Mad and answered his question. "Like Roman said, Vanessa came on during the campaign. She was a technical writer fresh out of Brown. She's now in charge of proofing everything that runs through the press office and yes, that means she's had access to my computer at times. I don't know if you realize this, but my job can get chaotic. I don't always have time to properly e-mail a statement and wait for someone to proofread and e-mail it back to me."

On a hard news day she sometimes barely had time to breathe.

"Who hired her?" Mad asked. "Can I see a picture of her? She's got a social media account, right?"

"I hired her, but she came highly recommended," Liz replied, then sighed as she remembered. "Well, of course. Joy vouched for her."

Roman turned his phone Maddox's way. "This is Vanessa."

Mad looked at the device and gasped. "I've seen her face... Hang on."

"She hits on Zack a lot," Roman said.

"She does what?" Liz felt her ire rise again.

Roman's lips turned up slightly. "When you're not watching, yes."

"Well, she's the person you should be questioning because she's the only one besides Gus who could have used my computer without anyone questioning her. She must be one of the Russian insiders."

"Um, yeah." Mad nodded enthusiastically. "I know where I've seen her now. She was at Zack and Joy's wedding."

"No, she wasn't," Roman insisted. "I never saw her there."

"I didn't remember her, either. We were kinda busy... But she was definitely there. She signed the guest book. I found a picture of that day. I've been studying it, and I couldn't figure out why it was bugging me... Let me make a call with your phone."

Roman scowled but punched in his code to unlock his

device. Seconds later, Mad had Sara on the line. "Hey, can you text Roman that picture you and I have been staring at? Yeah, the one where those three chicks are straightening Joy's veil. Thanks, baby. Love you." Then he hung up and looked at Roman with an expression that said *I told you so.* "Give her just a minute."

"If Vanessa is a Russian asset, there may be more. Joy hired a bunch of people," Liz pointed out. "Why don't you look at them?"

"Liz, it's not that easy. We have other evidence against you," Roman said quietly. "The 'secret meeting' I told you Zack intended to have with the energy director the Friday following our trip to Camp David? It wasn't real. It was a test of your loyalty. And you failed. Shorn came storming into the Oval, demanding to know why he hadn't been informed or invited."

She gaped. "I didn't tell anyone about that. Not. A. Soul. The only thing I did was make a note about it in my phone after the fact to follow up and ask how the meeting went. If Vanessa is smart enough to route an e-mail through our network to make something that originated from my office look like it came from the Oval, then I'd say she's smart enough to dupe my phone."

"But you can't prove that?"

"Can you prove she didn't?"

Roman's jaw tightened. "Can you tell me how it's possible that Krylov was ever in your building and yet no one was able to find any proof of that? He would have been forced to check in unless you gave him the code to get inside."

"Didn't Gabe say there was a back way in that wasn't covered by security cameras?" Mad was still staring at the phone, waiting for Sara's text, but he continued to play the part of her advocate. "Krylov could have snuck in and out with a little help."

"Exactly. Vanessa could have given him the code since she also lives in my building, along with three other members of the press office. I could have told you that had you given me the courtesy of treating me like a friend, rather than an enemy combatant."

"See," Mad put in again. "I'm telling you, Vanessa was at Zack and Joy's wedding. She's been involved far longer than we ever imagined. Liz, Roman thinks he's been doing the right thing. It's not that he doesn't care about you. He's made himself sick trying to figure a way out of this. The problem is he doesn't have a creative bone in his body and he always expects the worst. Zack...well, Zack has never been in love and he's clueless how to handle it. It's not fair to ask you to be the bigger person, but the truth is they need you to be. Please don't leave."

"I don't think I'm allowed to right now." She settled back in a huff, Mad's speech rolling through her head. It wasn't that she didn't hear what he was saying, but how on earth could she ever believe in Zack again, especially when he so obviously hadn't believed in her? If he changed his mind because he suddenly had enough evidence to prove she was innocent and he deigned to sleep with her again, she would merely be a convenience. Liz refused to let herself be used by him anymore.

"I think it would be a good idea for you to talk to Zack." Roman stood. "I'm sorry you're angry with me. I like to think you would do the same thing if you were in my position. There's so much at stake here. I have to take it seriously because no one else will. Stay here. I'll talk to Zack and have someone find Vanessa Jones."

A second later, Roman's phone dinged and Mad's face lit up. "Here you go."

Liz leaned in to see the image at the same time Roman did. Sure enough, there was a teenage Vanessa standing beside Joy, looking at her with something close to worship as she straightened the woman's veil.

Holy shit.

Suddenly, the door slapped open, Zack tore inside, wearing the wildest look in his eyes. She'd rarely ever seen him truly emotional, but right now he seemed out of control. His gaze careened wildly around the room until it landed on her. With shaking hands, he reached for her. Before she could retreat, he hauled her into his arms and held her so tightly she could barely breathe.

"Elizabeth…" His whisper was harsh against her ear and his whole body trembled. "I thought I would walk in here and find your body. Oh my god. Roman, we need paramedics. Now. Mad find me a cup. Something. She has to throw up."

"What?" She pushed out of his embrace. "I felt like I needed to a minute ago, but now I'm just mad."

Zack barely allowed a few inches between them. He gripped her arms, and the tension rolled off him in waves. She saw tears in his eyes. Actual, real tears. They felled her like nothing else because she'd never imagined she would see him shed any for her.

"I don't care how furious with me you are. I'm not letting you die, Elizabeth, you can't… You're my reason for living. I can't be in this fucking world without you."

"Zack, what in the world is going on?" Roman demanded.

"She's been poisoned. The Russians have several operatives here and one of them put a toxin in her coffee, according to Mr. Harding," Freddy said, walking into the room.

Liz glanced at Thomas, who had joined them, too, and was heading her direction. She'd never seen the Secret Service agent look so worried.

He flung off the sunglasses he often wore even indoors. "I'll hold her, Mr. President. We shouldn't wait for the

EMTs. You have to get your fingers down her throat far enough to hit her gag reflex."

He'd done that a couple of times before but not with his fingers.

Liz pushed against him. "I'm not sick."

"It hasn't hit you yet." Zack had lifted her off her feet and dragged her toward the trash can Mad had found. "Paul said it took a while. When did you get that cup of coffee this morning? Who gave it to you?"

If she didn't stop this, she would be forced to endure a few really nasty minutes for no good reason. "Are you talking about the latte one of the interns brought me? I never drank it. Zack, it's still sitting on my desk, utterly cold by now. I made myself coffee in the residence this morning. I filled up my thermos and I haven't touched anything else."

Thomas backed off. "Before your run, I did see a thermos on her desk, sir."

"And you didn't drink a drop of the stuff the intern gave you?" Zack demanded, slowly setting her on her feet.

She knew she should still be mad, but he was so distraught and unlike himself that she couldn't help but cup his face and soothe him.

He wasn't a man worried that, if she died, answers about the vast global conspiracy against him would be gone. He was terrified for *her*. He looked as if his whole world might crumble, depending on her next few words. He'd also just learned that he'd been betrayed by his wife and her family. He had the weight of the free world on his shoulders. But it was the possibility of losing the woman he loved that had truly undone him.

"I didn't, Zack. I didn't touch it. Ever since you bought me that coffee from Finland I love so much, I haven't touched the other stuff."

He'd changed up the residence in the last few weeks, ensuring it was stocked with all of her favorite things, even going so far as to import coffee from Helsinki because she'd fallen in love with it when they'd gone to a conference there years before. She'd been touched that he'd remembered.

Zack let out a deep, shaky breath. "Thank god, baby. Thank god."

"Mr. Harding is dead. I checked. He apparently ingested poison before we brought him in," Thomas supplied as Zack threw his arms around her.

"He claimed it was something new," Freddy explained, actually sounding excited. "I've heard a couple of covert groups have been working on a poison that allows the victim to seem perfectly normal until it activates a few hours later. Some of my contacts will have serious hard-ons to read that dude's toxicology report."

"Dead?" Liz wriggled out of Zack's embrace because he seemed to be in control of himself now and they still had a million things to discuss.

Or did they? Maybe there was nothing to discuss at all. The simple fact that he hadn't wanted her dead didn't mean he'd believed her when he should have or that she should forgive him for what he'd put her through.

"Give us the room." Zack stared at her as everyone else filed out. Even Thomas seemed to understand Zack needed to be alone with her now.

Once the door closed behind everyone else, Liz faced the man she'd thought she would spend the rest of her life with. "Don't worry, Zack. I'm fine. I'll have my office cleaned out by the end of the day. Gus can pick my things up from the residence."

"Elizabeth, I—"

"No. Don't. I understand why you investigated me. I really do, but I don't think I can forgive you for using me. You knew you didn't love me, knew you thought I was capable of betraying you, and you still had sex with me. Hell, you let me think you loved me."

"I did," he argued. "I do. I've loved you from the minute I saw you."

"You don't treat people you love this way."

"I don't know how to treat people I love because I never loved a woman before I loved you," he said, moving into her space. "Please. I'm sorry. I know I'm asking a lot. Forgive me."

She shook her head and backed away from him. She could not go easy on him, no matter how tempted she was. "It doesn't matter. The next time I do something Roman thinks is suspicious, all this will happen again."

He prowled closer. "The next time Roman so much as whispers even a suggestion you're not the angel who saved me from a ridiculously lonely life, I'll fire him."

Liz retreated again. This time, her back hit the wall. Zack kept coming until his chest brushed against hers and she felt the heat of his body. "Zack..."

"Elizabeth." He braced his hands on either side of her, caging her in, and dropping his forehead to hers. "I spent my entire life preparing for one role—president. I never wanted anything else until I saw you. No woman ever loved me before, not even my mother. I can count on one hand the number of times she spent more than an hour with me. We didn't take family vacations. I didn't have parents who taught me how to love. What they taught me was that everyone will tear me down if I let them, so I should be pre-emptive and beat them to it."

"I'm sorry to hear that, Zack. But that doesn't make what you did to me okay."

"I know, but it's the truth and the only reason I can give you for being so wrong. I'm asking you—begging you—to forgive me." He leaned even closer, his hands roaming her as if he couldn't quite stop himself. "I've felt so lost and trapped. The Russians...they played me perfectly. They knew exactly where I was most vulnerable. You."

"But you weren't. You readily believed everything they wanted you to because it was easy." Liz said the words with conviction, even as it was getting hard not to weaken under Zack's touch.

He'd been terrible to her, yes. But did that erase all his years of being so good to her?

"That's not true. I resisted at first. I resisted a lot. But the evidence kept coming, and I didn't know what to believe. I'm an incredibly smart man, but when it comes to relationships I'm truly dumb." He took a shuddering breath. "I know this may make me seem even guiltier in your mind, but even when I thought you might be conspiring against me, I'd already planned to cover everything so I wouldn't even have to pardon you. I was going to force you to marry me so you wouldn't ever get into trouble again. When I suspected you might have betrayed me, all I thought about was the ways I could keep you."

His words made her both melt and want to slap him.

"How could you even think I would betray you?" she asked, trying so hard to resist his nearness, but their chemistry was working its magic. She could feel his heartbeat, the way his body still shuddered from the fear of losing her. The reverence in his touch.

"I don't know what I was thinking. Everyone's lied to me, Elizabeth. Everyone. My in-laws. My wife. Even Maddox. I know I shouldn't be angry, but I am. I'll get over it, but all of that had me thinking that I couldn't possibly have someone as true and wonderful as you seemed. You've been the reason I wake up in the morning for so long it actually made sense in my twisted head that your devotion wouldn't be real. How fucked up is that?"

A lot. Then again, his whole life had been fucked up. His parents had hollowed him out as a kid and refilled him with ambition. He'd married Joy to further his singular goal. Then someone had used that very drive against him.

What would Zack Hayes have been like if he'd been allowed to be his own man? Would he have been able to trust her? Would he ever truly be able to trust her if she stayed?

Was she willing to walk away from him and never even try? Or would she regret it for the rest of her life?

Liz dragged in a deep breath. She couldn't believe she was doing this. "Zack, you have to pick me over Roman."

Something like hope lit his eyes and he cupped her shoulders. "Absolutely. Roman is my brother. He always has been and he always will be. But…"

"But what?" She pushed him a little more. After what she'd been through, she needed reassurance. She deserved it. "What if I asked you to fire him?"

"Then you wouldn't be my Elizabeth," he shot back, a ghost of a smile on his face. "I was always good at tests, my love. You are the kindest, most forgiving woman I've ever met, and you would never ask that of me. Here is what you will ask—and you should. You need to be more important than any of my friendships. You have to be my first, best partner. You have to be the one I come to, the one I face everything with."

Yes, he was very good at tests. He'd certainly managed to come up with the right answer. "I'll never come between you and Roman or any of the others. Not willingly. I know the Perfect Gentlemen are only looking out for your best interests, but you have to believe that's what I've always done, too."

"You're right. So right. Please forgive me. I don't want to waste another moment. I want to start our lives. I've fucked everything up—first because I was trying to protect you and then because I was protecting myself. None of it worked. I should have done the most natural thing of all, simply love and trust you. Nothing in my life works without you, Elizabeth. Marry me."

She smiled and cuddled against his chest. "All right."

"Just like that?" He pulled away just enough to search her eyes.

Life was as easy or as hard as she chose to make it. That was something her mama had been fond of saying. Perhaps if they hadn't been in such a perilous position recently, if someone hadn't already tried to kill him today, she might have held on to her anger for a while longer. Maybe she would have even been able to cling to it long enough to choose her pride over love and walk away from him. But this man was half her soul, and denying that was futile. She couldn't not love him.

Besides, if he'd truly never learned how to love, shouldn't she be setting the example and teaching him so they could have an amazing life together?

"Just like that," she replied, caressing the face she adored.

He was alive, hopefully the worst was behind them, and now they could get through anything together.

"But this mess isn't completely over," he warned. "I still might be Russian born, so if I have to step down…"

"Then I'll be by your side." She would never leave him.

"I'll do everything I can to protect you—everything except give you up. That I can't do, ever." He kissed her, his arms winding around her, giving her the physical affirmation of his words.

Relief filled her. They still had things to work through, but Liz knew this was the moment she would look back on and think here was where her life had truly begun.

With a warm smile, Zack picked her up like she weighed nothing and carried her out of the room.

Roman hovered near the door, looking grim. His eyes widened as he saw Zack emerge with Liz in his arms. "Where are you going? We're still rounding up people we need to question, and the press is going to need a statement about the assassination attempt. You can't just carry Liz through the White House in the middle of a crisis."

"I can," Zack vowed. "I am the motherfucking president and she's just agreed to be your First Lady, so we're going to celebrate alone for a few minutes. Handle shit, Roman."

"Congrats. What do you want me to do with the dead guy?"

"Get a shovel, buddy. Or better yet, call the police and tell them everything. Come hell or high water, we're making every single one of those bastards pay."

At Roman's shocked expression, she cuddled closer to Zack and smiled. He was quickly learning to put her first.

Mad gave her a thumbs-up.

"Where are you taking me, Mr. President?" she asked, not really caring. As long as they were together, she was perfectly happy.

"Home," he said.

It sounded like the perfect place to start their future.

* * * *

Smiling from ear to ear, Mad watched Zack walk off into the sunset. Well, he was really heading to the bedroom, since he couldn't go anywhere right now. And in this version of Zack striding off into their happily ever after, they wouldn't get much quality time before duty called. And Thomas and a second Secret Service agent trailed them while they ignored the mountain of reporters outside the gates of the White House.

Damn, Mad had never been happier not to wield Zack's kind of power.

"I didn't mean to hurt Liz," Roman called to their retreating forms. "Sorry."

Zack didn't reply.

"He'll forgive you eventually. So will Liz," Mad promised. "Hell, if she could forgive him, then she'll come around. Though you should expect a serious talking to from Gus."

Roman grimaced. "Maybe Liz doesn't have to mention this to her. It would make everything so much easier if my blushing bride-to-be never knew about the interrogation."

"I don't think Liz is that forgiving." He was pretty sure Roman would be paying for a long time.

"What are we supposed to do about the body?" Roman nodded toward the second interrogation room that still held Paul Harding's corpse.

"Can I have it?" Freddy asked, sounding far too excited.

Mad shook his damn head. "No, you cannot have it. The man's corpse is not a toy."

"Well, if I don't take him the Agency will," Freddy pointed out.

"What the hell would you do with a dead body?" Roman asked.

"Study it, of course." Freddy shrugged like the answer was completely obvious. "He's been exposed to a new type of poison. I know some people who would love to isolate it so we can start coming up with antidotes. Wouldn't it be great if we had a way around this poison before the Russians really started unleashing it? I mean, we have to do it anyway. Public safety and all. You would be surprised how often someone mistakes their coffee creamer just lying around for a neurotoxin."

"You live in a strange world, my friend." A world Maddox Crawford was saying good-bye to. As soon as the rest of the conspirators had been dragged under an international spotlight, he was going home to New York with his wife and their baby and he was going to be the most boring dad in the world. He was already hoarding bad-dad jokes to use on his daughter. He wanted a normal, humdrum, fabulous life where no one ever tried to murder him again. "I say we let Connor decide while Zack is...fixing things with the new First Lady."

Roman pulled his cell phone out. "I'll give him a call now."

One of the remaining Secret Service agents stepped forward. "Mr. Calder, I'm afraid I'm going to have to ask you to not do that."

Mad looked back and the agent had a gun pointed in their direction.

Shit. It looked like his nice safe life would have to wait.

Chapter Nineteen

Zack carried Liz all the way up to the residence. She'd joked about his back going out, but he'd utterly refused to set her down. He'd held her in the elevator, ignored the few people who'd seen them in the hall, and kept heading toward their bedroom, despite the fact that two Secret Service agents, Thomas and Glen, kept vigil behind them.

"You know we have to do a press conference soon," she said as he managed to open the door to the residence.

After the agents swept the interior of the residence, they fell into place on either side of the portal, standing stoic and patient.

With the door closed behind them, Zack finally set her on her feet. "I know, but I need a couple of minutes alone with you."

And he needed to change his clothes. If he was going to start an all-out war with the enemy, he couldn't do it in a torn T-shirt and sweat pants splattered with blood. He had to look the part of a powerful world leader.

She reached up and smoothed back his hair. "Are you

really okay? You weren't hit?"

"Fine. Thomas banged me up a bit when he covered me, but he also made sure I wasn't hit. Mike wasn't so lucky. Later, we'll need to follow up and see how he's recovering from the surgery on his arm." Zack gripped her hips and pulled her closer. "But right now, I don't want to deal with any of this. I want to take you to bed so we can forget the whole world."

"I wish we could. I miss touching you. I was terrified for you." She nuzzled closer to him, aching for the chance to spend hours connecting to him again. For now she shared him with a whole country, though. She had to be content with the fact that they would have time to themselves later. "But so are the American people. There was an attack on the president of the United States. We can put out a statement, but that's not what the country needs. They need to see you, Zack. You have to show them you're alive and well and utterly defiant."

"I know. If I don't get in front of some cameras soon, the financial markets could take a hit." He kissed her, drugging her with arousal and intimacy. "I want you by my side."

"Yes." She would be with him as they faced whatever storm was coming their way. They needed to let these conspirators—and the rest of the world—know that nothing would tear them apart and that Zack would never compromise his scruples or his country. And damn it, no one would ever think she was his weak link again. From now on, she would be the woman who made him strong, the one he could always count on.

"If you're sure…?"

He nodded. "Of course."

"I've been thinking… Should we tell the public about everything? If we do, I'll have to be honest about what we know…and what we don't," he said with a grim face.

"Baby, I realize we both want to be married as soon as possible, but maybe we should wait until you know exactly who you're marrying."

Because he intended to find out one way or another if he was really Zachary Hayes, son of Frank and Constance Hayes. The trouble was, she didn't care. "I know exactly who you are, Zack. I want to marry you as soon as I can, no matter what. For better or worse. I'm not in this to be the First Lady. I'm in this to be your wife, and that means I'm beside you come what may."

He sighed, a sound of deep satisfaction. "If we choose to expose everything, it won't be easy. We'll be subjected to a ton of hearings. My political opponents and enemies will use this against me, try to make me step down, paint me as dangerous, call for my impeachment."

"If it comes to that, we'll handle them." Of that, she had not a single doubt. Together she and Zack could do almost anything. "We can't back down. We have to face every adversary and every threat and stand tall. They have to realize that they won't break us."

"They can't break us." He said the words like a mantra.

"Speaking of adversaries...you weren't in the room with Roman, Mad, and me when we figured out that the mole in our press office is Vanessa Jones." She was almost certain Roman would have already given the order to find Vanessa, but Zack needed to know. "She's the only one I can think of who would have access to my computer. Over the years she's worked her way up to a position of trust. She edits all of my work. Someone should be interrogating her by now."

"Vanessa?" He looked surprised, then paused to consider. "I suppose that makes sense. These conspirators are very careful and very smart. Of course they knew how I felt about you. They'd put someone in place both to keep a handle on all our official communications and to watch us."

"Exactly. I hear she hits on you a lot, too. I'm sure they

would have loved to put one of their own in your bed." As soon as the words were out of her mouth, she winced. "Okay, so I can understand why you had some reservations about me, but I still think you should have asked me before assuming the worst."

His lips turned up into a jaunty grin. "I assure you Vanessa Jones never got close to my bed. You're the only woman I want there. And I promise if I'm ever worried again that you're a foreign operative, I'll ask you the question."

"Deal." She rose to her tiptoes and pressed her lips to his, a sweet, slow joining of welcome and forever.

Zack sank into her, tasting her, clutching her as if he never wanted to let go. Then reluctantly he pulled away with a groan. "I'm going to step out and talk to Thomas, ask him to get me an update on Vanessa." He pulled Liz in, holding her close. "We need to make sure they've brought her in for questioning. I want someone to have eyes on my father, too. I'm going to have him moved out of the White House."

"But why? You don't..." Liz didn't finish her reply. Zack didn't need an argument now, especially when neither of them knew if or how dangerous Frank might be. After all, they'd been surrounded by Judases for years. Removing anyone they suspected would be prudent until they'd separated the bad actors from the good ones. "We can move him to a hospital until we figure out where to put him and play it off as a health crisis. We'll make it work."

This was what she did well. She smoothed things over. She made everything run like clockwork.

"Perfect. I'll be right back," Zack promised. "As soon as I've asked Thomas to inquire about Vanessa and ensured that all of our friends are secure, I'll come back and change. Then you and I need to prepare for this press conference. We'll have to think about what I should say, how much to reveal about the assassination attempt. And we don't have time to write a proper speech, merely jot a few notes. If you could stand to be around Roman…"

Because he needed to be deeply involved, too.

Liz rolled her eyes. Roman was basically her asshole brother-in-law who truly loved Zack and the sister of her heart, Augustine. Eventually, they would be okay because they all loved the same people. "He's family and we've worked together for years. I'll talk to him. We'll create a rough draft, but I don't want you too prepared. It will be more convincing if you look natural. You're a man who's faced death today and you're still standing. After you give your statement, we'll tell them that the police will answer questions about the shooter as they're ready."

He nodded. "As soon as I finish with Thomas, let's do it." He started to turn away but stopped himself and pulled her close again. "I love you. I can't say that enough. I'm humbled and blessed to have you. Thank you for forgiving me."

This was her Zack, and he was all she needed. "I love you, too."

With a smile, she watched him leave the room before turning toward the bedroom and stepping into the massive closet. It made the sparse selection of her clothes here even more obvious. She would have to power through for now, find something presentable and get cleaned up. And she had to lay out a fresh suit for Zack, something solid with a strong tie.

As she identified a couple of possibilities and hung the garments on a nearby hook, she glanced in the mirror. Yikes, she needed to clean herself up before she faced the public. That was for sure. At the moment, all she could do was smooth her hair into place and refresh her lipstick because Zack had kissed off what little she'd had left.

Then again, Liz had a feeling Zack was going to kiss her a lot from now on and she doubted he would hide it.

They were going to be a very lovey-dovey first couple.

As she set the tube aside, it hit her. She was marrying Zachary Hayes, the most amazing man she'd ever met. She was also marrying the president of the United States. Never in her wildest fantasies had she believed it could happen. Happy tears pooled in her eyes.

Liz took a moment because she couldn't face Zack crying. He would be concerned about her, and he didn't need that now. They had too many things to do. Later tonight she could break down and feel every bit of terror and joy the day had brought, but for now she had to be strong.

In her pocket, her cell vibrated and Liz pulled it free, glad to see it wasn't one of the many members of the press she'd been ignoring.

She slid her finger across the screen to answer the call, putting the call on speaker as she strode back into the closet. "Hey, Gus. Is everything okay?"

"Everything is chaos," Gus replied. "Where's my fiancé? The Secret Service has locked down most of the press office and won't let us go anywhere. But I can't get hold of Roman. He's not answering his phone."

"He's down in the basement, probably in the middle of an interrogation. It's a long story but I saw him not five minutes ago and he was fine. So is Zack."

Gus heaved a long sigh over the line. "Thank god. I was so worried."

"Everything should be fine now. Why do they have the press office locked down?" Worry turned Liz's smile into a frown. What if the point of the assassination attempt hadn't been to kill Zack but to cause chaos so they could engage in other dirty work? "Where is Vanessa?"

"She's why we're in lockdown. Some suits came to take her in for questioning but no one can find her. So they wanted everyone tucked away safely until they do. Is she a Russian spy? I knew I never liked that bitch for a reason."

Liz tried not to panic. Maybe Vanessa was in custody now and they just hadn't released the press office yet out of an abundance of caution. Still, she ought to check. "Apparently she's been using my computer, she probably duped my phone, and she set me to up to look like the bad guy, which is why Roman—and therefore Zack—suspected me. Don't worry; it's all okay. I didn't kill Roman."

"But I might. Bastard! I knew he was up to something," Gus swore. "I'll make him pay."

"He had his reasons. We're fine now. So are Zack and I. But you should know all hell is about to break loose. He's considering telling the American public everything."

"We should talk about that first. Has he thought about all the implications?"

"If you mean about whether he's Russian born or not, after today, I don't think he cares." Liz tried not to let it, but foreboding continued to eat at her composure. "Let me call you back. I need to talk to Zack. He's conferring with Thomas. We need to find out what's going on with Vanessa. Then I'll let you know. Do you have an agent with you now?"

"There's one outside the door."

"Be careful. We hadn't finished vetting them all yet, so we don't know if some are colluding with the Russians." She walked toward the front of the residence, eager to reach Zack. "And as soon as I hang up, call Connor. Tell him we might have a situation. We need him to bring in reinforcements he trusts." Better safe than sorry. "We have no room for error on this."

"Liz, you sound worried. Are you okay?" Gus asked.

No. What if Vanessa was still on the loose? What if she'd used the assassination attempt to separate Zack from all his loved ones and put them all in the hands of the Secret Service, where they'd planted their own people?

Zack might still be in danger. Hell, all of them might

be.

"Call Connor now." She hung up and hurried to the bedroom door.

She had to find Zack.

The second she strode through the portal and into the living area, she realized that she wasn't alone. Trouble had found her.

Vanessa stood in the entryway, gun in hand, right beside Zack.

Liz's day was far from over.

* * * *

As Zack looked into Liz's warm blue eyes, he nodded, his heart so full of emotion. Maybe it didn't sound manly, but he couldn't deny that he found the devotion on her face so comforting. "I love you. I can't say that enough. I'm humbled and blessed to have you. Thank you for forgiving me."

The guilt still sat like a boulder in his gut and probably always would. How could he have ever doubted her? He would never make that mistake again. She was steadfast and loyal and in the years to come, he would learn how to be the best husband to her.

Her chin tilted up and he could see the love on her face. "I love you, too."

Three words that eased his soul.

With a sigh, Zack forced himself to walk away from her—for now. The next couple of hours wouldn't be pleasant. He had to get out in front of the press and reassure the country that he was perfectly healthy and fine, and that the government was still running smoothly. Then he needed to sit down with all of his friends and figure out their next steps because he was done playing this game. If ridding the country of this insidious Russian menace cost him his presidency, then he would pay the price, but one way or the other, he would ensure these tyrants wouldn't be able to infiltrate his country and try to corrupt it again. As far as he could tell, this had been going on for decades, and it stopped with him.

He glanced back. Elizabeth had disappeared into the residence. Already, he knew she would head for the closet and lay out his clothes because she would want him to look as polished and normal as possible. She would do what she always did—make life easy for him.

Moving beyond this conspiracy would be difficult, but Elizabeth would be by his side, so he could handle anything. Even disgrace, if it came to that.

He opened the door expecting to find Thomas there.

He did—but Thomas was on the ground, face down and eerily still.

Then Zack realized he wasn't alone. Adrenaline blasted through his system as he saw a gun pointed directly at his head.

"I think you should go back inside the residence, Mr. President," the Secret Service agent standing over Thomas said. Glen Warren. He'd been working with the Secret Service for years. In fact, he was one of Thomas's best men.

Thomas. Loyal and true. Thomas had two kids and a wife he'd been married to for over twenty years. Thomas shouldn't be lying on the ground.

He stared at the gun in the agent's hand. There was a suppressor on the end, explaining why he hadn't heard anything. Not surprising these criminals were prepared. The assassination attempt had been nothing more than a way to herd him here. And what else? What more had they sought? "I thought you were supposed to take a bullet for me, not put one into your boss."

Glen shrugged. "You don't pay as well as the others. Sorry about Thomas. He wasn't a practical man, so I had to deal with him. Now we get to find out how practical you are, Mr. President."

"Zachary?" a familiar voice asked.

He turned to find his father coming down the hallway. He wasn't alone, either. Apparently his nurse wasn't as invested in his well-being as he'd sworn because the man also held a gun, as did the woman by his side.

He was seriously outnumbered.

"Hello, Ms. Jones." Zack tried to calm his thundering heartbeat. Violence would go down today, especially if he refused to bend about the pipeline. But he had to keep them away from Elizabeth. Hopefully, Roman would figure out something was wrong, or Connor would return. For once, he even hoped Freddy was stalking him.

Then again, Roman might decide he'd interfered enough and give him alone time with Elizabeth. Connor might still be tied up with the shooter at the police station. And Freddy...who knew?

"Hello, Zack," she said. "I'm going to call you Zack from now on because I assume my father carried out his mission today. That means I'm running the show now. Tell me something. How will you explain his body in your White House?"

"Your father?" He glanced at his own father, who seemed equally confused.

"You still haven't figured it out? Joy was my half sister. Both your father and mine had liberal definitions of the word faithful." Vanessa smirked. Now that Zack really looked at her, he saw some physical resemblances between Vanessa and Joy. "Sex is such an easy way to manipulate a man."

He could see they'd tried to handle him that way, too. "It didn't work with me."

The smile grew but oddly lost any amusement. "Oh, but I think it will work in the end. Get inside or I'll kill your father right here."

"Zachary?" His father looked around as if he wasn't quite sure where or when he was. "What's happening?"

And Zack simply wasn't buying the con anymore.

In the past, he'd thought it was an ironic twist of fate that his father had developed dementia just as they'd reached the White House. In some ways, it had felt like justice. But now…it seemed a bit too coincidental.

"I think you know exactly what's happening," he accused. "I find it interesting that you can't remember your name most of the time, but you fought like hell until we hired the nurse you wanted. We went through so many, then magically found the one who could handle you. Tell me something." He turned to the nurse. "*U tebya khoroshiy russkiy yazyk, moy drug?*"

How is your Russian, my friend?

The nurse, who was still in his scrubs, sighed like he couldn't care less. "*U menya prekrasnyy russkiy yazuk. Takaya zhe, kak nasha zapadnya.*"

My Russian is perfect. So is our trap.

His father's demeanor changed, his shoulders straightening and the vacant look he adopted for three years suddenly leaving his eyes. "Don't look at me like that, boy. Do you think I wanted things to happen this way? That I'm enjoying this?"

"I think you don't really care about anyone but yourself. How long have you been a traitor?"

Zack mentally kicked himself for not realizing his own father's perfidy. He should have immediately suspected that Frank's illness was fishy, but again, the Russians had known exactly how to play him. His father's mental state had appeared to be slipping the last few months of the campaign. Joy had hired his specialists—all phonies, he supposed—then unwittingly given her life to get him elected. In the first hectic year after he'd taken office, Zack hadn't had time to think about anything except keeping his head above water...and he hadn't tried harder to spend time with his father because of their odd, strained relationship.

God, he'd been so easy to manipulate.

"I am not a traitor," his father snarled back. "Do you think I liked being put in this position? I fought like hell when my father told me the family's secret loyalties. I meant to serve the US with honor in that embassy post. It was your mother who screwed everything up. She deserved what she got."

Zack stared at his father in horror. "You arranged her death?"

Frank couldn't look him in the face. "The Russians thought she was a liability. We all agreed she would have been an embarrassment when you began your presidential run. Before you even announced your campaign, questions were arising about her mental state. Ah, but how much more sympathetic would voters be if she died suddenly and tragically? So Joy flew to Paris for a 'shopping trip.' From there, she found it was easy enough to reach Constance, disguise herself with a blond wig, and check your mother out of the hospital. No one asked many questions when money talked. Krylov's men took care of the rest."

Vanessa put a gun to the back of his father's head. "Thank you for the history lesson, Sergei. Now shut up and get inside the residence so we can talk. Or I'll do what my father should have done long ago and blow your brains out."

The Secret Service agent pressed the hard barrel of his gun against Zack's spine. "Let's move, Mr. President. We've taken control of the White House, but that doesn't mean we won't still have trouble."

He bit back questions, held his hands up, and prayed Elizabeth would stay in the closet. She was smart and if she could get a message out, perhaps one of the others would call for help.

Vanessa followed them into the entryway of the residence, then looked Glen's way. "I need a status report."

The rogue agent closed the door behind them. "PEOC is under our control. I've got confirmation that we have Calder and two others in custody."

"Two others? I thought Calder was the only one down there." Vanessa turned to glare at Zack. "Who are your other friends? Sparks? Spencer?"

So they still didn't know about Mad or Freddy. Thomas had been the only one in on that secret.

"I have no idea. You know it's a big house. There's always someone coming in and out." He sent them a humorless smile. "Why did you call my father Sergei?"

That was the name he'd feared for months. If he could get an answer now, it might both buy him peace and Elizabeth some time.

And while they talked, he needed to figure out their play. What was their endgame? If they'd wanted to kill him, they would already have shot him. They'd had plenty of opportunity. Instead, they'd isolated him. But they couldn't keep him here forever and they couldn't keep the White House in lockdown. There would be too many questions.

Vanessa stared at him, as though considering whether answering was worth her time. Finally, she sighed. "Natalia hated the name Frank. She said it reminded her that he had other loyalties, including his vows to another woman. She was somewhat possessive of him."

He was about to ask questions about his father's affair with Nata and the baby she'd given birth to, when his worst nightmare happened. Elizabeth exited the bedroom, carrying her phone. It looked as if she'd just hung up.

When she caught sight of them, her eyes widened with fear.

"Welcome, Ms. Matthews." Vanessa turned her gun Elizabeth's way. "Join us. After all, you'll soon be spending some time with friends of mine."

Zack held a hand out to Elizabeth, and she ran to him, her heels clicking against the marble floors. Their fingers tangled. He could hear her shaky breaths. He could practically feel her fear. "Stay calm, sweetheart. I don't think they're planning to take us out here and now. I believe they have other arrangements to make, don't you?"

"Well, you didn't leave us with many choices," his father complained. "If you had just been more reasonable, none of this would have happened."

"What's going on?" Elizabeth asked. "Other than your father being surprisingly lucid."

"My father is and always has been. He's also a part of this scheme. Apparently, he joined the merry band of Russians shortly after I was born. Is Natalia Kuilikov my mother?"

He wanted answers. He fucking deserved to know. And he had to find out now, before they made their next move. And Zack feared he knew what that was.

They needed him compliant, and he could only think of one way to ensure that: they intended to take Elizabeth with them and hold her hostage so he had little choice but to do their bidding.

Zack hoped like hell they would fail because he had friends—amazing friends who had never let him down—and there was no way they allowed the Russians to compromise their country or to break him. Roman, Mad, and Freddy might be under their control—good luck with that—but he'd heard nothing about Dax and Gabe. Or Connor, who hadn't even been in the White House. They would find a way to rescue Elizabeth. Then, Zack swore, these Russians would feel every ounce of his wrath.

His father looked confused for a moment, but not in the vacant way he had previously. "What are you talking about?"

Zack felt Elizabeth squeeze his hand, trying to lend him her strength. It gave him the courage to keep asking the questions, despite the answers terrifying him. "I know why you institutionalized Mother. I heard the tapes. She accidently killed a child. Was that the real Zack Hayes?"

Vanessa laughed, shaking her head the nurse's way. "I wondered if that was what he thought."

His father frowned. "You honestly believe I would pawn off some bastard as my own?"

"He was still your son. You were having an affair with Natalia, and she was in love with you. The way I heard it, both women were pregnant at the same time. What a bad boy, Frank..." she scolded. "But Constance was upset about Natalia's pregnancy, so you sent her back to the States to give birth under the guise of ensuring there would be no question that Zack had been born on US soil."

"I had to. Constance didn't understand that Natalia was a lovely convenience. Or I thought she was. She promised me she couldn't get pregnant." His father paced like a lion in a cage. "She lied. The whole fucking affair was a mistake. I talked to her about an abortion. She refused. Shortly after she gave birth, Krylov and a KGB officer came to me. I realized they'd plotted to shame me into working for them all along. Natalia was just the Jezebel they'd sent to trap me. But I didn't care. I already knew my political career was going nowhere, so I laughed in their faces. After all, I had a healthy, properly born son, and I just knew that Zachary would be the Hayes who finally became president. But then your stupid bitch of a mother ruined everything by smothering Nata's baby."

His stomach twisted. "So my mother killed my half brother?"

"Yes," his father croaked. "She smothered him. She was drunk, as usual. I managed to keep her from the gin until after you were born. The minute she recovered from your birth, she was right back at it. I stayed with her because her father had more money than God and she was his only heir. I knew that inheritance could fund your political career, but that damn old man stayed alive forever."

"And your dad wasn't around to stop Constance's big oops because he was in bed with Natalia at the time. And so your son died, Frank." Vanessa made a pouty face.

"My son is alive and right here in this room." His father's hands had fisted at his sides, face mottled as he regarded Zack. "I protected you after that. I wouldn't allow Constance near you. But the KGB, they came after the boy's death." He swallowed. "You have to understand what a scandal it would have caused if anyone knew that Constance had committed infanticide, even accidentally. I couldn't call the authorities. They would have arrested your mother. It would have ruined my career and her father would have never given you a dime. I needed his wealth for your career. We had money, but nothing like your mother's family."

"You chose cash over your country?"

"I chose your future over my freedom," he argued. "You don't think I would have wanted to be cut loose from Constance? Let them haul her away and bid good riddance? But I didn't so that you could have a future." He held out his hands. "This future."

"Don't pin this on me. You sold me out, even though you knew they would later want to use my position to compromise our country." Zack intended to break the decades-long stranglehold Russia had on his family. "You were too weak to say no."

He would never put his own son or daughter in such a position. Elizabeth wouldn't allow it. Unlike his father, he'd picked a truly great partner to spend his life with. Elizabeth would always check his worst qualities. She'd been doing it for a long time, and he'd only really gotten in trouble when he'd stopped trusting her.

"If I'd had my way, you would never have known about this sordid past."

"You've been giving the Russians intelligence," Elizabeth said. "You thought if you spied on Zack and passed along classified information, they would leave Zack himself alone. You have almost unfettered access since everyone thinks you're not lucid enough to know what you're doing. So no one questions it when they find you in the Treaty Room, playing around your son's desk." She turned to Zack. "Remember I told you I found him in there two weeks ago. The Secret Service didn't stop him. They came down to ask me what I wanted to do about it."

So the men in black suits either hadn't understood how to deal with the president's crazy father or they'd wanted to set Elizabeth up to make her look guilty of spying. Zack's money was on the latter since the nurse had hustled his father out and she'd been found in his office alone. In fact, the nurse hadn't been honest with him about the incident. Another way to isolate him.

"I can't believe you would be so naïve." Vanessa tsked at Frank like he was an idiot. "We were always going to want more. Zachary Hayes is the culmination of decades of work and careful preparation." She turned back to Zack. "Do you know how we regard you in my community? You're a myth. A unicorn. You're the thing we whisper about in shadows and pray for. The ultimate tool. You *will* do your job. Lives were sacrificed to get to this point. My half sister and father are gone, and I will not allow their sacrifices to be in vain."

"What did Joy willingly sacrifice? Your father already told me she didn't know she was going to die that evening in Memphis. So what did she really give up for the cause?"

"Not enough. By the time others decreed that she should give her life for Mother Russia, I believe she was corrupted and, therefore, useless. She'd spent too much time with your friends. I read through her correspondence with Roman." She sneered. "If you weren't elected, Joy thought she would be free. She was always naïve."

Maybe it shouldn't, but the idea of Joy trying to be free gave him a measure of peace. Because that meant not everything between them had been a lie. He'd reached her, affected her. If she'd found her independence from this conspiracy, she might have even become an ally someday.

Elizabeth leaned against him as though she knew what he was thinking. "If he gives in on the pipeline, what will you want next?"

"I don't make those decisions." Vanessa nodded toward the Secret Service agent. "But whatever it is, you will be a good boy and play along. If you do as you're told, we might even allow you occasional access to your girlfriend. Not too much, of course, since you'll be a newly married man."

So they were relying on that old playbook. "I assume you're my new bride."

Vanessa shrugged. "Someone has to stay close to you. My sister wasn't smart enough to handle you. I'll be better at it. We'll be married in a few weeks. In the meantime, your little whore will find herself enjoying Krylov's hospitality in Moscow. Her treatment will be dependent on your behavior."

The idea of Elizabeth under their control made Zack sick. He refused to let that happen. They would not take her out of the country. Hell, they weren't taking her from this house.

He tightened his hold on Elizabeth. "No one will believe I'm in love with you. And Ms. Matthews is not exactly an unknown figure. She's my damn press secretary. There will be questions when she disappears, especially since she literally talks to reporters all day. They like her. If you want to tank my presidency, piss off the reporters who love her. They're not stupid. They know I'm involved with her."

"I'm convinced they do," Elizabeth affirmed. "It's a genuine sign of their affection for me that they haven't floated more than rumors and innuendo about our relationship. How do you think it will look if the president dumps his well-respected, beloved press secretary for a younger woman, who quite frankly most people can't stand, and installs her as First Lady? You've worked in the press office long enough to know how that's going to go."

"I'll make it work," Vanessa vowed stubbornly. "And if matters here go to hell, Zack can always have a heart attack, and we'll deal with your mealy-mouthed VP. We have him in our pocket now, too. Everyone has a weak point. That pipeline will not go through. We have a stranglehold on the European gas market and it will stay that way. And soon we'll talk about those sanctions the US has had on Russia for years. You're going to bring our countries closer than ever."

"I might be amenable to a discussion, but if you so much as remove Elizabeth from this room, I promise you I will fight to the death. You want any chance of my cooperation? You leave her alone. She'll stay with me in the residence. She'll remain my press secretary. Anything less will raise too many questions, and we already have a ton of them to answer."

He used his last bargaining chip, hoping he could make her see reason.

"Do you think you're in charge here, Mr. President?" The nurse's dark eyes narrowed. "Your will means nothing. You are a pawn and we will move you around as we please. Vanessa, take her now. Our comrades will have already secured the garage, so we can smuggle her out in secrecy."

Elizabeth stiffened beside him. Zack held her tighter. They had not come this far and dedicated themselves to each other to simply give up now. He couldn't choose between Elizabeth and his country. He'd made vows to both. He wasn't so naïve as to think that they would ever return Elizabeth to him. And how much would she suffer at their hands?

But one asset in his back pocket the Russians had underestimated time and time again? His friends. He believed in them.

He stepped in front of Elizabeth. "I won't let you take her. I'll die before I allow you to leave with her. You think about that. You need me on camera within an hour or two or this country will start asking questions that will lead to your whole plan falling apart."

"Or we go to plan B," the turncoat Secret Service agent said. "Sorry, Vanessa. This looks best if there's a scapegoat. Turns out the president was unfaithful, and Ms. Matthews took exception."

He fired, the sound pinging through the room, and Vanessa's eyes widened as she stared down at the hole in her chest. Bright red blood bloomed across her white shirt. The gun she carried dropped from suddenly lax fingers as she fell to the floor and blood began to pool on the tile.

The nurse simply shook his head. "You were supposed to wait to do that."

"He's not going to cooperate," Glen argued. "My mission was to assess the situation and deal with it. I think our new course of action is to frame Ms. Matthews for killing her lover and her rival. Then we'll set up the vice president in the Oval. I think he'll be much more compliant."

"We don't have a choice now." The nurse raised his gun.

That was when Zack sprang into action.

He gave Elizabeth a shove, pushing her behind a heavy couch as the nurse fired. He felt something burn against his arm, but he ignored the fiery sting and dove for the gun lying on the floor.

"No!" A masculine shout broke through the room, and suddenly someone tackled Zack as he heard another bullet ping.

His father. Frank had covered his body with his own.

Seconds later, the door to the residence crashed open. Then he heard roaring gunfire. Whoever had just entered the fight was not using a suppressor.

"Stand down!" That deep voice belonged to Thomas. "I will kill you, Glen. You'll be just as dead as that fucking nurse and I won't regret it."

"Or we could question him." A sardonic voice joined the fray. Connor. "I promise we'll make it hurt, but we could use him to find out who the others are. Because clearly we've got a problem in your department, man."

"Why do you think I've taken to wearing a bulletproof vest even in the White House?" Thomas replied.

"Never meant to hurt you," his father, who was still draped over him like a blanket, muttered.

Had his father taken the bullet meant for him? Zack was scared to shift him and risk injuring him more. "Dad, are you all right? Elizabeth? Elizabeth, where are you?"

"I'm here." She was suddenly kneeling beside him. "Connor, call an ambulance."

His father shook his head. "No ambulance. Sparks is here? Roll me off my son."

Suddenly, the bodily weight lifted off him, then Elizabeth was above him, her beautiful eyes sparkling with tears as she reached for him. "Don't you ever do that again. They could have killed you."

They would have killed him if his father hadn't leapt in front of him. His right arm hurt where the first bullet had grazed his skin, but he clapped a hand over the wound to stem the bleeding and rose to see that Connor and Thomas had everything in hand. Connor shoved the traitorous agent on his knees while Thomas put on the cuffs.

Zack knelt next to his father, whose skin had gone a pasty white while the spreading blood quickly stained his pajamas. The man was clearly dying. "Dad, we need to get you to a hospital."

Elizabeth was on her knees beside him. "Quickly."

His father managed to shake his head. "No. Cover this up. Sparks will know what to do. Start over. Hide everything. None of this was your fault. I should have been stronger, but I wanted everything for you. I thought I could manage them. Thought they would leave you alone. I had no choice. No other way to protect our name."

Shock, anger, denial—they all rolled through him at once. Had his father ever truly cared about *him* or merely their name and the glory he could bring to it by becoming president? Zack feared he knew the answer. He had been nothing more than the means for the Hayes family to have a sparkling legacy.

"What about protecting me? Mom? The baby—your son—who never lived to see his first birthday?"

"Only you were important. History books don't remember pawns, only great leaders who do great things." A nasty gleam hit his father's eyes. "You've always been too soft to understand that."

And then his father was gone.

"Damn, this is a lot of bodies," a new voice said. Mad. "Are we planning on calling the cops or should we grab some shovels? Then again, I think someone will notice us burying a bunch of people in the Rose Garden."

"This is not the time, babe." Sara was with him. "Zack just lost his father."

He stood, turned. And they were here, all his friends.

They had saved him, just like he'd believed they would.

Roman moved in, reaching for Zack's shoulder. "You okay? Connor was already on his way back when Gus called him. Connor stealthed into the garage before the Russians could secure it, and he sent Dax to check on us. There are some bodies down there, too."

"You didn't answer Roman. Say something." Elizabeth wrapped her arms around him. "Are you okay?"

Suddenly, a smile broke across his face. The danger was past. Elizabeth was in his arms. He was surrounded by his brothers. "I'm not okay. I'm great."

Chapter Twenty

"Are you sure we're going in the right direction?" Lara asked several hours later, just before she stumbled into the Red Room.

At the sound of her voice, Zack glanced up and motioned her inside. Connor followed. Now, they were all gathered here, his family.

He was still dressed in the suit Elizabeth had selected for him to wear after he'd had a couple of stitches in his arm to close the bullet wound and before he spoke to the American people. He'd given a brief but reassuring press conference, promising the people that he was well and that he would give a full prime-time address the following evening with more complete details about the assassination attempt. As he'd stood behind the podium and done his best to both soothe Americans while projecting strength, he'd unashamedly held Elizabeth's hand.

He'd heard Twitter was abuzz about their public display of affection and he didn't care.

Now it was almost midnight, and the White House was

finally quiet again.

Connor and Thomas had taken over the grisly scene in the residence and worked miracles. Not thirty minutes after the bullets had flown, a grim-looking man and a silent woman with her pale-hair twisted in a severe bun had shown up, dressed in all black. CIA agents, ones Connor trusted. The man he'd introduced as Josiah Grant. The blonde woman Connor had merely referred to as Kim. Neither had been big on talk. Instead, they'd gotten to work right away and soon cleared the scene until he would have sworn it had never been the epicenter of a multiple-death event.

He didn't even know where they'd taken the bodies. He probably didn't want to.

Connor cupped his wife's shoulders as he kissed the top of her head. "You made the right call, Zack. I know you would far rather have given a press conference where you told the American people about this whole Russian conspiracy. But it's best for everyone that you didn't."

Roman nodded, tossing his arm around Gus. "If the truth got out, it could shake financial markets across the globe."

Dax looked reluctant to agree...but he did. "I'm a truth, justice, and American way type of guy, too. So I know concealing this bothers you. But the idea that the Russians were nearly able to compromise our president and our government would shake up all our alliances and embolden our enemies."

"Sadly, he's right," Holland put in as she dropped her hand to her husband's thigh.

"Then how do we explain all the other details?" Everly leaned against Gabe. "All the other deaths? It's not like people aren't going to notice..."

Gabe had a glass of Scotch in his hands. "You want to let us in on the plan, Freddy?"

Once again, the former intelligence officer, while

whacko, had proven invaluable. Now his eyes lit up like he'd been given the greatest gift in the world—the green light to build a conspiracy from the ground up.

Freddy stood with a bounce in his step. "Well, the president's father had a heart attack when he learned his son had been shot. It's very sad, but not terribly shocking since he was in poor health. Zack will mourn appropriately, at least for the cameras. His long-term nurse will give a statement, explaining the situation."

Sara cocked her head. "But his nurse is dead."

"Totally and rotting in hell, but no one knows that. So we've chosen a CIA agent who has lots of practice covering things up. He'll play nice for the cameras, and his part of the story won't even end up being a footnote in history. We've already got Frank Hayes's death certificate signed. His body will be cremated within the hour, along with his Russian nurse."

Connor led his wife to a chair where he sat and pulled her down on his lap. "And since the nurse apparently had no real ties to anyone except the conspirators, no one will make pesky inquiries later."

"What about Vanessa? Washington insiders knew who she was, even if her reputation was more twatwaffle than press secretary in training," Mad put in.

"She's more difficult," Connor acknowledged. "But Freddy has a solution for her, too."

"We trace everything back to our amazing assassin," Freddy explained. "He's got well-known ties to Krylov. Magically, he's going to disappear from custody this evening. He's a badass, after all. And"—he gasped—"we'll learn that he'd been using Vanessa to gain access to the president's schedule. They had to have some pillow talk, right? But after he escaped, he decided to clean up his loose ends and sadly, Vanessa's usefulness was at an end. We'll stage her murder at her apartment. It's really exciting. I'm looking forward to being in on the action."

"Won't forensics prove she died while the assassin was in police custody?" Gus asked.

Connor waved that off. "Trust me. We have ways around that."

"So you're saying we're simply going to let the assassin go?" Elizabeth said as she stood beside him.

Zack tugged on her hand, and like Connor had with Lara, pulled her onto his lap. He didn't want an inch of space between them. "He's a paid contractor with no loyalty to anyone. And he was never actually going to kill me. He was only on the scene to cause sufficient chaos so that two things could happen. First, to close off the entire White House so their agents could take over and second, to allow Vanessa to nab you so they could force me to do their bidding. They just didn't count on Thomas being a super-cautious badass."

Thomas, who stood in the corner of the room, almost smiled. "I might never take this vest off, sir. And I probably won't let you out of my sight again."

The man had been a six-and-a-half-foot mother hen all evening long.

"Have we figured out who our bad agents are and what we'll do with them?" Zack asked.

"Connor and Freddy helped me identify three," Thomas explained. "I'm certain we've cleaned house now."

"One died tragically saving Zack's life," Freddy explained. "The other two are already in holding pens. Connor will take them to an undisclosed location, debrief them, get all the intel we can, then...permanently relocate them. Later, we'll find proof they were in on the plans to assassinate the president. They were also on Krylov's payroll. We'll play the Russian mobster's motive as having a vested interest in killing the pipeline deal. A kernel of truth is always best."

"And bonus, we'll be taking Krylov himself down since our assassin was more than happy to admit he'd been hired by the man and we caught the bastard at the airport, trying to flee the country." Connor looked awfully pleased with himself. "Even if Krylov mentions the president's father or that past crap, no one will care. At this point, the Russian government will deny all knowledge of him or his activities and let us do whatever we please with him. And soon, look for a new head of that syndicate. They know they can't reach you now. Too many of the assets they had in place are dead or compromised, so we fully believe they'll cut their losses."

Elizabeth shifted so she could look into his eyes. "Then it's really over?"

Zack nodded. "It's over. I trust my friends on this. I know now that we'll have no constitutional crisis about where I was born. I'm exactly who I say I am. No one can blackmail me again, and I can get on with protecting and growing our country. You know, I've thought a lot about whether I should really run for reelection."

"Bowing out, especially with the election less than a year away, would be a bad idea," Gabe argued.

"The country needs you." Dax stood. "If you step down, Shorn might make a run at the White House. Having been the VP of a popular president, he'll likely do well. We know he's compromised, and it will embolden the Russians to try this again."

He'd already known what they were going to say, and he'd already begun formulating counterarguments in his head. In the end, Elizabeth had convinced him he had to run again for the good of the people. Besides, he wanted to see what the country would think of their gorgeous, intelligent, gracious and tough–as–hell First Lady.

He held up his hand to stay their debate. "I'm running. And it's for that very reason Shorn will see reason and step down before my next term. He 'wants to spend more time with his family.' Because I agree that we can't let those bastards win, and Connor has agreed to go back to the Agency to run a special division focused specifically on threats against the presidency, Secret Service, and our intelligence officers. We won't let them infiltrate us like that again. Dax, we're hoping you'll come on board, too. I know you two had plans to start your own firm."

Dax waved a hand. "They can wait. I would be more than happy to serve my country again."

"Mad, are you ready to make your debut? We'll schedule a splashy press conference in the next day or two." He sent his friend a wry grin. "Do we have a reason you faked your death besides dodging angry drug dealers?"

Mad managed to look hurt. "I don't mess with illegal substances. Well, not anymore. I'm a perfectly respectable husband and almost-dad now, thank you very much. And I faked my death because I caught wind of the assassination attempt and spent weeks underground putting all the pieces together so I could help foil it, of course."

Trust Mad Crawford to come out of this situation better than ever before.

"And I was in on it." Sara slipped her hand into Mad's. "We can say our relationship developed then, too. It's less tragic, and makes him seem way smarter than he actually is."

Mad simply grinned and gave him a thumbs-up.

It seemed his friends had everything handled. And now, he was almost ready to retire for the night. Today had been the longest of his life, and more than anything he wanted to put it behind him. He needed time to process everything, especially that, despite his father's arrogance and disregard for Zack as a human with wants and feelings, old Frank had still saved him in the end.

Elizabeth stood, stifling a yawn, and took charge. "I'm

going to head to bed. Thomas, I cannot thank you enough. Go see your wife."

Thomas frowned. "I'm not sure I should leave."

"We're one hundred percent sure about our remaining agents, and I've got a couple of Agency operatives I trust implicitly watching the residence tonight," Connor assured. "Go home. Kiss your wife and hug your kids, Thomas. Tomorrow we'll be back to work."

Elizabeth turned Zack's way and kissed him as the other women all stood and headed for the door. "I'm going to get Sara and Mad set up in a more comfortable bedroom upstairs."

"We're fine where we are." Sara squeezed Mad's hand before following Elizabeth. "We're actually kind of fond of the place."

"We've made some awesome memories there." Mad winked. "Besides, I don't want to prematurely spoil my big back-from-the-dead surprise."

Liz laughed, just like he did. "What about you, Freddy? The Lincoln Bedroom is lovely."

"Nah." Freddy shook his head. "I like the air ducts. They're very comfy."

Zack rolled his eyes. Eventually, he'd have to deal with the phantom of the White House. But for now, Elizabeth and the women all wandered out in a cloud of soft chatter. He was alone with his closest friends.

"How about a nightcap, guys?" Roman started pouring Scotch into the crystal glasses.

Zack could certainly use one. Then he would join his fiancée—he really needed to get her a ring—and hold her all night. But first, he had to take a moment with these men who had formed the foundation of who he was, and today had helped to save his life. If it hadn't been for Mad, Gabe, Connor, Dax, and Roman, he would have become exactly the man his father had tried to turn him into. He would have been taught that only his name mattered, that the only thing of value he had to give was his legacy. These men, his brothers, had shown him the true meaning of family.

"You okay?" Roman patted his shoulder and pressed the glass in his hand. "That was one hell of a rough day."

"But it's over." Gabe reached for his cocktail. "And we can move on with our lives."

"We still have to be vigilant." Connor smiled. "But I think we're back in control."

Mad held his glass up. "Then let's get ready to have some fun because we have two of our own to marry off in style."

Zack shook his head. "Since I'm president, my wedding will be very circumspect. And very soon."

"How soon?" Dax asked, brows raised.

"Next week...if I can wait that long. I want Elizabeth to be my wife now. We've already lost too much time. We'll have a small ceremony here at the White House. You guys, your lovely ladies, and her family will be the only guests in attendance." He turned to his chief of staff. "But Roman's wedding...that will be a blowout."

"Hey, let's talk about this..." Roman began.

"Nope, you're getting the full treatment, brother, because then we'll all be married and having kids," Dax explained.

"Tell me you and Liz aren't going to try to have a couple of little monsters soon," Gabe challenged. "I know Everly and I are going to announce our first at a proper time and place when she's ready to talk about it. But not now. Even though it's happening."

Everly was pregnant? He reached out and shook Gabe's hand. "That is amazing news, brother."

"You knocked up my sister?" Mad demanded.

"I couldn't let you do the dad thing alone," Gabe answered with a grin.

Mad gave him a shoulder bump. "No, you could not. Good job, man."

"But seriously, Everly wants to have a party and make an official announcement. Pretend to be surprised," Gabe insisted. "But I had to tell my brothers."

Zack raised his glass. "To the Perfect Gentlemen. We found our perfect ladies. Let's try our damnedest to be perfect dads."

They all agreed, though Zack knew there was no such thing as perfect.

But these men and his bride-to-be were pretty damn close.

He was content.

Epilogue

Connecticut
Twelve years later

"Does anyone know what this is about?" Mad slipped off his Yankees cap as he entered the small waiting room to the principal's office.

He and Sara had moved out to this small Connecticut town, though they kept a place in the city because neither he nor Gabe would ever leave the city behind. Zack and Elizabeth had followed them to this sleepy suburb after their Washington years.

Zack shrugged. "I don't."

That made Mad's frown deepen. "Are we here for the OGs or the next generation?"

They'd grouped their children in three groups. Mad had named the first six the OGs out of his love for gangsta rap and not at all because their oldest children had formed a gang themselves that often made Zack long for the days when he could call in the National Guard. Maddie

Crawford, Alex Bond, Karlie Sparks, Jordan Spencer, Helena Calder, and Nicholas Hayes had all been born within a year and a half of one another and they'd been tight ever since.

Nick and the OGs were all in fifth grade, and apparently had taken the place by storm, despite the fact that school had only been in session for two weeks. Now they'd been called into the principal's office.

"I didn't get any details," Sara admitted softly.

Mad sighed. "I know it's not the crazy babies or we'd be at the preschool, and I was just there yesterday when our son decided to explain to his teacher that she was outnumbered."

"He really said that." Sara winced. "He was leading a revolt because they changed the milk from chocolate to plain."

Zack shook his head and tried not to laugh. "I'm pretty sure we've been summoned to deal with the older kiddos because Roman and Gus are on their way, too."

"I suspect deeply that ours led the charge," Holland said, but there was a tiny smile on her face as though she genuinely enjoyed the chaos. After all, her life had significantly grown quieter after leaving NCIS a few years before to work on private investigations with select security firms, including the one her husband and Connor had opened after leaving DC behind.

Dax and Holland had been waiting when Zack had arrived at the school. They'd had an enjoyable few minutes catching up since they hadn't seen each other in a week or so, following the group dinner at Connor and Lara's. The rotating weekly get-together was at his and Elizabeth's place this week, and he needed to remember to pick up the ribs or his wife would be very cross. Freddy had even called from wherever Freddy lived these days—that was undisclosed—and he would be joining them. All the kids would look forward to seeing crazy Uncle Freddy.

The door opened, and Roman and Gus stepped inside. They were both dressed casually since they were taking some time off to be with the latest addition to their family, a newborn boy they had adopted a mere three weeks before. He was tucked into a sling she wore over her jeans and T-shirt.

"I will kill them all," Gus vowed. "I'd just gotten him to sleep when I got the call."

Roman shook his head. "She's not talking about the kids, guys. On our way here she devised four different ways to sue the school. I'm too tired to come up with any legal arguments right now. I need a nap."

"Don't worry," Zack told Roman. "Everyone knows I'm the brains of our operation."

Everyone chuckled.

After serving his second term as president, he'd been way too young to retire. So he and Roman had done what they'd always wanted to—practice law. They ran a nonprofit that aided Americans in trouble overseas. And in his spare time, he'd written a book or two about political history while Roman taught at Yale two days a week.

Their ladies were the ones who brought in the cash these days. Elizabeth and Gus ran a publicity firm in Manhattan that specialized in crisis management. After all, they were damn good at it.

Not that they were the most successful of their group. Lara had written a book of her own about a fictional president finding love in the White House. She had her own groupies now and was way more popular than even he was.

According to Lara, publishing was its own form of heaven and hell.

"Sure you are," Roman replied with a yawn. "Hey, Mad, you know what's really good at putting a person to sleep? Your movie. They're running it all month long on cable. I swear the title flashes up on the screen and I'm gone."

Gus shushed him. "It's a good movie, damn it."

"I love it," Holland admitted. "*From Dead to Dad: The Maddox Crawford Story* is the best title ever."

"Roman is still upset the actor who played him had a receding hairline," Sara teased.

Roman touched his head. "I still have a glorious full mane, despite the gray."

Gus leaned over and kissed him. "You're still hot as hell, babe. Best I ever had, and that's saying something."

Zack was well aware the school's office staff was watching them, but he supposed even in this wealthy suburb it wasn't every day they saw a man who'd led the nation for eight years. Or maybe they were excited about Mad since he did have a movie about saving said president. When it had first come out, they'd made a drinking game of it.

The door opened once more, and sunshine walked in.

Zack stood and made a beeline for the gorgeous woman who'd agreed to marry him twelve years before. They'd had a quiet ceremony that had been the exact opposite of his first over-the-top wedding. Only he, Elizabeth, their dearest friends, and immediate family. Some wouldn't consider it much of a wedding, but they had a hell of a marriage.

Even all these years later, she took his breath away when she entered a room. She'd given him a son and a daughter. She'd also given him a life more wonderful than he'd dared to imagine.

"Hey, sweetheart." Zack pulled her into his arms and held her for a moment. She'd been gone a whole four hours, but that felt too long to him.

She sighed against him as though she felt their connection, too. "Hi yourself. I caught a ride in with Connor and Lara. Is Nick okay?"

He nodded the couple's way as they crowded into the

room. "Thank you for picking her up."

"No problem," Connor said, his hand in his wife's. "We spent the whole ride in trying to figure out what our hooligans did this time. My money is on some kind of con."

Lara shook her head. "I'm almost positive it's about Karlie's latest investigation. She's convinced the cafeteria is taking kickbacks from the beef industry, and I overheard her talking to Jordan and Nick about how they could bug the principal's office. I probably should have warned her against that, but I was really proud of the stance they're taking on red meat."

His son lived for hamburgers, but he would do almost anything Karlie told him to because he'd been pretty much in love with the girl since they were babies.

Dax groaned. "I will check my inventory when I get back to the office. I'll bet I have missing surveillance equipment. I should have known there was no way our boy wanted to spend a Saturday at the office with his dad."

"Well, look on the bright side. At least there are three lawyers here, and the kids can get good PR advice," Elizabeth said, a grin on her lips.

"I get the feeling we should be more upset," Gus began, "but I'm kind of excited to see what they've gotten into this time."

Gabe strode in, followed by Everly. "Please tell me Alex didn't do something stupid like try to hot-wire a helicopter. I've been worried ever since I heard the school was flying in a police chopper for law enforcement day."

"Well, that's what happens when you let him fly yours," Everly complained, but she winked her husband's way. "And the event isn't happening until next week."

So there was something they could all look forward to.

The principal stepped into the waiting room. "Ladies, gentlemen. We need to talk about your children."

Zack grinned and glanced around to find all of his

friends smiling, too. They were all probably thinking what he was. They'd been those kids, but they'd been alone. They'd only had each other all those years ago.

But their kids were surrounded by family.

"All right, Principal Smith, let's talk." Zack rose.

He couldn't wait to find out what they'd gotten into now. He hoped it was epic.

After all, the younger generation had a reputation to uphold.

Want an alpha male who seduces his enemy, only to realize she's stolen his heart?
Meet Clint Holmes.
I romanced her for revenge…but what if she's not the enemy after all?

Check out MORE THAN TEMPT YOU, part of the steamy, emotional More Than Words Series.

MORE THAN TEMPT YOU
by Shayla Black
Coming April 30, 2019!

I'm Clint Holmes. I was an ambitious guy with a busy life and a growing business. Sure North Dakota wasn't a tropical paradise, but I was happy enough—until tragedy struck. Now the only thing that matters is finding the person responsible and making her pay. But Bethany Banks is a Harvard-educated shark used to swallowing her enemies whole while playing dangerous corporate games. How can a blue-collar oil man like me possibly beat her?

The moment I lay eyes on my beautiful nemesis, the answer is obvious. I seduce her.

On Maui, where she's fled, I get to know the man-eater who caused my family so much pain…only to find she's not the brazen ballbuster I assumed. She's skittish, secretive, vulnerable. For some reason, my instinct is to protect her. I can't abandon my plan…but I can't stop wanting her. Night after night, I pry her open with my touch until I'm drowning in our passion. Soon, I'm questioning everything, especially the fine line between love and hate. But when the past comes back to wreak vengeance and the truth explodes, can I prove that I'm more than tempted to love her forever?

More Than Words Series
By Shayla Black

Sexy contemporary romances that prove sometimes words alone can't express the true depths of love.

Each book can be read as a standalone. You may enjoy them more in order, but it's not necessary for your reading pleasure.

More Than Want You
More Than Need You
More Than Love You
More Than Crave You
Coming Soon:
More Than Tempt You (April 30, 2019)
More Than Pleasure You (novella) (Nov. 12, 2019)

Courting Justice

A new series from Lexi Blake
Now available

A fast-paced contemporary romance series where passion for the law isn't the only thing heating up the courtroom.

Order of Protection, Book 1, Now Available

To high-end defense attorney Henry Garrison, Win Hughes is a woman he met during one of the most trying times of his life. She's soft and warm, and he finds solace in their brief relationship. But Win has a secret. She's actually Taylor Winston-Hughes--born to one of the wealthiest families in the country, orphaned as a child by a tragic accident. Win moves in the wealthiest circles, but her lavish lifestyle hides her pain.

When her best friend is murdered in the midst of a glittering New York gala, Win's charged with the crime, and the only person in the world she wants to see is Henry.

Henry is shocked at the true identity of his lover, but he can't reject the case. This trial could take his new firm into the stratosphere. Still, he's not getting burned by Win again. And yet every turn brings them closer together.

As the case takes a wild turn and Win's entire life is upended, she must look to the people she's closest to in order to find a killer. And Henry must decide between making his case and saving the woman he loves...

* * * *

Evidence of Desire, Book 2, Now Available

Isla Shayne knows she's in over her head. As former all-star linebacker Trey Adams's personal lawyer, she's used to handling his business dealings and private financial matters, not murder charges. She needs to find an experienced criminal attorney who speaks her client's language. David Cormack of Garrison, Cormack and Lawless is exactly what she needs in the courtroom--and the only man she wants in the bedroom.

For David, taking on the Adams case means diving back into a world he thought he'd left behind and colliding head on with tragic possibilities he's in no mood to face. There's a reason professional football is in his past and no matter how close Isla gets to the truth he intends to leave it there.

But long days working on the case together lead to hot nights in each other's arms. As their feelings grow, the case takes a deadly twist that could change the game between the two lovers forever.

About Shayla Black
LET'S GET TO KNOW EACH OTHER!

ABOUT ME:

Shayla Black is the *New York Times* and *USA Today* bestselling author of more than seventy novels. For twenty years, she's written contemporary, erotic, paranormal, and historical romances via traditional, independent, foreign, and audio publishers. Her books have sold millions of copies and been published in a dozen languages.

Raised an only child, Shayla occupied herself with lots of daydreaming, much to the chagrin of her teachers. In college, she found her love for reading and realized that she could have a career publishing the stories spinning in her imagination. Though she graduated with a degree in Marketing/Advertising and embarked on a stint in corporate America to pay the bills, her heart has always been with her characters. She's thrilled that she's been living her dream as a full-time author for the past eight years.

Shayla currently lives in North Texas with her wonderfully supportive husband, her daughter, and two spoiled tabbies. In her "free" time, she enjoys reality TV, reading, and listening to an eclectic blend of music.

LET ME LEARN MORE ABOUT YOU.

Connect with me via the links below. The VIP Reader newsletter is packed with exclusive news, excerpts, and fun surprises. You can also become one of my Facebook Book Beauties and enjoy live, interactive #WineWednesday video chats full of fun, book chatter, and more! See you soon!

Connect with me online:

Website: http://shaylablack.com
VIP Reader Newsletter: http://shayla.link/nwsltr
Facebook Author Page:
  https://www.facebook.com/ShaylaBlackAuthor
Facebook Book Beauties Chat Group:
  http://shayla.link/FBChat
Instagram: https://instagram.com/ShaylaBlack/
Book+Main Bites:
  https://bookandmainbites.com/users/62
Twitter: http://twitter.com/Shayla_Black
Google +: http://shayla.link/googleplus
Amazon Author: http://shayla.link/AmazonFollow
BookBub: http://shayla.link/BookBub
Goodreads: http://shayla.link/goodreads
YouTube: http://shayla.link/youtube

If you enjoyed this book, please review it and recommend it to others.

About Lexi Blake

New York Times bestselling author Lexi Blake lives in North Texas with her husband and three kids. Since starting her publishing journey in 2011, she's sold over two million copies of her books. She began writing at a young age, concentrating on plays and journalism. It wasn't until she started writing romance that she found success. She likes to find humor in the strangest places and believes in happy endings. She also writes contemporary western ménage under the name Sophie Oak.

Connect with Lexi online:

Facebook: www.facebook.com/lexi.blake.39
Website: www.LexiBlake.net
Instagram: www.instagram.com/Lexi4714
Twitter: twitter.com/authorlexiblake
Pinterest: www.pinterest.com/lexiblake39/

Sign up for Lexi's free newsletter!

Other Books by Shayla Black

CONTEMPORARY ROMANCE

MORE THAN WORDS
More Than Want You
More Than Need You
More Than Love You
More Than Crave You
Coming Soon:
More Than Tempt You (April 30, 2019)
More Than Pleasure You (November 12, 2019)

THE WICKED LOVERS (COMPLETE SERIES)
Wicked Ties
Decadent
Delicious
Surrender to Me
Belong to Me
"Wicked to Love" (novella)
Mine to Hold
"Wicked All the Way" (novella)
Ours to Love
"Wicked All Night" (novella)
"Forever Wicked" (novella)
Theirs to Cherish
His to Take
Pure Wicked (novella)
Wicked for You
Falling in Deeper
Dirty Wicked (novella)
"A Very Wicked Christmas" (short)
Holding on Tighter

THE DEVOTED LOVERS
Devoted to Pleasure
"Devoted to Wicked" (novella)
Coming Soon:
Devoted to Love (July 2, 2019)

SEXY CAPERS
Bound And Determined
Strip Search
"Arresting Desire" (Hot In Handcuffs Anthology)

THE PERFECT GENTLEMEN
(by Shayla Black and Lexi Blake)
Scandal Never Sleeps
Seduction in Session
Big Easy Temptation
Smoke and Sin
At the Pleasure of the President

MASTERS OF MÉNAGE (by Shayla Black and Lexi Blake)
Their Virgin Captive
Their Virgin's Secret
Their Virgin Concubine
Their Virgin Princess
Their Virgin Hostage
Their Virgin Secretary
Their Virgin Mistress
Coming Soon:
Their Virgin Bride (TBD)

DOMS OF HER LIFE (by Shayla Black, Jenna Jacob, and
Isabella LaPearl)
Raine Falling Collection (Complete)
One Dom To Love
The Young And The Submissive

The Bold and The Dominant
The Edge of Dominance

HEAVENLY RISING COLLECTION
The Choice
Coming Soon:
The Chase (2019)

THE MISADVENTURES SERIES
Misadventures of a Backup Bride
Misadventures with My Ex

STANDALONE TITLES
Naughty Little Secret
Watch Me
Dangerous Boys And Their Toy
"Her Fantasy Men" (Four Play Anthology)
A Perfect Match
His Undeniable Secret (Sexy Short)
HISTORICAL ROMANCE (as Shelley Bradley)
The Lady And The Dragon
One Wicked Night
Strictly Seduction
Strictly Forbidden

BROTHERS IN ARMS MEDIEVAL TRILOGY
His Lady Bride (Book 1)
His Stolen Bride (Book 2)
His Rebel Bride (Book 3)

PARANORMAL ROMANCE
THE DOOMSDAY BRETHREN
Tempt Me With Darkness
"Fated" (e-novella)
Seduce Me In Shadow

Also from Lexi Blake

ROMANTIC SUSPENSE

Masters And Mercenaries
The Dom Who Loved Me
The Men With The Golden Cuffs
A Dom is Forever
On Her Master's Secret Service
Sanctum: A Masters and Mercenaries Novella
Love and Let Die
Unconditional: A Masters and Mercenaries Novella
Dungeon Royale
Dungeon Games: A Masters and Mercenaries Novella
A View to a Thrill
Cherished: A Masters and Mercenaries Novella
You Only Love Twice
Luscious: Masters and Mercenaries~Topped
Adored: A Masters and Mercenaries Novella
Master No
Just One Taste: Masters and Mercenaries~Topped 2
From Sanctum with Love
Devoted: A Masters and Mercenaries Novella
Dominance Never Dies
Submission is Not Enough
Master Bits and Mercenary Bites~The Secret Recipes of
Topped
Perfectly Paired: Masters and Mercenaries~Topped 3
For His Eyes Only
Arranged: A Masters and Mercenaries Novella
Love Another Day
At Your Service: Masters and Mercenaries~Topped 4
Master Bits and Mercenary Bites~Girls Night
Nobody Does It Better

Close Cover
Protected: A Masters and Mercenaries Novella
Enchanted: A Masters and Mercenaries Novella, Coming
June 18, 2019

Masters and Mercenaries: The Forgotten
Lost Hearts (Memento Mori)
Lost and Found
Lost in You, Coming August 6, 2019

Lawless
Ruthless
Satisfaction
Revenge

Courting Justice
Order of Protection
Evidence of Desire

Masters Of Ménage (by Shayla Black and Lexi Blake)
Their Virgin Captive
Their Virgin's Secret
Their Virgin Concubine
Their Virgin Princess
Their Virgin Hostage
Their Virgin Secretary
Their Virgin Mistress

The Perfect Gentlemen (by Shayla Black and Lexi Blake)
Scandal Never Sleeps
Seduction in Session
Big Easy Temptation
Smoke and Sin
At the Pleasure of the President

URBAN FANTASY

Thieves
Steal the Light
Steal the Day
Steal the Moon
Steal the Sun
Steal the Night
Ripper
Addict
Sleeper
Outcast

LEXI BLAKE WRITING AS SOPHIE OAK

Small Town Siren
Siren in the City
Away From Me
Three to Ride
Siren Enslaved
Two to Love
Siren Beloved
One to Keep
Siren in Waiting
Lost in Bliss
Found in Bliss
Siren in Bloom
Pure Bliss
Chasing Bliss, Coming April 23, 2019
Siren Unleashed, Coming May 21, 2019